PENNY'S SECRET MISSION

RACHEL WESSON

LONDONGATE PUBLISHING

To those brave men and women who gave their lives so we could be free. Thank you.

PROLOGUE

"Run, *ma cherie*, run. Leave before that *putain* takes you in place of your mama. *Il est le fils du diable*."

Drenched in sweat, Penny struggled to wake up. She sat up and rubbed her eyes, as if trying to rub away the memory of yet another dream about Alain, her mother's murderer. In this one, her old friend Madame Bayard, who she could see clear as day in her dream, had been warning her to run away. She had escaped him, but he was still out there, and Penny would have her revenge. Some day, that man would pay for the death of her mother. She'd get back to France and see him sentenced for his crimes.

There was a knock on the bedroom door and Cook's niece, Emma, came in.

"Pardon me, Miss Penelope, but Cook says you'll be late if you don't put a shift on..." The girl turned scarlet. She was so nervous, she jumped at every noise, having lived in the dockland area of London during the worst of the bombing raids. "Sorry, Miss, I mean you need to get up now. Please."

Penny gave her a smile to reassure her. "Thanks, Emma. Tell Cook I'll be down in a minute. I'm on the late shift today."

Emma nodded before turning and almost racing out of the room. As she got out of bed and began getting ready, Penny wondered if she should tell Emma about having grown up in France – where she'd been as poor as Emma and her family. Her eyes closed as she pictured Madame Bayard. How was she coping now, with the Nazis on her doorstep? At least they weren't goose-stepping through London. Not yet.

CHAPTER 1

"Cheerio, Penny, keep smiling."

Penny waved to the Barts nurses as they crossed the road to the nursing home, their faces pale with exhaustion despite their smiles. St Bartholomews, like most London hospitals, was stretched to breaking point by the constant stream of casualties.

She knew how they felt; the last eight months of almost constant bombings had taken their toll on everyone. She smoothed down her red jumper and green tweed skirt, thankful the dark colours didn't highlight the evidence of the night before. Despite wearing the uniform of the Women's Voluntary Services, she spent most of her time practising her first aid skills alongside the overworked nurses these days. She'd have become a nurse herself, but for her aunt Louise's objection. But Meme, her grandmother, had gently suggested Penny could seek experience as a volunteer until the Blitz was over and Louise was more like herself.

Penny pushed the hair back from her eyes, exhaustion making every bone weary – not that she should be complaining. An unexploded bomb had gone off near the back entrance of the hospital just as the all-clear sounded, scattering the female volunteers and male ARP wardens like pinballs. Miraculously nobody died, but some of the WVS would spend the next few days in hospital. She'd been incredibly lucky to walk away unharmed.

She smiled at the men in uniforms she passed as she walked towards the station, the blue grey of the Royal Air Force mingling with the khaki green of the army. There were some sailors around, too, looking for some rest and relaxation before returning to battle.

The London streets, which had become so familiar to her in the last few years, were unrecognisable; piles of rubble all that remained of familiar landmarks. The Underground had become almost a permanent home for those residents who used it as a shelter. As Penny walked past St Paul's, she stopped to marvel at the old building, still standing amidst the ruins of the city. People came here as if to prove to themselves that Hitler wouldn't break them. The tombs and banners from previous wars and battlefields seemed to give people confidence.

She heard a voice say, "We ain't ever lost and we won't start now."

Penny looked at the leathered face of the old cockney man who had spoken to her. "What do you think it will take to convince the Germans of that?" she asked.

"I don't know, girl. That Hitler is pure evil. But he won't win. He can't win." The old man shuffled off, and she headed down into the station to take the Tube home. It didn't take too long to reach Hyde Park and daylight. The Underground was much faster than taking the bus, but she didn't enjoy dwelling on just how far below ground the trains moved.

She walked past Hyde Park, marvelling at the field of daffodils in front of her. Nature just carried on, although the world seemed to have turned upside down. The fountains may not be working and the statues protected by mounds of sandbags, but the flowers kept growing. She stared up at the sky. It would be a clear night tonight, another perfect night for bombing. She wondered if Churchill had already left London. The papers said the prime minister wanted to stay, but his advisers felt that Chequers, his home, and 10 Downing Street would prove too tempting a target for the German raiders.

Penny quickened her pace, hoping to get a few hours of sleep before evening. She had promised her uncle that she would go with him to Queen's Hall to see Sir

Malcolm Sargent conduct *Dream of Gerontius*. She wished they were going to Haymarket Theatre to see *No Time for Comedy* with Rex Harrison, an actor she loved, but that treat would have to keep for another day.

Bombs had hit several streets in Belgravia, and many of the owners had closed up their houses and moved into hotels. Penny knew it was only a matter of time before her uncle took a similar step. Cook and Perkins were too old to be living in continual danger. There was too much work to do and not enough staff available. The younger members had left, either to join the services or to work in factories that offered higher pay.

Thankfully, her aunt wasn't around when she got home. The house was quiet. She slipped into the kitchen to speak to Cook but found her asleep at the table over-taken by exhaustion.

Penny slipped a cardigan around the old woman's shoulders, being careful not to wake her. She went up to her bedroom, falling asleep almost as soon as her head hit the pillow.

∼

THE MUSICIANS WERE EXPERTS, but the theme of life and death was a little too much for Penny, given the events of the previous months.

"Let me treat you to dinner at The Savoy, Penny,"

Uncle John said as they left the theatre arm in arm. "That will make up for depressing you."

"The music was excellent, Uncle John, it's just … we're surrounded every day by people dying. It's hard to appreciate what Newman was trying to say."

"Some would say it's always difficult to figure out religious pieces, Penny. Thank you for accompanying me. I needed something to take my mind off things."

Penny glanced at him, wondering if she should say anything. "You're worried about Hugo, aren't you?"

Her uncle's face paled, but otherwise he pretended he hadn't heard her.

"Uncle John, you can't just ignore his existence."

"He chose his side in this war. Please don't mention it again."

Penny sighed. She liked her cousin Hugo, even if she didn't understand his interest in Germany. She couldn't believe he was a Nazi, despite the evidence against him. He'd taken trips to Berlin to see his friends from college. One friend, Hans, had joined the Luftwaffe, but Hugo hadn't joined the services even when war broke out. She thought he was working in the war office; he spent a lot of time away from home. She'd just assumed he was protecting Britain. He wasn't a conscientious objector like Ralph, the worker on Meme's estate. Nobody had been more surprised than her when the police caught Hugo red-handed, distributing Nazi propaganda. He was now languishing in a jail cell somewhere; nobody knew where or if they did, they weren't telling. Uncle John had announced Hugo was dead to him. Penny's cousin Harriet still protested her brother's innocence, but few listened to her.

The air-raid siren wailed just as they finished dinner.

"Come on, Penny. Let's grab a taxi and see if we can make it back home. I don't want to leave Louise on her own during a raid."

They hailed one of the few taxis still operating but had to stop on their way because of an incendiary bomb. Penny watched as the firemen put it out. Some injured people were waiting for an ambulance.

Penny turned to her uncle. "Uncle John, we should give them our taxi. We can walk back from here."

Her uncle agreed. As they walked down Oxford Street, the scene of devastation left them speechless. There was glass everywhere.

"Penny, there are people hurt over there. Look." Her uncle pointed to several people lying in the gutter outside Selfridges. "Oh my, they don't appear to be wearing any clothes."

Penny edged forward, eager to help. Then she burst out laughing.

Her uncle looked at her in shock. "Penelope Hamilton, pull yourself together. Now is not the time to be laughing. These people deserve some respect."

Penny's hand shook as she brushed her hair from her eyes. "They're not real, Uncle John. They're shop dummies, which must have blown out when the windows shattered."

"Are you sure?" He moved closer and bent down to examine an arm. "Oh, thank God." He looked around him, a bewildered look on his face. "I could do with a drink. What was I thinking of? I should get you to a shelter rather than try to make it home to Louise."

"For goodness' sake, Uncle John. I'm not a child. If you weren't Lord Hamilton, I would have been out at work from the age of fourteen earning my keep. I have my first aid training and we should help where we can." Penny swallowed hard, waiting for a reaction.

To her surprise, her uncle laughed. "You are so like your grandmother. Okay, my girl. Let's see what you're made of."

"I think we should head down there." Penny pointed towards a crowd gathered at the bottom of the street. "They may need help."

They made their way towards the crowd, passing blown-out windows and shattered glass. Several firemen had extinguished a small fire and were now pulling at some rubble with their bare hands.

"What can we do?" asked Penny, as they reached the front of the crowd.

A fireman looked up at her, giving her costume a once-over. "Nothing, miss. This isn't suitable work for a lady. There was a family sheltering down here. They lived above the shop."

"I would like to help," Penny insisted. "Please. I know first aid. There must be something I can do."

The fireman appeared to hesitate, his gaze drawn to two figures a few feet up the road.

"Who are they?"

"That's the dad with one of his kids. He won't let us have her."

CHAPTER 2

Penny looked at the man cradling the child. "Why don't I see if I can help? The child may be hungry or thirsty."

The fireman looked as if he was going to say something, but he just swallowed hard and turned back to his work. Penny walked towards the man. He was sitting on the side of the road. The child's clothes were black with debris, but she didn't have any obvious injuries, though her eyes were closed. He had red welts covering his fingers, his nails broken and dirty. The gash on his head was deep and full of debris. Penny worried about his head injury. Scalp wounds always bled a lot. He needed medical attention. She sat beside him on the ground. It took him a few seconds to acknowledge her.

"I should never have left them." He looked at Penny. "I tried to get them all out. I could only reach the little one. There were too many bricks. The firemen won't let me help any more. They said I could bring the lot down on top of them. The wife, my girls and my boy are still in there." Tears mixed with the blood running from his wound.

"Shush, now. I'm sure you did all you could. What's your little girl's name?"

"Millie. Millie Taylor. She's four and doesn't like strangers. She's asleep. I daren't wake her up. I don't want her asking for her mam."

Penny nodded, inspecting the child. "I'm good with children, Mr Taylor. Can I please look at Millie? Maybe she's hurt. You are. That gash on your forehead needs stitches."

It took a few minutes for her to convince Mr Taylor to hand over his little girl. Penny choked back her tears, looking down at the perfect, innocent little face surrounded by what was once a blonde circle of curls. She looked like she was sleeping. There wasn't a mark on her. "She's pretty."

"Aye, takes after her mam," Mr Taylor responded, his gaze focused back on the firemen.

"Mr Taylor, please let me take you to the first aid station. You need to see a doctor." Mr Taylor shook his head, but Penny continued. "Millie needs a bath and a blanket. We don't want anyone seeing her covered in dirt. Your wife wouldn't like that, would she?"

At the mention of his wife, the man groaned. "My wife won't come out of there, will she? I should never have left them. But I had to find out when my next ship was going out."

"It's not your fault, Mr Taylor. You didn't know there was going to be a raid. Nobody deserves this, least of all your wife and kids."

They both looked up when the firemen started shouting at one another. They watched the men pull another body from the wreckage. Mr Taylor ran towards the firemen, leaving Penny carrying Millie, following slowly behind.

"Oh, sweet God, that's the wife. Is she dead?"

The fireman nodded. "I'm sorry, mate. You couldn't have done anything."

Mr Taylor grabbed the fireman's arm. "Where's my other kids? Please, you got to find them."

Penny caught the look in the fireman's eyes. They all looked back at the pile behind them. How could anyone survive being buried alive? Penny held back her sobs, focusing on Mr Taylor.

"Let's get you to the doctor now, Mr Taylor."

"No, I'm not leaving. Can't you hear the baby crying?"

The fireman looked at Penny and shook his head.

"I know they're still alive in there and I'm not leaving. If you won't do anything, I'm going in myself." He darted towards the building and two firemen grabbed at him to hold him back. Tears rolled down his face, mixing with the soot to form black streaks intermingled

with blood. "Shirley, Betty, are you in there? It's Daddy.
I'm coming to get you. Hold on." He fought hard, but
the two firemen stood firm.

Penny couldn't bear to see his distress; she knew
the man believed what he was saying. She turned
towards the remains of the house. What if he was right
and there were children alive under there? What if they
could hear their father shouting? They'd expect
someone to come get them. She couldn't walk away. It
wasn't right.

She looked closely at the mound of rubble. There
seemed to be a small hole to one side.

"Look, can't you go through there and have another
look?" Penny asked.

The firemen conferred for a couple of seconds. "It's
no use, miss. None of us could get through that space.
It's too small and we would only bring the whole thing
down on top of us. Other people need our help. We have
to focus on those who may have a chance of survival."

"No, we have to put the children first. They're innocent victims. We need to make sure that Mr Taylor is
wrong." Penny shrugged off her coat, leaving the
fireman staring at her pale peach shawl shouldered
evening dress. It couldn't have been less appropriate for
the task in hand. "I can fit through that hole."

The small crowd of onlookers around them muttered
between themselves.

"Penelope, I forbid you to go into that house. You

don't have any experience. You could die." Sir John looked at the firemen for backup.

"Uncle John, I know you're only trying to look out for me. But I know what it's like to lose your family and your home." Penny looked back at Mr Taylor. "I can't walk away. Those children could be alive. I couldn't live with myself if I did nothing. Could you?" Penny didn't wait for an answer but turned to the officer in charge. "What should I do?"

The man frowned for a few seconds, then said, "It's going to be dark and dusty in there, miss. You best stay as close to the floor as possible – it will be easier to breathe. Try not to move anything, as you could end up bringing the whole thing down on top of you. I'll secure this rope around your waist. If you want to get out, pull on it and we will guide you. If you feel us pulling on it, that means you need to leave fast. Is that understood?"

Penny nodded, but the fireman put his hand under her chin, forcing her to meet his direct gaze.

"Miss, I'm serious. I can understand why you want to do this, but that doesn't mean I'm going to risk any of my men by sending them in after you. If we pull, you come out."

"Yes, sir." She turned back to Mr Taylor. "What ages are Betty and Shirley?"

"Six and eight. The baby is Joe. Please try to get them all out. Please."

"I will, on one condition. You must get medical

attention for your head. Let the Red Cross people look after you."

Mr Taylor took her hand in his and kissed it. "Thank you, miss. May God go with you."

Penny moved towards the rubble, her heart beating so hard she didn't think she could breathe. Don't think – count one, two, three … She crawled forward on her hands and knees, ears straining to hear a child. The hole in the mound of bricks looked too small to squeeze through. She didn't know what part of the house she would find behind the stones. She couldn't risk moving any of the wreckage surrounding her. The structure could collapse at any second. Her nose twitched in the dust, she held her breath trying to stop a sneeze. She inched forward into the darkness.

"Shirley, Betty, are you in here? My name's Penny. Your dad asked me to come get you."

The silence mocked her. Maybe the firemen were right, the kids were dead. She shuffled on, her hands searching the floor as she crawled. She felt something. A foot. Please, God, let the owner be alive, she prayed. She tickled the surface of the skin to see if there was any response. The person moved a little.

"Hello? Betty? Shirley? Can you talk, sweetheart? I can't see you as it's so dark. Are you hurt?"

"No, but I can't find Shirley. Mum will be so angry. I'm supposed to look after her." Tears choked Betty's voice.

"I'm going to move closer to you, darling, okay?" Penny moved slowly, stopping when some bricks fell beside her, causing a cloud of dust to surround them. Betty screamed.

"Shush, love. We don't want to scare the others. Now, can you move towards me? Hold my hand."

"Can you hold Joe, please, as I can't move?"

Penny's heart soared. "Sure, sweetie. Give him to me. Careful now." Using her hands, she sought and secured the little bundle. Penny used the baby's blanket to secure him to her chest, tying the ends together around her back. She needed her hands free to crawl back out. The baby's face felt warm against her neck, but she could tell his heartbeat was weak. No time to lose.

"Okay, come on, sweetheart. Creep towards me." She reached for Betty's hand, but the child pulled away.

"No, I can't. I have to stay here. The dark and the bricks falling will scare Shirley, she needs me."

Penny fought the urge not to panic. She had to get out, not only because the baby needed medical attention, but she was finding it harder to breathe. She was fighting the dizziness, which would only get worse the longer they stayed.

"Betty, you need to come now so you can mind Joe when I come back for Shirley. Come on, now. You know that's what your dad would want you to do. The baby needs you."

Betty crawled forward with a sigh.

"That's great, darling. Don't worry about Shirley. I'll come back in and bring her out, too. I just want to get Joe out to your dad as soon as I can. Now, keep your head down close to the floor, the air is better there. Use the rope to help you feel your way out."

After what seemed like hours but was likely only minutes, they saw the crack of light up ahead of them. "Go on, Betty. Your dad is waiting for you. Keep heading towards the light."

Penny could hear that her voice was husky because of the dust and debris. Slowly, the three of them moved forward. Large hands pulled Betty to safety, followed by Penny and baby Joe. Betty ran to her dad, who was sitting on the kerb with a huge bandage on his head.

"Well done, young lady. Is the baby okay?" the fireman asked Penny.

Penny touched the baby's chest and shook her head. "I can't feel a heartbeat any more. There was one. But it's gone. He needs a doctor." She untied the blanket and handed the little bundle gently to the fireman, turning back towards the rubble.

"Wait, where do you think you're going?" The fireman took her arm, not too gently.

Penny looked at the fireman in surprise. "Shirley is still in there. I'm going back."

"No, miss, you can't. The structure is even more

unsound now. You must have heard the rubble moving above you."

Penny glared at the fireman. "I'm going back in, I promised Betty I wouldn't leave her sister. I can't break my word."

Uncle John stepped forward. "Penny, please. You have done enough. Let the firemen take over now."

"No, Uncle John. There's a child in there and I have to try. I promised that little girl."

Once more, Penny crawled in through the little hole, feeling her way in the darkness. She moved in further than before, using her hands to search the surrounding darkness. "Shirley, are you here? Can you hear me?" she called, but nobody answered. She felt the rope tugging around her middle. The signal for her to leave. Reluctantly, she turned back. Then she heard a cry. "Mummy, is that you?"

She moved towards the sound. "Shirley, I'm Penny. Your mummy sent me in here to take you outside. Can you move?"

"Me leg's stuck. I can't get it out. Where's Mummy? I want her."

The child's pitiful cries helped Penny locate her. She rubbed her hands along the small body, checking for injury, feeling something heavy that was sitting on Shirley's foot. She tried to move it, but her actions caused the child to scream, and they were both showered with dust and small pieces of debris.

"Sorry, darling. I don't want to hurt you, but I have to move it to get you out of here. As soon as I lift what's on you, can you roll to your side?"

"I think so," Shirley said.

"Great. I need you to be brave, okay?"

"Yes, miss," Shirley whispered.

Penny stood up as much as she could and, using all of her body weight, shifted the debris off the child's foot. The child rolled free just in time before Penny had to let go and the debris fell back.

Penny crouched down and held the whimpering girl for a couple of seconds. "Okay, darling, we need to get out of here now. Can you crawl?"

Penny half carried, half dragged the child out of the ruins towards the light outside. The fireman pulled Shirley out first, but just as they reached down to help Penny, there was a loud creak – Penny heard an almighty rumbling as the ruined house collapsed. Something struck Penny's head, and the light went out.

CHAPTER 3

Nell Thompson looked at the smiling faces peering out of the front page of the local paper. She had known the boys since childhood. She had fed them, wiped their tears when they cut their knees and given them a cuff around the ear when necessary. Now they were missing, presumed dead. She'd gone round to their mothers when the telegrams had come, but somehow seeing their pictures in the paper made it more real.

She brushed the tears away and told herself firmly to stop being defeatist. There was still hope, hadn't she thought the worst when Stan's plane had gone down. Although many had given her son up for dead, Nell's daughter Gracie believed her twin was a survivor. Sure enough, weeks after they had posted him missing in action, they'd got word Stan was a prisoner of war.

Nell looked up as the front door banged and her husband came in, looking older than his years, his skin tinged with grey. She worried about Tom. He'd always been slender, but now he was skin and bone. Like most of their neighbours, he spent his daylight hours at work and the evenings doing voluntary fire-watching. There was only so much one person could do, yet they carried on regardless. She put the newspaper away and plastered a smile on her face, rather than burdening her husband with her grief.

"Hello, love. Did you have a good day? Bill called round when you were out," she said.

"What did he want? I suppose he was wondering if there were any spare vegetables from the allotment."

"No, he didn't mention food. He checked our preparations for more raids. There are some families who don't have buckets or blankets ready in case of a fire. I showed him your supplies. He seemed impressed, particularly when he saw your axe was so well maintained." Bill hadn't commented on anything, but Nell knew it would make Tom feel better to think that he had.

Tom frowned. "Of course we're prepared. What does he take us for? We've been ready since before the war started. Weren't we the first house on the street to get our Anderson shelter?"

"Keep your hair on." Nell looked at Tom. The war was taking a toll on his mood, too. He never used to be so quick-tempered.

Tom looked guilty. "Sorry. It's just that man. The

Blitz has been raging for months and he comes to check on our supplies today?" He shook his head.

Nell patted his arm and nodded towards the table. "Come and eat your tea while it's hot. It's only scrambled egg and a bit of rabbit leg on toast. Do you have to go out again later?"

Tom shook his head. "The gaffer told me to take tonight off. Seems I could use some beauty sleep."

Nell smiled at his attempt at a joke as she sat down with him and they ate their dinner in silence. Sleep. They'd be lucky. Like most people, they had taken to going to bed after the 9.30 p.m. news to get some sleep before the bombers came. With an average of ten hours' sleep a week, when the raids were at their worst, they needed to grab whatever opportunities came along. She only hoped it would be a quiet night. They'd had three alerts and all-clears last night, although thankfully no bombs. She didn't know how some people could sleep through the siren. It was loud enough to wake the dead.

She looked across the table at her husband, who had fallen asleep, his head dipping forward towards his empty plate. The combination of rationing, exhaustion and constant bad news was enough to get anyone's spirits down.

She picked up the paper again, hoping to read some good news. Her eyes moved to a piece on a society heiress badly injured rescuing children from a bombed-out building. As she read the article, she couldn't believe it. They were talking about Penny, Gracie's friend, who had called just the other day with a wedding present for Gracie and Charlie. She had told Nell about her new role doing translation work and how excited she was to be starting at the office. There would be no new job now. Not when she was lying dangerously ill in hospital. Her tears dripped onto the newspaper. It didn't say whether they expected Penny to survive.

Nell had to let Gracie know what had happened.

With gritted teeth, Nell pushed back the chair and started clearing the dishes to the kitchen. When was this all going to end? She wondered if she could visit Penny. Perhaps it would be family only. Tomorrow, she would see Cook at the big house. Cook would fill her in.

Now there was nothing to do but get themselves to bed and pray that the young girl they loved so much would pull through.

CHAPTER 4

LONDON HOSPITAL

Penny woke with a throbbing headache. Her stomach roiled at the potent smell of antiseptic surrounding her. Gingerly, she opened her eyes and tried to sit up, but the pain in her arm outweighed the pain in her head and she found she couldn't move it.

"Don't move. The doctors said you have to keep still."

Penny relaxed back onto her pillow. She tried to smile. "You look awful, Uncle John."

"Humph, you should see what you look like. You have given us all a fright, young lady. Now stay still while I go find the doctor."

He got up and left, closing the door behind him, leaving Penny alone in the small room. She closed her eyes and tried not to think about the pain as she waited.

When he came back with the doctor, the doctor looked almost as tired as he did. He examined her, asking many questions. "Can you move your toes? Can you feel this? And that?"

"Ow, that hurt."

The doctor turned to Uncle John. "No lasting damage as far as I can tell." He directed his next comments to Penny. "You had a lucky escape, Miss Hamilton. That was a nasty bump on your head and you have been asleep for some time. Your arm broke in two places, hence the splint. You need to get a lot of rest and allow your body to heal. No more heroics for at least a month." He smiled at Penny before leaving.

"I could strangle you, Penny. Your aunt and I have been so worried. I haven't told Mother yet. I didn't want her travelling up to London with all these bombs." Her uncle moved his chair closer to the bed, taking hold of Penny's good hand. He brushed her hair out of her eyes. "I'm so proud of you. We all are."

Penny noticed the tears in his eyes and, feeling uncomfortable, she said, "Never mind about me. How are the kids? Did the baby make it?"

Her uncle swallowed hard and then shook his head.

Penny sank back further into her pillow.

"Poor Mr Taylor." She turned her head into her pillow, letting the tears fall.

"Darling Penny, don't cry. You did everything you could, and more. You were so brave. Your father would have been so proud of you."

"It wasn't enough, though, was it?" Penny heard the

anger and resentment in her voice, but she didn't care. Nothing mattered now.

Uncle John opened his mouth, but instead of saying anything, he stood and went to the door. "I will be back shortly."

He came back with company. Betty was holding his hand and behind them Mr Taylor pushed Shirley's chair.

Penny struggled to sit up, not quite believing her eyes. "You are okay?"

"Thanks to you, miss," Mr Taylor stopped to remove the hat he was wearing before offering his hand for Penny to shake. "I can't ever repay you. I don't know what I would have done if I had lost my girls as well. Go on, girls, say thank you to the lady."

"But I didn't save the baby," Penny muttered.

Betty edged shyly towards the bed, taking Penny's outstretched hand. She climbed up on the bed and wiped the tears from Penny's cheek. "Don't cry, miss, you couldn't have done anything more. Joe would have wanted to be with Mum and Millie. She was always his favourite."

The tears flowed even stronger. Penny put her good arm around the little girl, ignoring the dart of pain this caused. "You are such a wonderful girl. Thank you, Betty."

Then Penny turned to Shirley and gave her a warm smile. "I see you have a new chariot. Does it go fast?

I'm going to ask the doctor for one, too, and we can have a race."

Shirley giggled at first, then grimaced as she tried to lift her leg up for Penny to see. "My foot fell off. See?"

Penny darted a quick look at Mr Taylor, who nodded. She clutched the bedsheets to stop the tears starting again. "Oh, Shirley, you are so brave. I'm proud of you."

Mr Taylor turned to Penny's uncle. "Thank you, sir, for paying for my girls to be here."

"Please don't mention it. I will cover all costs, including your accommodation, so you can stay near your girls. When's your next ship?"

"Due out next Tuesday, Sir John." Mr Taylor glanced at his girls. "Lot to do before then."

"I bet there is. I must go now, too. Betty, will you make sure that Miss Penny doesn't get up? The doctors have said she must stay in bed, but she might be naughty."

"I won't let her, sir, I promise."

The door closed behind the two men. Penny chatted to the girls, marvelling at their resilience. If adults had gone through the nightmare they had endured, they would not have coped as well.

After a couple of minutes, a middle-aged, stern-looking nurse arrived to escort the girls back to their ward.

"Oh, please, Nurse, let us stay a little while longer," the children begged.

"That's quite enough. Lady Hamilton needs her rest. Now, come on, girls. You shouldn't be sitting on the bed. Matron won't like it."

"Please, Nurse, don't blame the children. It was my fault. I encouraged them," Penny said, trying but failing to charm the older woman.

"That's as may be, Lady Hamilton, but these children should know their place."

Penny sat up straighter, ignoring the sharp twinge of pain in her arm. "Excuse me, Nurse, but my aunt is Lady Hamilton. My name is Penelope Hamilton. You can address me as Miss Hamilton. I expect the girls to come visit me every day. I'll clear it with Matron. Is that understood?"

The nurse's cheeks flushed with annoyance and embarrassment. "Sorry, Miss Hamilton. Matron said to address you as Her Ladyship. Come along, girls. You're making this area untidy. You look like you both could use a good wash."

Penny disliked both the tone used and the way the nurse was looking down at the children who seemed scared of her. "Nurse?"

"Yes, Miss Hamilton."

Penny clenched the blanket as she tried to quell her annoyance. She'd never used her family status before, but she'd watched her aunt do it often enough to see it

got results. This seemed like a suitable moment to
practise.

"I have a special interest in these children, as does
my uncle, Sir John Hamilton. He's a good friend of
many of your senior surgeons. Treat Shirley and Betty
with kindness and concern, as if they were my family."
Penny glared at the nurse. "Do I make myself clear?"

She held the nurse's gaze, not missing the flash of
irritation followed by a glimpse of fear. She would have
felt guilty if it hadn't been for the nurse abusing her
position by being unkind to the Taylors.

"Yes, Miss Hamilton. Crystal clear."

Penny turned to the girls. "Betty, come here and give
me a kiss. You look after yourself, and Shirley and I will
see you tomorrow." When the girls shrank from the
nurse, Penny continued softly. "Go on, now, Nurse is
right. I'm tired, but I *will* see you tomorrow."

Penny smiled at the girls, but as soon as they left,
she sank back against her pillow and the tears flowed
again. She couldn't believe the nurse's attitude. She
obviously felt the children belonged in the infirmary
across town. Its location beside a cemetery didn't help
to offset the fear the locals had of being admitted to that
hospital. Perhaps Uncle John could have the nurse transferred to the infirmary. With that happy thought in mind,
Penny fell asleep.

CHAPTER 5

Penny woke later to find an RAF officer sitting by the side of her bed, smiling at her although concern filled his blue eyes. She couldn't believe he was here. She stared, the lines of exhaustion around his eyes were more pronounced than before, his hair curling over the edge of his collar. He looked worse than he had the night of the Café de Paris bombing.

"Hello, Penny. I'm thinking you have a death wish."

Penny tried to sit up. "Hello, David. What are you doing here?"

"I saw you were in hospital and called in to say hello. How are you feeling?" he said.

"I'm okay. I should be out of here, but the doctors are insisting I rest. Then Uncle John wants to take me to stay with my grandmother for a while. I think he wants to fatten me up."

"More likely, he wants to keep you away from the bombs. First the Café de Paris and now this."

"David, what did you mean by 'you saw I was in hospital'?" asked Penny, puzzled.

"Did you not see your lovely picture in the newspaper? You are quite the celebrity. It's not every day an aristocrat goes digging through rubble in her evening wear." David chuckled at the look on Penny's face.

"I grew up on a farm, remember?" Penny said, plucking at the bedcovers, trying to cover her embarrassment. Now she thought about it, she had vague recollections of a camera flashing. The firemen had been angry at the reporter getting in their way.

"You may have grown up on a farm, but you are a true blue. You come from one of the oldest English families. I'm sure your aunt can trace your lineage right back to the War of the Roses. Perhaps further," David teased.

Penny pouted. "Stop teasing me, David. I don't like it."

"Keep looking at me like that and I will start calling you Harriet."

Penny burst out laughing, causing him to laugh, too. They chatted for a few more minutes before David rose to go.

"Take care of yourself, Miss Hamilton. Even a cat only has nine lives."

"Yes, sir, Mr Andrews." She wanted to ask if he

would come to see her again, but couldn't. That wasn't ladylike, and despite what her aunt might think, she had paid attention to some lessons on etiquette.

At the door, he turned back and said, "Seriously, Penny, what you did was marvellous. You are a brave young woman. But you have to look after yourself now."

"I did nothing special. The firemen do that type of job every day and I don't see anyone taking their pictures."

David laughed. "Modest to the end. Good luck, Penelope Hamilton."

"That sounded like a proper goodbye? Are you…?" She couldn't continue, having failed to keep her voice from sounding squeaky.

"Yes, I have received my orders. I ship out in the next few days. Can't tell you where, of course."

"Yes, walls have ears and all that." She wanted to ask him to write, but didn't. They'd only met a couple of times before now, and she didn't know whether he shared her attraction. He had called to see her after the Café de Paris bombing and taken her for a walk around Hyde Park. That showed concern, didn't it? Now he was visiting her in hospital. Was that just a friendly gesture? "David, be careful."

After he left, Penny couldn't face any more visitors. She even pretended to be asleep when the Taylor girls poked their little heads around the door.

David was leaving, and she hadn't told him she liked him. Did he like her? He had visited her but … Oh, drat this war anyway.

～

PENNY SPENT the hours following David's visit analysing everything he had said and done. She couldn't sleep. Why had he come to see her? Was it only to say goodbye? He had an odd look in his eyes when he looked at her. It wasn't love, though; at least, she didn't think so.

The Taylor girls arrived at visiting time the next day, giving her a welcome distraction from her thoughts, the youngsters looking prettier and cleaner than before. They were also both clutching new dolls.

Betty said, "Your uncle gave them to us, miss. Aren't they lovely?"

"They are, and so are you two. You look so pretty. I take it you had a bath."

"That horrible nurse made us. I had to take a proper one, but Shirley had to have a bath in her bed." Both children giggled.

"I have to have a bed bath, too," Penny said.

The girls laughed again. Visiting time passed quickly. Once again, a nurse came to collect the girls. This one was younger and much friendlier.

"Come on, children, it's time to go now. Miss

Hamilton needs her rest." The nurse smiled and offered her hand to Betty to help her down from the bed. She tidied the covers. "We can't have Matron knowing you were sitting on the bed, young Betty. She wouldn't like that."

"Thank you, Nurse." Penny smiled. "The girls seem to like you. I can see why."

"Ah, sure, aren't they just gorgeous, the poor wee mites? After all they have been through, you couldn't be anything but nice to them, now could you? I'd give them cuddles all day long, if I could."

"I'm sure they would get better quicker."

"I think so, too, but I can't let them hear me say that as I was lucky to get this job at the hospital. I've only started my training, so I'm not a proper nurse yet, you know," the nurse whispered, throwing a glance over her shoulder.

"Well, we think you are wonderful, don't we girls?" said Penny.

Shirley and Betty nodded.

"Aw, you're making me blush now. Come along, kids. We don't want Matron to come looking for us. See you tomorrow, Miss Hamilton."

CHAPTER 6

David walked away from the hospital with a heavy heart. Since the first time he met Penny in the Café de Paris, there had been something special between them. At first, he had believed what he told himself. She reminded him of his little sister. Beautiful, brave and kicking against convention, just like Amy. Even their colouring was similar. Amy had inherited her father's jet-black curls, whereas David's blond looks were from his mother's side of the family.

He had adored Amy from the moment she was born, and her death in a horse-riding accident at fourteen had left him devastated. Father had told her over and over that the Arabian horses weren't a suitable ride for a young lady. Amy refused to accept it. She believed herself to be the best rider in their county and, to be fair, she was probably right. It wasn't a lack of skills that had killed her, but a crazy horse.

Amy would have been nineteen this year, just like Penny. She would also have been biting at the bit to join the services. He could see her flying planes for the Air Transport Auxiliary. Their father had been a pilot in the First World War and taught his boys to fly from an early age. Amy had made him promise to take her up on a flying lesson for her sixteenth birthday. David smiled at how excited his sister would have been, had she lived to see that day.

When he had walked into the hospital room, Penny had been asleep. She looked so fragile, her white face a stark contrast to the jet-black hair spread out on the hospital pillow. She was so young. The resemblance to Amy was never more striking, but his feelings for this girl lying on the bed were anything but brotherly.

"Pull yourself together," he muttered to himself, shaking his head. He wasn't free to court a young girl, no matter what feelings he had.

The newspaper had reported that her injuries had been severe. David was glad to see that had been a gross exaggeration. True, she had a severe concussion and had remained unconscious for a long time. She seemed to have bounced back. She would have to rest and look after her shoulder, but she would recover fully.

He wondered how she would cope with the emotional impact. Two children and their mother had died in the incident. He hoped she would focus on the fact that she had saved two kids. In war, it didn't help to dwell on the numbers killed; you had to remember those you saved.

Penny's Aunt Louise had told him that Penny would spend the duration of the war at her grandmother's estate in Suffolk. David sincerely doubted that would happen. Penny might go there to recover from her ordeal, but he would bet his pay cheque on the fact that she would soon talk about joining up once more. He wondered which service she would pick. Feeling guilty, he regretted putting her name forward to his boss as someone who may be suitable for work in his field, after the incident in Café de Paris. Given her recent injuries, it was unlikely they would call on her.

He hadn't told Penny what part he played in the war effort. Like most people, she believed he was serving with the RAF. She thought he was a pilot. Understandable, given that he wore the uniform, which is exactly what his bosses wanted. There would be no chance of writing letters from where he was going.

Before heading out the exit toward West Smithfield, he stopped to read the inscription on the World War I memorial in the inner courtyard. Skilled stonemasons had chiselled the headline, 'These gave their lives for King and Country counting not the cost in defence of right.'

Five thousand soldiers passed through the wards of St Bart's during the last war. He wondered how many of them survived. How many people would this hospital treat during this war? How many would still be alive in the end? Unlike the last one, civilians now made up a huge percentage of those injured and killed in the conflict. Would there be another set of memorials raised to the dead from this war?

He heard a clock strike four. Realising he was late, he put his cap on his head and marched off quickly to his next destination. Duty called.

CHAPTER 7
LONDON

Over the next few days, the girls came to see Penny every visiting time. Usually, they were in high spirits. Penny was sure they were helping her to recover.

She was looking forward to seeing them today. She wanted to tell them she would soon go home, and she planned to ask Uncle John if the girls could stay with her at his house in London for a few weeks to allow them time to get over their ordeal.

Uncle John arrived shortly before the girls burst through the door. This time, the tears were theirs.

"Daddy says today is the last time we will see you. We have to leave tomorrow. A lady is coming to take us somewhere. We can't go back to our own house. Daddy has to go away again on his ship."

"I'm sure the lady will look after you..." Penny said, her heart twisting at the sight of the tear-stained cheeks.

"We don't know her, and we don't want to go. We want to stay here," Shirley cried.

Tears flowed down Betty's cheeks.

"Girls, stop that." Mr Taylor walked towards them. He looked at Penny. "There's nothing I can do. I have to get back to the ship and there's no one else. The girls have to go into a home. I've told them I'll come see them when I get back."

"Oh, Miss Penny, we don't want to go." Shirley held Betty's hand as if she would never let it go.

Penny looked at Uncle John with a question in her eyes. He shrugged his shoulders in response.

She turned to the children. "Betty, please take Shirley outside for a few minutes. I would like to speak to your daddy."

When the door closed behind the girls, Mr Taylor spoke, but Penny interrupted. "Please, let me take the girls. I'm going to Suffolk to my grandmother's home. It's safe there. There's plenty of room."

"No, miss, I couldn't ask you to do anything more for my family. You need to concentrate on getting better."

"They'll help me. They've already helped me. Their visits are the highlight of my day. I love children, particularly yours. My friend's brother and sisters already live down there, so your girls will have friends. Please say yes, Mr Taylor. I have volunteered in children's orphanages and I know the staff do their best, but they're not always cheerful places." Penny took a breath. "There's also the possibility that they'll separate the girls. I wasn't much older than Betty when I lost my home and family. I didn't have any siblings to help me through that time, but I can't bear the thought your girls would experience the same isolation and loneliness I did. Please say yes."

Mr Taylor stayed quiet for a while before saying, "What happens when you get better and come back to London? Who will look after my girls then?"

Uncle John spoke. "My mother, although in her seventies, is young at heart. She has staff still working on the estate who will take care of the children. Please don't worry. Your girls will thrive. There is plenty of food and love to go around, everything your children need to get over the trauma they have suffered."

"Thanks so much, Your Lordship, and you, too, Your Ladyship. But Shirley needs to have more operations and treatment on her leg. The children's home said they'd make sure that happens."

"My good man, I have access to the best surgeons and doctors in the country. I will ensure Shirley gets all the treatment she needs. Now, please give my niece the answer she wants. We have both seen what she is likely to do when things don't go her way."

"Daddy, please, please say yes and let us stay with Penny." Betty poked her head through the door.

Mr Taylor looked from his kids to Penny and back

again. "Okay, I think I know when I'm beat. You can go with Miss Hamilton."

"Thank you, Daddy." Betty put her arms around her dad, leaving Sir John to push Shirley's chair nearer the bed. He lifted the little girl out and put her lying beside Penny.

"Thank you, Miss Penny," Shirley said, before putting her arms around Penny's neck. "I love you," she whispered into Penny's ear.

Penny couldn't respond. She hugged the girl closer.

Penny asked Nell Thompson to come with them to Suffolk. Nell hadn't seen her younger children for some time, and Penny knew how much she missed them.

She couldn't believe the difference in the estate from the last time she had visited. Vegetables grew in beds that took up almost the whole lawn. Food was in short supply. Before the war, Britain had imported at least fifty per cent of the food consumed. With the losses at sea, this was no longer possible.

"Oh, look, Penny, there is one of them land girls," said Nell.

Penny looked at the girl wearing army breeches, boots, a khaki shirt and a green V-necked jumper. She had a felt hat on top of her head. Running after her was a young boy. He seemed to help until he spotted the car. Then he raced over.

"Mam." Kenny stopped, excitement draining from his face. "You've not come to take us home, have yer?"

"Well, that's a lovely welcome," said Nell, trying to laugh, although Penny saw she was also blinking back tears. She watched as the older woman got out of the car. She gave her son a bear hug, but Kenny squirmed away. "Leave it out, Mam. I'm not a kid any more." He stood up straighter, trying to puff his chest out. "I'm a vital war worker."

"You've stretched, our Kenny. You're nearly as tall as your dad now. Where are your sisters? Are they farm workers as well?" asked Nell.

"Nah, they are at school. They don't do actual farm work. Just collect eggs and feed the hens and stuff like that. Oh, hello. Who are you and what happened to your foot?" Kenny asked Shirley, whom Penny had helped out of the car.

"I'm Shirley Taylor. It fell off. That's my sister Betty."

Kenny gave the girls a big smile, showing all his teeth, "Are you going to live here, too? There're loads of room. The house is enormous."

Penny and Nell exchanged an amused glance. Anyone would think the house was his. Penny prompted the boy to be a bit more welcoming to his mum. "Kenny, can you show your mam where to put her bag? I want to introduce the girls to Meme." Penny caught the look of thanks Nell threw at her. She squeezed the other woman's hand once before turning to the Taylor girls. "Come on, girls, let's go find my grandmother."

Meme was waiting at the front door. She looked rather tired. Penny wondered if she'd done the right thing; maybe having two more refugees would prove too much for her? She hugged her grandmother warmly before introducing her to the young Taylors. The girls were a little overawed at first, taking in the house's size and the grandeur of their surroundings, their eyes wide.

"Welcome to my home, girls. I hope you will treat my home as your own." Meme glanced around and beckoned a young man to join them. "Ralph, could you please carry Shirley to her room, please?"

Penny said, "Her chair is at the station. Could someone collect it? It wouldn't fit in the car."

"I can do that, Miss Penelope." Ralph smiled warmly at the young girls. "Miss Shirley, your carriage awaits." He bent down to pick her up, tickling her and making her laugh as he did so.

Betty went off with her sister, leaving Penny alone with Meme. "He really is a nice young man, Meme."

"Oh, my darling. Let me look at you? How is your arm?" Meme put her arm through Penny's good arm and together they walked towards the conservatory. Cook had sent up a cold luncheon. Meme rang for some tea.

"I'm fine, Meme, please don't fuss. I had enough of that in the hospital," said Penny.

"Your uncle wrote and told me all about it. You were brave, Penny. We are all proud of you." Meme paused.

"I sense a 'but' coming?" teased Penny.

"No buts. Just please don't get mixed up in any more dangerous activities. I can't bear to think what I would do if I lost you, too."

"Meme, you of all people know I can't make promises that aren't mine to keep. There's a war on. As the Taylors found out, nobody is safe now. Not mothers, little girls … or even a tiny baby." Penny's voice was barely a whisper as she struggled to contain herself.

Meme came over and sat down on the couch beside her. "Don't hold it in, my darling. That's not good for you. Let it go."

Penny needed little persuading. She sobbed in her grandmother's arms until she had no more tears left. Hiccupping, she apologised.

"You have nothing to be sorry for. You have been through a horrible ordeal. Now it's my job to make sure you recover, physically and mentally." Meme looked at Penny sternly. "Before you argue with me, young lady, may I remind you I'm the mistress of this household. I believe you may have inherited my stubborn streak, but remember I have had many more years of practice in getting my own way. It would be easier on everyone if you just accept defeat now and do as I say."

Penny nodded. She didn't have any energy left to argue.

"That's settled now. Will I pour, or would you like to wait for Mrs Thompson to join us?"

"Pour away, Meme. I imagine Nell has made herself comfortable in the kitchen with Cook. She may have come to terms with her daughter being my closest friend, but I don't think she is up to having tea with Your Ladyship just yet."

The sound of her grandmother's laughter filled the room. Penny sighed. It was good to be home with Meme. Now, maybe she could sleep without the nightmares that had plagued her since the raid.

CHAPTER 9

Nell had a fantastic time on the estate catching up with Helen and Mary, her young daughters. The first week passed so quickly she almost forgot about the war and the bombings. It relieved her to see Kenny was a real help on the farm. Her son had learnt so much in such a brief space of time. He showed her how he milked the cows, and tried to persuade her to milk one, but she declined. Her nose wrinkled at the smell in the milking area despite it being cleaned daily. The air may be fresher in the country, but the pungent odours associated with cows and pigs took some time getting used to.

"Mam, why don't you like cows?"

She eyed the nearest cow, keeping well clear of her swishing tail. "I prefer to help Helen and Mary with the hens. They're smaller and won't kick me."

"Cows won't kick either, Mam, not if you treat them

properly." Kenny sounded like an old farmer, making Nell laugh.

"I'll leave you the cows, Kenny, I'll stick to hoeing and weeding and helping Cook with some odd jobs as well. It will keep me busy while the children are at school."

Kenny kicked a stone around the yard as they left the milking shed.

"Mam, will Miss Penny be better soon? She looks so sad."

"She will be fine, darling. Her arm is healing nicely."

"I wish she would start smiling again. She has a friendly smile," Kenny said.

Nell felt the tears prick her eyes. She hugged her son. "She has a lovely smile."

"Aw, Mam, stop being mushy. I'm all grown-up now. I'm not a kid any more."

Nell smiled. Her son was growing up. The fact he had picked up on Penny's hidden wounds was a testament to that. Nell hoped she was right. Although the haunted look in Penny's eyes was easing and the black circles weren't as obvious as before, her experiences in the bombing raid were a lot for anyone to get over.

"Look, Kenny, there is Miss Penny now. She looks happy, doesn't she?"

They both looked over at Penny walking towards the

stables. She had spent most of the past week looking after the horses. Besides exercising them, she also groomed them and even tried to muck out the stalls, despite one arm still being in a sling. She didn't ask anyone to do anything she herself didn't do. Nell admired her courage.

"Mam, come on, let's go over and say hello."

"You go on, son. I've got to get back to help in the kitchen."

She didn't fool her son, who picked up on her fear of horses.

"Mam, you don't like horses any more than you like cows, do you?" Kenny laughed. "You'd never survive living in the country."

Nell watched her son run over to Penny. She was glad that Penny's grandmother had helped her convince Penny she would do nobody any favours starting a new job in less than full health. Although the raids over London seemed to be a thing of the past, life was more difficult in the capital. The bombing raids weren't a nightly event, but the piles of rubble everywhere would remind Penny of the night the Taylor family lost everything. Not that she needed reminding.

Nell walked back to the kitchen where Cook was preparing lunch. Yawning, she set the eggs on the table. "I found a few extra when I went to pick some lettuce and tomatoes for lunch."

"Still finding it hard getting accustomed to the country air, are you?" Cook asked.

"I don't know what it is, but I'm so sleepy. Her Ladyship said it was because of the higher levels of oxygen than those found in the London fogs."

"I reckon it's a mixture of that and the excellent food. You don't get fresh, decent food in the cities. Didn't happen before the war and it sure won't start now," Cook muttered. "All that pollution isn't good for your health, you know."

Nell nodded. Another thing she loved about the country was staring out at the clear night sky. She had wished on more than one falling star, before crossing herself and praying for forgiveness for indulging in such foolishness.

~

THEY STAYED on the estate for two months. Finally, Penny insisted it was time she got back to help with the war effort. Nell felt pulled between wanting to stay with her children and being there for her husband back at home. It wasn't fair to leave him home alone when he was working so hard. Her children were lucky and well looked after. She decided her place was with her husband.

Meme packed a large case with provisions from the

farm. Nell was looking forward to seeing her husband's face when she presented him with a cooked ham for the first time in years. What would he make of her new muscles? She'd always been a hard worker, but helping with the harvest had defined the muscles in her arms and legs, toned and flattened her stomach, despite the excellent food.

Her Ladyship embraced her at the door when she came to see them off. "Thank you for all your help while you were here, Nell. I hope you will come and visit again soon. Not just to see your children, but to see me. I shall miss our chats."

Nell smiled at her host, no longer intimidated by her wealth or social status. She was a lovely woman, just as she had always seemed to be when Nell worked in her kitchen all those years ago. She'd never spoken to her before, but she remembered the warm smile.

The train journey back to London took forever and was extremely uncomfortable. Nell shifted in her seat, trying to give Penny more space. Her arm had recovered, but Nell didn't want to do anything to hurt her.

"Did you see the dirty look that woman opposite gave me?" Penny whispered. "Everyone's staring at me for not being in uniform."

"Penny, don't you worry about what other people think. Maybe they recognised your picture from the papers. You're a hero, remember?" Nell glared back at the old woman who'd looked down her nose. Uniformed personnel travelling back from or going on leave filled every available space. The surrounding faces were gloomy, but that didn't dispel Penny and Nell's good mood.

"Thank you, Penny, for asking me to come and help you with the Taylor girls. This trip has done me the world of good. I feel like I'm ready for anything the Germans are going to throw at us."

Penny looked at Gracie's mother with fondness. "I know what you mean. Meme, the kids and the estate have a way of making you feel ready for anything."

"When do you start your new job?" asked Nell.

"Monday morning, bright and early. I will work as a translator. I'm a little nervous to be honest, I've never worked in an office before. Uncle John says this is more useful than being a nurse, as they don't have enough native French speakers in London."

"You'll be fine. When you turn twenty-one, you can make your own choices. You might make some new friends at the office. Other girls your own age." Nell paused before adding, "They will call you up if this stupid war doesn't end soon. Might be a good idea to have your choice of occupations now."

"At least I won't have too long to get under Aunt Louise's feet." Penny sighed before looking at Nell. Nell rolled her eyes, her brief encounters with Lady

Louise in the past having been enough for a lifetime. They both giggled like schoolgirls, causing the other occupants to look at them curiously. *They must think we are out for the day from the loony bin.* The thought made Nell dissolve in giggles once more.

CHAPTER 10

LONDON, SEPTEMBER 1941

Penny turned up for work on her first day wearing a smart new blouse and skirt with her hair rolled up. She had a packed lunch in her bag, courtesy of Cook.

She found the address easily, an old Georgian home converted into offices. The dark blue door with a white painted frame looked well maintained despite the rubble from the bombings that dotted every street in London. After pressing the doorbell, she waited, glad she'd worn gloves as her hands felt clammy.

An older man, perhaps someone who'd come out of retirement, opened the door and told her to walk up the stairs to the second floor and ask for Miss Kennedy. Her heels clicked on the wooden stairs as she made her way. She could hear the clacking of typewriters and several telephones rang in the distance. Despite it being before nine, the office was already busy. Penny swallowed down her nerves, knocked on the door and entered.

The large room was brighter than she'd expected, with white painted walls dotted with a few picture frames. Two large sash windows and a high ceiling meant it didn't feel claustrophobic, despite the number of desks placed at regular intervals. She guessed it would have been the drawing room when the house was originally built.

Miss Kennedy, her manager, was tall, thin and wore her glasses at the end of her nose. She seemed quite stern.

"Good morning, Miss Hamilton. My name is Mary Kennedy, but you can call me Ma'am. Now follow me."

"Yes, Ma'am." Penny smiled, but the woman turned her back. She followed the older woman into another room where three other girls were quietly working. Each table had a typewriter, a jotter and about five buff-coloured files. As she walked past, one girl with dyed blonde hair winked at her before returning to the work on her desk.

"Girls, this is Miss Hamilton. She is replacing Miss Allen. I'm sure you will help her settle in. Now, Miss Hamilton…"

"Oh, please call me Penny."

Miss Kennedy glared at her. "Miss Hamilton, please take a seat. I believe you don't know how to type. Is that the case?"

"Yes, Ma'am. I never learnt. This is my first office job."

"Well, I suggest you take an evening course and brush up on your skills. In the meantime, your first task will be to translate three pages of French into English. I want to see how good your language abilities are."

Her tone suggested that she expected to find Penny lacking.

"Please come up to my desk when you have completed your task."

"Yes, Ma'am."

Penny settled herself at the desk and looked at the document in front of her. She recognised the text. Guy de Maupassant had been one of her father's favourite writers. After her mama died, she had found a book packed away in her bedroom. It was a copy of The Necklace. It was one of the few things she had brought with her to England.

She worked quickly, and as soon as she finished, she walked up to Miss Kennedy's desk. The woman looked up at her. "Don't tell me you can't understand it?"

"No, Ma'am. I've finished."

"Finished?"

"Yes, Ma'am," Penny said, worried she had misunderstood. "You said only three pages, didn't you, Ma'am?"

"There is no need for impertinence, Miss Hamilton. Please take a seat while I correct your work. I must warn you I do *not* view mistakes in a good light."

As Penny returned to her seat, none of the other girls

looked up. As she waited, she looked around the room. A large map of France covered one wall. The opposite wall had a similar-sized wall map, but of the world rather than one country.

How on earth am I helping the war effort sitting here translating old books? she wondered.

Miss Kennedy approached her desk. Penny caught her breath, even though she knew she had translated the work properly.

"Excellent work, Miss Hamilton. I didn't find one mistake. You must have gone to school abroad?"

"Well, yes, Ma'am. I was born in France, but my father was English, so I grew up reading and writing both languages."

"Wonderful," said Miss Kennedy.

Penny thought the woman was going to clap, she looked so animated.

"You should see the standard of some translators they send over to us. Here's some more useful work for you to complete. Lunch is at one."

Penny worked steadily through the document, translating it carefully. She didn't want to risk getting on the nasty side of her new boss. As soon as one o'clock arrived, the other girls stood up.

The girl with the dyed hair came over to her. "Hi, I'm Margaret, but my friends call me Mags. That's Denise and Sarah. Good, I see you brought lunch with you. It's such a lovely day, we're going down to the park. Do you want to come with us?"

Penny nodded, pleased to be invited. The girls seemed to be a friendly bunch.

As they walked to the park, Mags said, "Oh, I wanted to laugh out loud at the look on old Kennedy's face when you said you grew up in France. She can be such a witch."

"Leave it out, Mags. She's only doing her job. You will scare Miss Hamilton off and she won't come back tomorrow." The brunette who'd spoken turned to Penny, holding out her hand. "I'm Denise. Did you say your name was Penny? That doesn't sound French?"

"It's short for Penelope. Nice to meet you. Have you worked for Miss Kennedy long?"

"I've been here about a year now. Sarah's been here about six months, but Mags is the old-timer." Denise laughed before adding, "She's been here almost as long as Miss Kennedy."

Mags pulled a face. "Don't hold that against me, will you? So, what brought you to our office?"

Denise gave Mags a warning look. "I would have thought that was obvious even to you, Mags."

"Yeah. I know she can speak French," Mags retorted before turning to Penny. "I'm guessing you've never worked before. You don't get clothes like yours on a secretary's wage. I would bet a week's wages that your stockings are silk. Is this job a sort of hobby for you while you're waiting on some lord to sweep you off your feet?"

Penny looked down at the clothes she was wearing. True, they were the same colour as the other girls, but her blouse seemed whiter, and her skirt had a better cut.

"Mags, stop. You are embarrassing her." Sarah smiled at Penny. "Take no notice. I think your clothes are beautiful."

"Thanks, Sarah." Penny turned to look directly at Mags. "You are right, this is my first office job. And I guess I don't need to work, not for the money anyway. But you are wrong about the waiting for romance. I don't want to be any man's accessory. I want to do my bit for the war and, being underage, this was the only job I could get my uncle to agree to."

Mags looked slightly uncomfortable. "Okay, sweetheart, keep your hair on. I was only joking."

Penny burst out laughing, causing the other girls to stare at her.

"What's so funny?" asked Mags.

"Me. That's what. The lords and ladies you talk about don't accept me, as I grew up on a farm. They look down on me for being working class – and the first job I get, the girls I work with think I'm doing it for a hobby."

"I'm sorry, Penny. Trust me. I didn't mean to upset you. I have a big mouth. Don't you take any notice of those toffs, anyway. They are so stuck up, they don't even know there's a war on." Mags grinned at Penny. "Stick with us, love, and we'll show you how to have fun."

The lunch hour passed quickly. Penny spent the afternoon translating more documents until shortly after 5 p.m. Miss Kennedy collected her work. "Very good, Miss Hamilton. You can leave now. See you tomorrow morning, at half-past eight."

Penny grabbed her coat and, with a quick wave to the other girls, almost ran out of the building, desperate to be out in the sunshine.

CHAPTER 11

Penny gradually got into the office routine. She loved spending time with girls of a similar age. Miss Kennedy gave her more intricate documents to translate. They were busy, which helped the time pass quickly, but Penny still felt there was something more she could be doing.

Friday evening, she buttoned her coat as she stepped out onto the street, saying goodbye to the other girls and getting ready to head home. "Glad to see you made it through the first week. You're coming back on Monday, aren't you?"

"Yes, Mags. Just try stopping me."

Penny waved goodbye, smiling so hard her face hurt. She liked all the girls, but Mags made her laugh the most. She'd miss them over the weekend.

"Hey, Penny, wait."

Penny spun round, surprised to see David standing

there, looking very dashing in his blue-grey RAF uniform. He pushed the blond hair from his eyes; he wore it longer than most servicemen she'd seen around. "Oh, David, how nice." She immediately cursed herself for sounding like a lovesick puppy. "I mean, what are you doing here?"

"I had a meeting just around the corner and thought it would be nice to see how your job was going."

Penny grimaced. "It's okay."

"Only okay? What's wrong? Don't tell me you would prefer to be back making tea with the WVS?"

"The other girls are lovely, and the work is easy. But…" Penny looked at her feet.

David put his hand under her chin, forcing her to meet his eyes.

"So, what's the problem?"

Penny's heart raced at his touch. She looked into his smiling face. What beautiful eyes he had. Blue like the…

"Penny?" He was still smiling, but a look of concern crossed his face.

She clenched her hands; the nails digging into her palms. *Focus.*

"Sorry, David. There's no problem. I'm just being silly. It's just that I can't see what the work I'm doing has to do with the war."

David laughed. "Oh, to be so young again. You should have a little more patience, it's only been a few weeks. You may see soon enough what opportunities this job opens up."

"You said before that the RAF needed people who spoke fluent French. I think teaching your colleagues would be more useful than translating correspondence."

"Perhaps. We can discuss that further when I get back."

"Get back? Where are you going?" Penny stopped. "Sorry, I shouldn't have asked that." She laughed self-consciously.

"No harm done. I have to go see my parents. We're on embarkation leave."

"Again? You were going abroad the last time I saw you." Penny coloured. "Sorry, I have no right to ask you to account for your movements."

"That's okay, Penny. Curiosity is normal. I won't mistake you for a German spy, I promise." He smiled at her before continuing, "The last trip was a relatively brief tour. We were only away for about eight weeks. This tour will be longer, but then that goes with the territory. I can't complain. Plenty of my RAF colleagues don't get home half as often as I do."

They walked down the street in silence. Penny debated whether she should ask him in for something to eat. Before she knew it, the invitation came stumbling out of her mouth.

"Do you want to stay for dinner? I'm sure Cook can

rustle up something." Penny wondered if she was being too forward.

"No, but thank you. I have another appointment. Marianne has booked a table for us at the Ritz."

"Oh, I see. Sorry. I mustn't keep you." She tried desperately hard to keep the disappointment from her voice. Who was Marianne?

"It's okay. I wanted to see you to check you had fully recovered from your ordeal. My parents are in town and I have seen little of them since the engagement announcement."

"The engagement? Sorry, what?" Penny knew her voice squeaked, but that wasn't her primary concern. She was going to be sick. Her stomach turned over and over, making her feel quite giddy.

David looked at her oddly. "I'm surprised you didn't know. It was all over the society pages. Marianne Henry. Do you know the Henrys? They own most of England. Mother is so proud."

His bitter tone surprised her. He didn't seem happy to be sharing the news of his engagement. She looked at his mouth, which was still moving, but she couldn't focus on what he was saying. She swayed slightly.

"Are you sure you're okay? You don't look well. Perhaps I should look for a taxi?"

Penny's stomach lurched at the thought of having to sit beside him, even on a brief journey. "No, don't.

Please. I'm fine. I just need to get used to the light after being in the dark office all day."

"Okay, if you're sure." David didn't look too convinced.

Penny gathered her wits and started walking as fast as she could in the general direction of home. "So is Marianne in the services?"

"She's in the FANYs but is intent on resigning her commission once we get married."

A fiancée. Why hadn't Harriet told her?

"A wedding, how wonderful. Congratulations. Oh, I almost forgot. I promised Harriet I would collect something for her from Selfridges. Please excuse me, David. Nice to see you again. Take care of yourself."

Penny put out her hand to shake his but didn't look at him. She didn't think she could bear that.

"Oh, okay. Good luck with the job. See you," David said, clearly confused by her sudden change of mind.

"Bye." Penny crossed the road so quickly, she nearly got run over by a bus. *How could I have been so stupid, thinking someone like him would be available, much less interested in me? Harriet's right. I don't fit in. Not in their world. It's time I went home. Back to France.*

CHAPTER 12

Penny slept badly over the weekend, going over the scene with David again and again. At work on Monday morning, all she could think of was what a fool she had made of herself with David. *Honestly, the first man who looks at me, and I have us walking up the aisle.* She sighed wearily, wishing she had something to do to occupy her mind. But it looked like Miss Kennedy wasn't in a hurry to dish out work.

Mags, Denise and Sarah all smiled at her as they came in and made their way to their own desks. They immediately started working. Left alone with nothing to do, her thoughts kept going back over her meeting with David. Why would an engaged man call on her? Why wait for her outside the office? Perhaps it had been just a coincidence, but something told her that wasn't the case.

At last Miss Kennedy gave her some letters to translate, and she spent her morning deciphering love notes, which made her feel even worse. At lunch time, the girls took their sandwiches outside to sit in the park on some seats opposite the embankment. Penny wished she could jump on a boat and head down the river.

"So who's the gorgeous young man who met you after work on Friday night?" Mags asked.

Penny's face flushed. "He's an old family friend, that's all."

"You don't expect us to believe that, now, do you? He's RAF, isn't he? Everyone knows what those pilot boys are like."

"He isn't a pilot, he's a medical student." As the girls looked at her in confusion, Penny stammered, struggling to keep tears at bay. "Well, he was before … actually I don't know what he does in the RAF."

"For an old family friend, you don't seem to know much about him," Mags teased. "I could get up close and personal if you're not interested."

"Stop it, Mags. Ladies like Penny don't want to listen to that type of talk," Denise said.

Horrified, Penny realised that they once started, her tears wouldn't stop.

"Now look what you've done." Denise glared at Mags before rooting in her bag. She produced a hanky with the initial D embroidered in the corner. "Mam sews them for me, so I don't lose them. Here you are. It's clean." She handed the hanky to Penny.

"I'm sorry. He's a family friend – he's known my cousin for a long time – but I only met him the night they bombed the café. He said he was a medical student, though he was joining the RAF, and he was so nice, and then he called to the house after that and then to the hospital, so I thought – but now he has a fiancée and—"

"Slow down girl, you're talking so fast it's hard to keep up." Mags lit a cigarette, taking a pull before offering it to Penny, who declined.

"Are you saying that you were dating him, not knowing he had a girl already? What a cad. You're better off without him, regardless of how good-looking he is." Mags offered Penny another drag. Penny shook her head.

"With your looks, you won't be on your own for long. You can come with us to the Palace at the weekend. We'll set you up with someone nice. Someone single."

Sarah said, "My mam keeps warning me to stay away from pilots. I thought she was exaggerating, but that's awful. Imagine taking a young lady like you out when he was already engaged. I thought gentlemen would behave better, but I guess under all those posh clothes, they are just the same as any other man."

Penny shook her head. "No, David's not like that. He…"

"If you're going to say he told you he's not really in love with this other girl, I'll shake you. That's the oldest line in the book, right up with 'my wife doesn't understand me'," Mags said. The other girls giggled.

Penny panicked. "No, what I mean is that I met him at the Café de Paris. He wasn't my date." She ignored Mag's raised eyebrow. "David helped look after some people wounded in the blast. He was wonderful."

Mags rolled her eyes. "Penny, you are going all dewy-eyed again. This is the guy with the fiancée he didn't tell you about, remember."

"Yeah, but that was my fault, not his. He was so nice to me and he called to check I was all right. He talked my aunt into letting me take this job. Then after my injury when he came to see me in hospital ... I thought he liked me, and…"

"Oh, you poor chicken. He's the first guy you ever had a crush on, isn't he?" Mags said. "Wow, you really have had a sheltered life. If you lived where I grew up, you'd be married now with a kiddie on the way."

"What happened to you then, Mags? Had a lucky escape, did he?" Denise teased.

Mags responded by sticking out her tongue.

Penny felt her cheeks grow hot. "My aunt is strict. She doesn't like me going out, but I don't think she's afraid I will meet someone. She just worries I will let her down."

"Your aunt sounds like such a pleasant woman," Sarah said sarcastically. "Don't worry about David, Penny. First love is hard, but you get over it. Believe me. It's happened to us all, even to Mags, although she'd never admit it. The good news is that he's a man, so he may not realise that you had feelings for him. They take a while to figure us women out."

"Oh, look at the time." Mags stood up. "We're going to be late back and then we will all be in tears. Penny, I promise we will take you out one night and you'll forget all about this RAF fellow of yours. Now, chin up. There's a war on, remember?" Mags gave her a pat on the back as they walked back to the office to face a seething Miss Kennedy.

Despite getting into trouble for being late, Penny felt better. These women, although strangers, had shown more compassion than her own family had done. She decided never to let Harriet get to her again.

CHAPTER 13

Penny didn't see or hear from David for the next few months. She threw herself into her work and spent every spare hour volunteering. Mags kept her promise to take her dancing at the Palace. On the way, they stopped at a café, just off Denham Street, called Chez Moi. A cartoonist worked there, and his drawings of pilots and other aircrew decorated the walls.

A couple of pilots tried to talk to them, but Mags dismissed them. "Sorry, boys, but we aren't interested in the RAF tonight. We want to find us some nice sailors."

Penny giggled at the look of indignation on the pilots' faces. She guessed they were so used to being treated as stars they couldn't understand why Mags behaved as if they were naughty schoolboys. The girls left Chez Moi and headed to the downstairs bar in the Regent Palace. The number of single girls sitting around on their own surprised Penny. She declined Mags's suggestion to have an alcoholic drink. Her friend Gracie's story of what had happened to her the night a pilot had added alcohol to her drink had put Penny off for life. She preferred the taste of lemonade. They had a good night out and it led to many more, but she didn't meet anyone special.

Although she enjoyed the social side of work, as time went by, she became more frustrated. She wanted to do more – to feel she was helping to bring the war to an end.

~

AT THE END of her six months, she waited behind until the office was empty.

"Miss Kennedy, could I speak to you please?"

"Yes, Miss Hamilton."

This was more difficult than she'd expected. "I wanted to say thank you for the opportunity and experience of working here. I enjoy my job, but I think it's time I joined the forces. I'd like to be more involved."

"More involved?"

Penny resisted the urge to run. Instead, she held Miss Kennedy's gaze. "I believe my language skills could be more useful, perhaps serving in a more direct field."

"I see."

Penny wondered if she understood. She waited for

the other woman to speak until the silence grew uncomfortable.

"I'd best go now. I don't want to keep you from your work any more. Goodnight, Miss Kennedy."

"Could I ask you to hold off on joining up for a week? I've had an idea about how you could help the war effort, but I need to check a few details first."

"You have?" Penny bit her lip. She sounded like an overexcited child. "I mean, yes, I can wait."

Miss Kennedy shocked her by smiling. "I have recommended you for a promotion. There's a position you may be suitable for, it will involve extra secrecy and some additional training, but I believe you would be eminently suitable. Good evening, Miss Hamilton."

Penny wanted to ask more, but she knew a dismissal when she heard it.

"Thank you, Ma'am."

A few days later, a note arrived, asking her to attend an interview at the Northumberland Hotel.

～

WHEN THE DAY CAME, she dressed carefully, wanting to appear older than nineteen. She teamed a short-sleeved, cream silk blouse with a black scalloped collar jacket and black skirt. Together with a fresh pair of stockings and court-heeled shoes, she hoped she looked professional and capable. Her palms were sweaty, and her stomach was turning over. She regretted having eaten that morning.

Although she didn't know who she was meeting, it was obvious they were expecting her. An older woman wearing spectacles, a tweed suit and brown brogues showed her into a sparsely furnished room. All it contained were two folding chairs, a blackout screen and a naked light bulb. The woman didn't announce her and withdrew from the room without comment. A tall and thin, clean-shaven man with greying hair in civilian clothes stood there, apparently waiting for her. He evidently knew who she was but didn't introduce himself. Speaking English, initially, before switching to French, he asked several questions about why she wanted to leave her position as a translator, which she felt she answered adequately.

"It must have been difficult for you and your mother, after your father died in June 1929. You were seven."

Penny held her hands together on her lap, keeping a fixed expression on her face. What did this man know of her past? He stared at her, expecting a reply.

"A little."

His eyes widened a little, but he didn't correct her. "We wondered why your mother didn't bring you here to live with your father's family. You could have grown up in altogether different surroundings."

Irritated at the insinuation her mother was to blame,

Penny couldn't stop herself. "My father and his family were estranged. Mama believed we wouldn't be welcome. She did the best she could. She was a wonderful mother."

His expression remained a mask. He looked at his notes and the silence in the room grew. Penny wanted to smooth her hands on her skirt, but she wouldn't show any sign of discomfort.

"She died suddenly. A suicide, wasn't it?"

Penny swallowed. How could she answer this? Agree and betray her mother, or disagree and tell the man the truth: that her landlord and abuser Alain had murdered her because she wouldn't allow Penny to take her place in his bed.

The man coughed.

"That was the opinion of the local police." Glad to hear her voice sounded firm, she hoped that was enough to close those questions.

"You left quickly afterwards, came by train to London and from there arrived, more or less unannounced, on Lord Hamilton's doorstep."

Penny bit her lip – what could she say?

"You seem to know everything already. Why are you asking me?"

The man stared at her, again his face not giving her any hint of what he was thinking. He was waiting for her to talk, maybe give away the true story. Let him wait. She'd hidden the truth for years from Aunt Louise and her cousin.

"We know a lot but haven't been able to find out why you left so quickly? Couldn't a friend in the village have given you shelter? Madam Bayard perhaps."

Penny's eyes swung to his. He knew about Madam Bayard. She needed another tactic. She didn't have to force the tears.

"Sir, it was a very traumatic time for me. I was young, just lost my mother and found out I had family in London. Madame was a good neighbour, but she didn't offer me a home. In those days, when money was scarce, few people would take in an orphaned girl." Penny's gut twisted with guilt. She'd made Madame Bayard, the lovely old lady who'd looked after her so well, sound cold and hard-hearted.

"Mama's belongings included an address in London and enough money for a one-way train ticket. Madame decided for me. Mama had tried to contact my father's family before. Perhaps Madame thought that if I turned up unannounced, it would be harder for them to turn me away."

She held his gaze the whole time, willing him to believe her.

He lit up a cigarette, taking a deep drag before expelling a stream of smoke.

"Do you have contact with Madame Bayard now?"

"No, sir." This was easy to answer. "We were in

correspondence, but that stopped with the invasion. No letters get through now."

"So she wasn't a close family friend, yet you continued to write to her?"

Penny almost cursed aloud. How had she not seen that trap?

"Sir, Madame Bayard showed concern for me. She wanted to be sure I was happy and safe. She put me on the train after all."

He flicked the ash from the tip of his cigarette.

"What do you think of the Germans?"

The sudden change in his line of questioning was a relief, and she spoke freely.

"I hate the Nazis and everything they stand for. We must stop them, and the sooner the better. They seem to intend killing anyone who opposes them. But I..." She wondered if she had said too much.

"Go on."

"Well, I can't help feeling sorry for the ordinary German women who worry about their fathers, brothers and sons, and of course the children who are missing their fathers. They didn't ask for this war."

"But the Germans killed your father, didn't they?"

"My father died prematurely because of the wounds he sustained in the last war. But he never blamed the German people. He blamed the war. He didn't believe in hating people because of their nationality, although my mother didn't share his sentiments. She hated the *Boche*, as she called them, for killing my father and other members of her family."

"How do you get on with your aunt and uncle?" he asked.

This threw Penny. "Um, fine."

"Really?"

"Well, according to my aunt, I'd get on better if I behaved more like a lady and less like a common farm girl."

He smiled, but the smile didn't reach his eyes. "How do common farm girls behave, then?"

"I don't know how to do needlework or play bridge, but I can milk a cow, ride a horse, plough a field and bring in the harvest. I'm also quite good at cycling, but I'm not a talented dancer. She would prefer me to be more charming and less practical. In short, I guess she would prefer me to be more like Harriet, my cousin."

"Ah, yes, the beautiful and most honourable Harriet. Tell me, do you see yourself as being French or English?"

She thought the answer to that should be obvious to him, but he waited for her to reply. "I'm French. I was born in France to a French mother. But England is my adopted home and the birthplace of my father."

"So you would fight for England?"

"As they are on the same side as France, I would fight for both countries, would I not?"

The man contemplated her, she decided, as though

he was trying to decide something about her. His expressions and demeanour gave nothing away. Then he continued with his questions. She felt like she was being interrogated. The meeting lasted about forty minutes, although it seemed like hours. Just as she thought she couldn't bear another question, he abruptly stood up and brought the interview to a close.

"Please come back next Saturday for a brief chat. In the meantime, you must tell no one about our meeting or what we discussed. Is that clear?"

She had barely nodded when the door was closed in her face. She stood staring at it for a couple of seconds, trying to work out if she'd convinced him, she was keen or if she'd failed whatever test they'd set for her.

CHAPTER 14

"Oh, she sounds so fed up, Charlie. Maybe I should talk her into coming down here for a visit. Like a holiday?" said Gracie.

Charlie smiled at his wife. "Not sure that a holiday would be essential travel now, do you? Plus, with all the signposts being removed, she might get lost."

Gracie gave him a look, making him laugh.

"Seriously, Gracie, the trains are busy transporting rubble from bombed-out buildings to the airbases."

"What do they want rubble for in airbases?" asked Gracie, momentarily distracted from the contents of Penny's letter.

"To build runways, I suppose," said Charlie. "What else does Penny say? Has she seen your mam?"

Gracie quickly scanned the contents of the page. "Yes. She said Mam took her with her to visit the neighbours. Mam was collecting for the Red Cross fund."

Charlie shook his head. "I wonder if the soldiers and sailors getting those parcels realise it's old women like your mam who are going door to door collecting coins."

Gracie looked at her husband lying in his hospital bed. His bandages, changed that morning, were snow white. She wondered whether the new drug Dr McIndoe was using would help Charlie recover quicker. If the rate of operations kept up, Charlie would gain entry to the so-called 'Guinea Pigs Club'.

Gracie thanked God once again that Charlie was being treated by Dr McIndoe. The thickset, medium-height man with his horn-rimmed glasses may not have looked like anyone's idea of a hero, but he was hers. He not only repaired burn victims' physical injuries, but he also understood their mental suffering as well. Gracie believed he was a walking saint who could do no wrong. She turned her attention back to the letter she was holding.

"Honestly, darling, I could wring Penny's neck, complaining that she isn't doing anything to help the war effort. She wants to be more involved. What more does she want?"

"Maybe she could become a VAD and then I could have two beautiful women nursing me."

"Charlie! Be serious. I think Penny is going to do something stupid."

"Like what, darling? She will have to join up now.

She's almost twenty. Remember how you felt. You couldn't wait to serve your country."

Gracie ignored him. She read the letter through again. Penny's work in the translation service was valuable to the war effort, yet Gracie knew Penny wanted to feel more useful. Just how was the question Gracie didn't want answered. She would write back to Penny later.

~

GRACIE CRADLED her stomach as she paused in writing her reply to Penny. Two babies. How was she going to cope? She chewed the end of her pencil, wishing her friend was sitting opposite her. She was excited, of course, but also scared. How was she going to look after two babies and an injured husband?

She looked over at Charlie, who sat reading contently. The latest operations had been successful, but his treatment continued. Gracie's hand moved protectively over her tummy.

"Are you feeling all right, darling?"

Gracie looked up, realising Charlie had asked her something.

"Yes, I'm fine. Don't fuss."

"Are you telling Penny the news?" Charlie asked, smiling.

"Yes, she will be so excited. You know what she's

like with babies. She missed out so much on being an only child. I bet when she meets someone, they'll have ten or more kids."

Charlie laughed. "Glad I'm spoken for, then. Two is more than enough for me."

"You're happy, though, aren't you? I know you wanted to wait until the war is over. But nature knows what it's doing."

Charlie smiled at his wife. "At least someone does. I admire you so much. Nothing fazes you, Gracie. Few women could cope with an invalid for a husband and a baby, never mind twins."

I have little choice now, do I? "You are not an invalid. I wouldn't have planned it this way, not two together, but it might be fun. At least our children will never be lonely. They will always have each other to play with."

How would she feed them both? Would she be able to do it herself? Thank goodness the raids had stopped. Imagine having to feed babies in a public shelter.

"Gracie, are you there?"

"Sorry, Charlie, I was miles away. Can I get you something?"

"You were frowning. Stop fretting. You know the midwife told you, you need to keep calm. Expectant mothers don't need to add high blood pressure to their list of ailments." Charlie looked at his wife. "You will be careful, won't you? Any signs of swelling ankles and you have to rest."

"Charlie Power, if you don't stop fussing this instant, I'm going to ask Dr McIndoe to keep you in hospital for the duration."

Charlie laughed but wisely said no more. Gracie went back to her letter. She didn't tell Penny about the midwife's concerns about having twins at home, especially as she was a first-time mother. Gracie had refused to book a maternity hospital as it was too far away from Charlie. If Penny had been beside her, she could have discussed her fears, but it didn't feel right putting them into a letter.

Penny arrived when she'd been told to on Saturday, and again her interviewer didn't keep her waiting.

"Morning, Penelope, thank you for being so punctual. Now, how do you feel about our conversation? Do you have questions for me?"

"Yes, sir. I can't help but wonder what position you were interviewing me for?"

"Well, I believe you would be interested in a position that required local knowledge of the French countryside, and the ability to converse fluently in French?"

Penny looked at him. She wasn't sure if she had understood. It seemed he was implying she'd go to France, but that couldn't be right. That was where the Germans were. Unless he meant he wanted her to work behind the enemy lines – but he couldn't, as she was a woman, and they didn't send women over there. Did they?

He watched her carefully as she digested what he had said. Before she responded, he said, "Yes, I mean, go to France. We need to send people with local knowledge and the ability to pass themselves off as French citizens. Given your upbringing, you're ideally suited for training to undertake the role in question. But I would like you to give this some thought. This is a life-and-death decision. You must decide whether you will risk your life for France and your adopted country, England. You must promise not to look up any old neighbours."

Her eyes flickered to his, but she stayed silent.

"And we have to decide whether we want to let you."

"I would like to do my bit, sir, but I'm not sure what you'd want me to do. I don't have any skills."

"That's not true, my dear. As a native, you speak the language fluently and you also know the area where we intend to send you very well. That type of knowledge is valuable, especially in our line of work. Don't worry about the rest for now. If you're accepted, suitable training will follow. All I need to know for now is whether you will proceed. Before you decide, know that only about half of the agents we send into France will come back alive. You may wonder why we would ask anyone, let alone a young woman, to take such a risk given those odds. The answer is that we believe the coordinated resistance offered by our agents and the people who help them will shorten the war by several years, thus saving hundreds of thousands of lives. Their work is vital to the success of our troops."

Penny nodded, but couldn't speak, so he continued.

"You can't decide in five minutes, so why don't we meet again on Thursday? I must remind you, you are not to discuss this with anyone, no matter what rank they hold or who they are. That includes your aunt and uncle and your manager at the translation unit, although she is aware of what we had in mind. This conversation is strictly private. Do you understand?"

"Yes, sir. Can I ask another question?"

He nodded his assent.

"What would I tell my family? It's not as if they would readily accept me disappearing for days or weeks on end? They have rather strong opinions about what is suitable work for a young lady."

He smiled. "I'm familiar with your aunt and uncle's views on the role of young ladies in society. If you join us, we'll post you to the First Aid Nursing Yeomanry's in a secretarial role."

She was about to interrupt, but he continued.

"I'm sure your family will have no objection to you mixing with other society girls. Now, consider what I have said carefully. We will speak on Thursday."

PENNY LEFT the building in a daze. Outside, everyone was going about their business as normal, yet she felt different. The man who interviewed her seemed to know everything about her, yet she didn't even know his name. She couldn't really believe that she might go home to France. "Yes" was the only answer, regardless of what the work entailed. Home. She missed her old home, although she knew it would be different now.

She sat watching the world go by. A young mother pushing her pram caught her attention. Gracie. She must write to congratulate her on the news. She couldn't imagine how her friend was feeling. Probably a bit scared and excited. For a moment, Penny wished she could put her application on hold and go to visit Gracie. No, she would only try to talk her out of it. It was best to write.

She thought of all the people who had lost their lives already in this damn war. If she could do something that would help end it quicker, she was definitely going to do it. She would be glad to get away from her aunt and Harriet for a while. When she came back, she would visit Gracie and her new family at the first opportunity. Humming to herself, she hopped onto a bus and headed back to Belgrave Square.

~

SHE HAD JUST REACHED the top of the staircase when Harriet came rushing out of her bedroom.

"It's about time you came back. Where were you? I have been looking for you for ages. Peter is taking me out for a special dinner tonight, and I want you to dress my hair. There is no one else to do it, not since Gracie left," said Harriet.

Penny let the comment about Gracie slide. She was used to her cousin winding her up at every given opportunity, but she couldn't believe who Harriet was going out with. "With Peter? I thought you had forgotten about him. He doesn't deserve you, especially after what happened that night in the Café de Paris." She might not get on with her cousin all the time, but she didn't hate her enough to want her to marry someone as selfish as Peter; someone who'd so readily leave her to die in a bomb blast while saving himself.

"That was over a year ago. Anyway, I told you before. He explained what happened. It wasn't his fault that Lady Agatha insisted he escort her to safety."

Penny looked at Harriet in disbelief. "You don't seriously believe that story, do you?"

"Enough. What has it got to do with you, anyway? It's not like you care about me. Not really. Now, I want you to do my hair in that Lana Turner style you did a few weeks ago. I need to look my best tonight, as I suspect something special is going to happen. Mummy's lending me her diamond hairpin. I intend looking fabulous."

Penny knew it was pointless trying to talk Harriet out of something she was sure her cousin would live to regret. She despised Peter, not only because he was selfish and totally spoilt but also because he had a wandering eye and couldn't keep his hands to himself. She had fallen victim to those hands pawing at her once and resolved never to be caught alone with him again.

Penny couldn't tell her cousin where she'd been, so she lied. "Sorry, Harriet. I went to the hospital to see if I could help. They are so short staffed. Maybe you could offer to help. It would give you something useful to do, rather than just decorating Uncle John's office."

"Me in a hospital? Are you mad? God only knows what germs I would pick up. Actually, have a wash before you touch my hair. I don't want to catch anything. Anyway, the work I do in Daddy's office is important war work. I'm doing my bit for the war effort, despite what you may think."

Penny decided it was best to keep her thoughts to herself. She didn't want to upset Harriet and, by extension, Aunt Louise, just as she was on the brink of finally being able to join up.

After helping Harriet to get ready, Penny was glad to make her excuses and head to bed. With Harriet and her uncle out for the evening, she didn't relish the thought of spending an evening with her aunt. She was keen to be alone with her thoughts and, for the first time, was glad that Gracie wasn't there. She would have known straight away that Penny was being less than truthful. It's bad enough that she suspects I may be up to something from my letters.

She couldn't wait until Thursday. She only hoped that the man had decided she was worth taking on.

CHAPTER 16

Thursday finally came and Penny arrived early for her appointment, walking there through the bombed-out streets, piles of rubble, and houses that looked like someone had cut them in half. Her aunt and uncle presumed she was going to her translating job. Miss Kennedy was already aware of where she was, having set the whole thing up. Arriving early, she paced up and down outside the office building, looking at the people coming and going. Were any of these people back from France? What was it like back in her homeland? Was Mrs Bayard suffering at the hands of the Nazis? Shuddering, she took a deep breath and entered the front door.

As she climbed the steps, she wondered what she'd do if they said no. Now the chance to go home had been dangled in front of her; it was all she wanted. Some special agent she would become if she got this nervous over a meeting.

As before, the man was expecting her, but this time there was another person present, an attractive, well-groomed blonde wearing a tweed suit who introduced herself as Miss Vera Atkins. "Hello, Penelope. How are you feeling?"

Despite the cultured accent, Penny knew Miss Atkins wasn't British. She may fool most people sounding more English than the English themselves. She wasn't French either despite the woman's flawless French. Penny focused – the woman's nationality wasn't the issue. "Fine, thank you, ma'am." Penny tried to stop her foot tapping on the floor.

"Relax, Penny, it's good news. You passed the first hurdles and will be enlisted in the First Aid Nursing Yeomanry. The uniform will help you explain to your friends and family why you will be away for such long periods of time."

Penny nodded but sensed there was another reason. She was almost tempted to take the cigarette Miss Atkins offered her. Miss Atkins lit up, taking a drag before she spoke again.

"There's another reason we want you in uniform. If you are captured, we hope the Nazis will abide by the Geneva Convention. In theory, the uniform and rank should protect you."

"In theory…" Penny repeated.

"It's not one anyone wishes to test."

Feeling a little stupid, Penny looked around the room. Nothing about it gave away any secrets. But for the discussion about France at the last meeting, and the question of the uniform, she could be at any job interview.

"I suppose you are wondering what's in store for you."

Penny nodded, so Miss Atkins continued.

"The initial assessment and training will take three weeks and will include a psychiatric evaluation. Once you pass this step, you will then learn about parachuting, explosives, Morse code and hand-to-hand combat."

Penny swallowed hard, trying not to show any emotion. Hand to hand? But there was no time to think, Miss Atkins was still speaking.

"Each team comprises three agents, being a courier, wireless operator and an organiser. The role of wireless operator is by far the most dangerous, as they are carrying incriminating evidence should the Nazis or the *Milice* should stop them. But the success of each network depends on keeping in contact with London, so the role is vital.

As the name suggests, the courier carries messages between members of each circuit or network. As a security measure, a different and totally independent network covers each area of France. If one circuit is betrayed to the Germans, those members can't endanger the other networks."

"But surely nobody would betray their friends?" protested Penny, before realising she had rudely interrupted. "Sorry."

The thin man looked soberly at Penny. "Everyone who is captured talks eventually. All we ask is that our agents do their best to hold out for forty-eight hours to give other agents a chance to escape the eventual round-up that will come. Don't underestimate the lengths the Nazis will go to in order to get information."

Penny looked at him in horror before switching her attention back to Miss Atkins, who explained more.

"We feel women are naturally suited to the role of courier as men of military age risk being arrested and sent to Germany as forced labour. Female couriers are less likely to arouse suspicion, particularly when they have an excellent cover story for having to move around, such as being the local nurse.

"The organiser is usually male, simply because the role requires a lot more experience in sabotage and recruitment of more agents from locals. Men have been doing this job for longer so are, therefore, more experienced. There is also the fact that most French men hold very traditional views on what roles women should undertake, and being their boss is not one of them. Now, have you any questions?"

Questions – she had tonnes of them. She thought

quickly for one that sounded intelligent. "Who decides which position I will hold?"

"Your course tutor will make a recommendation about which position you are most suitable for depending on what strengths and weaknesses the training highlights."

"When would I start?" asked Penny.

"You will receive your orders in due course outlining where and when you must make yourself available for duty, but be prepared to start a week on Monday." Miss Atkins smiled at Penny.

Penny was totally bemused. She had just about got over her excitement at being accepted when the nerves hit. Parachute training! Now was probably not the time to admit to a fear of heights … Hardly trusting herself to speak, she mumbled a reply. Her superiors were obviously used to the effect this speech had on raw recruits. The thin man reminded Penny that she was free to change her mind about serving with the unit until she actually departed for France.

The man started speaking again. "It's normal to be scared. In fact, if you didn't show a little fear, we wouldn't have recruited you. People who don't show fear are a liability in the field. The Germans are ruthless, but at least they are the enemy in plain sight. What you have to be really careful of is the French collaborators."

Penny opened her mouth to refute this slur on her people, but the man didn't let her speak.

"Before you get all patriotic, all communities have those elements who are only concerned for their own survival. They would sell their grandmother into slavery if it bought them some extra money or power. Beware of all contacts you make, including any that you may have had from your childhood. Sharing a common background doesn't mean that a person's political beliefs or opinions now mirror your own. You need to be wary of everyone and only allow yourself to be friendly with someone when you are completely sure that you can trust them with your colleagues' lives. Remember, if you get caught, you will betray those on your team."

Penny glowered at the man, wanting once more to protest, but again he cut in before she opened her mouth.

"Don't look at me like that. Everyone goes out there hoping they won't, but if you survive forty-eight hours of the torture techniques that the Gestapo use, you will do very well. The training will help to answer questions you may have. You will learn how to recognise those who may be helpful to our cause. We will also teach you how to master various weapons. By the time we have finished with you, your skill set will include being able to shoot a man dead with your eyes shut, jump out of a plane, blow up a railway and, perhaps just as importantly, know how to transport explosives without blowing yourself and those around you to kingdom come."

Penny was reeling, wondering just what she had got herself into.

As if sensing her thoughts, the man continued.

"Some would-be agents find that the work doesn't suit them. Others decide not to proceed for personal reasons. If you have any doubts about whether you still wish to go into the field, then please come and tell us. We are not in the game of sending unwilling operators into danger. Now go home and tell your family that you have been ordered to attend training somewhere in Scotland and will be gone for several weeks."

The man walked to the door. Penny took the hint. She thanked both of them for their time. As she strolled home, she didn't notice anything around her. It was really true; she was going home.

Back to France. And to him.

CHAPTER 17

Penny told her aunt and uncle at dinner that evening. Harriet was out with Peter. She sat at the table, waiting for the right moment to break her news. Thankfully, her uncle gave her the opening she needed.

"How was your day, Penelope?"

"Actually, Uncle John, I got my papers today. I have to report for duty on Monday week."

Aunt Louise looked up. "Your papers? What about your translation job? Surely that was a reserved occupation?"

Her uncle grinned at her, but despite his smile, his eyes were stormy, pride and frustration warring in their depths. "I rather think our young niece volunteered. Am I right, Penelope?"

"Yes, Uncle, I did volunteer." Penny figured being direct would cut off any arguments. "I'm almost twenty and liable to be conscripted. I've joined the First Aid Nursing Yeomanry's. They've ordered me to Scotland."

"Congratulations, Penelope. Your aunt and I are very proud of you. Many of our friends' daughters are in the FANYs. It seems like the right sort of outfit for someone of our background. Don't you agree, Louise?"

Penny looked at Aunt Louise, who seemed to be about to say something but then changed her mind.

"Do you know what you will do?" asked her uncle.

"Oh, probably some secretarial work and more translation. I won't know for certain until I get to Scotland."

Louise's smile was almost warm as she leaned forward. "Penelope, that is wonderful. You could find a nice suitable husband among one of those officers. Lady Sybil was only telling me the other day how her younger daughter is walking out with the son of an earl whom she met when driving an officer around."

Penny looked at her aunt in disbelief. "The FANYs aren't a match-making service."

Her uncle laughed. "Despite the war, my wife still believes finding a suitable husband is the most important thing in a girl's life."

Louise pursed her lips before rising from the table, her tone barely civil. "Just because I have standards doesn't give you the right to laugh at me. I have better things to be doing than sitting here being abused. Excuse me." Her aunt swept out of the dinner room.

Penny was struggling not to laugh. She darted a quick look at her uncle and was relieved to see that he was trying to cover the sound of his laughter with a napkin.

"Penny, I'm very proud of you and I'm sure your father would be, too. I will leave it to you to write to your grandmother to tell her what you have done. Now try not to get in Louise's way over the next few days as she may start measuring you for a wedding gown." He laughed at his own joke and they finished their meal in companionable silence.

∼

ALTHOUGH PENNY HAD BEEN TOLD her services were no longer required at the translation department, she wanted to say goodbye to the girls. They had been very nice to her and were her friends. She went into work the next day to see them.

"It's my last day today. I have joined up," she said.

"Is that what you have been doing? I knew you were up to something," asked Mags when they all went to lunch. "Why did you do that? We're doing important war work and having fun at the same time." Mags looked almost disappointed.

Penny avoided answering. "I'll miss you girls. All of you. Thank you so much for being my friends."

"Sure, we will keep in touch. We can write and

when Penny is back in London, we can head to the Palace again," said Denise, ever the peacekeeper.

Penny smiled gratefully at Denise. "I'm not sure where I'll be posted. Scotland was mentioned."

"You'll get leave though, won't you?" asked Mags.

"Not at the start, as you have to work up some time. But I should be home for Christmas, and then we can all celebrate together. I'll write when I can. I'll want details of all the latest love affairs."

"Okay, you got it. But before you go off, let's celebrate. You haven't seen *Gone with the Wind* yet, have you? It's on at the Empire in Leicester Square." Mags looked so excited, Penny didn't have the heart to say she'd seen it about ten times already. The other girls nodded. "We can all go tomorrow night."

～

PENNY SPOTTED Denise and Sarah as she arrived at the agreed meeting place in Leicester Square. Mavis ran up behind them, breathless.

"Sorry, I missed the bus," Mavis stammered.

The girls became so immersed in the film they couldn't believe that nearly four hours had passed from start to finish. As they walked outside into the darkness, they chatted about the film.

"That scene of Atlanta burning reminded me of London early last year," said Denise.

"I know exactly how Scarlett felt in the bit about the radishes." The other girls laughed. Sarah was always hungry and never stopped complaining that their daily rations weren't enough to survive on.

As they chatted and laughed, for a split second Penny had second thoughts about volunteering. These girls had given her their friendship, and she'd be leaving them behind. Just like Gracie.

Mags put her arm through Penny's. "Are you okay?"

Penny smiled at her friend. "Yes, of course. Just thinking how much I will miss you all."

"We'll miss you as well. The office just won't be the same without our own poor little rich girl." Mags gave Penny a hug. "You look after yourself now, and don't go getting into trouble. Remember to stay away from those RAF boys."

Penny smiled at the reference to David. It had been so long since she had seen him, and she'd been distracted by work and her new role to come, that she'd barely had time to think about him; yet she could still remember how he looked, smelt and the touch of his lips on her cheek.

"He's not your Rhett, darling, but your Ashley. He belongs to someone else," Mag whispered.

Penny blushed. "I know that."

"I hope so." Mags's tone suggested that Penny didn't.

"Come on, you two, you're falling behind. We'll never get a table at this rate," said Sarah.

Mags laughed. "You and your stomach."

CHAPTER 18

Nell brushed the hair from her face, impatiently wiping away the sweat rolling down her forehead. At least the scorching weather gave people something else to talk about. The war news was so depressing. She switched off the wireless. She didn't want to hear about another ship sinking or the battles being lost in Egypt.

She missed her children. Frank away with the army, Stan in some prisoner-of-war camp, Gracie down south with her husband, the younger children evacuated to Penny's grandmother's home. Thank goodness for Penny, otherwise she'd be fretting even more. And at least Kenny and his sisters were well cared for and enjoying life on the farm.

She scrubbed the new potatoes and cabbage before putting them on to boil. She had put the lamb stew on a low heat since morning. Hopefully, by the time her husband came in, the lamb would be edible. Lamb?

She'd wager a shilling it was more likely mutton the butcher was offloading. Thank goodness Alf kept an allotment. The vegetables he grew had helped feed their growing family during the difficult years of the 1930s when jobs were scarce. At times, both her husband and her eldest son, Frank, had been out of work or on shorter hours. Now the potatoes, cauliflowers, cabbages, peas and other vegetables helped stretch the rations, not only for them but their neighbours benefited, too.

Rations. What would they think of next? Banning pleats, pockets and long socks to save material? Reducing the soap ration to three ounces a month? It was a wonder anyone kept their house and family clean.

Oh, stop it now. She needed to get a grip of herself. Fretting about rations and other nonsense when the actual issue was her daughter's pregnancy. Her own twins, Stan and Gracie, had been good babies, but two babies caused so much extra work. Being pregnant during the war was bad enough, but how would her daughter cope so far from family and friends with twins and Charlie's injuries?

The knock on the door was a welcome distraction from her thoughts. Opening it, she was surprised but pleased to see Penny standing on her doorstep.

"Sorry, Nell, I didn't have time to send a note. Is now a good time?" asked Penny.

"Come in, Penny, please. You're a sight for sore eyes. I've been having an off day today."

Penny blanched. "You haven't had bad news, have you? Is it Gracie?"

Nell shook her head. "Gracie is fine and well. No, I was listening to the news on the wireless. Where do the Russians think we will find the men to start another front? Then there're the ships being lost and those poor men fighting over in Egypt."

Although she motioned for Penny to sit, Nell couldn't stand still. She kept talking and walking backwards and forwards. Eventually Penny stood up and, taking Nell's hands, pulled her into a chair.

"You put your feet up and I'll pour the tea. It's the weather. The heat is getting to all of us," Penny said.

"It's not the weather, Penny. I'm worried – about Gracie. What on earth is she playing at, having babies in the middle of a war? I would have thought she had more sense. With Charlie injured and everything…"

Penny put a strong cup of tea in front of Nell. "Drink that. A good cup of tea is the answer."

Penny took her own cup and sat down opposite Nell. "Gracie will be fine. She's surrounded by doctors and nurses at the hospital. Charlie is getting better every day. They'll manage."

"You are a dear girl coming over to see me. Did Gracie tell you it's twins? One baby is bad enough, but two together?" Nell played with her hands.

Penny leant forward, placing one hand on top of Nell's. "They will be fine. You can go down and help them out. Imagine having more grandchildren to spoil. Now I hope you don't mind, but I brought over some things from the attic for the babies when they come."

Nell couldn't hide her excitement. She picked up each little piece. "Oh, don't you forget how tiny babies are? These are gorgeous. Are you sure your aunt doesn't mind?"

"Meme will be happy someone is getting use out of them. They aren't safe in that attic any more. We can protect them from moths, but Hitler's bombs are a different story."

Nell picked up a matinee coat. "Isn't it ever so soft? It looks like nobody ever wore it."

"Maybe they didn't. There were so many things up there. I just picked out some more practical items. I knew that you would have to carry them down by train. When are you going to see Gracie next?" Penny asked before sipping her tea.

"Next month, maybe. It depends on the shop. Did Gracie tell you I have a little job now? I work a couple of days a week. I love it. It's so nice to chat with other women. Some ladies have sons who are prisoners of war just like our Stan." Nell stopped to drink some tea.

"Have you heard from Stan lately?" Penny asked.

"We got the usual brief letter last week, but it's hard to know whether he is telling the truth. Anyway, he should get his first parcel soon. That should cheer him up." Nell poured some more tea for herself and Penny.

"So what about you? Any news to tell me? How is the translation work going?" Nell asked. It surprised her when a couple of seconds elapsed before Penny answered.

"I've joined up, Nell."

"Why? I thought you enjoyed the translation work. It would have kept you out of the war, too. It's a reserved occupation, surely?"

"Yes, it is, but I want to do more. So I joined the FANYs."

"The FANYs? Don't they drive the officers around in nice cars? How is that more important than your translation job?" Confused and suspicious, she looked at the young girl closely. "Where will you be based?" Her suspicions mounted as Penny picked up her gloves, saying she had to get back.

"Penny? What is it? Is there something you're not telling me?" asked Nell. "You're not running away because of the chap Gracie mentioned? I know she was worried he had hurt your feelings." Nell swallowed, hoping she'd not spoken out of turn.

"Who? Oh, David? No, not at all. I just wanted to do something useful and see more of the country. I only ever go to Suffolk. Now I'm being sent to Scotland."

"Scotland? That's far, isn't it? What are you going to be doing up there?"

Penny was almost out the door. "You know, Nell, a

bit of this and that. They won't be more specific. Walls have ears, you know."

"Hmm. I think there is something more to this, Penelope Hamilton. It smells fishy to me." Nell went quiet, seeing the red flush take over Penny's face. The young girl wouldn't meet her gaze. "It's okay, sweetie. You don't need to tell me anything. Just mind yourself. Okay? You are precious to my daughter. And to us."

"Thank you, Nell." Penny gave her a quick hug and ran out the front door, leaving Nell staring after her.

God be with you wherever you are going. She would bet a shilling it wasn't Scotland. At least not for long.

Nell watched until Penny had disappeared from sight before she closed the front door. She had bread to make yet. Her husband would have to do with home-made brown bread. There wasn't a slice of white bread to be found in any shop. Scotland – what on earth do they want with young girls up there in Scotland?

It was a good thing, she hadn't had time to visit Meme. She wouldn't have been able to keep anything from her.

If they saw how badly I handled the visit with Nell, they would sack me already. Some spy I'll make, Penny berated herself on the journey to Wanborough Manor in Guildford. As usual, the train was delayed many times. Passengers around her moaned about being late or missing their connections.

She looked out of the windows of the train carriage, the green fields reminding her of home. Closing her eyes, remembering how she used to play on the ramparts with her friends, she heard her mama's voice reading from *Les Misérables*. She would soon be home. Biting her lip, she tried not to smile with excitement.

Her stomach churned as she wondered how Madame Bayard was faring under the Nazi regime. She prayed her old friend was safe and well. Soon she would see her in person. *And I will also see him.* She couldn't let anyone know she had another motive for going home. Her new training would help her deal with Alain. Her throat felt dry from thirst. Breathing quicker, she searched through her bag looking for a sweet to suck on. Her mind went over and over the reasons she wanted to go back to France. It wouldn't do for her boss to guess that personal revenge was her primary motive.

~

The house she had been told to arrive at reminded Penny of Meme's home in Suffolk, only not as nicely decorated. She left her case at the front door and was directed into what had once been the dining room, where a few people were already sitting in armchairs or chatting as they drank cups of tea and coffee. Blackout curtains hid the original red velvet curtains adorning the bay windows. The mantel over the ornate fireplace was free from dust and ornaments, and someone had set the fire, but it wasn't lit.

Penny looked around at the other recruits. There were three other girls, and the rest were men. One girl, speaking with a French accent, was introduced as Juliette by the female officer who had shown Penny in. It was presumably a code name as Penny was introduced to the other trainees as Simone. It would take some getting used to being called by another name.

A couple of uniformed WAAFs were handing out teas and real coffee, a luxury that Penny couldn't resist. They could be at an afternoon tea party if everyone wasn't in uniform. Penny joined one of the smaller groups chatting amongst themselves. One soldier was talking loudly about how excited he was to be going into France.

"This is a jolly splendid show, isn't it? My name's Leon and, personally, I can't wait to get over to France. It's about time we showed those Frenchies how to fight properly. They need to have some backbone. Cowards, the lot of them."

Penny bristled, but before she could make a comment, an army major walked into the room.

"Ladies and gentlemen, if I could have your attention. My name is Major Hunter, and I will be your commanding officer during your time here at Wanborough House. Now does everyone have a drink?"

He waited for a few seconds for everyone to take their seats before continuing.

"First, let me remind you all that you are not to disclose any personal details to anyone in this group. Yes, I know that some of you know each other from school or society functions, but we must pretend we have all only just met. This is for your own protection. Try as we might to ensure against it, there could be a traitor standing amongst us. They will be happy to tell the Gestapo everything he or she learns about you. So no girly gossip." Two men sniggered, but soon shut up when the major looked at them before adding, "And no bragging designed to impress a date.

"Now, some of you will be more prepared than others for what lies ahead of you during your time here. There are a couple of people here who have already been working behind enemy lines, so will know better than most the dangers you face." The major looked directly at Juliette and a couple of men standing beside her. "We are delighted that you have joined our group and look forward to learning from you over the course of the next few weeks."

Juliette and the men nodded.

The major continued, "On the course, you will learn several sabotage and assassination techniques. This is war, ladies and gentlemen, so the first thing you do is forget about behaving 'properly'. We are not interested in winning a fight fairly, we just want to win."

He drank some water.

"There is no place for pity in your work. Your job will mean working with and perhaps recruiting local resistance fighters who can help us. The risks are enormous. There are many men and women who are making a living by collaborating with the Nazis. If a member of your team is a collaborator, your orders are to kill them, regardless of age, sex or relationship. You can't risk those making false promises not to report back to their masters."

The officer looked at the group sternly.

"We will teach you how to break into premises without being caught. We have some of England's finest criminals in our employment who are ready to teach you everything you need to know. In the field, you may need to enter a property to take photographs, conduct a search or carry out an assassination.

"When you shoot someone, use two shots – aim for the stomach and the heart. The first may kill him, but the second will make sure. Again, remember you don't want to leave witnesses behind you. The risk of identification is too high."

Penny exchanged a look with one of the other women. She'd wanted Alain dead for a long time, but when it came to it, could she really kill someone?

"Yes, Simone, you could, and you may have to."

Penny jumped as the officer, staring directly at her, read her thoughts so clearly. He continued to address the group.

"Those of you who took up boxing at school will be familiar with the list of fouls under the Queensberry Rules. Here, we encourage you to practise these fouls as it's the simplest way to overpower your enemy. It isn't enough to know how to think and move quickly. Every action you take must have a serious consequence for your opponent, preferably his death. You can't afford to be sympathetic, as not only your own life, but the lives of your fellow agents depend on you. If your opponent is injured, this is a good thing as it makes him or her easier to kill."

He gazed around the room, taking time to look at each would-be agent individually.

"If you have to search a prisoner, you should first kill him. If that isn't possible, or if you wish to keep him alive for questioning, render him unconscious. A kick or hard blow to the head usually works."

One girl gasped, but the officer ignored her.

"Finally, if the Gestapo arrests you, try not to become defeatist and believe the worst. All may not be over as they may not realise who you are. They will often pretend to know more than they do, so stick to your cover story at all times. We will issue you with a cyanide pill when you go into the field. You may not agree with suicide, but after time spent in the hands of the Gestapo, you may find your attitude changes. There is no way back once the pill has been taken."

The officer took a sip of water from the glass on his desk before turning back to look at the assembled group.

"Does anyone have questions?"

"Sir, do you make allowances on the training for the young ladies amongst us?" asked Leon.

Penny bristled. Everything about Leon irritated her, and it wasn't just because of what he had said earlier about the French being cowards. He reminded her of

Harriet's fiancé, although he was better looking. That was probably his problem. People would have doted on him since he first arrived in the nursery.

His obvious disdain for the female members of the group didn't appear to endear him to the major.

"No, Leon. I think you will find that underestimating our 'young ladies' could be a deadly mistake. Mr Churchill certainly thinks so. They may look pretty and decorative, but in our experience, the combination of brains with beauty has proved quite lethal to more than one German officer. We don't go easy on the ladies as the Germans won't treat them any differently to the men should they be captured." He paused before asking, "Any more questions?"

"Sir, how do we know when we are ready to go?" the red head asked. Penny wondered if her hair colour was natural and whether she'd change it. Miss Atkins had mentioned they were supposed to blend into the population and this woman stood out like a lighthouse.

"By the time you are finished with this training, you will eat, sleep and think like a Frenchman – sorry – woman." The group laughed but were silenced by a look.

"By nature, you will walk on the correct side of the road, eat in the French fashion, make tea by putting in the milk last, not first as we do in England, and dress appropriately. The ladies won't smoke in public as cigarettes have been rationed for women since 1941 in

France. The men will all have excellent reasons why they haven't volunteered to work in Germany. Now, any more questions?"

"Someone mentioned the course involves a visit to the dentist. Is this mandatory?"

"Scared of the dentist, are we, Pierre?"

"Well, I wouldn't say scared, exactly, sir, but I would rather avoid it if possible. I hate getting fillings." Pierre made a funny face, causing the group to laugh.

"Had some fillings already? One look into your mouth would tell the Germans you were English, so they have to come out. Don't worry, our French dentist will have them removed and replaced with gold ones before you can say 'Bonjour, Paris'."

Pierre blanched, causing more laughter.

"Now any more questions? No. Good. Then please disperse to your quarters. You will be shown where to go. We eat at 7 p.m."

Some WAAFs appeared to show them to their rooms and divided them into groups. Penny's group climbed up two flights of stairs. The runner of carpet held in place by brass rods showed some wear, and Penny thought they were not the first recruits to stay there. She looked at the other three recruits climbing the stairs ahead of her. As she had suspected, Juliette was foreign, as opposed to pretending to be. Penny wondered what part of France she was from. There was an air of sadness about her. She had looked shy earlier when the major had mentioned her work behind the lines.

The other two girls reminded her of Harriet by the way they spoke, walked and acted. They were full of excitement at what was ahead of them. They didn't appear to be nervous. One of them had already been trained as a home signals operator, so she was used to receiving coded messages from the field. She told the others a bit about her work and how she had decided that, given her knowledge of French, she could be more usefully employed in the field. Her superior agreed, and they transferred her across.

Surprised to find that she would share a bedroom, she was thankful the two society girls were put together, leaving her with Juliette. A WAAF opened a door into a room furnished with two wrought-iron beds, the white linen a stark contrast to the bare floorboards. The only other furniture in the room was an old but sturdy wardrobe and a chest of drawers. The cobwebs on the fireplace and the slightly damp smell made Penny wonder just how often this room had been used. Despite the warm August sun streaming in the small window, the room was chilly.

"It's not luxurious, but the beds are clean. The major doesn't want anyone getting used to home comforts. I'll leave you to it. Don't be late for dinner."

When the door closed behind their guide, Juliette and Penny looked at each other and started laughing.

"Which bed would you like?" asked Penny.

"This one, please. I enjoy being near the window."

Penny sat on her bed. She should unpack, but she wanted to take a few minutes to let everything sink in.

This was it. There was no going back now.

CHAPTER 20
GUILDFORD

Their training began immediately. They got up at 6 a.m. and after a quick but ration-free breakfast, they started with a physical exercise class. Both men and women trained together, and the class tutor expected both sexes to complete similar exercises.

Penny soon found out they had let them start gently. On the second day, Juliette and Penny were woken before sunrise. The beaming WAAF turned on the electric light, clapping her hands together.

Penny groaned, her leg muscles protesting after yesterday's workout.

"Come on, ladies. Up and out, as they say. You have five miles to cover before breakfast." The WAAF walked to the curtains and pulled them open, giving Penny a glimpse of rain. The woman was enjoying this far too much.

Juliette protested, "Five miles before we eat? That's torture."

"You haven't seen anything yet, miss. You're running late, he'll make you do extra laps if you don't get downstairs now."

Penny threw back the covers and pulled on her uniform slacks and blouse. Whoever designed it hadn't counted on them running for miles in it. Still, this was what she'd signed up for. Juliette beat her out the door, but they were among the first to arrive at the meeting point just north of the big house.

"The village is five miles there and back. Off you go, and no shortcuts. We have lookouts along the way. Real coffee and bacon will be waiting for your return."

He whistled, and they set off. Some men took off like rockets, but Juliette and Penny kept to a regular but slower pace. Neither had run five miles before and didn't want to fail their first test.

After the first mile, Penny's heels blistered. The second mile saw them burst and by the time they returned, sweating and groaning to the mansion, her blisters had blisters. Juliette wasn't in a much better state. Two men who'd passed them en route, threw some towels in their direction as they puffed their way up the drive. The taller of the two men winked at his mate before commenting, "Not bad for two ladies."

Penny gave him a dirty look, but Juliette aimed a torrent of French at him. It was too fast for the

Englishman to understand, but the words made Penny laugh, though it hurt her stomach muscles.

They staggered up to their room where they tried to remove their socks. The blood had crusted into them and it was agony trying to pull the wool from their wounds.

A WAAF came in as they were struggling. "Put your foot, sock and all into the water. It's easier that way."

Penny could have kissed her. She was a different WAAF from the one who'd woken them up. She handed them a jug of warm water and some fresh socks.

"I think someone should tell the boss you need to exercise in the same uniform the boys use. Those trousers weren't designed to be abused in this way."

Juliette rolled her eyes. "My body wasn't either. Sometimes I think the Germans would be nicer than our instructors."

Penny sensed this was only the start. Their training became progressively tougher as the weeks went by, but their fitness levels were increasing. Their soles and heels grew harder and soon running five miles came easily.

Then one morning the PT instructor smiled that smile. Penny groaned silently and exchanged a look with Juliet. They both knew they were about to be pushed.

"Ladies and gentlemen, meet your nearest and dearest friend."

The instructor stood aside as his assistant rolled some bicycles in their direction. "Since the occupation, travelling in France is difficult. Nobody but the Germans have access to petrol so you, my friends, will have to cycle your way around the countryside. We expect those of you becoming couriers to cover thirty miles a day.

"Thirty miles? That's insane."

The instructor glared at the man who'd dared to protest. "Insanity is doing something twice and expecting a different result. Haven't you learned by now that I don't tolerate objections? On the ground and give me twenty."

The man fell to his stomach and began the push-ups. Someone laughed and was soon doing the same. The instructor gazed around the group as if daring anyone else to join them. Penny kept her eyes on the bicycle. She hadn't ridden in years.

"Not only will you be able to cycle but you will also be able to change a wheel, fix a puncture and keep your bicycle in top condition. They don't come cheap. In some parts of France, you would pay a year's salary for one of these." The instructor hesitated a second before ordering them to mount up.

It took a while to remember her co-ordination but soon she was just as fast as the other women and faster than some of the men.

Next, they learnt to handle many firearms, from revolvers through to light automatic weapons.

"This is the favourite weapon of most agents," said the trainer, holding up what looked like a small machine gun. "Don't let its size mislead you. In the right hands, this little baby is lethal. It's also easy to carry and to hide. If you get stuck, you can use Luger rounds, too, although they can jam."

They had to learn not only how to fire the different guns, but how to break them down and put them together. Penny learnt quickly and impressed her trainer, growing in confidence as she handled different guns.

CHAPTER 21

In the evenings after dinner, most of the trainee agents were too tired to do anything other than go to bed. But even then, they couldn't always rest. The staff would often come in, using a very bright light to wake them up, checking whether the agent would curse at them in French or English. There were also other tests, which included being dragged downstairs in the middle of the night for "questioning" by staff dressed as Nazis.

One afternoon, Juliette was helping Penny to learn the uniforms of the German forces. They needed to know not only the different divisions but also the ranks. Penny was finding it hard to differentiate between them, so Juliette had volunteered to help her.

"Are you afraid of going home?" Juliette asked Penny, who looked back at her in shock. "Oh, don't look so worried. I'm not going to ask you your life story, but I know you're as French as I am."

"Yes, I am, but I think I'm a little more afraid of not passing the course. Can you imagine the look on Leon's face if we girls don't pass?"

Juliette giggled. "He thinks he is above us all."

"But of course. He is a man, and we are just ladies," Penny said sarcastically.

One of the WAAF drivers interrupted them.

"Oh, sorry, first time here. I thought this was the dining room. Good job my driving isn't as bad as my sense of direction in this old house." The WAAF smiled at both girls before turning her gaze fully on Penny.

"You're Penny Hamilton, aren't you? Harriet's French cousin. I thought you were up in Scotland. At least, I'm sure that's where Harriet said you were."

Penny didn't know what to say, but thankfully Juliette covered for her.

"Typical, we got caught not going home on leave, but we didn't want to spend our two days trying to get back to London. We cadged a lift here from one of the girls who had to collect a Major somebody or other. Do you know it never stops raining in Scotland? Ma'am saw we were both fed up so gave us permission to come up with Felicity. You won't tell the family now, will you?"

Both girls saw that the WAAF didn't believe Juliette, but it had dawned on her she shouldn't be asking questions in these surroundings.

"I'm frightfully sorry to interrupt you. Don't worry, your secret is safe with me. Cheerio."

The WAAF closed the door loudly behind her.

"Thanks, Juliette. I didn't know what to say to her," said Penny.

"You would do the same for me. Look on it as practice for any encounters with the Germans. Now, tell me, which uniform is this?"

Penny was relieved Juliette didn't probe into her background. She admired the girl's reticence as she was dying to know what work Juliette had been involved with behind the lines. She must have been part of the French resistance given she was going through the same training as Penny. She also wondered what had made Juliette so sad.

Thanks to Juliette's help, Penny passed the uniform test with flying colours.

Penny was glad of the marches, the runs and the cycling. Being physically fit would help her in her personal mission, too. Alain wouldn't be expecting the toned, fit, trained killer she was – to her amazement – being turned into.

Juliette moaned as they lay on their beds resting one evening. "I think I have muscles where you're not supposed to have them."

Penny was too tired to respond. She couldn't move.

A voice came from the open doorway. "Juliette, Simone, you're wanted downstairs. Major's office."

All thoughts of not moving disappeared as both of them jumped to attention. Penny risked a glance in the mirror to check she didn't look too bedraggled and then followed Juliette out of the door.

Downstairs they knock on the major's door, and he called them in.

"Good job, ladies. You should be proud of what you've achieved. I'm sending you both to Manchester. Ringway Airport to be precise."

"Sir?" Juliette queried but Penny knew what that meant. They'd been selected for parachute training. She clenched her hands to restrain herself from jumping up and down with excitement. She was one step closer to home.

"You'll learn how to jump out of an aircraft safely. Can't risk losing my agents, now, can I? I expect you to conquer the five jumps and then you will be on your way to Scotland for further training. Well done, ladies."

They stared at him before he pointed to the door. Once outside they hugged each other. "We did it!" Penny said, and they ran back up to their room together, two steps at a time.

~

PENNY CLAMBERED over the old fuselage, wondering why she'd ever been excited about taking this course.

"See that hole? You will drop out of that just like I

showed you in class. Not the real thing, of course, but the nearest we can come to showing you how to get out of the plane without a real one."

The expression on the sergeant's face suggested he'd prefer to be doing the training on a proper flight. Penny shuddered. She didn't mind jumping, but she hated enclosed spaces and the experience at the Taylors' house hadn't helped.

"Come on, girl, you're holding everyone up. In you get. Go on now, it won't bite you."

Gritting her teeth, Penny pushed herself into the old fuselage, adopting the correct position to drop out. She thought she'd done it properly, but the trainer ordered her to do it again. On the third attempt, she sensed he was riling her and spoke up.

"What's wrong with the way I did it? I adopted the position just as you said."

"I gave you an order, girl."

She imagined how Harriet would deal with him. "I'm not 'girl'. My name is Simone and as I have a higher rank, you should address me properly."

She saw the anger before he quickly doused it. He gestured towards the direction of the balloon. "Go on then, if you think you're ready."

She was more than ready. There was plenty of space in the balloon.

One of her fellow recruits moved to her side. "About time you stood up to him. He would have had you repeating that move for the rest of the day. Afraid of heights, are you?"

She sensed he was trying to be helpful. "No, not at all. I just don't like small dark spaces." She glanced back at the fuselage and shuddered.

"You did great. Don't let him tell you otherwise. Got any tips on how I conquer a fear of heights?"

Gaping at him, he held her gaze for a couple of seconds, his eyes sparkling before grinning.

"You're teasing me, aren't you?"

"Yes, but it isn't much fun when you didn't fall for my helpless act. Care to have a drink with me later to mend my fragile ego."

Penny smiled. He was nice and not full of himself. "I'll go for a drink, but I think your ego is safe enough."

~

SHE COMPLETED ALL FIVE JUMPS, although on the last one she landed badly, hurting her ankle.

"Should have spent more time with me. I'd have taught you how to land properly."

She didn't respond to the sergeant's gloating. His sort wasn't worth wasting time on.

CHAPTER 22

Finally, the last week of the course arrived. One trainer said that as they had worked so hard, they all deserved to take the night off. A party had been organised in a nearby hotel and they had arranged overnight accommodation. Once there, he said, the recruits could let their hair down and behave normally for once. The only rule was that they had to use their cover names.

They were shown to their rooms at the hotel and, this time, weren't expected to share. Penny's room was a sight for sore eyes. A walnut wardrobe and matching chest of drawers occupied one side of the room, a dressing table with a gilded mirror the other. In the centre of the room stood a double bed. It was dressed in sparkling white linen offset by a beautiful, flowery eiderdown. The same material had been used to make the curtains, already closed over the blackout blinds.

With joy, Penny sank into the feathered quilt. Maybe I'll skip dinner and just sleep.

~

IN THE EVENING, refreshed after a nap on the luxurious bed, Penny, wearing a rose-coloured gown and white gloves, went down for dinner. Some support staff remained in uniform. The male recruits looked very attractive in their dinner suits, while the women shone in their glamorous frocks. Juliette looked like she'd visited a Parisian dressmaker. Her hair and make-up was also perfect. Looking at her dainty appearance now, it was hard to believe she was a trained killer.

The alcohol was flowing, and the food was plentiful. Penny noticed some of their group were drinking heavily. She allowed herself a glass of wine with dinner, but switched to lemonade when they went dancing. The doors on one side of the ballroom opened out onto the lawn. Nobody seemed too concerned about the blackout.

"This is the life, isn't it?"

Penny looked at the young man in the RAF uniform who had spoken to her.

"I suppose," she answered non-committedly.

"You suppose? Where would you prefer to be?"

"At home in peacetime with my family and friends. Wouldn't you?"

The officer grinned. "When I could spend the evening with a beautiful woman like you? Not a chance."

Penny smiled, despite wanting to roll her eyes. Why did men think such a line would win over any woman? "Are you based around here?"

She had expected to be told off for asking questions, but to her surprise the officer not only told her where he was based but described at great lengths recent missions he had flown.

"What about you, miss? Sorry I didn't introduce myself. Richard Talbot, at your service." He bowed slightly.

"Simone Moreau." She let him kiss her hand. "What about me?" she said.

"Well, you aren't wearing a uniform, so I just wondered what you were doing for the war effort."

"You mean aside from looking beautiful and entertaining heroes?" Penny flirted back, but didn't answer him. The conversation continued that way for most of the evening. The officer told Penny more and more about his day-to-day job, but all she would volunteer was that she had signed up and was awaiting her orders. His questions grew more direct as the evening progressed. No matter how hard she tried to change the course of conversation, he kept returning to the war. Finally, her patience exhausted, Penny made her excuses and went to bed.

~

THE NEXT MORNING, after a sumptuous breakfast, they drove the recruits back to the manor. Penny was summoned to her superior's office. As she drew near to the door, it suddenly opened and Leon stormed past her, almost knocking her over.

The secretary told her to take a seat until the commander was ready to see her. She sat, twisting her fingers.

After what seemed like ages, the secretary told her to go in. It surprised her to find the RAF officer she had spoken to the previous night standing talking to her boss, wearing a khaki uniform.

"Good morning, sir."

"Good morning, Simone. I take it you have already met Sergeant Walters."

"Sort of, sir," Penny replied.

"Pardon?"

"Well, sir, I met Sergeant Walters, but he gave his name as Flying Officer Talbot and wore an RAF uniform."

Both men smiled before Walters/Talbot replied, "I assure you, Simone, my correct name is Walters and I have never flown a plane in my life."

"But why did you tell me all those things last night?"

"It was a test. By being deliberately indiscreet and

providing you with what you thought was vital information, I hoped to gain your trust so you would reveal your true self to me."

"You hoped to trap me into betraying myself?" Penny retorted angrily.

"Calm down, Simone," ordered her commanding officer before continuing, "Last night was a training exercise and I'm very pleased to congratulate you. You passed with flying colours."

Penny couldn't resist sending a dark look at Walters.

"Now, before you go blaming Sergeant Walters, know that this is one of the few times he has failed in the role assigned to him. His job was to trick you into telling him details of your training or your mission. Don't be angry at him. He was only carrying out my orders."

Penny mellowed slightly but didn't return the grin flashed at her by the sergeant.

"We are very pleased with your performance. All three ladies performed well. It's a pity the same couldn't be said for your male contemporaries."

Penny thought of the look on Leon's face as he had exited the office earlier that morning. She didn't say anything.

"Are you not going to ask me who failed the test? I thought curiosity was part of the female psyche."

"It is, sir, but knowing how much my fellow trainees

want to serve their country, it doesn't seem the right thing to ask."

"Well, that's as may be. The fact remains that Leon and Gilbert won't be attending any more classes. Leon couldn't resist the charms of a pretty woman last night and spent the night engaged in pillow talk. He was frightfully indiscreet."

"Pillow talk?" Penny blushed.

"Yes, Simone. You must have thought it curious we gave you a double room for the evening. We employ many people here, some of whom are prepared to give their all for their country. I'm only thankful that we found out now, and not when Leon fancied one of the many beautiful courtesans employed by the enemy."

"Yes, sir."

"Gilbert couldn't stop drinking and, once drunk, took to telling silly stories about his supposed exploits. I thought the French could hold their liquor. Such a waste."

It was obvious her commander was extremely angry.

"What will happen to the men now, sir?"

"Oh, they will go to the cooler."

"The cooler, sir?"

"During training you will have learnt information that could prove very useful if it fell into the wrong hands. Therefore, if agents can't complete their training, we send them to one of our properties in Scotland until we deem that the information they have learnt is no longer critical."

"Oh. I see, sir."

"As the men were quite advanced in their training, they can expect to spend as long as six months enjoying everything the peace and solitude the most northern tip of Scotland offers." Penny flinched at his sarcasm, even though it wasn't directed at her. She waited for him to continue. "I will tell everyone what has happened when we meet for dinner this evening. I didn't expect to lose any people at this stage in the training. Is that clear?"

"Yes, sir."

"Very good. Now, congratulations again on a job well done. Be a dear and escort Sergeant Walters back to the principal building, will you please?"

Penny left the office, followed by the sergeant.

As the door closed behind them, he flashed her what he must have thought was a charming smile. "Now you know the truth, am I forgiven?"

Penny didn't hide her annoyance. "There is nothing to forgive. You were just doing your job."

"I guess I would feel the same if I were in your shoes. All I can say is that it's true what the commander said. I'm usually very successful in getting people to talk. I'm quite embarrassed by my failure."

"Well, I'm not!"

Walters laughed. "No, I dare say you aren't. Good

luck, Simone, with whatever it is you're doing for England. Goodbye."

"Bye."

CHAPTER 23

Juliette passed as well so both girls travelled to their next course together. They were heading to Scotland, not to the cooler but to learn more about planting explosives, picking landing areas and self-defence. Penny wrote a few letters to Meme, the Taylor girls, Nell and Gracie. In all of them, she kept to the script. She was working hard but loved her job. She would be home when leave became available but, in the meantime, they were to write back to her at the address on the letter. Vera Atkins arranged for the letters to follow the recruits to their next training ground.

"Simone, you have to thrust down. Head for the..." The instructor coughed, as some of those assembled around the straw stuffed mannequin giggled. The instructor flushed, muttering something about wishing he was back in the Far East with his men. "The upper part of the body is well protected with bones including the rib cage. The lower area has more exposure. If you thrust in and down, you will hit the stomach and other regions. It works best."

Simone took note of everything he said. The skills this man gave her could save her life.

She was the first he picked for the next training exercise.

Simone bit her lip as they walked through the dawn mist to the far edges of the estate. "I don't have to shoot the stag, do I?"

"Not much of a hunter, are you?"

"I'll kill for food and to win the war but I can't destroy an animal just because I have a gun."

The officer rolled his eyes but he didn't say anything. They continued in silence. He pointed in the direction he thought they would spot the deer. She saw the magnificent brown animal with enormous horns standing on a small hill, looking like the prince he was as he surveyed his kingdom. Then he turned to look directly at her, or so it seemed.

"And you're dead," the instructor said, as he turned away and walked back in the direction from which they had come.

"What did I do wrong?" Penny struggled to catch up with the man's longer strides. The dew made the grass slippy, or was it the constant rain? Every part of her was soaked even though it was only a drizzle not a full downpour.

"If you can get within a hundred yards of a stag without it noticing you, you can slit the throat of a German sentry." He stopped moving and gave her his full attention. "You're good, Simone, but you need to be excellent. Tomorrow, forget the perfume. Scents carry on the wind."

"Yes sir, sorry sir." She walked back to the house annoyed with herself for making such a stupid mistake.

The next morning they didn't see any sign of the stag. It seemed to have been scared off. Penny concentrated on the other parts of the training.

She joined the rest of the recruits in the drawing room.

"I've divided you into teams for the next task. You will plant a dummy charge on the railway track. The train drivers are aware that an attempt to sabotage their trip will be made. If they catch you, they will pelt you with coal pieces from the tender. Let's hope they aren't lit."

He let the laughter die down before continuing, "The losing team will return to the scene and collect the coal pieces for the mess fire. We can always use extra fuel to heat up this old mausoleum."

Penny and her team laid the charge successfully without being spotted. Juliette wasn't so lucky, coming back with a few bruises from the coal being hurled at her. Her ego was bruised further when the officer made good on his threat and sent the losing team back to collect the coal pieces.

Penny had a bath drawn for Juliette's return, using some of the scented soap Meme had sent her a gift.

"Thank you, Simone, you're an angel."

"Just be glad tomorrow is Sunday and nobody will complain about how good you smell."

There was no sign of Penny getting a chance to repeat the exercise with the stag. Summoning up her courage she approached the officer.

"Please sir, can we go hunting the stag tomorrow morning if you are free."

"You want to try again?"

"Yes sir."

He flicked his pen a few times in his hand before nodding. "All right then. See you in the morning."

"Thank you, sir."

～

THE NEXT MORNING, she got so close to the stag she could almost pet it.

"Well done, Simone. Now you're ready."

"Ready, sir?"

"I've signed off on your training. You're heading

back to London. It's up to Baker Street what happens next."

She was going home, back to France. Overcome, she almost threw her arms around his neck, but a last-minute instinct stopped her. "Thank you, sir. Oh, thank you."

"It's me who should thank you, Miss Hamilton."

She froze. He knew her actual name – but was this a test?

"Relax, it's not a test. I know your cousins and your uncle John. He would burst with pride if he knew how hard you've worked. You are a credit to your family, young lady."

"Thank you, sir."

She saluted and was dismissed. She walked a few steps, and when she thought it was safe, broke into a run. She was going home. Back to France. Back to Madam Bayard. She slowed to a walk. And back to avenge her mother.

~

BACK IN THEIR ROOM, she hugged Juliette and wished her "*Bonne chance*". She had two weeks' leave and was heading to Suffolk to stay with Meme. She couldn't wait to see how the Taylor children were. But she was nervous about seeing her grandmother. She sensed from the tone of her recent letters that she didn't believe the story about Scotland, but the last thing Penny wanted to do was cause her more pain. After everything she had done and how close they had become over the last few years, she wouldn't understand why France was and always would be Penny's home.

CHAPTER 24

Penny sighed as Meme's home came into view. She loved the old house, half covered in creeping ivy. The original property had been built hundreds of years ago, around the time of the War of the Roses. Each generation of the family had made their mark, but the fact that the property had survived all these years was a comfort. No matter how bad things got, the house would still be standing.

The trees lining the drive up to the house were well maintained, their evergreen colours not as vivid as they'd been when she was last here with Nell. She spotted smoke coming out of two of the chimneys, the back kitchen and the front drawing room. Shivering in the cold air, she couldn't wait to sit down opposite an open fire with a cup of cocoa in her hand. That's if Cook had any cocoa. Penny didn't know how easy it was to buy these days.

She hoped Meme was just the same as she always was. She didn't like to think about how old her grandmother was or the effect of the war on people of her generation.

"There you be now, Miss Penny. Home at last."

She glanced at the young man who'd driven her back from the station. Unlike many their age, Ralph didn't feel the need to fill silence with chatter. He seemed to sense she had a lot on her mind.

"Thank you, Ralph. I'm so glad I bumped into you at the station. I hate to think how long it would have taken me to walk in this weather."

Ralph grinned. "Best get used to it, Miss Penny. They say that the rain will only stop when it's cold enough for snow."

Penny smiled back at the young man, getting out of the car and taking her bag from Ralph. She knew others thought him to be a coward as he refused to fight, but she felt he was the brave one. It took a lot to stand up against the rest of the world who believed that a man's place in war was on the battlefield.

The shouts of the children alerted her to their presence, and they ran into view.

"Miss Penny, you're back. We missed you."

Betty Taylor hugged her legs as her sister Shirley looked on. The two young girls bore little resemblance to the children Penny had taken from their bombed-out home. Both of them looked much healthier; the country diet of nutritious food, fresh air and plenty of love was working wonders.

"Betty, I'm sure you have grown another five inches. Shirley, how are you?"

"Great, Miss Penny. We had a letter from our dad. He's coming to see us soon. He might even be here in time for Christmas."

Penny hugged the children closer. "That would be fantastic, girls. Where are Kenny, Mary and Helen?"

"Kenny is out in the stables. He's always out there. Mary and Helen are with Cook in the kitchen. Meme is having a nap. We are supposed to be quiet."

"How is my darling Meme?" asked Penny.

"Old," said Shirley, making Penny laugh.

A girl dressed in brown breeches and a green jumper walked towards them, a disapproving look on her face. "Mind your manners, Shirley." The girl winked at Penny to let her know she wasn't being horrible. "Hello, Miss Hamilton. I'm Rose. Rose Walsh. I'm the new land girl. Cook asked me to look after the young ones while she made dinner." Rose looked a bit flustered. "Not that I mind the kids every day or anything. I'm usually busy on the farm, but…"

Penny shook Rose's outstretched hand. "Nice to meet you in person, Rose. Please call me Penny. I've heard a lot about you from my grandmother's letters. You have made quite an impression in the short time you have been here."

Penny saw the blush creep across the younger girl's face. "Thank you, miss. Sorry. I mean thank you, Penny. I love it here. It's so different from the city."

"Rose does all sorts of jobs, including horrible smelly ones like mucking out the pigs." Shirley wrinkled her nose, causing everyone to laugh.

"Lady Hamilton is resting. Would you like me to wake her?" asked Rose.

"No, thank you, Rose. Let her sleep. If I know Meme, she has been working too hard and could do with the rest."

All thoughts of exhaustion vanished as Penny walked into the kitchen, greeted Cook with a hug and ran upstairs to leave her bags in her bedroom. She changed quickly before racing back downstairs and out towards the stables to see Kenny and to check on her horse. She'd missed riding and hoped to take the horse out for a quick turn around the estate before dinner. She was relieved her grandmother was lying down. She tried telling herself it was best to let the older woman sleep. In reality, although she was dying to see Meme, she wasn't looking forward to her questions about her part in the war effort.

~

As Penny had suspected, Meme wasn't convinced by her explanation for the extended trip to Scotland. They were sitting in the drawing room, huddled by the small fire. Her grandmother had a rug wrapped around her legs. The beautiful old house was difficult to heat at the best of times, but more so now that coal was rationed.

"Penny, darling, I may be old but I'm not yet senile. There is no need to send you all the way to Scotland to join the FANYs. The translation work you were doing was important to the war effort. I just don't believe you gave that up to act as a secretary to some officer."

"Meme, you know the FANY do more than drive, do secretarial work or nurse officers. Many of the women are trained on how to fix vehicles, not to mention helping the Home Guard." She was about to say other woman had been sent to different countries but caught herself just in time.

"You went to Scotland to learn how to fix an engine?"

Meme's piercing blue eyes settled on her grand-daughter's face. Penny hated lying to her. She couldn't meet her gaze.

"Meme, please don't ask me. I can't tell you anything." Penny gazed into the fire, hoping her grand-mother would give up.

"You've changed, darling. Don't look so worried. Not in a bad way. You are still beautiful but you have a … presence you didn't have before. You walk taller, more confident in your own abilities. I sense you've learned a number of useful skills while you have been away." Meme sighed. "Your hands resemble those of someone who works for a living not a secretary who types all day. I watched you out riding. You're stronger and fitter than when you went away."

"Meme, you make me sound like a prize bull."

Meme ignored her attempt to make a joke.

"John stayed here a few weeks ago. He mentioned something about Churchill wanting to organise a revolution in France. He thinks our best chance of winning is a combination of traditional war tactics combined with those learned from our experiences in Ireland and other places. Guerrilla warfare, I think he called it. It has something to do with sending French-speaking people into France behind enemy lines. Their role is to organise the French resistance. What do you think of that?"

Penny risked a glance at her grandmother, but she couldn't hold her gaze. Trust Meme to have worked it all out. Instead, she focused her eyes on the painting above her head. It was of some great ancestor who'd been given the estate in return for loyalty to the Crown.

"I don't know, Meme. Does Uncle John believe Mr Churchill is right?"

Meme snapped, "Don't play games with me, Penny. You are going to France, aren't you?"

Penny didn't answer.

"Darling," Meme spoke more softly, "I can understand you wanting to do your bit for the war effort, but do you not think you are taking this too far?"

She was glad Meme had softened her tone, but it made little difference. Penny stood up and walked over to the window, looking at the view across the lawn. She took a second to try to calm her tone. "Meme, if I was born a boy, I would be fighting by now. How would you feel if the Nazis were to march across the estate, through your land?" Penny clenched her fists before turning to face her grandmother. "I can't stand by and watch while they destroy my country. France is my home. I have to do something."

"Oh, Penny. If only your papa and I had not fallen out. Then you would have grown up in England. You wouldn't be so strong-willed or so…"

"French? I would always have been French, Meme. As for strong-willed, I believe that I may have inherited that from your side of the family." Penny smiled at her grandmother, the tears in the older woman's voice making her feel so guilty. She hated hurting the old lady, but her mind was made up. She was going home. Nobody would stop her now. God help her but she hated upsetting her grandmother. She rushed to Meme's side.

"Meme, I love you and I'm very grateful for everything you have done for me. But I have to go home. You understand that, don't you? I need to go. I must."

"Yes, Penny, I understand. I don't want you to, but if the Germans were to march into England I would feel the same way. Just promise me something. Please take care of yourself. I've already lost your father. I couldn't bear it if something happened to you as well."

"Oh, Meme, please don't cry." Penny wrapped her arms around her grandmother as the tears coursed down their cheeks.

CHAPTER 25

When Penny went back to London a few days later, her overwhelming feeling was one of relief, despite the guilt at causing her grandmother pain.

Her orders were to report to an office at Whitehall. She hoped to be told she was leaving for France. She arrived on time but was kept waiting for over two hours. Her nails were non-existent by the time they called her in.

"Penny, I'm sorry for keeping you waiting. Please come in." Miss Atkins stood back, gesturing for Penny to walk into the room. The air crackled with tension. Penny looked at the faces of her superiors.

"What's wrong?"

"The circuit you were to join has been betrayed. As far as we know, the Germans have either killed or captured almost every one of our agents in that sector."

Miss Atkins lit a cigarette, throwing the match into an overflowing ashtray.

Penny sat down without requesting permission. "How?" she whispered.

"We don't know. We got a last-minute warning from Victor, an agent who has been in the field for over a year now. He advised against the landing. We will know more in the next few days."

"What happens now?" Penny fought the urge to be sick. She had waited for so long, and now it had all been taken away from her. On the other hand, she was lucky not to be landing straight into the hands of the Germans. She didn't want to think about the captured agents and the terrible trials they would face now.

"We will have to arrange another drop for you. It's likely to take several weeks to get everything sorted. Assuming you still want to go?"

Penny couldn't hide her disappointment. "Of course I want to go. Now, more than ever. With the agents in custody, you must be very short of people on the ground."

"Yes, Penny, we are, but that doesn't mean we will rush anything. We can't take any chances. Don't look so upset. You will go, but not until the New Year. For now, I suggest you make the most of your leave. I understand you probably don't want to spend more time with your family as you may face some awkward questions regarding your leave being extended. Is there anywhere you would like to go? I will arrange a travel warrant for you."

Penny thought for a couple of minutes. She couldn't face seeing her grandmother again and having to say another goodbye. Staying in London with Aunt Louise wasn't an option. *Not if I want to stay sane.*

"East Grinstead, please. My friend is married to a pilot who was injured last year. He is being treated by Dr McIndoe. I have my first aid certification. I would like to volunteer in the hospital while I'm waiting to leave, if that can be arranged."

Miss Atkins looked at Penny with approval. "I'm sure that will be just perfect. You will be in uniform so that should help avoid questions from people wondering why you haven't joined up."

～

PENNY CALLED to see Nell before she set off, and came away laden with presents for Gracie. The train journey to East Grinstead didn't take too long. Soon, Penny was walking along the high street, looking at the timber-framed houses. She shivered. If a bomb were to fall here, the fire would be horrendous.

She followed the directions Gracie had provided. Her friend's house was located just outside the village. Penny had to walk past Sackville College and St Swinthun's Church, resisting the urge to stop and gaze

at the buildings. It might not be raining now, but the
sky was very dark. Rain was forecast. Gracie's new
home was a semi-detached Edwardian property over-
looking a park. The owner, a lady in her late seventies,
had a grandson on the same ward as Charlie. When she
heard Gracie was looking for somewhere to live, she
had invited her to share her home. Gracie had written to
say that Mrs Matthews was a sweet, if somewhat
eccentric, old lady who spent most of her time in
Cornwall.

Gracie flung herself at Penny as soon as she reached
the front door.

"I can't believe you're here at last. Was the journey
awful? Are you wet? Hungry? Come in quick and close
the door. It's bitterly cold out there."

Penny came in, closing the door carefully behind
her. Taking off her coat, she burst out laughing. "You
are a right mother hen, aren't you? Stop fussing over
me. Let me look at you."

Gracie was blooming. Pregnancy gave her skin a
translucent glow and made her blue eyes sparkle. She
looked so happy and healthy. Penny gave her a big hug,
trying to stop the tears from flowing.

"You look fantastic, Gracie."

"Go away with you." Gracie walked towards the
kitchen. "I'm fat and I can't walk any more. I'm ready
to burst. I swear that these two will come any day now."
Gracie's voice bubbled with happiness. "You don't

mind sitting in the back room, do you? It's much warmer than the front of the house. I haven't lit a fire in there yet."

"You sit down. Let me make some tea."

Gracie sat down gratefully. "Oh, Penny, I'm so glad you're here. One day, I'm excited and the next, I'm nervous, I get twitchy. How will I cope with two babies?"

"You will be fine. Charlie can help you. Speaking of the man himself, is he here?" asked Penny. Gracie started plumping the cushions on the chairs beside her.

"Charlie just popped out for a little while. He had to go up to the hospital."

"Is he okay?" asked Penny.

"Yes, he's fine. If you really want to know, I asked him to go out. I wanted to talk to you. Penny what's going on? What are you doing here?" Gracie's foot bounced up and down as she moved a cushion from one hand to the other. "Don't give me any story about you volunteering at the hospital."

"I'm going to work there," said Penny.

"Penny Hamilton, there are hospitals all over England. Why here? Why now? How can working in a hospital be more important to the war effort than your translation work?" Gracie glared at Penny. "Tell me straight. What's going on?"

Penny had a lump in her throat. She needed a few minutes to gather her thoughts. She poured the boiling water into the teapot. Stirring rapidly, she took a deep breath before turning to face Gracie.

"Please don't ask me any questions. I can't answer them. I've signed the Official Secrets Act. Let's just enjoy some time together. It's been so long. I want to hear all about you and the babies. What are you going to call them? Do you want boys or girls or one of each?"

"Put that teapot down before you break it. Come sit beside me, Penny. Please."

Penny sat down.

"You are going to France, aren't you? Don't answer that. I know. I can feel it. You always said you would go back."

Penny stayed silent. She couldn't lie to her friend, but she wasn't about to betray her training, either. For a couple of seconds, she found herself wishing things could be different, that she could stay in East Grinstead with her friend. But she knew she would go to France as soon as she could. She had to. This was war.

Gracie hugged Penny close to her. "Just promise me you will be careful. No damn heroics. I have had enough of those. Speaking of which, how are the Taylor girls?"

Relieved to find the subject changed, Penny squeezed Gracie's hand gratefully. "They are wonderful. Honestly, I don't think I could cope if I lost my foot. Mr Taylor is due home soon. I just hope nothing happens to him."

"That would be too unfair, wouldn't it? They have lost their mother and their sister and baby brother. That's enough for any family." Gracie stroked her stomach. "Thank God we don't live in London now."

"You would be evacuated. You could live on the estate, too. Meme would love fussing over you."

Gracie shivered. "No thanks, Penny. Meme is wonderful, but I'd always feel like staff, however welcoming she was. And between the smell of the cows and the pigs, I'm better off here."

Penny noticed Gracie rubbing her stomach again. "Are you all right?"

Gracie nodded. "It's just a touch of stomachache. I've had it all morning. It's nothing. You get aches and pains when you are pregnant. Now, where is that cup of tea you promised me?"

～

THE HOURS PASSED QUICKLY. Charlie came back with some fish and chips.

"A special treat for dinner," he said smiling, extending his hand to Penny. "Welcome to our home, Miss Penny."

"Charlie Power, don't you call me 'Miss'."

"Yes, ma'am."

Gracie smiled at her friend. "Don't worry, Charlie,

it's her French side which makes her temperamental. She can't help it."

They all laughed. Penny was glad Gracie was smiling, but she couldn't help feeling her friend wasn't comfortable. She kept shifting around in her chair.

"We are both delighted you came to stay with us for a month or two. The hospital will be very glad of your help. It seems as if more pilots arrive every day. Some of them are hideously injured."

"I hope I will be a help, not a hindrance." Penny said, hoping Charlie wouldn't ask her how long she intended staying.

"Will I turn on the news?" asked Charlie.

"No, thanks all the same. I'm going to wash up and then head to bed. It's been a long day. Gracie, why don't you go on up. I can tidy these away."

"Are you sure, Penny? I'm so tired I could sleep in my clothes." Gracie didn't argue for long. "See you in the morning."

CHAPTER 26

Penny woke early the next morning. Hearing noises downstairs, she jumped out of bed and dressed quickly.

"Are you feeling better this morning?" she asked Gracie, noting her friend's pale face. She didn't look like she'd had much sleep.

"The midwife is calling this morning. I have the kettle on and some clean sheets and towels ready."

Penny's stomach flipped. "The babies? Are they coming? Now?" Penny was torn between excitement and fear that her friend would go into labour in front of her.

"Relax, Penny. I'm fine. She'll be here soon. I have sent Charlie up to the hospital. I don't want him getting in the way."

Penny marvelled at Gracie's calm. "What can I do?"

"Help me upstairs, please. I'm not sure I could manage on my own."

Once Gracie was safely back in bed, Penny walked up and down the street looking for the midwife. *Some special agent I am if the thought of labour scares me.* She felt giddy when she saw the middle-aged midwife coming down the road towards her, a picture of good health with her rosy cheeks.

"Are they coming, then?" the midwife asked Gracie when Penny showed her to the bedroom, pushing Penny out the door. With relief, she retreated to the kitchen. She'd seen plenty of horrible injuries in the Blitz but maybe the midwife thought she'd be a hindrance. She wouldn't do anything to put Gracie in danger. The midwife would know best.

Penny made several cups of tea using her rations to supplement Gracie's and took them upstairs. Each time, the midwife greeted her at the bedroom door, took the tray and dismissed her.

She washed the dishes, mopped the floor and sat down to read the paper but the cries from the room above sent her out to the scullery. There she did some laundry and hung it out to dry on the line in the small garden at the back of the house.

This was worse than any part of the training had been. Gracie's screams sounded like she was in agony. Penny paced back and forth across the living room. She tried to sit and do some mending but she couldn't concentrate on anything. *This is ridiculous. I can kill someone with my bare hands but can't be by my best* friend's side to comfort her. Pushing her shoulders back, she made another cup of tea and took it upstairs. She entered the bedroom and ignored the midwife's glare. She was sitting in a seat by the side of the bed as if she couldn't see Gracie was in pain.

"I made you a sandwich downstairs. Take your time."

"I will not…"

"Mrs. Medlock, I worked through the Blitz and can handle a patient in childbirth. You won't be any good to Mrs Power unless you have some refreshment. It won't take you long and you deserve a little rest." Penny couldn't look at Gracie as she spoke for fear she'd laugh.

The midwife stood up and checked Gracie one last time before leaving. "I won't be long."

As soon as the door closed, Gracie giggled, and that set Penny off. "You sounded just like your Aunt Louise then. All posh and stuck up."

"Sorry for intruding but I couldn't bear it any more downstairs. You sounded like you were in agony. What can I do?"

"Will you rub my feet if that's not too horrible. It helps to relax me." Gracie glanced away.

"What?"

"Penny, I'm terrified. What if something goes wrong? It seems to be taking ages."

Penny took some of the scented talc she'd given Gracie as a gift and rubbed it into the soles of her feet. "All first-time mothers say that. Everything will be just fine and in a few hours you will have two bouncing babies to hold. Have you decided on names yet?'

"I want Ruby for a girl and Charlie wants William for a boy. If we have two boys, the second one will be called Stanley. I thought it would please Stan when we write to him to tell him he has a nephew named after him."

"He'd love it. How is he?"

Stan was a prisoner of war in Germany but he sent regular letters home. Nell sent him packages every so often through the Red Cross.

"He seems bored, to be honest. Says he doesn't hear from Alice much but I told him she's busy. She's working herself to death, I think she finds it almost harder than Stan." Gracie gasped as another pain hit her. No sooner had it ended than there was another one and then another. "Penny, get Mrs. Medlock. I think the baby is coming."

Gracie insisted she needed Penny to stay with her and Mrs Medlock reluctantly agreed. After waiting so long, everything moved fast. Penny stayed at the head of the bed, holding Gracie's hand. Her friend's nails raked her skin but she didn't flinch. Tension filled the room for a few seconds as the first baby, a girl, arrived without a cry. But a swift slap on her bottom and she screamed. Penny took the child from the midwife, swaddled her in a towel, and held her as the second baby arrived.

Charlie arrived home just a few moments after the twins had been born; they heard him racing up the stairs but Mrs. Medlock refused to let him enter the room. Only when the midwife deemed it proper was he allowed to see his children. Penny slipped out of the room to allow the little family some private time. She took the sheets and other washing downstairs and put them in a bucket to soak.

About half an hour passed before the midwife called Penny. "Mrs Power would like to see you now. Don't stay too long. Mother and babies need their rest."

Penny peeked in the bedroom door. Gracie looked so beautiful, lying in bed cradling one baby. Charlie held the other. He looked up at her as she came in, gently shutting the door behind her.

"Thank you, Penny, for helping my wife bring our beautiful children into this world."

"Gracie did everything." Penny blinked, trying to stop the tears from falling.

Gracie looked up. "Penny, come meet Ruby Penelope and William Stanley properly."

"Oh, Gracie, they are beautiful." Penny couldn't say anything else. The look of total happiness on her friend's face had taken her breath away.

～

PENNY ENJOYED WORKING in the hospital over Christmas and early New Year. The twins thrived, growing bigger every day. She helped Gracie as much as she could, and the days passed quickly. William was a quiet baby, content to sleep in his cot once he had been fed and winded. Ruby was a handful. Her eyes followed you around as if she was desperate not to miss anything. She slept badly and cried unless someone carried her around.

Penny was holding Ruby in her arms when the telegram arrived. Taking her daughter from Penny's arms, Gracie handed the brown envelope to her.

"They have ordered me back to London." Penny looked up at Gracie, who was biting her lip. "I go tomorrow."

"Penny, you will come back – come back to see the babies again, won't you?"

Penny choked back the tears. "Yes, Gracie, I will. I promise."

～

GRACIE DIDN'T COME with her to the station. They both agreed to say goodbye at the house.

"Gracie, it's not goodbye. It's *au revoir*. It means until we see each other again."

"Yes. Remember, you promised, Penny. Look after yourself, please."

Penny gave her friend a quick hug and ran down the street without looking back. She was thrilled to be going to France, but the goodbyes got harder every time.

Nell scrubbed the sheets with Sunlight carbolic soap before kneading the soapy garments furiously. It was all well and good that the Allies were finally making headway in North Africa. She was thrilled to see the Germans and Italians retreating. Then Mr Churchill had to go and ruin it. She was sorry she had listened to his speech on the wireless. What did he mean – it was the end of the beginning? She knew the war wasn't over, but how much longer did he think it was going to last?

Aside from the war, everyone was talking about the Beveridge Report. She didn't understand it but it seemed like everyone would get a pension in old age. Did that mean men could give up working early and still have money to live on? What would she do with Alf in the house all day under her feet?

Nell sighed, wiping the sweat from her brow. It was

unnaturally warm for the time of year – the kids would be disappointed if there wasn't snow for Christmas. She scrubbed her husband's trousers up and down the washboard. It was useless; those stains were never going to come out. He would just have to make do. It's not as if they could go and buy new ones. Clothing coupons were in short supply, especially for men. Oh, drat this war anyway. Nell's tears of frustration ran into the washing water. Her hands, red and raw from soap exposure, worked even faster as she took her temper out on the clothes.

Her husband would have to make do with chicken soup for dinner, made from Sunday lunch leftovers. She cut up a small onion and added an Oxo cube. She didn't have time to go and stand in queues for groceries. She had to get the washing finished and hang out or it would hang around damp for days. Then she had to get to the charity shop and work for a few hours.

As she worked, she thought about her children. Some Christmas it was going to be without them home. It was hard to believe that this was the third year running she had spent apart from her kids. She wanted them to come home, but people said there was still a risk from bombs. They were safer where they were. Nell closed her eyes, picturing Kenny and her girls racing around the farm.

Maybe I could go see Gracie and her precious bundles. The twins were thriving. Gracie had taken to mothering like a duck to water, even if Ruby was proving to be rather challenging, and Nell was so proud of her daughter. Charlie was helping, too. She had almost forgiven him for believing that Gracie had been unfaithful in the days of their courting. Almost, but not quite.

~

THE SHOP WASN'T AS busy as she expected when she went to work that afternoon. Most people were well-prepared for Christmas. Nell had her cake made. She had saved and dried her own fruit from what was available in the allotment and the countryside around Suffolk. It may not taste like the traditional Christmas cake but it would be a treat. She was quite proud of the fact she had all her Christmas presents sorted, too. She had knitted sweet little matinee coats for the twins, made some stuffed toys for her own girls and Kenny had a new hat and gloves to keep him warm. She had bought some nice hankies, which had been donated to the shop, for Charlie and Alf. Gracie would get some writing paper and a couple of envelopes.

The door of the shop opened, distracting Nell from her thoughts. A little girl not more than ten came in. Her appearance made Nell want to grab her and put her in a bath.

"Can I help you, child?" she asked.

The young girl nodded, her cheeks flushing, her eyes darting from one item to another on the counter. "Do you have a small dolly I could buy? I only have a halfpenny." She stared at the floor.

"Is it for yourself?"

The girl looked up when she spoke. "No, missus. It's for my sister. She's only four, not grown-up like me. She's sad as our dad was away and he ain't coming back." The child's voice cracked before she whispered, "He was somewhere called Egypt. Mam says we won't ever see him again. Mary, she's my sister, won't stop crying."

Nell's heart contracted with pity for the young girl.

"Well, let's see what we have. We don't have any dolls left but we have a couple of animals. Would your sister like a bunny rabbit?" Nell held up a soft black-and-white stuffed toy she had knitted herself. The girl's eyes sparkled.

"It's lovely. But…"

"Yes?"

"I only have a halfpenny."

Nell handed the girl the bunny. "Buy yourself some chips on the way home. This is a present. Tell your sister her dad sent it to her."

The girl's eyes widened. "Thanks, missus, I will. Happy Christmas."

"Merry Christmas to you too, sweetheart."

The door shut behind her visitor, leaving Nell

feeling worse than she had felt that morning. Poor little mites. Losing their dad at Christmas of all times. If only I could get near that Hitler. I'd beat ten bells out of him.

~

NELL WAITED outside the Lyons tea shop, looking around her hoping Penny wouldn't be late. She would be warmer sitting inside but she felt self-conscious. She picked at an imaginary thread on her good coat, wrinkling her toes in the shoes she rarely wore. What was she doing here, looking like mutton dressed up as lamb?

"Sorry Nell, I didn't mean to leave you standing. Things got a bit chaotic at the hospital. I volunteered to help on the children's ward this afternoon. The girls like to see ladies in uniform as they say they are just as good as the boys at fighting." Penny grinned.

Slightly taken aback by the fact Penny was in uniform, Nell fingered her coat again hoping she looked smart.

"You look wonderful. It's so good to see you." Penny put her nerves at rest and continued chatting as she guided Nell inside. The server gave them a big smile before directing them to their table.

"The special is a toasted ham-and-cheese sandwich, heavy on the cheese."

Nell couldn't find her voice and was glad when

Penny answered on her behalf, "We'll take two and a pot of tea, please."

"Thank you for treating me, Penny, but you really shouldn't have gone to so much trouble." Nell glanced around her. Most of the tables were occupied by courting couples, men in uniform and some women, too.

"I told you in my note I was treating you for Christmas. So eat up and then we have to get going."

"Where?" Nell tried not to stare as the toasted sandwich arrived. The smell was so good. Food you didn't cook for yourself always tasted so much better.

"A carol concert. Gracie told me how much you enjoy them and I thought, with the children being away, Frank in Italy and … well, you know, you could do with cheering up. I would have invited Mr Thompson too, but I believe he'd rather stick pins in his eyes."

Nell giggled like a schoolgirl. "That's so true. Tom thinks it's mushy. He's exhausted anyway between work and his job with the Home Guard. He's happy to sit at the fire with his feet up."

"I hope the alerts don't go and he gets to enjoy it. Meanwhile, we best get a move on."

They finished their tea, Penny insisted on paying, and soon they were walking toward the Albert Hall.

Nell's hands shook as they reached the fabulous old building. There were crowds of people outside, many in uniform like Penny but some dressed up like Lady Louise would be if she were here. She pushed down the feeling of discomfort in her stomach. Penny had gone to a lot of trouble on her behalf.

"Are we going in there?"

"Nell, stop looking like a German is going to drop out of the sky any second. You are my guest and we are going to sit in the Hamilton box and have ourselves a lovely Christmas evening. We can forget about the war, just for a few hours."

Nell knew it was pointless arguing when Penny used that tone. She might as well enjoy herself now she was here. She ignored a couple of looks from ladies dripping in furs and diamonds and followed young Penny to her box.

Malcom Sargent conducted the orchestra and from the first note Nell was transported into another world. Her eyes filled with tears as Megan Foster and Norman Allin, the soloists, sang the most beautiful carols.

"Are you enjoying yourself?" Penny whispered.

"This is so magical, thank you." Nell didn't take her eyes off the stage for fear she'd miss something. At the interval, a man came with some drinks. A port and lemon for her and a lemonade for Penny.

Nell looked around the hall. There wasn't an empty seat in the place. The choir ladies all wore white dresses; she'd hate to be washing them tomorrow. Pinching herself, she smiled.

"Penny, thank you. I can't wait to write to Gracie and the others about my incredible evening. Imagine

Stan when he gets my letter telling him how I spent the evening in the Albert Hall listening to Christmas carols." Her voice wobbled as the need to see her son again nearly consumed her. Penny's eyes shone in the dark as she gripped her hand. "Soon, Nell. The war will be over soon and he'll be home."

CHAPTER 28

Penny stared at the full moon. This was it. Finally, the flight could leave and she would soon be in France. The long wait through the winter months had been difficult but it seemed there was no alternative transport available. At least not for the female agents. It was rumoured some men had been sent by boat via the naval section of SOE but she hadn't met anyone who had confirmed that.

Penny had thought the waiting would never end. Now her chance to return home was here. She wrapped her arms around her body in a big hug.

Penny rehearsed her cover story again. She was going into Soucelles as Isabelle Michiels, a young married woman whose husband was missing, presumed dead. Given her job in the translation service and the need to keep the cover story as real as possible, she was to act as a qualified secretary looking for work. Her identity card and ration book would be in the name of Isabelle. Simone was only to be used with members of the network. Confusing as it seemed, Penny knew this was one way to protect the agents from being discovered by the Gestapo. From Soucelles, she would travel to Paris and other areas as necessary. Vera had instructed her to buy a first-class season ticket. "It's safer. The Nazis are less likely to quiz you if you don't turn up at the station office buying regular train tickets. I hope you have been practising your cycling."

Penny grimaced at the memory. The first few weeks of training would be hard to forget. Even if she did, she had the muscles to prove her proficiency.

There was a knock on the door and a senior WAAF, Christine Brown, whom Penny had met earlier, came into the room. "Miss Atkins would normally come to see you, but she's been held up elsewhere. She asked me to wish you bonne chance!"

Penny pushed her nerves down.

"Please, can you strip?"

Shocked, Penny repeated, "Strip?"

"I need to check that every item you are wearing is French. I also need to check the contents of your handbag."

Christine was very thorough as she went through each individual item of clothing, including the spare suit in her luggage. The department employed a Jewish refugee tailor to ensure that all costumes worn by the agents were "genuinely" French. As instructed, Penny had been wearing the clothes for the last few days, helping her to feel like Isabelle Michiels, and also to make the clothes lose their newish look.

Penny watched as Christine laid the contents of Penny's handbag bare on the table. Christine glanced briefly at the pictures of Penny's "husband" and her "parents". "You were a lucky woman to be married to such an attractive man," she joked, and they both laughed.

"Okay, that's it. Well done, all present and correct. You wouldn't believe what I find on some agents. One lady had a pack of playing cards covered in the Union Jack while another man had cut out the crossword from The Times to help keep his mind off things!"

Christine smiled at her before adding, "Good girl, now come and have your breakfast. It will soon be time."

Penny sat down to eat, although she wasn't hungry. She didn't want to faint on the flight because of an empty stomach. She had a boiled egg, followed by two rounds of toast dripping with butter and marmalade, particularly thankful for the strong tea. She released her tight grip on the bone china cup, afraid she would break it.

"You ready?"

Already sitting at the edge of her chair, Penny

leaned forward. "Yes, ma'am." Her heart was beating so fast she hoped Christine couldn't hear it.

"Okay, Penny, this is it. Take these two packages. One is for you and the other is for Victor. Betty will drive us to the airfield, so from now on we will use your cover name, Simone. It's imperative that nobody knows your actual identity, and that includes the guys flying you to France. Now you have everything, your ID, ration book..."

"*Oui, madame*, I have everything. *Merci.*"

Tessa, the driver, was obviously used to driving agents, or "Joes" as they were known, to the planes as she didn't comment or ask questions. Penny, grateful for the silence, clutched her hands together to stop fidgeting.

Tessa drove up to the gates of RAF Tempsford, checked in with the sentry, and was waved on towards the barn where the crew were waiting.

"Simone, take these with you, but remember, don't smoke in public." Christine handed Penny some packets of *Gauloises*.

"Thank you, Christine, but I don't smoke."

"Take them all the same, they may come in useful. It's amazing how much information one cigarette can buy." Christine smiled grimly. "*Bonne chance*, Simone."

"*Merci, au revoir.*"

Penny held her head up and tried not to run over to the plane. I'm going home.

~

FOR A SMALL PLANE, the engines seemed very loud, and she wondered if the Germans would hear them approach.

Penny's stomach churned, and her fear combined with the smell from the nearby spare petrol cans was overwhelming. She could no longer feel her feet or hands. If only the sergeant who'd made fun of her at the fuselage training could see her now. He'd have no time for her complaining about the cold. All he'd care about was that she left the aircraft in the correct position. There wouldn't be a second chance to get it right tonight.

She glanced at the dispatcher, who responded with a wink and motioned her to move to the exit hole before turning his attention back to his job. She waited for the red light to change, willing it to turn green but hoping that it wouldn't and she could return to relative safety. The seconds dragged, but then it was time.

She barely heard him shout "Go!" as she plunged downwards, relieved that her parachute had opened. Her relief was short-lived when she realised the wind was carrying her canopy away from the source of light below and by implication the reception committee. She hoped she hadn't been blown too far off course, but didn't have too long to worry about it as the ground rushed up to meet her.

She landed safely, thankful for the tight bandages on her ankles that had done their job. She hit the harness release button, sending the billowing parachute silk into folds at her feet, and removed her overalls. As she'd been trained, she was busy burying her parachute when the first member of the reception committee reached her side.

She looked up into his melting brown eyes. Their gaze locked before he greeted her with a kiss on the cheek, saying softly, "*Bonsoir, Simone. Je suis Paul.*"

Penny couldn't think clearly. She was home; she fancied she even recognised the smell of France, which was silly, never having been around Poitiers before.

Paul put his hand on her arm, guiding her out of the field. He, too, appeared concerned that the noise of the engines could have alerted the local German division. They needed to hurry to get her to safety.

"We must move. We've had a minor problem, nothing for you to worry about."

Bristling, Penny snapped. "I've just dropped from a plane. Please don't treat me as if I'm brittle or made of glass."

He laughed, turning it into a snort at the look she gave him.

"*Pardon.* Your safe house fell through. For now, there is no option but to take you to my grandmother. It's not ideal, but…" He shrugged.

She didn't want to ask for details.

Paul took her to his grandmother's house where she could stay until he could arrange a more permanent safe house. He introduced Penny as Madame Isabelle Michiels, the name on her forged identification papers.

The old lady provided her with warm food and a drink. As she shared the meal with Paul, he explained she was to meet with Victor, the leader of the group, the next day at the local café.

"Will you come with me?" she asked, fighting her desire to move closer to him.

"I have another appointment." He held her gaze for a few moments.

Penny felt the heat rising up her neck and across her face.

"Unfortunately, I must leave immediately." Paul stood up. Speaking in a low voice as he kissed her cheek, he said, "Annette will tell you everything you need to know. Take care, little one. You couldn't have landed at a more dangerous time." His lips briefly brushed her cheek and then he was gone.

Her mouth was so dry, she could barely breathe. She crossed her arms, conscious that Annette was watching her closely.

"My grandson is very brave."

Penny swallowed, hoping her voice would sound normal. "As are you, madame."

Annette shrugged her shoulders. "I'm an old woman

who has lived a long, happy life. Now, my little one, I shall show you where to sleep. You must be tired."

Penny was exhausted, but she couldn't sleep. She hoped Paul would return the next day. *You have a job to do. Stop it.* But no matter how often she berated herself, she couldn't help thinking of the man she had just met.

~

WHEN PENNY WOKE the following morning, Paul's grandmother greeted her with a hot drink.

"I'm sorry, Isabelle, but we don't have any tea, coffee or chocolate. We have a little milk. The *Boche* take everything for themselves and leave us with nothing," the old lady continued. "We have to make coffee from barley."

"Thank you, madame. I'm very grateful for you putting me up for the evening. Please don't apologise."

"*Bon.* Now, you must call me Annette. Madame is far too formal for the granddaughter of my closest friend." She smiled at Penny. "Our story is that your grandmother and I met in Paris some years ago and stayed in contact until her untimely death. It's only natural that you would call to spend a few days with me." Annette smiled mischievously. "I have already told the neighbours that I'm hoping Paul falls in love with you, as a match between our families would be wonderful. That will give them something to gossip about."

Penny should have laughed at the idea of the old lady matchmaking, given the seriousness of the situation. Instead, she found the idea intriguing. Giving herself a mental shake, she pushed her shoulders back and sat straighter.

"Thank you, Annette, for doing all of this."

"I'm doing it not just for you and Paul, but for France. I hate the *Boche*. They took my husband the last time they were here. Now they are putting my grandson at risk. But now we must get to work. I have had a message. Unfortunately, Victor can't meet with you today. He suggested you have a wander around the town to get used to being back in France once again. He will make contact to arrange a meeting as soon as he can."

Penny took Annette's advice and went out exploring. She went to a café to kill some time, pondering how everything about France had changed. It was different to London; the buildings remained intact. Despite the lack of war damage, unlike London where the atmosphere had been one of relief that the constant bombings had ceased, here you could almost taste the fear.

The people walked around with their eyes downcast, as if afraid to look into anyone's face for fear of what they might see. Even the children didn't play in the carefree way they should. The lack of young men was obvious. She knew this was because of the Germans' habit of sending all able-bodied men over the age of sixteen off to Germany as forced labour. And then there were those who had been killed or wounded while fighting for France.

After ordering what the locals called coffee, she sat

at an unoccupied outside table, watching the world go by. The changes she saw around her were upsetting, but she knew she was apprehensive about her meeting with the circuit leader. What if he didn't believe she had what it took to be a courier?

She thought about Paul and his grandmother. They seemed like such ordinary people, yet they were involved, too. The world had gone mad. Paul's grandmother should be playing cards and visiting her family, not fighting the Germans. She shook her head.

"Is this seat taken, madame?"

Penny looked up into Paul's smiling face. "No, please sit down, monsieur."

Leaning towards him, she pushed her hair behind her ear.

"My grandmother said I would find you in the town," Paul said. "I think she might take this matchmaking story a little too literally." He laughed, but she noticed he had moved so he sat nearer to her.

He reminded her somewhat of David, being around the same age. But where David was blond and blue-eyed, Paul was dark. His hair matched his deep brown eyes. When he smiled, his eyes looked like melted chocolate.

"How do you move around so freely? Are the Germans not suspicious?" she whispered, wanting to hear him talk. His voice had a funny effect on her, making her stomach feel all fluttery.

"No. They think I'm a coward or a sympathiser, having heard I refused to fight them. They have seen the prison records showing I spent time in custody."

Penny remained silent. To her horror, Paul seemed to interpret her silence as a personal attack. His nostrils flared as he moved his face closer to hers. "I'm no coward, Isabelle. Those records are false. I grew up a long way from here, volunteered as soon as war broke out, and fought for my country until the very end. I was on my way to England. But then Dunkirk happened. I couldn't go home. I had to come up with a story, and being a coward was the safest I could think of."

Irritated he'd misunderstood her, she apologised. "I didn't mean to insult you. For the record, I have a friend who is a conscientious objector. He isn't a coward, just someone with a powerful sense of what is right and wrong. I may not share his views, but I can see it has taken a lot of courage to stand up for his beliefs."

Paul burst out laughing. "Relax, little one. We are on the same side, remember?"

Penny rose, desperate to get away. Her reaction to him was confusing and distracting. She needed to put some distance between them. "I best get back to your grandmother's house."

"I have a couple of errands, but I will see you later for dinner." Paul stood up as Penny left the table. She could feel his eyes on her as she walked down the street, but she pretended not to notice. They both were professionals and had a job to do. This was no time to get involved with anyone.

~

SHE WAS close to Annette's house when she came across a family being arrested. She was tempted to help and started forward, only to be restrained gently by a woman standing next to her. The woman whispered, "You can't do anything for them and will only get yourself shot."

Penny adopted a vacant stare, but she noticed every detail, looking on as the stick-thin mother and three young children, all dressed in ragged clothes, were manhandled by the soldiers, forced into the back of a lorry. One of the little girls dropped her doll on the street and screamed for it. She tried to jump down to get it. A soldier gave her a hard slap. A young boy darted away from his mother, into the road to pick up the doll for the little girl. He turned to one soldier, looking at the man as if he should know better.

Holding the soldier's gaze, the little boy explained, "Lily goes nowhere without her dolly. She is my friend. Why are you taking her?"

"Shut up, boy, and return to your mother if you know what is good for you." When the boy didn't move as quickly as he wanted, the soldier aimed his gun at him.

Penny started forward but stopped as a priest

quickly moved, putting himself between the gun and the boy. She clenched and unclenched her fists as she listened to him trying to remonstrate with the soldier.

"He's only young. He has yet to learn your ways," the priest said as the boy's mother hugged him close.

"Well, see that he does!" said the soldier before deliberately stamping on the doll. He then laughed and jumped into the lorry and they all disappeared.

The priest made the sign of the cross before turning away without saying a word. The townspeople dispersed, with the silence only broken by the little boy's pitiful sobs. Soon, Penny was alone with the broken doll lying in the puddle.

A wave of nausea overtook Penny. She emptied the contents of her stomach at the side of the road. Her cheeks flamed. Pressing her palm against her mouth, she ran as fast as she could back to Annette's home. She barely had time to close the door behind her before collapsing in tears.

Annette rushed to greet her, "What's the matter?"

"It was just horrible. They took a little girl and left her doll behind. It was all broken and wet and…" Penny's voice cracked.

Annette drew her towards her, "Shush. Who took a little girl and from where?"

"I was in the square and suddenly a van drove up carrying some soldiers. They jumped out and ran into this house. They dragged a mother out into the street, followed by her three children. One was carrying a doll."

Annette stiffened. "The little girl was Lily?"

Penny stopped crying and looked up at Annette. "How did you know her name?"

Annette's eyes widened with fury. "Someone must have betrayed them."

"But why? Why would someone want to hurt a child?"

"They are Jewish and were in hiding. They would have been moved to safety soon, but now it's too late. If I could get my hands on whoever talked, I would..." The tears flowed unchecked down Annette's cheeks. "Some war this is, where grown men go around picking on women and babies. People like you must win."

Penny reached for the older woman's hand. "You mean people like us."

Annette rewarded her with a sad smile and a shrug, then turned to go back into the kitchen. Penny needed to be alone and went up to her bedroom.

～

WHEN PAUL RETURNED LATER that evening, she heard him speaking to Annette and then the sound of someone climbing the stairs. Penny heard the knock on the bedroom door. Thinking it was Annette, she called "come in". She was surprised to see Paul enter.

"Are you okay?" he asked gently.

"Yes, I'm fine," she replied.

"It doesn't look like it." Paul took a napkin and gently dried Penny's face. "We will make sure the person who betrayed Lily and her family will never make the same mistake again."

Penny thought of the little girl, and the scene brought back memories of all the stories that the kids from the orphanage had told her. She tried, but failed, to stop the tears from falling. Paul put his arms around her and she cried for a while on his shoulder. When the tears subsided, she drew back, feeling embarrassed. Paul leaned closer and, using his thumbs, gently wiped the last of her tears away. Their eyes locked, she couldn't tear away her gaze. His hands moved to the side of her face, but then they heard Annette's voice calling dinner.

Paul jumped back as if burnt. "I'll go down. Perhaps you should wash your face first so Annette doesn't see you so upset. She feels awful she couldn't help the family even though she did all she could."

She couldn't help but be impressed by his care for her host, and she tried to ignore the butterflies in her stomach.

She freshened up before joining Paul and his grandmother for dinner. Tension sizzled in the air. Annette did her best to lighten the atmosphere by telling stories of Paul and his sister, Chloe, from when they were younger.

Penny went to bed early and cried herself to sleep. The escape didn't last long. She woke desperately trying to breathe. Feeling claustrophobic, she got up and opened the little window. Was she really cut out to be a secret agent? From the stories she'd heard in training, she'd face much worse than what she'd seen that day. If she did as she was trained and sabotaged the German war effort, they would take reprisals out on the townsfolk. What if they shot people because of something she did?

She got out of bed and paced back and forth. She had to toughen up, develop a thicker skin and do the job she was sent here to do. She was the one who wanted to make a difference. If the Germans got to England, that would be Shirley or Betty. She sat on the bed. People could be tortured and die as a result of her actions, but they would help end the war, saving thousands of lives in the process. That was what she must focus on. *Easier said than done*, she thought as she wrapped her arms around her knees, rocking back and forward. Every time she closed her eyes, she saw the little girl crying for her doll.

CHAPTER 30

When Penny got up the next morning, Paul had already left. Annette put some day-old bread and preserves on the table along with a cup of steaming liquid.

"I made a tisane. It tastes better than the muck we drink as coffee."

The scent of ginger and lemon lingered around the kitchen. Penny took a sip before asking, "How can you be so cheerful?"

"We can only beat the Germans if we behave as if they don't exist. Don't misunderstand, I feel terrible about Lily and her family. They were such good people." Annette's hands shook as she spoke. "We don't know when death will visit us. I think we should treat each day as our last and live the best we can."

Penny noted Annette's use of the past tense in relation to Lily and her family, but she didn't probe. Sometimes it was best not to ask questions.

⁓

PAUL, appearing agitated, arrived back around lunchtime. Annette had gone out to the village, leaving them alone. Penny wondered if he felt uncomfortable because of her lack of control over her emotions. Was he questioning her ability to do the job she'd trained for? She waited for him to speak first, but when he didn't, she apologised.

"Sorry for the tears last night. It won't happen again."

He didn't seem to register what she'd said, but stared at a mark on the wall above Penny's head. "Looks like you landed at the right time. London wants to blow up a local oil refinery."

Penny gaped at him. "And they want us to do it?"

Paul laughed harshly. "No, they don't expect miracles. Well, not big ones like that. We won't demolish it. London is sending in a team to do that. Our job is to make sure that when they get here, they can do their job. They have asked us to put the site under surveillance and report back on security, number of employees, timelines, etc."

Forgetting about what she'd told herself about not getting emotionally involved, her first thought was for the workers, "What about the people who work there? They won't be killed, will they?"

Paul looked grim. "I'd like to kill the owner with my

bare hands. Monsieur Verger knows exactly what he is doing. He doesn't care about supplying the Germans with synthetic fuel, which they use for their tanks in North Africa. So long as he is still making a profit, he can sleep at night."

She could understand his feelings but the people working there may be innocent.

"But surely the workers don't all feel the same?"

"That's what we need to find out. If they do, then they can go to hell with their boss. If they don't, we need to find a way of complying with London's orders but without losing any innocent lives."

The fact he wasn't happy about murdering innocent workers made her feel good – proof they were on the same side. "You head back to Annette's and try to get some rest. The next few days will be rough going."

"I'm stronger than I look and don't need you to protect me," she retorted. His eyes widened, and she apologised. "Sorry, I didn't mean to snap, but I'm not a little girl. I know what I was sent here to do."

"I should hope so. We leave after curfew and will be gone for a few days."

❧

PENNY BLEW her wet hair from her eyes as she cycled after Paul along the back roads, keeping an eye out for patrols. The rain wasn't heavy but it had a way of getting inside her coat to drip down her back. Shivering, despite the pace they maintained on the bikes, she hoped they would come to the shelter soon.

Paul stopped to point towards a grove of trees, a small forest. She followed him as he veered off the road, dismounting and pushing his bike through the undergrowth. The trees provided some shelter from the rain and the wind chill. The spongy leaves underfoot were slippery, the branches of the bare trees scraped her skin. Paul kept going further into the trees. She hoped he was looking for a hut or shelter of some sort.

After about thirty minutes he stopped, laying his bike against a tree. He gestured for her to do the same but didn't speak. She followed his lead and watched as he covered both bikes with some branches. It wouldn't hide them from close inspection, but it was enough of a camouflage if someone happened to go for a walk and passed by.

He beckoned her to follow him as he moved to what looked like an abandoned hunting cabin. She eyed the structure with dismay; the roof was sagging, was it safe? Paul obviously thought so as he pushed the door open. She stepped inside, her nose wrinkly at the smell of decomposing leaves, animal droppings and goodness knows what else.

"This is home for the next while. You can have the bed and I'll sleep on the floor."

She eyed the old mattress. Shuddering, she put her bag on the ground. "I'd prefer the floor too."

"Let's eat and then get some rest."

She pulled out some of the picnic Annette had made them. The ham-and-cheese sandwiches were the best thing she'd ever tasted. They drank cold water from a stream to the rear of the property.

"We can't light a fire for fear someone will see the smoke. It's not what you are used to."

His words irritated her. "I didn't expect the Ritz."

He held up his hands in a gesture of surrender. "Easy. I didn't mean it as an insult. I just bet you thought your first mission would be more glamorous than this." He glanced around the hut.

She couldn't help but smile. She wasn't sure what she had imagined, but being stuck miles from nowhere in a freezing tumbledown dwelling hadn't been it.

"Tell me more about what we need to do."

Using a stick, he made a drawing on the floor. "The refinery is ten miles to the north of here. We know the guards are positioned here and here. The workers are checked going in and out through this main gate." He drew an x on the ground.

"If we know all this, why do we need to do more surveillance?"

"Patience, Isabelle. I heard this second-hand. I prefer to see for myself how the land lies."

She nodded in agreement. There were too many lives on the line to mess this up.

"You want the first watch or will I take it?" he asked.

"I'll do it." She was too keyed up to sleep. She put back on her wet coat and walked to the door.

"Watch out for bears."

She threw him a dirty look before closing the door behind her. He wasn't serious, was he? She gave herself a shake. Of course not, bears belonged in the Alps. Wild boars were a possibility. Even so, she'd prefer to come up against one of those than an armed soldier.

⁓

ASIDE FROM THE rustling in the bushes and the wind whistling in the trees, her watch was uneventful. Paul relieved her and she returned to the hut to sleep. She lay on her coat and fell asleep instantly.

Paul woke her later.

"We need to go now. You up to it?"

"Are you?" she retorted, standing up, ignoring the weariness in her muscles. Their work hadn't started yet.

They hid their belongings just in case of visitors, before cycling towards the refinery. They left their bicycles at the edge of the wood and continued on foot.

The refinery security wasn't what she expected. The guards seemed quite casual. Maybe they didn't believe it would be a target. She compared notes with Paul when they returned to the hut, and both had seen similar numbers of guards despite their differing viewpoints.

"We'll go back tomorrow night to make sure."

She nodded, too tired to comment.

He stared at her for a couple of seconds before commenting, "There aren't many who would put up with these conditions without complaint, yet you haven't moaned once."

"What would I complain about? Our lodgings are inexpensive, our food makes me lose weight, and then there is the company." She pointed to an inquisitive squirrel who was watching them from a nearby tree.

Paul burst out laughing, causing Penny to do the same.

Working together so closely, they quickly got to know one another and fell into a comfortable rhythm. She knew very little about him yet trusted him instinctively. He was meticulous, patient and didn't gossip. She didn't ask him anything about the other members of the network. One night, she asked him why he had got involved in the resistance.

A bitter look came over his face, and his eyes filled with hatred. "They killed my wife. She was pregnant with our first child."

"I'm so sorry, Paul. I shouldn't have asked."

"She wasn't French. She was Jewish, from Poland originally. I'm not sure which upset my mother more.

Our parents didn't agree with us getting married so we eloped. We went to live with my married sister, living in Paris. We were very happy. Then the Germans came."

"You don't need to tell me any more," she said, feeling she had intruded on his grief.

"I joined up along with Samuel, Rebecca's brother-in-law. We were fighting in the Ardennes when he was killed. The Germans moved into Paris in June 1940. It didn't take them long to show their true colours. Rebecca started bleeding because of complications with the baby. She needed medical attention, but they refused to allow her into the hospital. When a doctor tried to help her, they arrested him. She died a few days later."

Penny put out a hand but stopped just shy of touching his shoulder. "I don't know what to say."

"There's nothing you can say. I should have been with my wife. I should have protected her and our baby. Instead, I was fighting a lost cause." Paul stood up and grabbed his rifle. "I'll be back shortly. I want to check the perimeter one more time."

Penny didn't offer to go with him, sensing he needed some time alone. Damn this war, anyway. How many more innocent people were going to die before it was over?

It was some time before Paul returned.

"The Germans obviously trust Monsieur Verger to keep his refinery secure. I expected at least a few

German soldiers to be on guard duty. It will be a slice of cake, as you English people say."

Penny wasn't so sure but didn't like to contradict Paul, as he was her boss and more experienced. Why would they leave an obvious target sitting there unguarded? The Germans weren't stupid.

The next day, it was time to head back, but rather than go to Annette's, Paul instructed her to go to the nearest town.

"I've arranged, through a local contact, for you to take a job at a local café. We need to find out more about the workers, how they feel about their job, their boss. Don't ask too many questions, just listen."

"I can't walk into a café to take a job looking like this." She looked down at her dirty clothes. She could smell her own sweat. "I need to wash and change."

"I've thought of that. The café owner's wife will take care of you. They are good people and have been with us since the start."

CHAPTER 31

Working in the café proved to be an enjoyable experience. Solange, the owner's wife, kept her amused with
comments about the different customers. A small,
bustling little woman with a huge smile, she was a firm
favourite with everyone.

"You'll have a dozen offers of marriage before you
leave us, Isabelle. Especially now. If they had seen you
when you first arrived..." Solange held her nose,
making Isabelle laugh. Any nerves she had disappeared.
She didn't have to do anything more dangerous than
listen, serve drinks and meals and, on occasion, keep out
of the way of groping hands.

Three days later, she met Paul for a quick meal at a
different café across town.

Paul was already sitting at a table, looking tired.
Could she not do more to lighten his load? He caught
her watching him. His smile caused her stomach to flip.

She accepted his kiss on the cheek before sitting down and they made small talk until their drinks arrived.

He picked up her hand as if they were on a date, his fingers caressing her wrist. "What have the workers been saying?"

Trying to ignore the flutters his touch caused, she waited until the server was out of earshot. "They, too, are fed up with Monsieur Verger. He is making all the money and they are getting a pittance. One even joked about blowing up the factory himself."

"You have done an outstanding job. I keep having to remind myself that this is your first mission in France."

Penny glowed from his praise.

"We are running out of time. The team arrives in the next few days." He hesitated, then said, "You will have to meet them at the landing site with me as one of my usual guys has yet to return from Paris."

Something in his manner made her ask, "Is it normal for him to be away so long?" She picked her tone carefully, not wanting to sound like she was questioning his authority. Things were moving too quickly and a little too easily. After all she had heard in her training, she'd expected more obstacles.

Paul caressed her face gently. "Stop being so nervous, little one. Everything is in hand. We are in charge here, not the Germans."

Penny didn't share his confidence. She pushed her

food around her plate, thinking of the conversations she had overheard from the workers.

"Paul, listen. The workers say the security is tighter on the inside. Surely they would know?"

"Their idea of security and ours would be very different, Isabelle."

She bit her lip, knowing Frenchmen hated to be questioned by a woman and it was her first mission.

"Do you not think everyone would guess the refinery would be a target?"

His eyes widened. "You haven't been here long enough to question orders."

She nodded, accepting the rebuke despite his gentle tone. He had plenty of experience. She had none.

Picking at her cuticles, she asked, "Have you a location for the landing site? Do you need my help?"

Paul put his hand on hers. "Stop fidgeting. Everything will be fine. I'll tell you on the night. Tell the owner of the bar that your aunt is sick and you have to look after her. You need to disappear now, well before the refinery goes up. We don't need the Germans asking questions. You can lie low at Annette's house for the next two to three weeks."

"Will it take that long?" she asked.

A teasing light lit up his eyes, "Are you in some sort of rush?" He didn't wait for a response. "London has had an issue with some people from the team. They are rushing a couple through training. Anyway, we need to leave a brief time lapse in case they have noted your absence from the restaurant. We don't want to raise any suspicions. I will contact you when I need you."

Paul stood up and threw some francs onto the table. He reached for her hand, pulled her to her feet and gave her a kiss on each cheek. "Go back to Solange now, and tomorrow return to Annette."

Louder, he muttered at her as if angered by something she'd said and marched off. The waiter approached. "Stupid man, leaving a beautiful woman like you behind. Would you like me to walk you home?"

"No, thank you. I just live around the corner." Penny walked away without glancing behind her. Had Paul seen someone? Was that why he'd been in such a rush to leave, or had he lost faith in her because she asked too many questions.

CHAPTER 32

The next day, she arrived back at Annette's home to find her host in unusual form. The older lady kept fiddling with the chain around her neck and glancing at the door as if expecting someone.

"What is it? Has something happened?"

The older woman just shook her head. Penny knew something was bothering her. Her host's unease increased Penny's sense of foreboding.

"Ignore me, Isabelle. I got up in a foul mood. My old bones are aching. What I wouldn't do for a strong cup of real coffee right now."

Penny didn't believe it was the lack of coffee, but if Annette didn't want to tell her, she wouldn't force her.

The older woman kept to her normal daily routine of Mass, followed by a trip to the market. Penny spent her time tidying up the spotless house.

When Annette returned, Penny tried to learn how to

knit, but her efforts only made Annette laugh. Penny would have loved to ask Annette more about Paul, like whether she had met Paul's wife, but decided not to. She didn't want to cause the old lady any pain. Annette didn't ask Penny about her previous life, either. Instead, she teased Penny about her grandson.

She smiled as she took the needles and wool away. "My neighbours think you and Paul make a delightful couple. You would have lovely children."

Penny blushed. She didn't want the old lady to know just how much of an impact Paul had made on her heart. Even if he was a little domineering at times. That wasn't it – he was protective. She wasn't sure which trait she'd find most irritating. But when he smiled … she shook herself, seeing the glint in Annette's eyes. "Paul is a lovely man and very brave, but…"

Annette teased, "But what? He is a man and you are a woman. You spend a lot of time together. Do you not see the attraction between you? The sparks flying could cause a forest fire."

"Stop it, Annette." Her sharp tone caused Annette to gape at her.

"Why? Do you have a man in England?"

"No. There was someone I liked, but it didn't work out. He is probably married now." She didn't like how the conversation was developing.

Annette sighed, "He wasn't right for you if he

marries someone else. Paul, he is free to marry where his heart takes him."

Penny stood, eager to end the conversation. "We work together. We have a job to do. You, of all people, should understand that."

Instead of putting a stop to the conversation, Penny's protests only encouraged the older woman.

Annette laughed gaily. "I think I have touched – what do you say – a raw nerve?"

"Not at all. I'm here to do a job. Nothing more. Now is not the time for romance. You must understand?"

"*Mais oui*, I understand. Working together under such stressful conditions will only push you together." Annette looked serious. "Remember, little one, you must live each day as your last. In times like this, tomorrow may never come."

Penny hesitated at Annette's remark. It was so unlike her, and together with her fidgeting and odd behaviour since Penny had got back, she had to know.

"Annette, what's wrong?"

"Wrong? Why, nothing, little one."

"I know something is bothering you. Can you not trust me?" Penny didn't even notice she was holding her hands on her hips.

"Isabelle, I trust you completely. Don't mind me. My old mind is playing tricks on me. There is nothing to be worried about. Now, I'm going to bed early. Perhaps you could clear up after dinner?"

Annette never went to bed before her, but Penny didn't argue.

"Yes, madame," replied Penny, knowing there was something up but that she wouldn't find out any more information until Annette was ready to talk.

～

THE DAYS PASSED WITHOUT INCIDENT. Penny cleaned, knitted and cooked but nothing made the time go faster. There was no word from Paul, although she made contact with his wireless operator. Annette tuned into BBC London so they could listen to the personal messages some of which were nonsense, others were coded messages for the resistance. A message for her confirmed London's request for more landing areas. She would have to examine the surrounding areas, which gave her a perfect excuse to visit Madame Bayard.

She hated leaving Annette, but the woman seemed to have put whatever was worrying her to one side.

"Annette, I have to go away for a day. If I don't come back tomorrow evening, it's because I have missed curfew. I will be back the next morning."

Penny couldn't return Annette's probing gaze. "You're going away? Now? But what if Paul needs you?"

"He won't for another week. The cloud cover is too dense and, anyway, London had to replace and train some of their team. This visit is important. I have to check something. For London." Penny hated lying, even if it was by omission, but she couldn't risk telling the truth. Annette would only tell her not to visit her childhood home as it was too dangerous. "I can't just sit around waiting." Not while my old friend might be in danger.

"Are you meeting a man?" Annette narrowed her eyes suspiciously.

Penny laughed. "Are you still matchmaking? I promise it isn't a man. We need more landing drops, that's all." Penny crossed her fingers, hoping to offset the lie.

"Okay, little one. But be careful." Annette gave Penny a hug.

CHAPTER 33

She travelled by the fast train to Paris and then took the slow train to Marly-le-Roi, trying to contain her emotions at returning to her old home. The war had changed her country beyond recognition, but she desperately hoped that some things had remained the same. Penny knew she was breaking all the rules, but she didn't care. She had to know her old friend was okay.

The train to Marly-le-Roi seemed to take even longer than before. She stepped cautiously onto the platform, telling herself not to be silly. Nobody will recognise you. You don't look like the scared little girl who left here all those years ago.

Penny walked up the street. She felt for her papers once more. The soldiers made comments as she walked past, but she pretended she didn't understand them. The years of working with the children from the Kindertransport in her first volunteering job had given her a fair understanding of the German language. It was information she kept to herself.

She wiped her hands on her dress a couple of times. She was afraid, not of Madame Bayard, but of her reaction to seeing her again. She hoped that her unexpected arrival wouldn't put the old lady in any danger. She hadn't given that much thought until now. She realised she had been so selfish, wanting to see her again. She hadn't even thought that her visit could place her in jeopardy.

Tears filled her eyes at the pink climbing roses covering the outside of the house. Mama had given Madame Bayard a small rose bush she'd grown from some cuttings. She walked past the old woman's house first to make sure she wasn't being followed. She didn't think anyone had taken much notice of her, but it was best to be sure. Only when she was absolutely certain nobody was around did she go up to the door and turn the handle. Relieved to find it was unlocked, she walked in, closing and locking the door behind her. She didn't want anyone coming in unexpectedly.

The familiar smell and layout of the cottage meant that the years disappeared. She was twelve years old again, delivering something for her mother. Madame had invited her in for some chocolate milk and something to eat. Penny could almost smell the chocolate.

She walked slowly through to the kitchen. Madame

was working in her garden at the rear. Overcome with emotion, she stopped to stare. The years hadn't been kind to the old lady. She looked frail and much older than Penny had expected.

I was wrong to come here. I should have left her alone. I'm only placing her at risk.

As if she sensed something, Madame looked up to catch Penny looking at her. Penny watched the recognition light up her eyes, but they dimmed quickly. She realised Madame was frightened.

Penny wanted to rush outside to give the old lady a reassuring hug, but some instinct stopped her. Instead, she stood waiting in the kitchen. The old woman put down her work and plodded up the garden path.

"*Penelope, ma petite jeune fille.*" Tears coursed down the wrinkled cheeks as she looked up at Penny. "*Je n'en crois pas mes yeux!*"

"Madame Bayard." Penny hugged the old lady close, taking care not to hurt her. She could feel her bones through her clothes. "*Mon Dieu*, you are so thin. I know things are difficult, but surely you have sufficient rations to get by? Do your neighbours not help you?"

"Penelope, stop fussing and sit back down. Let me look at you. You are so pretty. Of course, you are the image of your mama, God rest her soul." Madame held Penny's face in her hands. "What, my dear, are you doing here? You are in danger. Do you not know that he still lives here?"

"Don't worry, Madame. Nobody knows I'm here. I will slip away quietly later. But tell me, how are things with you?" Penny looked at the lady she had long considered to be her grandmother. "Why are you so thin?"

Madame stood up. "You will have some coffee? Not the real thing, you know, but..." She shrugged. "Or perhaps you would like some soup."

Penny was starving, but she didn't want to eat her friend's dinner. "*Merci beaucoup. Une café* would be lovely."

"You haven't told me why you are here in France and not safe in England."

Penny shook her head. "Don't ask me questions I can't answer. Please tell me, how you are? How are things here in Marly-le-Roi? Do the *Boche* give you much trouble?"

"Things are very bad, Penelope. The people here are good people for the most part. But Alain, pft. The other day, he personally rounded up ten of the local men ... well, boys really. He handed them over to the Germans to be executed."

"Shot? Why?"

"The resistance tried to blow up the train track but the device didn't go off properly. In the shoot-out that followed, one German soldier was injured. He died later that day. Alain decided that one *Boche* was worth ten of our fine men." Madame looked at Penny. "You didn't come to hear stories of our troubles. Why are you here?"

Penny noted how her friend's hands shook. She had to persuade her to come with her. She took her friend's shaking hands in her own. "Madame, will you not come with me? I can't get you out of France, but at least you can live somewhere else. Away from Alain."

Madame Bayard shook her head.

"I'm sure your husband and sons would understand," said Penny.

"I thank God they are not here to see what has happened to our beautiful country. They would be so ashamed. Angry, too. But it's not because of them that I stay. Here I can be useful." She looked like she was going to say something else, but stopped.

"Useful? In what way?" Penny thought she knew the answer but wanted to confirm her suspicions.

"Now, my dear, you know better than to ask questions like that. I'm guessing our work is not so very different." Madame smiled.

"Oh, Madame, it's too dangerous for you."

Madame's eyes glittered, making Penny aware that she had annoyed the old lady.

"Dangerous for me? That is what the English would say, the kettle calling the pot black. I never left my home and I'm not going to let anyone make me. You..." She paused before continuing, "You were safe but you decided to come back. Why, Penelope? Why?"

"I had to see you. I had to say thank you for saving me all those years ago. If it wasn't for you, I don't think I would still be here."

"And?"

"And what?"

"Penelope Hamilton, I may be old but I'm not senile. You could have thanked me in a letter before the war started. You have come back here for something else." She looked at Penny, who stared back defiantly.

Madame Bayard paled and sat down with a thump. "It's him, isn't it? You have come back to see Alain."

"Don't be silly…"

"How dare you treat me like a fool in my own house? You stupid little girl. What are you going to do to him? He will eat you up for breakfast. He works with the Germans now. He is completely in their pockets. I could have some respect for him if he believed in their message like Petain seems to. But no, Alain is only interested in power."

Penny's anger threatened to engulf her, but as she looked at the old woman wringing her hands together, she felt remorse. She moved to reassure her friend.

"I'm not the same frightened little girl who left here. I have changed. I will repay Alain for everything he did. Not only to Mama, but to you and everyone else. He will die. Not today, but it will be soon. I promise."

"Penelope, you are frightening me. You need to forget all about this and go home."

"This is my home and nobody, not the *Boche*, Alain or even you are going to make me leave it again. I have to fight back. I have a job to do. Now, I'm sorry, but I must go. I was wrong to come here."

The old woman sagged into a chair. Her voice trembled as she spoke, leaving Penny straining to hear her. "Penelope, don't leave on an argument. Stay with me for dinner. You can leave first thing in the morning. Please."

Penny wavered.

"I have all your letters hidden. I want to hear about Gracie and Meme and all the other people you wrote about. I even want to hear about Harriet."

At that, Penny burst out laughing. Madame Bayard opened her arms. Penny knelt at her feet, allowing herself to be engulfed in a big hug. "You are right, *ma petite jeune fille*. France is your home. Welcome back."

Penny spent the next couple of hours catching up with her old friend. She told her all about Gracie and Charlie, Harriet and Peter and everyone else.

With a twinkle in her eyes, the old lady said, "And you, my precious? Is there no special man in your life?"

Penny blushed. "Not really, although I have met two I liked."

"Two? Now I know you are truly French and not English."

Penny smiled at the teasing.

"David is English. He's in the RAF and I met him on the night I got caught in a bombing raid. He was very kind. We worked together to help the wounded. He came to visit me at Aunt Louise's."

"He sounds like a nice man. What was wrong with him? Was he ugly?"

Penny flushed. "Not at all. He is tall with blue eyes and blond hair. In fact, he could pass for a Nazi, but only by looks. He is very brave, and he isn't overprotective." Not like Paul.

Madame lifted her eyebrows. "He sounds perfect. So what was wrong with him?"

"He had a fiancée. He's probably married by now." Penny bit her lip. Why doesn't that seem to matter any more?

"Ah, and he didn't tell you about this fiancée? I can understand you being upset at him, expecting you to be the other woman."

"He didn't. Well, not really. At least I don't think he did." Penny knew she sounded confused, but after all this time she wasn't sure exactly what David meant to her. She'd looked forward to seeing him, liked looking at him and talking to him, but Paul made her heart beat faster. Nobody could make her laugh or seethe in anger so quickly. She missed him when he wasn't nearby. In the forest, she'd been lonely without him even if he'd only gone for a few hours. His face was the last thing she thought about every night and on waking every morning. She averted her gaze so Madame couldn't read her thoughts.

Madame Bayard laughed. "Okay, what about the other man? Is it as complicated with him?"

Penny thought of Paul. "Possibly more so."

The old lady stayed silent, leaving Penny to explain.

"Paul is French, so we share a bond. He's fierce and brave but kind, too. He is tall, like David, but is as dark as David is fair. He has beautiful eyes."

Madame smiled.

"He was married, but the *Boche* killed his wife and unborn child. He is involved, you know, in the fight against the Germans. He is determined that France will once more be free."

"Ah, you are worried that he is looking for a surrogate to replace his lost wife?"

Penny shook her head. Why hadn't she thought of that?

"No, I don't think so. But then, I don't know. Oh, Madame, I'm not very good at this. I don't know how I'm supposed to feel. I didn't come back to France to meet a man." Penny rubbed the back of her neck.

"Cupid doesn't care what your plans are, my darling. Falling in love is as natural as living. You will know soon enough whether he is the right man for you."

"We haven't known each other very long. His grandmother is trying her best to make us a couple." Penny smiled, filling Madame Bayard in on Annette's explanation of her presence to the neighbours.

Looking confused, Madame asked, "So what is the problem?"

"He makes me feel different. I want to be with him all the time. I haven't known him very long, yet I feel like I have known him forever."

"But?"

Penny smiled as her old friend picked up on her hesitation.

"He treats me like a woman."

Madame's puzzled look made Penny elaborate. "I mean rather than an agent who is equal to him. He tries to protect me and he doesn't always listen to what I'm saying."

Madame shrugged. "He's a man."

"Yes, but is that the way it should be? One minute I want to kiss him, the next to kill him."

Madame Bayard smiled. "Love doesn't follow a set of rules, my darling. Your father fell in love with your mama from the moment he saw her. She took a little longer to realise how much he meant to her."

"But if I'm in love with Paul, then what did I feel for David?"

Penny knew there was no comparison between her feelings for David and those she now had for Paul.

"Perhaps he was the first man who looked at you like a woman? Many people mistake that initial admiration for love."

Penny thought about that for a second before saying, "I don't think Aunt Louise would approve of Paul, although she loves David. She would be scandalised if she knew I was even speaking this way about two men I hardly know – one of whom may well be married by now anyway."

"It's natural to grow close to people when you don't know what tomorrow may bring. In war, you can't count on living a long life."

"That is what Annette says. You would like her. She reminds me a lot of you."

Madame Bayard smiled before adding, "As for your Aunt Louise, I would not be basing my decision on her reaction. You are not her." Madame Bayard took her hand. "My darling Penelope, you will know which man is right for you. Trust your own judgement."

Seeing the exhaustion etched on her friend's face, Penny suggested they go to bed. "I must leave early tomorrow. I will come again soon."

"Penelope, please don't take any risks. I couldn't bear to lose you, too."

"I'm not going anywhere. I'm home to stay. I'll live in Marly-le-Roi again. Not now, but soon. When the war is over."

Penny hugged the old lady before heading to bed. She left the next morning without saying goodbye. It seemed easier.

Penny's journey back was without incident. She cycled around some areas she'd discovered from a map of the area and found what she thought were two landing sights.

Annette welcomed her back with open arms. "Did you find some suitable places?" she asked.

Penny looked away, swallowing repetitively. She hated lying, especially to people she cared about. How she wanted to confess about where she'd been. "The trip was successful, but I may need to go back again."

Later that afternoon, Annette came back from the market with news about the mission. "It's tomorrow night. Meet Paul. He is happy with the first landing zone you found. The owner is a friend. Paul said to go to the hut." Annette looked at Penny strangely before giving her a big hug. "Be careful, my little one, and look after my grandson. He is a good man."

Penny spoke, but Annette held a finger to her lips.

"You can protest all you like, but I've seen the way you look at him. The look of disappointment on his face when you were not here the other night was enough for me to know he feels the same."

Despite the thrill her words gave her, Penny felt the need to deny it. "Annette, not now. We have to concentrate on the job in hand."

"Isabelle, life is for living. Remember that, especially in the coming days."

Before Penny could challenge her host, she had gone, closing the door behind her. Annette hadn't returned by the time she had to leave to meet Paul.

∽

IT WAS a perfect night for a landing. The moon glowed in the clear sky. Penny took care not to encounter any German patrol on the way to meet Paul. Despite her nerves, she was looking forward to seeing him.

There were six other men waiting for them at the appointed spot. She saw her fear and excitement reflected in the faces of these other *Maquis* members who formed part of the landing party. She didn't recognise any of them. Paul barely acknowledged her, and she wondered if he didn't want the other men to know that he knew her well. She pushed her feelings of hurt aside to concentrate on the job. She knew Paul was careful to keep people separate for fear of informers.

She craned her ears, listening for the sound of the plane. After what seemed like hours, they finally heard the engines.

"*Merde*, he is flying very low," Paul whispered.

Penny agreed, looking around, almost expecting the Germans to arrive before they could reach the plane. The noise seemed so loud and would carry on the wind. The RAF pilots were the best but perhaps the plane had been damaged on the route over.

Penny counted the parachutes as the team bailed out of the plane. Eight in all. Good job the Germans hadn't found them. They would have captured so many.

Paul was right. The pilot had flown in too low, and two agents landed badly. One dislocated his shoulder, and the other sprained his ankle. Everyone worked together quickly to dispose of the parachutes and to move the new arrivals to the relative safety of the farm-house. The other members of the landing party disappeared into the countryside, leaving the farmer, Paul and Penny with the soldiers.

The old farmer provided some bowls of soup, which Penny had to water down in order to feed everyone. Then she took out the field dressing kit to see to the men's injuries. An argument between Paul and the British captain in charge of the recently arrived team disrupted the meal.

Paul protested, "We must postpone our plans. Your men have been injured."

"Nonsense. We didn't need eight men to start with. London was simply being overcautious." The British man looked Penny up and down. "Are you one of us? Your English is almost perfect."

Penny wanted to roll her eyes, but she kept her face blank. She'd heard the accents of the men surrounding her. The ones who could speak French spoke it badly. One, Max, freely admitted he didn't speak a word of the language.

Penny glanced at Paul, who nodded.

"Yes, London sent me." She turned back to dressing Tommy's shoulder injury, but the captain addressed her again.

"You speak fluent French, I assume?"

Penny nodded. Paul, scratching his chin, spoke before the captain had time to reply.

"What are they doing sending people in who can't speak the language?"

"Max is an expert at blowing safes and could pick any lock. He wasn't picked for his command of the local lingo!" The captain reminded Penny of Leon, the guy who had been kicked off her course. Not as good-looking, but his height and stature probably made him popular with the ladies. He wasn't making any effort to understand the local situation, let alone hide his contempt for Paul.

He turned back to Penny. "You are bilingual. Good. You can take the two injured men back to Paris. I believe there are several escape routes there to help British soldiers return to the UK."

Penny stared at the captain, not bothering to hide her disbelief. "You can't just walk into the middle of Paris and hitch a ride on an escape train."

Her comments made the other soldiers laugh, annoying the captain further.

"I see London didn't impress the need for obeying orders as part of your training."

Penny ignored the bait. Instead, she asked Tommy and Max a few quick questions. She directed her suggestion to Paul.

"I can take the men by train to Paris. Tommy could pretend to be a Flemish refugee injured in a farming accident. His French is bad enough to pass for Belgian."

Paul nodded but didn't interrupt. The captain started to speak, but Penny pretended she hadn't noticed.

"I suggest Max pretend to be deaf and dumb. His ankle isn't broken but is badly sprained. I will travel as his companion. I'm sure the farmer will give us a stick to help him walk. Do you have any contacts I can use?"

Paul looked pensive. "Nobody who is directly involved, but I have a few friends who may help. I will give you their names later."

The captain stood, interrupting their plans. "I'm in charge here. Nothing happens without my say-so."

Penny's temper got the better of her. She rounded on the captain.

"This isn't a bloody game and we aren't your soldiers. Paul and his men know this area. They have been involved in various raids. You should really try to work with him."

"Listen, miss, I'm not in the habit of taking orders from children or civilians. I'm a British soldier sent here with a job to do. Now, do as you are told and get my men back to England. That's your job. Leave me to do mine." The captain turned back to his men.

Paul stormed out of the farmhouse, slamming the door behind him.

Penny was about to follow but was prevented by the captain's next words.

"Tommy and Max will leave with this young lady tomorrow. The rest of you grab some sleep. You won't get much of that over the next week."

Paul didn't reappear. Penny went upstairs to share a bedroom with the farmer's wife.

After a fitful night's sleep, she woke early the next morning to find Paul standing at the base of her bed, staring at her. She could hear the farmer's wife humming downstairs, presumably making breakfast.

Penny pulled the covers closer to her chest. "How long have you been standing there?"

Paul smiled, but it didn't reach his eyes. His pale face looked drawn, dark circles under his eyes.

"You need to leave now. Don't wait for breakfast. Take those men and get out of here now. This guy is going to send us all to hell. George, Solange's husband, brought us papers for Max and Tommy. They aren't the best as they were done in a hurry." He handed them to Penny. "Take the slow train to Paris, and for God's sake, travel first class. When you get to Paris, go to the Café Verlet near Gard du Nord and ask for Henri. He's the man in charge, about this tall with a stupid-looking moustache. Tell him Paul Le Clerc sent you."

"Will you not come with me?" Even as she spoke, Penny knew the answer, but she didn't want to leave him.

Paul shook his head and moved towards the bed. He bent down and kissed Penny on both cheeks. "You are very brave, my little one. I'm proud to have known you." He turned to leave.

She caught the past tense. Penny reached up, throwing her arms around his neck. "*Bonne chance, mon ami*," Penny whispered. Paul didn't reply, simply removed Penny's arms gently and left the room, closing the door softly behind him.

Penny dressed quickly. She found the two men waiting for her downstairs, Max sporting a bandaged ankle and a handmade crutch. Without looking back, she escorted them away from the farm.

CHAPTER 35

It took a day to reach the train station. There were German soldiers on the train, but thankfully they asked no questions. At Gare Du Nord, a disturbance at the station proved helpful; two men tried to break through the barriers and when the guards rushed towards them, Penny and her men slipped out.

Leaving the men in a park, she located the café relatively easily. Finding it empty, she went back to collect the men and ordered them a meal, giving them instructions to eat in silence before gesturing to Henri to meet her at the bar.

"Paul Le Clerc sent me to you. I need your help."

"You want me to take those two off your hands? What are they? Downed airmen?" he whispered, his moustache covering his mouth.

"*Oui*. Something like that. The injured one has no

French, the other sounds like a Belgian. Their papers were prepared quickly. You should replace them."

A car drew up outside the restaurant, the atmosphere inside fell at least ten degrees. Penny bit her lip, trying to quell the urge to run. She couldn't look at the British men, praying they didn't lose their nerve and bolt.

"Gestapo," Henri whispered. "They're after someone else tonight. Smile and pretend you are in awe of my handsome face."

Penny reached over the bar and brushed her lips lightly over his moustache. "*Merci*. Paul said to say hello to Madame Henri for him."

The Gestapo men didn't come into the café but entered the apartment building next door.

Henri rolled his eyes. "Trust Paul to ruin my chances with a lovely lady. *Bonne chance*. Now let's take those gentlemen to their new quarters. They will stay with me for tonight, you shall stay with my wife in our home. It's safer."

Penny felt a sense of relief handing over the two men. Henri would pass them on to an escape route run by friends.

≈

Despite Henri's offer to stay a few days in Paris, she only stayed one night with his delightful wife. She kept

Penny amused that evening, telling her stories of how they tried to resist the occupiers.

"The Germans must think we are so stupid. They ask for directions and we send them the wrong way. They take our food, we tell them we are on a diet. We wear our best clothes to prove we are still attractive women, but stare at them with disdain if they whistle or comment on our appearance. I rather enjoy it, but I wish I had some shoes like yours. Wooden soles are all we have left in Paris and they sound dreadful on the cobbles."

Penny agreed – the sound of shoes on the pavement had been one major change she'd noticed. That, and the signs all being in German. "I will bring you a pair if I find some on my travels. It's the least I can do to thank you for your hospitality."

The next day she took the early fast train back and hoped Paul and Annette had not yet had lunch.

She was surprised by how much she had missed them. Especially Paul. Perhaps Annette was right. The war was the reason people got emotionally involved so quickly. She got off at the station and headed towards the north side of town where Annette lived. She hadn't gone far when a child stopped her. "Madame Michiels?"

Penny stopped and stared at the brown-haired child with the chocolate eyes. She thought she recognised him but for a moment couldn't place him. Then it came to her. He was the same boy who had challenged the soldiers, who took his little friend away.

"*Bonjour.* Who are you?"

"Mama said you are to come with me." The little boy grabbed Penny's hand. "You can't go to Tante Annette's house." He tugged at her arm. "Please come before the soldier starts asking questions."

Instinctively, Penny trusted the child. She picked up her small bag and followed him. She had to hurry to keep up with him as he darted between the different streets. Finally, they came to a stop outside the bakery.

"Please go in, madame. Mama is expecting you," he said.

"Are you not coming in with me?" Penny asked.

"No, madame. I'm going to play out here. Mama said I have to sing if I see any soldiers." The little boy had a serious expression on his beautiful face.

Penny walked slowly into the bakery, the aroma of freshly baked loaves reminding her of how long it had been since she had last eaten. The woman behind the counter nodded at her but continued to serve a customer who wasn't in any hurry to leave.

"Is it true Madame Le Clerc was working for the resistance? What did she do? What of her grandson?" asked the customer.

The baker's wife smiled before saying, "Ines, go work for the *Boche.* You ask so many questions."

Ines coloured slightly but didn't seem too affronted. "Yvonne, that is what my old man says too," she said.

Penny's heart lurched as she realised that the woman had been talking of Annette and Paul. She pretended to study the flag hanging in the window. It had a picture of an olive branch, a pretzel and two wooden paddles, which she assumed were what the baker used to take the bread out of the oven.

"Well, you best get home and feed him or he will be cranky." The baker's wife gently but firmly escorted Ines to the door. "See you tomorrow, my old friend."

When she was satisfied that Ines had left, the woman turned to Penny. "Oh, thank goodness Jean was in time to meet you. Paul wasn't sure what day you would return."

"I'm sorry, madame, but I don't think we know each other. My name is Isabelle..." said Penny, her lips trembling so much it was hard to continue speaking.

"Don't tell me anything else. My name is Yvonne. I don't want to know." The woman opened the door to check on her son. "Paul is my son's godfather and one of my husband's closest friends. They have known each other since childhood. Paul doesn't involve my husband in his politics." The woman paused, looking around despite the empty shop. "He asked us to look out for you. He wanted to make sure you didn't go to Annette's house."

Penny's stomach churned, her early breakfast threatening to reappear, "Why?"

"The Germans are waiting there. The refinery was blown up last night. The Germans are furious and have taken many of the men from the town as hostages. They said they will shoot five men every morning until the resistance give themselves up. They started with the British soldiers they arrested near the explosion." The woman stared at Penny.

"Oh my God." Penny looked back at the woman. "Your husband?" she whispered.

"No. Thankfully he was away at my parents' farm. My daughter went to tell him not to go back. But my neighbours have lost their husbands and sons. Someone has talked, as the Germans got Annette and Father John."

Penny remembered the priest who intervened to save the boy. Unconsciously, she crossed herself.

"And Paul? Where is he?" she asked the woman, who was staring out the window at her son.

"Paul is injured and had to be sedated. He wanted to give himself up to save his grandmother. That's not possible, as he knows too much. He is much too valuable to the resistance to be handed over to the Germans." The woman turned back to Penny. "You must eat and hide today. Tonight, I will take you to him. You must get him out of this area."

"But what about the reprisals? So many of your townspeople will be killed."

"The Nazis think they have found their resistance. Father John has claimed leadership and taken full responsibility for the explosions. He will be executed as soon as the Gestapo have no further use for him."

"Annette?"

"Annette is dead. She shot a soldier when they came for her. His friends shot back, and she died almost immediately."

Penny thought of the gentle old lady who had been so welcoming to her. Tears glistened in her eyes, but she didn't have time to grieve now. She had to get to Paul. She couldn't do anything for Annette, but she might help Paul.

Both women tensed as the sound of singing came from the street outside.

"Quickly, wait in the back kitchen. Hopefully, they're just passing."

CHAPTER 36

Sweat trickled down Penny's back as she stayed as silent as possible, praying the Germans wouldn't come into the bakery.

When the baker's wife came back, Penny tried to apologise for putting her in danger.

"No, madame. It's not you who should apologise. You didn't invite the *Boche* to set up home in my country. Those savages need to be beaten. France will rise again. The last few weeks have proved that it's impossible to live safely under Hitler's yoke. One day, all of France will recognise this." She placed her hand on Penny's arm. "Eat and then get some sleep. We will leave when it's dark."

∼

PENNY THOUGHT she wouldn't sleep, but the combination of the hot food and exhaustion proved otherwise. She had nightmares. In her dreams, she saw Annette face the soldiers. She smelt her fear. She felt her conviction not to be taken alive in case she betrayed others. The realisation that Annette had died rather than risk giving way under torture woke Penny up.

In the morning, Yvonne took her via the backstreets to a dentist on the outskirts of the town. They were lucky, as they didn't meet any patrols on the way. Once inside, Yvonne made the introductions.

"Monsieur Beger, this is Isabelle."

The dentist shook Penny's hand and kissed her on both cheeks.

"Paul has been asking for you. It will do him good to see that you are safe," he said.

"For now. They must leave soon," said Yvonne. "Is Paul any better?"

"Physically, he is on the mend. Mentally..." The dentist shrugged his shoulders.

"Can I see him?" asked Penny.

"*Mais oui.* He is in here. Thankfully, one bullet went right through his shoulder. The second grazed his face. Neither hit any vital organs. He has a nasty wound, but he won't die. Still, it would have been better if he had seen a doctor. There is always the chance of infection." The dentist opened the door to another room. "The Germans have rounded up all the doctors in the town."

Penny gasped when she saw Paul. His ashen face made the ugly wound stand out even more. She saw where the dentist had bound up his shoulder, but the blood had seeped through the bandage. She moved closer. He opened his eyes. "*Dieu merci*," he whispered.

She bent closer, her lips grazing his forehead. "*Mon ami. Je suis ici*." She looked back at the dentist. "When can we move?"

"Do you have somewhere in mind?" asked the dentist. "His condition could deteriorate if he has to travel far. I'm concerned about an infection. The Germans are looking for him. They know he was Annette's grandson." The dentist blessed himself when he said the old lady's name. Penny's eyes filled with tears once more.

"I have friends who will help me. They aren't too far away and are expecting me." Penny crossed her fingers to offset the lie. Could she involve Madame Bayard in this? She had little choice. She couldn't leave Paul here. He would die. There was nobody else.

Yvonne said, "I can lend you the horse and cart. It's already in the stables outside. The horse is old, it belongs to my father. Nobody will be interested in stealing it. If you keep to the country roads as much as possible, you may just make it. But you must leave now. The dentist can take me back into town in the morning. People will just assume we are having an affair."

"*Merci*," said Penny.

The trio moved Paul as gently as possible onto the cart before they covered him with a rug after the dentist gave him a shot for the pain. He gave Penny a couple of extra shots, with instructions on how to administer them. "Use it sparingly, as it's very strong – I usually use it on the horses. But it will stop him groaning in pain should you have to go through a checkpoint."

They placed some wood on the cart, so at a cursory glance it looked like Penny had been collecting firewood from the forest. "Thank you very much, both of you. I don't know how we can repay you," said Penny.

"Set France free," the dentist said, putting his arm around Yvonne's shoulders.

Maybe they are *having an affair after all*, Penny thought.

Penny took the reins and set off on her journey. She took Yvonne's advice and travelled as much as possible via the country roads. She checked the map she had drawn to make sure she was on the right route. Twice she gave Paul a shot and hid the trap under some trees while she went foraging for food and water. She dressed Paul's wounds every day, constantly checking for signs of infection. The wound looked a little red, but she wasn't sure whether it was natural healing or something else.

"You wouldn't make a good wife. These berries aren't ripe yet. If we eat them, we will have trouble." He tossed a berry at her, making her laugh before she retorted, "You go and find food then."

He put his good arm across his chest, pretending to be affronted. "Me? I'm the man. It's not my job to go foraging."

"So you want to starve?"

He laughed, the sound sending a frisson of delight through her. She caught him looking at her sometimes but he pretended not to be and she didn't show him she noticed. She wasn't above stealing glances at him, too. Even dressing his wound was more complicated as the days went by as touching his skin gave her goosebumps.

Penny felt different around Paul. She watched him, wondering how he felt, but he was hard to read.

"Why did you come to France, Simone?" he asked.

"To fight the Germans."

"Yes, but why? Did they do something to your family, or do you just like living rough in a foreign land?"

Penny shrugged. "It's not foreign to me. I had to come. France and its people should be free. To live safely and happily in their own homes. Surrounded by family and friends."

"So, where are yours?" he asked.

"My family? Dead. Well, the ones who mattered. Papa died after the last war, Mama a few years later. I have been on my own since." She didn't tell him about living with Louise and Harriet. He wouldn't understand.

She closed her eyes, thinking of Meme, Gracie, the Taylor girls. They were her family now, but she couldn't dwell on them. She had to concentrate on Paul's recovery and contact London. Somehow.

Paul told her stories of his youth, growing up in the south of France. He made out that he begrudged looking after his younger sister, but he obviously adored her. She noted the pain in his eyes as he talked about the last time he had seen her. The argument over his marriage had left a rift in the family that had yet to be mended.

"If I live through this, I will make it up to Chloe some way," he said.

"Don't talk like that. Of course you will live to see her again," she said, trying hard to sound convincing. "Paul, what went wrong at the refinery?"

"You were right, and I was wrong." He clenched his teeth, but from pain or the apology she didn't know.

"What do you mean?"

"You had doubts about the security, but I wouldn't even let you voice them."

She stared at him, waiting.

"I was too stubborn. I didn't think a recruit could size up the situation better than me." Paul looked into the distance. "The Germans were waiting for us, but they let us cut through the perimeter fence. The captain set some charges, set for ten minutes, but it was more like fifteen. His men beat up a few of the French workers like we had agreed. One of the French men tried to warn us, but the captain wouldn't listen. One worker turned to me and told me to run."

"So you ran but still got shot?"

"Yes, I ran, but only when the Germans had come out. I'd studied the factory plans. I went to the other side of the plant, pretended I was a worker. The plan could have worked, but the Germans ordered the men onto the back of lorries. They intended to interrogate all of us. So I jumped from the lorry and ran. That's when I got shot."

Penny moved towards him but was afraid to touch him. She sensed there was more to the story.

"The Germans were going to come after me when two other men made a run for it. They ran in the other direction. The soldiers couldn't chase in both directions. They went after them. I crawled into a ditch and stayed there. I think I lost consciousness a few times. George found me later. He took me to the dentist and then you came."

They both sat in silence, sheltering under a tree as the rain dripped off everything around them. It seemed natural for Penny to rest her head on his shoulder. "You're not to blame. No one is. It's the war," she said. He said nothing, but he put his good arm around her, drawing her closer. They sat and waited for the storm to pass.

They continued to make their way through the countryside. Penny grew more concerned about Paul. His eyes seemed slightly glassy. The wound wasn't healing like she hoped. She wished she could take him to the doctor. Whatever doubts she had about going to see her old friend had taken second place to the concern she now felt about Paul.

After another restless night, she told him she needed to go to a nearby town. It would take more than a day and night to walk there. She couldn't take the horse and cart; it would be quickest if she took the train. Would he survive for four days until she came back? What choice did she have?

She gave him a shot, made sure he had plenty of water and some food, and then reluctantly left him. It was too dangerous to take him with her until she checked the situation in her old hometown and made sure her suspicions that Madame was in the resistance were correct.

CHAPTER 37

As before, nobody stopped Penny as she passed through the town on the way to Madame Bayard's home. This time, the old lady was in the kitchen. She seemed pleased to see Penny, but she was clearly concerned, too.

"*Ma petite cherie*, the risks you take give me even more grey hairs." She pulled Penny close, giving her a hug that took the edge off the rebuke.

"Madame, I need your help. You remember I told you about a man…"

"Paul, the French man you love?"

"He's hurt. He needs medical help. Is there a doctor you could trust?"

Madame Bayard shook her head. "Not while that fascist Alain holds the town in his hand. Where is your friend now? How bad are his injuries?"

"Hiding in the woods. They shot him. We got the

bullet out and, to begin with, he seemed fine."

"But?"

"I'm a little concerned about the wound. It looks rather red to me and he's running a slight fever." Penny's emotions made her voice quiver. She looked at her old friend, her eyes pleading for help.

"Sounds like an infection has set in. Was he wearing a jacket when they shot him?"

"*Oui.*"

"The jacket fragments can cause the wound to fester. You must apply a poultice on it and make him rest. You can't bring him into town, not after the recent show of force. Alain would relish the opportunity to torture a genuine hero."

Penny nodded, trying her best not to look disappointed.

"The Durand farm is close to the woods and far enough away not to entice unwanted visitors. Do you remember where it is?"

Penny nodded. "But we would put the family at risk."

"They sent the father and eldest son to Germany as forced labour. The younger sons left soon afterwards. Madame Durand stays in town with her daughter rather than at an isolated farm with land she can't use. It's not perfect, but it's safer than here." Madame stood up and put on her coat. "Stay here out of sight. I won't be long."

The time crawled by. Penny paced up and down, biting her nails, convinced someone had betrayed her friend and the Germans would arrive any minute. She took her frustration out on the floor, scrubbing it until it shone.

Madame arrived back with a small package. "A friend made this up for you. You have to first clean the wound and then apply this salve direct to the skin. It will sting, but it will help Paul heal. He must also drink this tonic and get as much rest as possible. I also visited Madame Durand. She gave me her blessing for you to use the farmhouse. She has some provisions hidden in the hay barn. You are welcome to take as much as you need. Don't worry, my friends won't betray Paul. They know nothing about you. They think I'm hiding airmen. Now you must go."

Penny hugged her friend, her admiration for the old woman spilling out.

"Oh, my dear Madame, how brave you are. Thank you so much for all of this."

Madame squeezed Penny's hand.

"This man, Paul, he is special to you, my darling. Please promise me you won't let your feelings of revenge for Alain destroy your chance of happiness."

Penny couldn't answer and looked away from the challenging gaze. Yes, Paul was important, but she'd make Alain pay for what he had done.

~

PENNY FOUND Paul running a high fever when she returned from Marly-le-Roi. Between the train and walking, it had still taken her almost two days to get back to him. She applied the poultice as instructed and insisted Paul drink the tonic.

After she had rested a little, she moved him to the relative safety of the Durand farmhouse. She gave the horse some feed and water for his hard work. Storing the cart in the barn, she returned to the house.

Paul's fever soared. He wouldn't lie still, but tossed and turned, calling for his wife and Annette. He was constantly muttering, but most of the time Penny couldn't work out what he was saying.

Caught between fear for Paul and fear for her friend, Penny fretted for the week. Could she risk returning to Marly-le-Roi to see if Madame Bayard could get a doctor to visit the farmhouse? It wasn't only her life at stake. She waited to see how Paul progressed, talking incessantly to him even though he didn't answer. She'd read somewhere that patients could still hear you if they were unconscious. Talking seemed to make the time go faster.

"I wonder what Nell and Gracie are doing now? Meme is probably going out of her mind worrying about me. I think it was a good idea to leave the Taylor and

Thompson children with her, don't you? At least it will give her something to focus on."

Paul didn't know any of the people she spoke about, but that didn't matter. Talking about her family and friends made them seem closer in some ways. She was breaking the rules about sharing her true background, but Paul was hardly going to tell anyone.

He opened his eyes a few times, and she got him to drink water, but that was all. He turned his head away when she tried to feed him soup. She couldn't blame him in all honesty. But for the fact she was starving, she couldn't stomach it either. It was impossible to make a tasty meal without proper supplies.

Her Red Cross training combined with the medicines eventually worked. At last Paul's fever abated, and he slept quietly for twenty-four hours. He was awake and staring at Penny when she opened her eyes the following day. He raised himself on his elbow.

"Do you ever stop talking? You were giving me a headache going on about all these people yesterday. I feel like I know them all."

He grinned to show he was joking and then fell back, exhausted.

"I'll keep talking until you walk out of here. You gave me such a fright."

He whispered, "You were worried about me?"

She turned away so he didn't see her cheeks flush.

His strength increased with every day that passed.

Penny continued to dress the wound, but now every touch made her nerves tingle. She loved the feel of his skin under her fingers. She had to resist the urge to run her hands over his chest.

She knew her feelings for him had deepened, but she wasn't sure of his. He hadn't called out her name when he was delirious.

Yet he seemed to watch her all the time. She felt his eyes on her. When she looked up and they locked eyes, he smiled. They talked non-stop about everything and nothing. She thought of him constantly as she went about the farm, collecting food for them to share.

To celebrate his recovery, they cooked a meal. Penny lit the fire and Paul prepared a rabbit stew. Penny washed and changed into some old clothes left behind by Madame Durand's daughters. She hummed as she rinsed out clothes and hung them on pieces of furniture around the room.

"Why are you smiling?" Paul asked.

"I was just thinking of what someone from my past would say if they could see me now." Penny giggled. Aunt Louise would have had a stroke if she had seen her dressed in little more than a nightdress, eating dinner on the floor in front of the fire. Since Paul had regained consciousness, she hadn't shared any more stories from London. She'd left that life behind. For now, at least.

Paul looked at Penny. "I would hope they would be proud of you. You are very brave. And very young."

"I'm not much younger than you." She stood, intending to move the dishes to the kitchen.

"Simone, do you think you could draw a bath for me? I stink to high heaven. I would do it, but I don't think my shoulder is up to it." He didn't meet her eyes; instead, he played with a loose thread on his trousers.

She nodded and heated some more water on the fire. Soon, she had enough for a bath. She found a fresh towel in a chest upstairs.

"Thank you," he said, smiling at her.

"You're welcome. I found these as well. They must have belonged to the farmer or his sons." Blushing, she placed the razor on the sofa near the bath before leaving the room.

She busied herself in the kitchen, clearing up after the meal. She wondered if she should offer to help. *Oh, stop it*. At the kitchen sink, Penny splashed some cold water on her face. She heard Paul curse loudly. Without thinking, she ran into the room, halting as she realised he was still in the bath.

"Sorry. I thought you'd hurt yourself," she stuttered, turning to leave.

"Simone, wait. I can't shave. It hurts like hell to use my arm. Could you do it? Please."

Penny stared at him, feeling the heat in her cheeks rising. "I've never shaved anyone before."

He chuckled. "It's okay. I trust you. Just don't make any sudden moves and it will be fine."

She hesitated, wanting to move closer but not trusting her trembling limbs to carry her.

"Come on. Please. You can't do a worse job than me."

Penny moved behind him, taking the razor from his outstretched hand. He had already lathered up his face. Gently, she moved the razor in the direction he showed her. He laid his head back against her as the blade moved slowly across his face. As her hand crossed his mouth, he kissed her wrist.

Penny held her breath, and he swore. "I'm sorry. I shouldn't have done that." He took the razor from her hand. "Thanks, I can finish this."

She moved closer to him. "I'm not that much younger than you. Why do you treat me like a child?" she said.

"It's better I see you as a child than as a beautiful young woman," said Paul, before he stared into the fire.

"Better for whom?" whispered Penny, willing him to look at her.

"Simone, don't play games with me," he said, looking at her closely before turning back to the fire. "I'm not an innocent schoolboy. My body has mostly recovered and responds accordingly."

Penny reached to caress the scar on his face. "I know what you are. You are gentle, yet fierce and brave. You show empathy to strangers, yet can kill a German without giving it a second thought." She paused. "You suffer from nightmares and…"

He placed his hand over hers. "How do you know that?"

"I have heard you cry out in your sleep. Paul, you couldn't have done anything to save Annette. She knew what she was doing. I've thought back to that last day. She was different, edgy, strained. I asked her what was wrong, but she wouldn't tell me. I think she knew her time was near. She told me to live each day as if it was my last."

"Is that what this is about?" he said gruffly. When she didn't answer, he caressed her face, the drops of water running down her clothes.

"You should leave and let me get dressed."

"Why?"

He looked at her, then kissed her gently on the lips. "Are you sure that you want this to happen, Simone?"

"I have never been with a man. You know what the invaders are doing to French women. I don't want my first time to be with a German," she whispered.

His hand fell away. "Talk about killing a romantic moment."

"Sorry. It's just that, when I look at you, I forget."

"Forget?"

"Forget the war, your wounds and the fact we are on the run. I want to be normal, Paul. I want to feel young and carefree, if only for a night." She took his hand and leaned in to kiss him once more. "I was so worried about you. I thought you were going to die."

"So now you want to pity me?" he teased.

"Please stop talking, Paul, and kiss me."

With a groan, he took her in his arms and kissed her, gently at first and then more passionately. She lost her balance and ended up in the bath with him. They laughed before being overpowered once more by the heat between them. They kissed over and over as he held her face in his hands.

"Simone, we need to get out of the bath. I would carry you, but I don't think my shoulder is up to it."

She stood, conscious that her wet clothes hid nothing. She didn't care. Reaching down, she helped him out of the bath. With his good arm, he pulled her towards him, moulding her against his body.

Pushing the bath out of the way, they sank to the rug in front of the fire. She let the sensations overtake her, marvelling at the passion he aroused in her. He was patient and knowledgeable. She was certain that his skills helped make her first time more enjoyable. She had heard whispered stories in England about pain and duty towards one's husband. The only one in pain was him when she accidentally hit against his wound. His sudden intake of breath caused her to stop in concern.

"Don't. It's okay. I'll live," he muttered, kissing her deeply, making her forget about his injury once more. A feeling of being safe and whole overwhelmed her, causing her to cry. He kissed the tears as they flowed down her cheeks.

"I'm sorry," he whispered. "Did it hurt?"

She kissed him tenderly on the lips. "No. It's not that. I'm happy."

He gathered her to him, holding her close. They lay in silence in front of the fire, his bare legs entwined with hers.

After watching the flames for a while, she reached up to pull his face down to hers for a kiss. "Thank you."

"That is so very British. Are you really thanking me for seducing you?"

Penny grinned before stretching out fully naked beside him. "I'm not sure it was you doing the seducing, are you?"

He gathered her to him, making her feel how excited he was. "You are going to pay for teasing me, you little minx."

They spent the rest of the night and most of the next day exploring each other's bodies. Finally sated, they fell into a deep and lasting sleep, curled up together.

Without discussing it, they spent another week at the farmhouse. They needed to rest and come to terms with what had happened to Annette, Father John and the British soldiers. For a while, they could forget about the war raging outside. They spent the time lying in front of the fire, again talking about everything and nothing. Neither of them spoke about the future.

CHAPTER 38

"Simone, it's time to move. I have to get back to my friends. And London will worry about you." Paul kissed the back of her neck. Once he started, he kept kissing her exposed skin. They made love once more, but this time it was more tender than usual. Penny tried to ignore the reason for this, but somehow she knew it was good-bye. Neither of them knew when, if ever, they would meet again.

As they were preparing to leave, Paul spotted something.

"Simone, someone's coming."

Penny looked out the window and saw a teenage girl cycling furiously, headed straight for the farmhouse.

"Hide, Paul, quickly. I can bluff my way out, but one look at you and she will know you have been injured."

Paul took his gun and clambered up the stairs. Relieved he was out of sight, Penny checked to see if her knife was hidden in its usual place. She didn't relish the thought of having to use it on a young girl.

The door slowly opened.

"Penelope? Are you here?"

Penny swallowed. The girl knew her actual name. She moved out of the shadows, causing the girl to jump back.

"Sorry, you startled me." The girl looked at Penny with open admiration. "You aren't much older than me."

Penny knew from the stories the *Maquis* spread that age didn't define a traitor. Many had been caught out trusting a child or an old woman. "What's your name and why are you here?"

"Sorry, my name is Anne Durand. This is, or was, my home, before the *Boche* took my father and my mother had to move into Marly-le-Roi. Madame Bayard told me to come. She said that the Germans have requested more troops and ordered a widespread search. They are due to leave Marly-le-Roi tomorrow morning. There are reports that some paratroopers bailed out and are in hiding around here."

Penny turned to get the girl a glass of water. She bolted it down.

"Thank you for coming here, but I don't know any Madame Bayard. I didn't know this was your home. I will leave today."

The girl looked startled.

"But you have to know Madame. She knew you

were here. She gave me this for you." Anne handed a small scrap of paper to Penny. "She told me to swallow it if anyone stopped me."

Penny looked at the scrap of paper. It was a tiny piece of a letter she had written. Not enough to implicate anyone but proof the girl was genuine. Impulsively, Penny gave the girl a hug. "You must go now. Thank you. I will leave shortly."

"I wish I was a little older. Then would you let me join you and fight for France, too?"

Penny shook her head. "You can fight the battle using your head and not a gun. There will be plenty for you to do once the Allies have come. In the meantime, please keep safe and tell Madame to do the same."

The girl nodded and left just as quickly as she had come.

Paul came down the stairs and put his arms around Penny. "We have to leave now."

Penny nodded.

"When this is all over, I shall go back to Annette's house. Will you meet me there?" he said, kissing her tenderly on her eyelid.

Penny didn't answer. The silence between them grew uncomfortable.

"What is it, Simone? I thought you shared the feelings I have for you?" he said.

"I do…"

"But?" He put his finger under her chin, forcing her to meet his gaze. "You don't think we will both live?"

"No, it's not that..." She looked over his shoulder, not wanting to see his face. "I have to go home first."

"Ah, you mean to England."

Her heart beat faster. Could she trust him with the truth? Or would he think her wicked?

"No, Paul. I mean home. Close to here, in France. There is unfinished business I must see to." She tried to hide the fact her hands were shaking. She didn't want him to see her weakness.

"This unfinished business? Does it involve a man?"

She heard the note of jealousy in his voice. "Yes, but not in the way you think."

He turned his face away, and when he spoke his sarcastic tone cut through her. "What other way is there? You told me your father is dead. You don't yet have children. So what man could be more important if not another lover?"

"My mother's murderer."

His loud intake of breath made her realise she had spoken out loud.

He put his hands on her shoulders. "Sit down. You're not leaving until you explain. The war can wait."

She sat down, but didn't move closer to him. "My name is not Simone. You probably heard the girl call me Penelope."

He nodded. "I assumed it was another alias."

"No, my proper name is Penelope Hamilton. I was born on a farm just outside Marly-le-Roi. My father, a British soldier, was injured in the last war. He married my mother, a local girl. They were happily married until he died. He had borrowed money unknown to my mother. His investments failed. She had no money, yet this man insisted she repay the debt." Penny paused, hiding her face behind her hair. "When he was tired of her, he started looking at me. I was twelve."

Paul pounded his fist against the wall. "*Merde*. Why didn't you go to the gendarme?"

"He was the gendarme, a local police inspector. He was a powerful man. Nobody crossed him. Mama tried. She died." Penny didn't realise she was crying until Paul wrapped his arms around her. He drew her close, holding her tightly as the storm broke.

"This man, he's still alive?" he said.

"He was two weeks ago. He's not the type to die in the line of duty."

"Tell me his name. I will find him and kill him with my bare hands," he said, his eyes cold with suppressed fury.

"No, *merci*." Penny kissed Paul gently on the lips. "He is mine. I have waited a long time for this. I want my face to be the last thing he sees."

"Simone – ah, I mean Penelope – that look on your face scares me. I don't believe you could kill someone in cold blood. Even for revenge. It's not what your mama would have wanted for you. It's not what I want for you."

"It's not your decision." Penny moved away from him. His mouth opened, but no words came out. She knew she had hurt him, but it was true. This was her battle, not his.

She went over to the table where she had left her things. "Hours ago, you said we must leave here. You were right. We have to go. Today. Your men need you. I have to find out what London has planned for me. We can't risk the Germans discovering both of us."

Paul moved to face her.

"Simone, don't do this. The revenge you seek won't bring back your mama. Instead, it will destroy you." He reached for her, but she pretended not to notice.

"Are you ready to leave?"

His eyes raked her face, "Jesus, but you're stubborn. Hasn't this man done enough to your family?"

Irritated, she snapped back, "Yes, and that's why it is I who must punish him. Only when I've avenged Mama's death will I be free," she said coldly, impatiently shoving the last of her things into the bag.

"Not if you die trying. I forbid you to go near this man," he shouted. When she didn't respond, he said, "Simone, you do this, and we have no future together."

She knew he was angry, but she couldn't understand the depth of his anger. He had known she was a trained spy before sleeping with her. Did he expect her to become a docile housewife once they defeated the Germans?

"I know you care for me and that's why you are acting this way." She looked at him. "Just because I lay with you doesn't give you the right to dictate my future choices. I don't need your permission or your blessing."

"Simone, please. Don't let us part like this."

She turned and kissed him, almost gently, on the lips. "It's too late. We have both said too much. I hope you survive the war and get your chance to reconcile with your family. Family is all that matters. Goodbye, Paul."

Without looking back, she left the farmhouse. They had agreed he would take the horse and cart. She had to go back to Marly-le-Roi, where she hoped Madame Bayard could put her in contact with London. She walked purposely on, hoping he wouldn't follow her. If he did, she didn't think she could break free of him again. She loved him, but it wasn't enough. She had to fulfil her destiny.

CHAPTER 39
MAY 1943

Nell Thompson stood near the Marble Arch entrance to Hyde Park. It was the closest she could get, given the number of people who'd turned out to see the Review of the Home Guard. The sun shone high in the sky and people were smiling as they milled around waiting for everything to start. She was so proud of her husband, who was part of this parade. Winston Churchill was right when he said they owed these men a debt of gratitude. Her thoughts flew to Penelope. She'd been on her mind lately. Nell hoped it wasn't a premonition the girl was in trouble.

"You all right, missus?" She glanced up to see a cheeky young lad, about the age of Kenny, by her side. "Fancy a rose? We're raising money for the men to sink a couple of pints in the boozer after. Thirsty work, this standing around waiting for the king and all."

Nell tried to hide a smile and failed. "Go on, you little tyke. You're collecting for yourself, aren't you?"

"Nah, missus." He met her eyes, and she saw the hint of honesty. "It's for my mum. My dad, he's ran off, silly bu … git." The boy corrected himself quickly. "Left her with three little ones and a bun in the oven. I don't know when she last ate properly. I mean, when I hear her stomach…" He gazed up at her with what looked like tears in his eyes. But for the glint of mischief, she almost fell for his tricks.

"You belong on the stage, you naughty little brat. Here, take this, but I'm only giving it to you as you made me laugh." Nell handed over a couple of coins. "Don't spend it on booze."

"Cor thanks, missus. I won't, I swear."

The lad ran off just as a distinguished officer in Home Guard uniform came out riding a magnificent white charger. *If only Kenny could see that horse. Look at the tail swishing back and forth – he knows he's majestic.*

Four police officers on dappled greys led the procession. Nell knew the king was in the crowd but she didn't see him. Not that it mattered. She beamed with pride as her husband marched along with the rest of the home-grown heroes, men who risked their lives running into burning buildings or crawling under mounds of rubble to rescue victims of the bombs. *I wish I had a movie camera and could film this and send to old Hitler. That would show him we will never let him win. No matter what he hits us with next.*

⌇

NELL PUT the key in her front door, wishing someone was home. Tom was going for a few drinks with his mates, a rare luxury for her husband these days. She put her coat on the rack behind the door and walked into the back room. The vision before her nearly gave her a heart attack.

"Frank! When did you get back? Look at you, you're all tanned. You look wonderful. How's Molly and the babies?"

"Settle down, Mam, I only just got in. Didn't know where any of you were. Haven't been to see the family yet as not sure whether they're here in London or down the country. Give us a cuddle. You look just the same as ever, Mam."

He gripped her so tight; she was almost breathless, not that she was complaining. Frank, her first-born, had come home.

"Let me get you a cuppa and a sandwich. I think I have some spam. Are you hungry? I could go to the chippy, I might be lucky and find some fish."

"Mam, sit down and put your feet up. I'll make you

a cuppa. I'm an army boy now, I can look after myself. After we chat, I'll go down the chippy and treat us all. Where's Dad?"

"Gone to the pub, but he won't be late. Never been much of a drinker and now…" She shrugged her shoulders. Everyone knew beer and spirits weren't freely available. "Frank, he'll be chuffed to see you. He's been following the news about the campaigns, wondering where you were. Somewhere hot, obviously."

Frank put his finger to his lips. "Walls have ears and all that, Mam. Now let me get that cuppa."

Nell sank into the chair by the wireless. Her boy was home.

"Frank, I made a rhubarb crumble for your dad. Plums, damsons and English rhubarb came off points, I guess they thought they'd go off or something. Not that cans should. Anyway, it's not as good as the one I made before the war when butter and sugar was plentiful but…"

Frank put his head around the corner from the kitchen and grinned at her. "Thank God you haven't changed a bit, Mam. Still talking the hind legs off everyone."

When her husband came home, she was sure she saw a sparkle hinting at tears in his eyes. But she didn't comment. He would be mortified and so would Frank. She went to bed leaving her men to chat. Despite the war, this was a happy day she'd never forget. If only she'd had the whole family around. She couldn't believe she had yet to meet her twin grandchildren.

Gracie sat in the tea shop on London Road, waiting for Charlie to arrive back from the hospital. She watched the kids walk up the road in the rain towards the cinema. She guessed they were going to the Hopalong Cassidy movie. The children from the town had a habit of going to the cinema on a Friday after school; it was a special treat and a chance to forget the war.

It was such a wet and miserable evening, Gracie wished she had stayed at home. Thankfully, the twins were asleep in their pushchair so she could enjoy her cup of tea. Charlie was late, as usual. Looking out the window, she watched the world go by. There were a lot of soldiers in the tea shop. She listened to their funny accents. It must be hard being so far from home. She moved the pushchair to allow one soldier to pass.

"Gorgeous kids you have, ma'am." The Canadian officer looked down into the pushchair.

"Thank you. They are when they're asleep." Gracie smiled at the twins, who looked like two little angels. Ruby was holding her brother's hand.

"I have two myself at home. Want to see a picture? They probably won't recognise me when I get back, I'm away so long."

Poor man. Gracie could tell he was lonely. She took the photograph to have a closer look. "They seem very nice. What ages are they?"

"Five and seven, ma'am. Don't think my wife would have liked to have twins. It must wear you out looking after two babies, especially in wartime. You look after yourself and those kiddies."

Gracie smiled as he walked back to his friends. She looked up when the door chimed and in came Charlie.

"Sorry, darling. I got delayed talking to one lad. He got a Dear John letter this morning."

Gracie bristled. It always bothered her when girl-friends dumped their aircrew boyfriends after the men had been injured.

"How's my son?" asked Charlie, looking down at the babies.

Gracie knew he loved both his children equally and was only teasing.

"Both your son and daughter are fine. They enjoyed their walk, but the motion of the pushchair finally lulled them to sleep."

Charlie took Gracie's hand in his good one. "And how is my wife?"

"Better, now you're here. Can you watch these two for a minute? I want to see if the shop has any new wool. I would have gone earlier, but I can't get the pushchair through the door."

"You could leave it in the street. It's quiet enough."

"Not in the rain, darling!" Gracie stood up. She heard the drone of a plane. Looking out the window, she could see a lone plane up in the sky. She assumed it was one of theirs on an exercise.

She was still watching as it released high explosive bombs over the town. The tea shop seemed to lift in the air with every explosion, teacups and plates smashed to the floor.

"The babies."

Charlie had reacted quicker, draping his body across the pushchair to shelter them from flying glass and other objects.

Gracie could see flames pouring from the cinema. She took a step towards Charlie and the babies, and glass crunched under her feet. She looked in horror at Charlie.

"Where's the nearest shelter?" someone shouted.

Gracie couldn't move. She was riveted to the spot. Charlie grabbed the handle of the pushchair and moved towards her. They hadn't yet got to the door when they heard gunfire.

"That low-down snake is trying to shoot us now," said the Canadian. "Take cover, quickly."

They heard the bullets ricocheting off the pavement outside. It seemed to take forever for the plane to pass over and then there was silence for a couple of seconds before everybody started talking and moving as one.

When the sky was clear, they headed out of the tea shop and into the high street. More devastation greeted them. The wool shop Gracie had intended visiting was no longer there. The ironmongers had exploded. Someone said it was due to the amount of paraffin the owner had stored on the premises. Several people lay wounded on the street. Some were dead, others hideously injured.

She couldn't understand why the Germans had picked East Grinstead. It was such a small town where everyone knew everyone else. She saw people trying to help the injured; one woman was insisting a man take off his jacket, not seeming to realise he was dripping blood.

"Charlie, take the twins and go home. I have to stay and help."

Charlie shook his head. "Gracie, I think we should stick together."

"No, darling. You go home. This heat won't do your skin grafts any good. You need to leave. Now."

Charlie kissed her before pointing the pushchair towards home. Gracie looked at the surrounding scene to see where she was most needed. Working in the hospital had given her plenty of expertise with burns. Flames were pouring out of buildings. Firemen struggled to get the fires under control.

There were hundreds of casualties. She wasn't sure whether she should stay and help or get to the hospital. She decided the hospital was the best option as she would be of more use there. She hitched a lift in an ambulance, taking the place of a doctor who would remain at the scene.

Looking out the window as they headed towards the hospital, she saw a woman pushing a young child in a pushchair in the same direction. The child had a large bandage around his mouth and chin.

The hospital resources were stretched to breaking point. The casualty ward sister was glad of Gracie's help once she explained her training and recent experience at the burns unit. She watched as the RAF men, themselves victims of horrific burns, tried to help the victims of the air raid.

The ones whose hands weren't injured helped her to bathe the burned children in saline. The screams were pitiful. Gracie forced herself to keep a smile plastered on her face.

Just as she thought they had seen the last casualty, more arrived and continued to do so.

"How many more can there be?" she wondered aloud.

"Not sure," said a nurse working alongside her. "The cinema took a direct hit. I heard that there are over one hundred bodies in the makeshift mortuary at the newspaper office." The nurse looked at the child they were bathing. "What has Hitler got against these kids, for God's sake?"

~

IT WAS twenty-four hours later when she got home to find Charlie asleep on the sofa, the twins asleep on the floor beside him. Nappies surrounded him, some dirty, some clean. There were some bottles of milk and toys dotted around the kitchen, along with a cup of half-drunk tea. Her poor husband had a hard time with the babies. She hugged both of them close, thankful her little family had made it safely home. The tears flowed down her cheeks thinking of all the youngsters who hadn't made it and those who would be scared for life.

She wanted the war to be over, to be back with her mam and Penny and the rest of the family. Would they all survive to see the end of this horror?

CHAPTER 41

The door was unlocked and Penny slipped inside. It was early evening. Madame Bayard was sitting at the kitchen table wringing her hands together. She looked worn out.

"Madame…"

"Penelope. Thank goodness you are okay. I was worried."

"I'm fine, thanks to you and Anne. Did she get back safely?"

"*Mais oui.* How are you? How is Paul?"

"He's fine." *Please don't ask me about him.*

"There is something wrong. It's written all over your face. You have fallen out. Sit down, tell me about it."

Penny sagged into the chair. Feeling hurt and angry, she blurted out a version of the last few days' events.

When she had finished, the old woman looked troubled. "Did this have something to do with Alain?"

Penny looked away. "It might have."

"Ah, Penelope. Please don't let that man ruin your life. He almost did once. Revenge is not something you should live to achieve. Hating someone only ends up hurting you. You should concentrate on your future. You are here to do a job, you must focus on that."

"I can't. I have to pay Alain back for destroying my family."

"You would give him more power? Do you not see he could kill you? I thought you had matured. It seems I was wrong."

"You are just like Paul, assuming Alain will get the upper hand. I know how to deal with men like him. It's what I was…" Penny stopped talking, realising she had already said too much.

"It's what you are here for? Is that what you were going to say?" Madame shook her head. "I can guess why you are here, Penelope. I can also guarantee that the people who sent you back to France didn't do that so you can put yourself and others at risk because of some vendetta. Do they know about Alain?"

Penny remained silent.

"I thought so. For someone so young, beautiful and brave, you have been selfish and foolish."

Penny spoke, but Madame's look stopped the words leaving her mouth.

"What now?" the old lady asked Penny.

"I have to get in touch with someone from our

network. My contacts are dead or missing. I have to make contact to see where I'm needed."

Madame Bayard stood up, taking her coat with her.

"Stay here. I will see what I can find out."

Penny stood, too. "Let me come with you."

Madame's face hardened. "What if Alain sees you? How many people would you betray by the time he has finished torturing you? I think you should tell your new leader to send you home. Here, you are more of a liability than anything else. Don't wait up. I would prefer not to have company this evening."

The door slammed behind the older lady. Penny stared after her. When did everything become so complicated? *Paul, and now I have hurt Madame as well. If they truly loved me, they would understand. I have to do this.*

She waited for ages, but there was no sign of Madame returning. Giving in, she lay on the bed in the room she had used previously. She replayed the last few days' events over and over.

∽

"You are to go to 10 o'clock Mass. Your contact, a man named Victor, will approach you. All I can tell you is that he has been an agent for a long time. He won't acknowledge you unless it's safe." Madame looked at Penny thoughtfully. "I hope you have thought long and hard about our discussion last night. You should go back to England."

Penny's eyes filled up. She looked pleadingly at the older woman.

"I'm sorry we argued. I don't expect you to understand. This is something I have to do. Alain took everything from me. My home, my mother, you, my country. I can't just let that go."

"You mean you won't. Penelope, I have lived longer than you. Alain is evil. Everything you say is true. He took all those things, but killing him won't return them. You can't change the past, but you can do something about the future. Alain will steal your happiness if you let him."

Penny remained silent. She didn't agree with Madame, but she couldn't argue with her again. Madame threw her hands up in the air before giving Penny a hug.

"Please take care of yourself. I loved your mama very much and you are like the granddaughter I never had." She put her wizened finger under Penny's chin, forcing the younger girl to look up. "Please, Penelope, promise me you give up this crazy idea of revenge. Nothing good will come of it."

Penny took the old lady's hands in hers.

"I wish I could, but I can't. *Au revoir, Madame.* Please take care. I love you, too." She kissed her old friend on the cheek and then turned to pick up her things.

Penny hurried to the station to take the train back. The tears ran down her face, but again, she didn't look back.

CHAPTER 42

When she arrived, Mass was just about to start, so she put her headscarf on and went indoors. There were only a few men in the church, but they all seemed too old to be the man she was looking for. She knelt in the appointed pew and imitated the act of praying. She tried not to make others aware that she was waiting for someone, although her nerves were getting to her.

Just then, to her shock, David walked in and moved into the pew beside her. She couldn't hold in a squeak of recognition. He gave her an angry look that silenced her urge to say hello. David was Victor, the man Paul worked for as well? There couldn't be two Victors, could there? Her face heated as she remembered the conversation with Madame Bayard. She'd poured her heart out about David and her feelings for him when she lived back in London. Had Madame known David, but hadn't let on? Or maybe she didn't know his actual name. That must be it. She looked at him, still disbelieving. This man bore little resemblance to the charming, handsome RAF officer she'd last seen in London. His hair was now darker, probably dyed, and he looked dishevelled. He was also limping.

"Sit up," he whispered and roughly pulled her into a seated position. Gradually, the church emptied and they walked outside towards the graveyard.

Penny was confused. Was he angry to see her or annoyed over something else? His words came back to her, all those conversations about her using her languages to do her bit. Was it David who'd recommended her to SOE?

Before she had the chance to ask, he pulled her into a full embrace, kissing and holding her close. Her stomach swirled with emotion as she clung to him, not out of love, but nostalgia and a kind of homesickness; he was a link to her family, to Meme and London.

But she was in love with Paul, not David. She put her hands on his shoulders to push him away and only then noticed the German soldiers walking by, laughing and making some comments.

Her chest tightened – she'd just shown her lack of experience. "Really, did you have to do that?" she muttered angrily as she sought, but failed, to gain her composure.

"Sorry, but would you prefer he checked your

papers? They'd have arrested you for being with a man who has a price on his head."

Penny felt ashamed. David must have been in the field longer than she had if both Paul and Madame Bayard knew him as Victor, although those she loved were in different circles of the resistance. Had he been an agent from those first days back in the Cafe de Paris? Fragments of their previous conversations came rushing through her brain. Was he married now? What did he tell his wife he was doing? He clearly wasn't an RAF officer like he'd pretended to be.

"Come on. We have to get out of here, but not too quickly as we don't want to attract any more unwanted attention. Listen, Penny, it's not personal. I suspect we have an informant in our circuit, but as yet I'm not sure who it might be. I have no concrete proof, just a suspicion that the recent arrests are not an accident."

Penny stayed silent.

"I thought I kept security tight. I warned all my new people that there were certain things they shouldn't do, like stay in hotels or boarding houses. Even if we change our names, the French or German police watching those places could easily find us by simply asking the staff to describe the person or people staying there."

He stared at Penny. "You are never safe here in France. The second you feel you are is the moment you tell me it's time to send you home. Always be on your guard. Betrayal could be round the next corner."

Penny shivered, remembering what had happened to Annette.

David frowned. He took her arm, guiding her as they walked out of the church and headed towards the woods. If anyone glanced at them, they would surmise they were courting.

"Sorry. It's been hell for the last few weeks. It's nice to see someone from home. Tell me, has Harriet joined up yet or has she finally persuaded that boyfriend of hers down the aisle?"

Penny knew he was trying to make up for scaring her earlier, and while she appreciated his efforts on one hand, on the other she was annoyed that he appeared to be treating her like a child.

"Please, don't worry about me. Unlike most of your agents, I'm French, not someone who is pretending to be. I know what acceptable behaviour is and how to avoid standing out in a crowd. I…"

David grabbed her by the shoulders. "Stop shouting, for God's sake. Do you want to bring the soldiers back?" At the look on her face, David burst out laughing.

She stiffened – he was laughing at her again. "Sorry!" she said grudgingly. "It has been a difficult few weeks for me, too."

His expression softened, gesturing at the grass.

"Just sit down. If the soldiers do come back, we can pretend we just had our first lovers' quarrel and now are looking for some privacy to make up."

He laid his coat on the grass and they sat down. Penny was conscious of just how close he was sitting to her. She tucked her skirts under her legs, trying to put a little distance between them.

"What do you mean by difficult?" he asked.

"The last job I was on ended badly. It was partly London's fault. The team they sent in wouldn't listen to the local men. It cost us dearly."

His eyes widened, his expression grave.

"Were you in danger? Did anyone who knew you get caught? Don't look at me like that, Penny. If they were caught, the Gestapo could be on your trail right now."

"They killed the lady at my safe house. I had never met the other contacts, apart from the British soldiers who didn't know my name. They were shot." Penny bit her lip. Why didn't I tell him about Paul? He was Paul's boss. Maybe she'd get him in trouble.

David stayed silent for a moment.

"I'm sorry that you had such a bad time. Are you sure you don't want me to arrange for you to go home?"

"Home? I *am* home." Penny glared at him. Why was everyone intent on sending her back to England? "What's my new job?"

David looked as if he was going to say something, but didn't.

She clenched her fists in her lap. "David, do you want me to work for you or not? I have other contacts who would welcome me."

"Calm down, Penny. Fighting with me won't get rid of your anger about what happened." He looked her in the face. "Of course I want you to work with us. I need a courier. Your role will be to collect, read, memorise the contents, then destroy all messages left in dead boxes. It wouldn't do to be caught with those in your possession."

"Oh, really? I was planning on asking the soldier at the next checkpoint if he would like to read them."

David didn't appreciate her sarcasm, looking at her sharply. "This is *not* some schoolgirl prank. People's lives depend on you. Even the best agents in the field make mistakes. It's easily done when you are exhausted, living on your wits and unsure just when you are going to get caught. As the days pass, your chances of surviving the war grow slighter. You said you had other contacts? Who are they? Are they reliable?"

Penny was going to tell him about Paul, but decided against it. "You already know one of them, she arranged our meeting. I've also developed some contacts in Soucelles, Châtres and in central Paris."

"You are to stay away from Paris for now. The

network there is too big, too exposed to traitors. Its days are numbered, not that Prosper is listening to me."

"Don't babysit me, David."

"I don't have time to do that," he snapped back. "I have to build another network, with people I can trust. You need to move away from here. There's a suitable place on a small farm. I remember you telling me about your experience of farming life so you will fit in easily."

Penny nodded.

"You can help the farmer in small ways around the place if you have time, but you will be away a lot."

Penny again nodded, deciding it was best to leave the decisions to David, or Victor, as she must come to know him. She had to bow to his better judgement, at least for now. She realised that David had stopped talking and was gazing at her. "Sorry, did I miss something?"

"No, I was just thinking that London did an excellent job at making you look French."

She smiled, although her cheeks flushed. "I *am* French."

"Yes, of course. Let me see your *Carte d'Identite* and ration book, please. What cover story did they give you?"

"My name is Isabelle Michiels. My husband is missing, presumed dead, having not been heard of since Dunkirk. I'm a secretary, but because of ill health was advised by my doctor to spend some time in the countryside. As I spent some time on a farm when I was younger, he thought I should find some work in the fresh air to give my health a chance to recover."

"Okay, good, but what was the ill health – you look fairly healthy to me."

"I had suspected TB. If questioned, I will bite my lip, cough and spit blood on the ground. That should help with my cover story."

"We need to come up with a good excuse for the amount of travelling you will do, but we will worry about that later. There isn't much call for a secretary in the countryside." He looked at Penny. "Don't worry. The farmer has an extensive family network, we will say that you are bringing farm produce to other family members to swap them for other goods."

"Have you worked with the family long?"

David nodded. "What are these stamps?"

Penny shrugged. "I had to travel a bit for the last job. London told me to buy an annual first-class ticket. I needed permission to cross into some areas." She didn't want to talk about Paul. "Tell me more about the arrests," Penny asked, not wanting to give further information on where she had been. She sensed David wouldn't approve of her visiting Madame Bayard, regardless of the need if he knew their shared history.

"I won't give you names or other details, just in case you get pulled in, too, but I have lost three good men in the last week alone. Thankfully, they haven't talked, at least not for the first twenty-four hours, so we had time to get people moved."

"Can you not rescue them?"

He smiled, but it was more of a grimace.

"I would give anything to go in and rescue those brave men, but it would be suicide. The Germans know we are aware of exactly what treatments they have in store for our guys. They rather expect us to mount a rescue. But the prisons are very well guarded, and they hold the men in solitary confinement. If we had more men and ammunition, then…" David swallowed hard before continuing, "For now, it's not possible."

She touched his arm. "It's better that you're not in their place. London relies on you."

David acknowledged what she had said with a slight nod, and then continued to fill her in on the type of work they would be doing. One priority was to stop the local car manufacturer from making trucks for the Germans. While they understood that the man couldn't just down tools and say he wouldn't do it, they could infiltrate his workers and start sabotaging stuff from the inside. They would need the owner's permission to do so, but David was adamant that he either gave it or they would blow his factory up. With Penny's help, they had to figure out how best to move forward.

"It's more difficult now we don't have a wireless operator. We have no choice but to use someone belonging to another circuit, which is obviously a security risk. But for now, it's unavoidable, as it's the only way of keeping in contact with London."

David turned to look at Penny. "A vital part of your role is to maintain contact between London and me. You will pass messages to him regularly until London sends us another pianist."

"What happened to the last wireless operator?"

David looked grim. "He was one of those arrested. You have seen for yourself the number of Germans around. We take every precaution possible, but it's just not the Germans you have to watch out for. There are many people who all have different reasons for wanting to make friends with the enemy. So make sure you stick to your cover story at all times. Only answer the question they have asked you. Don't start conversations with German soldiers. Some new agents think that this is a way to seem ordinary, but you immediately blow your cover. The soldiers are not used to beautiful young girls having a chat with them. So answer their questions and no more. Don't encourage intimacy, but don't be rude. You don't want to get their attention any more than you already will, by the way you look. Did London have to make you so pretty?"

Penny didn't answer, she couldn't meet his gaze. Only a few months ago, his words would have made her burst with happiness, but now they just embarrassed her. She knew now that she loved Paul.

"Your host Marie will give you some more details.

She has been helping us out and you can trust her completely."

"I won't let you down. I promise."

"I have to go. Be careful, and for God's sake, keep your head down. You couldn't have landed at a more dangerous time."

"David, when you know more about the traitor, you will tell me, won't you?"

"Only if I need to. Now, remember my name is Victor, and yours is Simone. Don't tell anyone your actual name. Use Simone for our people and Isabelle for everyone else. Clear as mud, right?"

Penny nodded again before asking, "How will you deal with him?"

"Penny, what makes you so certain the traitor is male? It's just as likely to be a woman. In fact, some would say more likely. Remember, you can't trust anyone, and I mean anyone. Now, go. I want to make sure nobody follows you, then I will leave."

Penny turned, but on impulse rushed back to give him a kiss on the cheek. "Take care, *mon ami*," she whispered before dashing away.

CHAPTER 43

Penny made her way to her new home, thinking about David as she walked. She had been pleased to see him and she sensed he was still attracted to her; after all, he had said she was pretty more than once. But she hadn't felt anything apart from wishing he was Paul. Damn it, she didn't want to think about him. She marched on, hoping to distract herself with physical exercise.

The safe house, a small farm holding, was situated near the coast at Cap Gris-Nez, between Calais and Boulogne.

They chose the house for many reasons, not least the fact that the ground behind the farm dwellings sloped sharply away, giving the occupants an unobstructed view of the countryside. Penny appreciated why David had picked this spot despite the proximity to the closely guarded coast. At least the Germans couldn't sneak up on them.

She walked down a well-worn path to the farmhouse, taking care to avoid the ruts made by the
farmer's wagon. They had harvested the wheat, leaving
behind yellow stalks in the fields. She saw a small
vegetable patch near the back door. A few cows and a
horse roamed free in the large pasture behind the L-
shaped old building. She sniffed the air, appreciating the
slight scent of salt in the wind. Hens clucked happily as
they pecked along the ground just outside the house. To
her left was a large barn, rusty machinery including an
old plough standing just outside.

Shielding her eyes with one hand against the setting
sun, she spotted two women coming towards her, a girl
of about seventeen and, judging by the extra-worn face,
her mother. Both had similar welcoming smiles, their
intelligent brown eyes searching the distance behind
Penny. Despite the welcome, the women were apprehensive, although Penny could see that they were doing
their best to hide their fears. Penny was reminded of the
risks French families like these were taking. If they
captured an agent, they knew what to expect. These
families would be shot and their properties burned to the
ground – yet they insisted on taking the risk. She
blinked away the tears in her eyes. If only all their coun-
trymen were the same.

"*Bienvenu*! Welcome, Isabelle, to our home. Oh, but
you are so young and pretty. What does your mother
think of you working for *La Belle* France?"

"Thank you both for inviting me to your home."

"Oh, no, don't answer me as I'm not supposed to ask you questions. It's not just your accent, but you look French." Marie looked happy. "You should hear some accents of the people that London sent to us. They would only have to speak for five seconds for any German to know that they're not French. But you, you're different. You are truly French, no?"

"Mama, you are talking so much that Isabelle will turn herself in to the Germans just to escape your questions. Please excuse my mama, she gets a little excited." The young girl laughed as she gave her mother a quick hug.

"*Merci*, Madame and Mademoiselle. Yes, I'm French and very glad to be back here in my country, although it would be better if the soldiers weren't here."

"Please call me Marie, and my cheeky daughter's name is Jeanne. Let me take your bag and show you your room – or would you like to eat first?"

Penny's stomach groaned in answer as the tantalising scent of garlic and freshly baked bread teased her nostrils. She bent her head to walk into the kitchen, spotting the table set with bowls, a bottle of red wine and some glasses. Marie apologised, "It's only soup but I've added a lot of vegetables. Fritz takes most of our harvest to feed their armies and then expects me to feed our family enough so that they have the strength to milk cows and tend animals and fields." Marie's eyes sparked with anger.

"It smells wonderful, as you can hear my stomach already appreciates your efforts."

Marie beamed at Penny's words before turning to her daughter. "Jeanne, take Isabelle to your bedroom and show her where to put her bag. I will see to the soup."

Jeanne led Penny up the stairs at the back of the house and into her room. The exposed eves made the ceiling low in places, causing Penny to duck. A large double bed with a beautiful quilt cover dominated the room.

Penny glanced at the marble washstand with the jug and ewer on top. She hadn't used one of them since she lived with her mother. She blinked away the memory. The bed was really comfortable, sinking under her when she sat down. She was tempted to swap the food for a nap.

"You don't mind sharing your bedroom, your bed, with me?"

Jeanne shrugged her shoulders. "I would do a lot more for *La Belle* France if mother would let me. She's overprotective."

Penny reached out to touch the younger girl's elbow. "She cares about you. You're lucky."

Jeanne smiled in acknowledgement before showing Penny where to put her things.

⌀

"WE BEST GET DOWN before Mama burns the soup. It smells wonderful, but she gets distracted easily. She's a better farmer than cook."

Jeanne laughed as she led Penny back to the kitchen.

Marie dished out the soup and bread, and the three sat down to eat. Jeanne explained how the Germans carried out periodic checks, arriving at different times of the day and night.

"They come to see my beautiful daughter. They're so stupid they believe that a good French girl like her would welcome a German boyfriend, although sometimes I can understand why they think she could be interested." Marie threw her daughter a look.

"Now, Mama. You know that I only pretend to be friendly. I make sure they know about Marc."

Turning to Penny, Jeanne explained Marc was her boyfriend, who the Germans believed was working for the Third Reich as a prisoner of war in Germany.

"Oh, Jeanne." Penny had been about to offer her condolences when she saw the glint in the young girl's eyes. "He's not in Germany, is he?"

Before Jeanne could answer, Marie interrupted.

"My daughter plays a dangerous game by playing with the affections of these German soldiers. Marc may also be in the resistance and understand why she's doing so, but our neighbours don't know her true intent. I worry about her, sometimes."

"Mama, you worry so much you get upset if you have nothing to worry about." Jeanne gave her mother an affectionate hug, but Marie remained serious. "Mama, I know what I'm doing. I've been involved since Dunkirk, no point in arguing about it now."

"Dunkirk?" Penny raised her eyebrow.

Marie answered. "Jeanne saved several French troops who would have walked straight into a German roadblock had she not run and warned them of what lay ahead. I don't think my heart has beat properly since."

"Mama!" Jeanne rolled her eyes at her mother while smiling. "Isabelle, my mother is too shy. She keeps a radio hidden in the barn's loft. We listen to the BBC. That is where you will pick up your messages, yes? We listen to the BBC Londres. Those garbled messages about geese and all sorts are messages, aren't they?"

"Shush, Jeanne, we have to be careful." Marie glanced at the door. Was she expecting someone?

"You worry too much." Jeanne dismissed her mother's fears, but Penny was inclined to agree with Marie. Jeanne appeared to think the war was a game, and that could be dangerous. For all of them.

"Of course I worry. Some of the bravest families have traitors in their midst."

Penny couldn't keep her eyes open, causing the two

women to laugh as her head flopped forward almost into her soup.

"Isabelle, you're exhausted. Please go to bed. We can catch up tomorrow. You need your rest. Go on now."

Penny thanked her "aunt" and gratefully did as she was told.

Once alone, she had time to think about David. Meeting up with him again had been such a surprise, but she wished she hadn't been so shocked. She could have asked him lots of questions – not least, was he married now? Had he heard anything of her family back in London? No doubt Harriet and Louise were fine, but what about Uncle John and Meme? She wondered what her grandmother made of her letters, all written prior to Penny leaving England. Miss Atkins promised she would post them at regular intervals from different parts of Britain. Another trick to convince her family she wasn't in danger. She listened to the sounds of an argument downstairs, but she couldn't make out what the couple were arguing about. Determined to remain awake until Jeanne came home, she lay on her side.

Her thoughts drifted to Paul. Although their last words had been said in anger, she missed him. He was like David in lots of ways: proud, brave, annoying, arrogant. But he'd been able to make her forget the war. Maybe it was a good thing he wasn't here. At least now, she could concentrate on getting the Germans out of

France. Then it would be time for revenge. Alain's face was the last thing she pictured before the combination of exhaustion, a full stomach and the softest feather mattress ever made meant she fell into a deep dreamless sleep.

CHAPTER 44

The next few days passed peacefully. Marie and Jeanne refused to let Penny do anything more than eat and sleep. They argued a couple of days of proper rest would do more for her – and, by extension, France – than her helping with the farm work.

By the third day, Penny was bored. She was ready to help while wondering when she would hear from David, or Victor, as she should remember to call him.

As the days passed, Marie seemed distracted and on edge. Jeanne had disappeared for a few hours. Penny tried to persuade Marie to trust her but the woman wasn't in the mood to talk.

"Best I keep busy when my mind starts thinking like this."

Penny wasn't sure what she meant. She stayed silent, watching as Marie chopped up the vegetables and added them to the pot simmering on the fire.

"Isabelle, have you ever wondered what France would be like if everyone felt like we did? If we had all stood up to Fritz and sent them back to Germany, where they belong? Instead, even the best families have traitors in their midst." Penny sensed Marie was trying to warn her, but their chat was interrupted. A farmer, judging by his clothes although they were fairly clean, walked into the kitchen, causing the atmosphere to grow frosty. Marie stiffened momentarily before greeting the man with a kiss on his cheek. Jeanne arrived just behind him, carrying a bucket of freshly picked vegetables, her eyes warily following the man.

"Jeanne, I thought I'd have to pick those vegetables myself. What took you so long? Daydreaming again?" Marie tutted, taking the pail from her daughter.

They want to hide from this man the fact Jeanne had left the farm, Penny realised, and looked at him again.

"Isabelle, this is my husband, Gaston. Gaston, you remember I told you that my cousin's daughter was coming to stay with us for a while until her health recovers. She's been helping on the farm."

Penny instinctively didn't like Gaston. He had a way of looking at her that made her feel dirty and exposed.

"You look too skinny to be much use on a farm. I don't need another useless mouth to feed, even if you *are* pretty." His rudeness didn't shock Penny as much as the reaction of the two women to the man. She could almost smell their fear, and Jeanne didn't make any effort to hide her contempt.

"I'm much stronger than I look, Monsieur, and I'm a hard worker." *I'll make certain to keep out of your reach, too*, Penny vowed.

Marie spoke, but her jolly tone sounded false. "Gaston, stop grumbling and come eat. The food will get cold."

The food, although plain, was hot and tasty. Gaston alternated between eating with his mouth open, sending spittle everywhere and complaining about the locals. He seemed to hate his French neighbours more than the invaders and didn't spare Penny from his comments. Gaston muttered about ungrateful brats and poor relations while Marie blushed. He drank almost a full bottle of wine with his meal. Once finished, he pushed his chair back so roughly it toppled over. He didn't bend to pick it up but headed outside.

"It's best you girls to go to bed now," Marie said.

"But Mama, he might hurt you again."

"Go on, child. I can deal with him. Goodnight Isabelle."

Penny put her hand on Jeanne's shoulder, but the girl shrugged it off and ran out the front of the house.

"Leave her, Isabelle. She'll come back when she's ready. I must go to him."

Penny put the dishes in the sink but didn't stay to wash them in case the man came back into the kitchen.

Taking the stairs two steps at a time, she closed the door to the bedroom, half wanting to put a chair in front of it. But she told herself she was being silly. After the lessons from camp, *I could kill him with my bare hands.*

The thought didn't bring her any comfort, and that night she dreamt of Alain and Madame Bayard, with the former threatening to hurt Madame. She tossed and turned for ages before exhaustion won out and she fell asleep. Jeanne hadn't returned.

CHAPTER 45

The next morning was a typical September day. The sun rose high in the sky and there wasn't a cloud in sight. For a few moments, Penny forgot why she was back in France, taking time to savour the memories living on the farm were invoking. Her pillow smelt like lavender. Jeanne's side of the bed was still warm despite the girl not being in the room. She must have got up early to see to the chores. Collecting eggs and milking cows didn't wait, even if there was a war on.

She got up, shuddering as her bare feet hit the icy floor, washed and dressed quickly, heading down to breakfast, ready and willing to take on what the day in front of her held. Marie had left a plate with some bread and cheese on the table. There was a jug of fresh milk too, and she drank her fill before stepping out into the farmyard. Marie waved at her from the barn. Walking over, it thrilled Penny to find there was no sign of Gaston.

"You should have called me. I told you, I'm here to help, not sleep."

"You needed the rest, Isabelle. Jeanne said you didn't even move when she got up. She was terrified she'd wake you."

"What would you like me to do? I wasn't lying when I said I can milk cows and do most farm chores."

"Useful as well as brave. Your parents raised you well. The cows are milked. I was just about to turn out the pigsty."

"Let me help. You can tell me what I need to know, the pigs won't be interested." With a smile, she took the rake from Marie's hands. The woman looked like she was going to protest but instead shrugged her shoulders and led her way into the barn. It took Penny a few minutes to adjust to the darkness.

Gaston roared for Marie just as they were about to start.

"You go, I can do this." Penny turned to the pigs and spoke to them in French as she cleaned their sty. It wasn't so bad, as Marie obviously kept the place well run and clean.

That evening she helped Jeanne with the milking, thankful Jeanne's father was nowhere to be seen. The girl was chatting about the German soldiers, warning Penny that although the younger soldiers were friendly, they were all afraid of the Gestapo and they could trust none of them.

"Where is your father today?"

"He's not my father," spat the younger woman. "My father died in the first month of the war. He hated the Germans. He died a hero. Mama couldn't run the farm alone, and rather than pack up and go to live with relatives in the town, she married Gaston. He had been a friend of my father's since childhood, and he seemed different then. Hard as it is to imagine, he was nice once, and funny. But not any more. All that bastard thinks of is money and how he can make more of it. He would sell his own mother to the *Boche* if he thought he would make a profit on it."

"Surely, he isn't that bad." Penny tried to sound convincing, although when she thought of the way he had looked at her over the last night, she couldn't even say his name without cringing.

"No, he's worse. He makes Mama work day and night while he goes off on his trips. We know he's making a fortune on the black market, but we never see a penny. He's always complaining he's poor. When he's not here making our lives miserable, he's off wining and dining with his new best friends. He isn't fussy. Anyone in a German uniform will do."

Jeanne turned away from Penny before continuing, "Make sure you stay out of his way when he comes home drunk. He believes any woman is fair game, and he doesn't take no for an answer. One of these days, he will go too far, and then…" Jeanne motioned for Penny to be silent. They both listened and then Penny heard it, too. Somewhere nearby, a bird whistled.

Jeanne rubbed her hands on her apron. "Stay here and continue the milking. I'll be back shortly."

The young girl wasn't away long, but when she came back her pretty face looked troubled.

"What is it?" asked Penny.

"There's going to be a raid on the local village, so some of our parcels must move. There isn't much time. I have to see somebody. Can you go back and warn Mama that we will have some guests later?"

"But how do you know there will be a raid?"

Jeanne stared at Penny. "Mama wasn't wrong when she told you I encourage the German soldiers. What she doesn't know is that one of them thinks that I'm his girlfriend. He came to tell me he couldn't see me tonight as he will be busy. I pretended to be jealous and upset, refusing to believe that he had to work, telling him I knew he was taking another girl out. That stupid boy believed I was really jealous, so he told me that there were British airmen hiding in the village and they were planning a raid tonight to catch them."

"Is it true? Are their airmen close by?"

"I don't have time to talk now. Go to Mama and tell her, but make sure she's on her own before you say anything. Don't tell her how I found out. Pretend it was from one of your contacts for now. I'll be back."

Penny returned to the main farmhouse, relieved to find that Marie was on her own. She told her what had happened. Marie's face turned white.

"You mean she has gone to move the men in daylight? She doesn't know what she is doing. Those airmen are injured – they can hardly walk through the town unnoticed. How does she know it's not a trap? Oh, my brave daughter. She will get herself killed."

Penny made her sit down. "Stop it, Marie. Trust your daughter. She knows what she is doing. All we can do is wait for her safe return. Does your husband know how you help the resistance?"

Marie turned to Penny. "My husband is a traitor. He should rot in hell for what he has done. I was a fool to marry him and bring him into this house. I believed he was like Jeanne's father, but he is nothing like him. He is a bully, a coward and a drunk. He spends all his time with his new friends, those German bastards, and then comes rolling home to me. No, he's not here. We couldn't hide those brave Englishmen if that idiot was here."

"But surely he wouldn't inform on his own family?" Even as she protested, Penny knew that's what he would do.

"Don't be such an innocent, Isabelle. He would do anything to keep in with the *Boche*. They give him the type of lifestyle he believes he's entitled to. Where else could he eat and drink as much as he wants for free? There's no such thing as rationing for friends of the Germans. I wonder what they get. But no doubt they think he's useful for some purpose – probably spying on his neighbours. I don't underestimate the depths that man would go to. But enough now, we have work to do." Marie stood up. "The men will be hungry. I'll have to prepare their food quickly, but make sure there's no sign of any extra portions if the Germans decide to come calling. We will make some thick soup – one that can be watered down to make extra portions, with no one becoming suspicious."

Penny followed Marie out to the barn to help prepare the hiding space for the airmen. She watched as her host moved to the furthest corner of the barn away from the pigpen and started moving some bales of hay out of the way.

Marie hissed as she worked, "Gaston doesn't know about this – my first husband's father built it in the First World War to hide things from the Germans. During those times, the Germans took everything they came across, so rather than starve many farmers had hiding places."

A soft look came over her face. "Pierre, Jeanne's father, loved hiding here as a child, but thankfully he didn't share his secret with Gaston, although they were best friends." Marie continued working as she talked, and soon Penny saw a trapdoor in the floor. When they lifted it up, a small cellar room appeared. It was deep enough for the two women to step into, although the men would maybe find it rather cramped. Marie had brought some bedding and some bottles of water, which she left in the cellar.

Penny tried to break the tension, "I hope they are good friends, sharing this space."

Once satisfied the hiding place was prepared, Marie shut the trapdoor and covered the floor space with some straw. They would replace the bales once the men had been sheltered. They returned to the kitchen.

Soon, they heard a motor car. Both women froze. Save for a few favoured French, it was only the Germans who had access to petrol. The car stopped outside.

CHAPTER 46

Jeanne burst into the farmhouse.

"Mama, come quickly, one airman needs your help – he's unconscious and has been badly hurt."

Both Marie and Penny rushed after Jeanne. It was the doctor's car that had brought the young girl home with her two airmen, whom they later found out were called Geoffrey and Jason. Both were injured. Jason had a twisted ankle, but Geoffrey had a head wound and the blood was still seeping through the bandage.

"Where is Dr Beauchene?" asked Marie. "Surely he would be better seeing to this boy."

"He has a head injury of his own but, hopefully, it's not too severe. We had to knock him out cold so that he wasn't implicated. We need the Germans to think we stole his car for the black market." Jeanne looked guiltily at her mother. "He told me to hit him, but I don't think he meant me to do it as hard as I did."

Marie told Jeanne and her friend, Michel, to carry the injured airman. As they moved towards the barn, Penny spoke to Jason as he spoke no French. He explained how they had been forced to crash-land and were the only survivors of their crew. He was anxious about Geoff, whose wife was expecting a baby. Penny was worried, too. Head injuries were a nightmare for medical staff in a hospital, never mind a countrywoman operating out of a barn.

"Try not to worry too much," Penny sought to reassure the young RAF man. "Your friend is in excellent hands. Please tell me what happened to you since the plane crashed. How many people know that there were survivors?"

Penny exchanged a glance with Marie, realising the woman hadn't understood the exchange, and translated quickly for her. Marie nodded. "Get as much information as you can. The more people who know about the crash, the worse for us."

Jason explained that the crash had been seen by a group of resistance fighters, and they had taken the men to the relative safety of the church in the town. The priest, while not an active resister, was on their side and wouldn't betray them. He had contacted Dr Beauchene who had dressed their injuries, but they couldn't risk taking the men to the hospital. The hospital staff had to report any suspicious patients or injuries to the Germans.

The resistance fighters had tried to buy some time by hiding the plane wreckage, but a German patrol had stumbled across it accidentally when searching the woods for an escaped prisoner. They knew some crew members had survived and the search that Jeanne's "boyfriend" had mentioned was ordered.

Penny translated everything for Marie, who blanched as the full story came out.

"*Merde*. The Gestapo will arrest the priest."

That wasn't what Penny expected her to say. "Why? Do they suspect him?"

"No Isabelle, it's what they do. They arrest the priest, the mayor and the doctors if there is resistance activity near a town. They know those people are most likely to be involved or know something. Teachers, too. Those they consider having the brains to resist. Farmers rarely make their list."

Penny ignored the contempt in Marie's voice. If they arrested the priest, her new friends were in danger. And so was she.

Despite being a trained agent, she knew Marie would have the best solution. "What should we do?"

Marie examined and redressed the head wound. "I have seen worse. It doesn't seem to be that deep, but the impact may have caused some internal bleeding. We just have to hope he's okay and try to keep him as quiet as possible. Now, we have little time. As soon as the *Boche* discovers there are no airmen in the village, they will widen their search."

She turned to her daughter and Michel. "You need to go now and dump that car somewhere close to the village. But be careful not to be seen. Leave some packaging and a couple of tins of stuff on the back seat and hopefully those stupid soldiers will believe they took the car for some black-market trading."

When Jeanne and Michel had left, Marie opened the cellar entrance. She turned to Penny. "Please explain to this young man he needs to stay in the cellar, no matter what noises he hears up here. Tell him to trust nobody but you, Jeanne or myself. In particular, he's not to trust Gaston. There's likely to be a financial reward posted for information. Now, let's move quickly as we have little time."

Penny explained everything to Jason and Geoff. Geoff didn't seem to listen, but Jason argued enough for both of them.

"We can't put women in danger. We'll hide in the forest. If they catch us, they'll send us to a camp. The Geneva Convention protects us." Jason's words sounded braver than he looked. He refused to hold her gaze, she guessed in case she saw his fear.

Penny reached out to touch his arm, making him look at her. "You should be so lucky. They may send you to a camp, but first they would torture you to find out who had helped you move from the crash site. They would see from Geoff's injuries that you didn't work alone but had help. If you provided them with any information, they would shoot the people who helped you."

"We wouldn't tell anyone." Jason protested angrily, shrugging off her arm.

"If you didn't provide any details, they would be likely to shoot you and a few villagers as well. As a warning. Either way, lives are already in danger, so it's best you stay here and do as you're told. The Germans aren't paying too much attention to the Geneva Convention!"

Jason looked chastened by Penny's outburst.

"I'm sorry to bring so much trouble to your door, madame." He narrowed his eyes as he looked at her. "Your English is very good. Are you British?"

Penny forced a laugh, speaking with a slightly French accent. "You flatter me. I spent a few summers over there with family. I learned a little bit."

He didn't look convinced, but Marie interrupted by gesturing towards the hiding place.

"Don't worry about us. We know what we are doing," she murmured as she pushed him to Marie's side.

"It isn't your fault that the Germans don't behave in the way the English would, should a Luftwaffe pilot be shot down over London. You're not responsible for us." Penny smiled at the young airman. "We chose to work against the Germans and consider it our duty to get you back to your squadron. So please try to get some rest."

Marie and Penny put the bales of hay over the trap-door, and only when satisfied that the place looked like an innocent barn once more did they return to the farmhouse.

Penny watched her host with admiration as Marie poured two glasses of wine with a steady hand. She handed one to Penny before downing the second one.

"What should we do now?" Penny asked. She glanced around wondering where Gaston was.

Marie caught her glance. "He's drinking with his cronies in the village. He won't roll in until later. You must contact Victor. We need his help."

Penny quailed inside. She hadn't been here more than a couple of days and they needed David already. He'd think she was a liability.

Marie paced back and forth over the stone floor. Every couple of seconds she glanced through the window as if by wishing her daughter to return, she would appear.

"Jeanne will be fine. She's a clever young woman."

"You can read my mind so easily. A mother always worries about her children – and Jeanne, she's special." Marie put the wine bottle away. Taking the two glasses, she rinsed them under the tap. Penny sensed she was gathering her thoughts. She waited in silence until Marie finished and turned to face her.

"Meet with Victor and arrange some transport for the men. They can't stay here for long, not with Gaston home every evening. Do you think London could arrange for them to be picked up by a ship?"

"Boat?" asked Penny. She didn't want to insult her host, but didn't Marie know how heavily the beaches were protected.

Marie frowned as she crossed her arms. "Yes, a boat. I can take them to a place further down the coast away from the principal ports, assuming Victor can sort out transport. The injured one obviously can't walk far. A cousin of mine is an angler. He has his own boat and lives in a fairly quiet village. At least, it was quiet before the *Boche* moved in. He might row them out to meet the English, under cover of darkness."

Penny's stomach muscles tightened. It sounded like Marie could walk into trouble. "I'll go with you."

Marie smiled and tucked a piece of Penny's hair behind her ear, "No, Isabelle. You'll stay here and complete whatever work Victor has for you. These airmen aren't part of his plans, and he'll have other duties for you to undertake. It will be dangerous enough without putting an English agent at risk."

Penny opened her mouth to protest, but Marie stopped her. "I have other friends who will help me. Now go, child, and see if you can get a message to Victor. Tell him about the airmen and warn him of the intended raid. I'll wait here for Jeanne to return and try my best to keep that stupid boar of a husband of mine away from the barn. Hopefully, he will get too drunk with his friends and will need to sleep it off in town rather than come back here."

Penny gave Marie a quick kiss on the cheek. "I will be back as soon as I can." She went outside to grab her bicycle and cycled off.

CHAPTER 47

David had given her a means to reach him in the event of an emergency, and she hoped he would see this as one. She was to contact the priest at the church a few towns away. She cycled hard, knowing every hour counted. Out of breath, with screaming muscles, she arrived to see the priest at the side of a freshly dug grave, leading the mourners in prayer. Penny waited for him inside the church. She covered her hair as she went into the building.

She was gazing at the statue of Mary, trying not to sneeze at the lingering scent of incense, when she noticed the priest moving towards the confessional box. She went inside, closing the door behind her.

"Forgive me, Father, for it's a long time since my last confession."

"The Lord forgives us all, my child. Now, tell me what brings you to see me today?"

"Father, I need to meet with a friend and he told me you would arrange contact with him."

"A friend? What type of friend?" asked the priest, rather suspiciously.

In her haste, Penny had forgotten to use the safe phrase David had given to her. No wonder the priest had been less than forthcoming.

"I'm so sorry. My manners are dreadful. Juliette said to thank you for the rosary you said for her mother."

The priest relaxed somewhat, but his eyes were still wary.

"Why do you need to see this friend, my child? Can I not help?"

"No, Father, it's really important that I see Victor. We have a situation and we need his help."

"Ah. I will do all I can, but it's going to take some time. This evening, go to Café Du Coeur and someone will meet you there. They'll ask you if you have seen Marc. You'll answer, 'Not for some time.' Now, while you're here, do you want me to hear your confession?"

"No, but thank you, Father. I don't think confession and my current line of work go hand in hand."

"God works in mysterious ways, my child. Have faith and believe he is watching over all of us. Now, be safe."

Penny left the confessional and prayed for a while so that anyone watching could see her doing her "penance". As soon as she could, she left the church, genuflecting and crossing herself on her way out. She didn't want Marie or Jeanne to be waiting and worrying about her needlessly, but she couldn't risk going back to the farm to tell them what was happening.

She arrived in town after 4 p.m. and hadn't been waiting long when David entered. She was surprised, as she had been expecting a stranger, and had been worried she would mess up the security question.

David greeted her like a casual acquaintance before asking loudly if she minded sharing her table. They engaged in idle chit-chat for a couple of minutes before David asked quietly, "What's happened? Are you in trouble already?"

She gave him a dirty look. Could he make it more obvious he had no faith in her? Her training kicked in and she pushed her personal feelings out of the way. "I need your help." She quickly explained what had happened.

His nostrils flared as he ran a hand through his blond hair. "Why did they have to land now?"

Penny hissed, "Well, I don't think that they had much choice in the matter. What's wrong? Can you not help them?" What was he getting so annoyed about? They hadn't turned up dripping blood at his home putting his family at risk. She swallowed hard. She was letting her fondness for Marie and Jeanne colour her vision. Still, he didn't have to act as if she had created a problem on purpose.

The pilots were heroes and deserved their help. She didn't understand why he seemed reluctant to get involved.

"So can you help us?"

His eyes widened at her use of "us". Looking closer at him, she saw the lines of exhaustion around his eyes. His hands clenched and unclenched. Maybe he wasn't angry, but worried.

"There was a rescue line we used, but it has been compromised."

Penny blinked to clear the horrible images his words brought to mind. He meant they had caught the brave men and women, possibly tortured or executed them. Her fear for Marie and Jean increased. They had to get the airmen away from the farm.

"Marie says she can do it, but she needs transport to move them. One can't walk. Can you not get a truck from somewhere?" she asked.

"Sure. I'll drop one of the many fully fuelled trucks I have at my disposal over to you some time this evening. How does that sound?"

Penny glared at him before retorting, "There's no need to be sarcastic."

He glanced around before moving closer to her. Taking her hand in his, he stroked it. "Sorry, it's just the timing. I've orders to move to Paris and to take you with me. In fact, I was on my way to see you when I got your message."

"Paris?" She couldn't hide her surprise. She'd assumed she would be involved in something more local to the farm.

"Yes. We leave in two days. You're to take the early train, the slow one, not the express. I'll meet you on the train. Now, tell Marie to sit tight for the moment. I'll sort something out for tomorrow evening. Go home and try to rest. We won't get much of that in the coming weeks."

Rest? Did he think she was inhuman. How could they relax with Marie's husband, a traitor, the injured men, and not to mention the location of the farm in a heavily guarded area? Her training hadn't prepared her for this.

He stood up and threw some francs on the table. With a last look at her, he walked out. She waited, watching the other café occupants under her eyelashes to make sure nobody followed him. She didn't see anyone behaving oddly.

Penny left, thinking how tired David looked. He seemed to have aged in the week since she had last seen him. She wished he trusted her more, but guessed that would only come when she proved she wasn't a naïve little girl.

CHAPTER 48

She took it as a good sign that nobody stopped her as she was leaving town. She cycled slowly at first, checking every so often to make sure she wasn't being tailed. Only when she had left the town some distance behind did she start pedalling furiously. She dreaded to think of what she would find back at the farm.

Jeanne was waiting for her at the turn into the farm.

"Trouble?" asked Penny.

"You could say that. The uninjured airman was worried about his friend and came out to find help. Mama told him off and got him back into hiding, but she thinks Gaston may have seen him. He's suspicious and threatening to tell his friends we are hiding something unless Mama comes clean."

"Oh, the stupid idiot. Why couldn't he have stayed where he was? He must have known that we would have checked on them soon. What's your mother going to do?" asked Penny.

"She's been buying time, waiting for you to come back. She wants to talk to you first."

"What do you mean – first?" Penny felt a chill down her spine, which increased in intensity when Jeanne didn't look her in the eye.

"Let's talk to Mama. She's in the kitchen. She cooked him his favourite meal. No soup for him."

Jeanne pushed the door open, Penny following in her wake. They found Marie plying her husband with wine and trying to persuade him he was imagining things.

"Gaston, please think about what you're saying. If the *Boche* come here and start searching, they're going to find all your black-market stuff. You know the penalty for that," Marie pleaded with her husband.

"They won't be interested in that stuff when they find out what you've been hiding. Why are you risking yourself for those men? Do they give you something I don't?" Gaston tried to move towards his wife, but his weight made him slow on his feet.

Looking at his wild eyes and the spittle gathering at his mouth, Penny thought she had never seen anyone so ugly. He was evil, inside and out. She put her hand on the small knife concealed in her jacket.

"Stop it. You're disgusting. I'm not doing anything with anyone, as there's nobody there. You're drunk and your mind is playing tricks on you. Now, shut up and eat your dinner."

Neither of them seemed to have noticed Penny and Jeanne come in. Gaston raised his hand. "Don't you tell me to shut up, you stupid woman."

Instinctively, Penny moved forward as the fat man threatened her host, but Jeanne moved faster.

"Back off, Gaston. Don't you dare lay a finger on my mother. She's worth ten of you."

"So much passion. So beautiful." He made a grab for Jeanne, but she backed out of his reach. "A slut just like your mother, but unlike her, you fancy our German friends. If I call them, they may not wait to take you to a fancy hotel. They will do you on the floor and allow me to watch."

Marie muttered something, but Penny was fixated on the horrible man. Gaston dribbled, making Penny want to retch.

"You're disgusting. You won't have time to call your friends," spat Jeanne.

Gaston moved forward, his face almost touching Jeanne's. "And how are you going to stop me?"

"She won't have to. I will." Penny surprised herself by speaking.

Gaston turned his attention to Penny. "Oh, yes, I forgot about you. The so-called daughter of my wife's mystery cousin. I'm sure the Germans will be very interested in you, as well. But then, they do like a pretty face." He shot towards her, but she was faster – he didn't see the knife in her hand until it was too late. She did just what she'd been taught. Straight in and cut down. He screamed, a sound she was sure would echo in her ears for a long time. He fell to the floor clutching the knife, trying to pull it out, but his blood spilled out, weakening him. The dark liquid pooled as the man breathed heavily, cursing them even as he lay dying. In seconds, he was silent.

CHAPTER 49

All three women stood, looking at the body. Marie recovered first. "We need to hide his body. The last thing we need is to have to explain this to the authorities. Jeanne, grab an old sheet from the closet. We need to wrap him up or we will leave blood tracks on the floor. Isabelle, help me, please."

Penny couldn't move. Her legs were frozen, although the rest of her body was shivering uncontrollably.

"Isabelle, I need you now." Marie moved away from Gaston to put her arms around Penny. "You had no choice. Now, come on, we have to get rid of him. We need your help. He's too heavy for us to carry on our own."

Marie wrapped the body, and between the three of them they dragged it outside and buried it in a shallow grave behind the barn.

"That will do until we can come up with something more permanent."

Penny turned away just in time to avoid vomiting over her friends. She retched until her stomach was empty, her entire body shaking. Jeanne gave her a wet cloth to wash her face as Marie put her arm around Penny's shoulder.

"How can you be so calm, Marie? I just murdered your husband."

Marie forced her to look at her. "Isabelle, you didn't murder anyone. You killed a traitor who was about to pass you over to the Germans. If you hadn't had that knife, we could all be in the hands of the Gestapo. I'm grateful to you for giving me back my freedom. I only wish I had the nerve to kill him myself. It would have saved everyone a lot of grief."

Jeanne paced back and forth, her hands shaking by her side.

"Mama, what are we going to tell everyone? He can't just disappear. There'll be questions."

Marie pulled her daughter towards her and, with an arm around both her and Penny, directed them back towards the farmhouse.

"We'll just tell them that Gaston went on one of his trips. He goes so regularly they won't think anything of it. I'll make sure they discover his body miles from here and news will filter back they killed him over black-market goods. I don't think there will be many crying over his demise. Now, come on back to the kitchen. Isabelle needs a potent drink. We all do."

Penny's admiration for her French landlady grew even more. Not only did she face risks daily by hiding the airmen, but she was obviously further involved in the resistance than she had previously let on. She had kept her head in a potentially dangerous situation and, given her plans for Gaston's remains, she obviously had a wide range of valuable contacts she could call on for help.

Jeanne stopped walking. "Mama, what about Gaston's horse and cart? Nobody will believe he left without it."

"*Merde,* I forgot about that. Jeanne, hide the cart and let the horse loose in the field. If anyone comes tonight, we will say Gaston took another horse as his usual one was tired. Tomorrow, I will have the horse and cart moved. They can carry their master on this last trip." With that, Marie walked into the house, leaving Penny and Jeanne standing in the farmyard.

"Your mother is very brave."

"So are you. I couldn't imagine killing anyone with a knife."

Penny couldn't speak or look at Jeanne. She'd planned on killing Alain. How often had she dreamed about it or wished it was him when she was practising on the straw dummies back in England? Yet the reality was much different. She'd taken a life. Maybe he deserved it but was it her place to act as judge, jury and executioner? "We need to wash up." Penny moved to the well and dragged up bucket after bucket of water to wash the blood from her hands. Even when they glistened, she kept scrubbing. If only it was as easy to remove the guilt.

"Isabelle, thank you for what you did. You saved us."

Arm in arm, the two girls followed Marie to the house. They found her standing at the sink, staring out the window. Penny wished she could go back and change things, but how? Gaston was prepared to betray not only her but his wife and stepdaughter.

"Marie, I'm sorry. I didn't see any other way out. I understand if you want me to leave now."

Marie turned to look at Penny, the tear stains clear on her face.

"Want you to leave? Why? You did what I have wanted to do for months. You have set me free. That man had no loyalty to anyone. Every day he lived, I was terrified he would betray us. I didn't care about me. I deserved it for marrying the creep. But Jeanne…"

Jeanne was on her hands and knees scouring the floor where Gaston's blood was still visible.

"Mama, stop. You didn't deserve that man. You thought he was like Papa. We all did. I'm glad he's dead. I hope he rots in hell for everything he's done."

After ensuring there was no evidence of what had

happened in the kitchen, the three women sat down at the table. Marie poured some wine, her hand shaking this time, until Jeanne put a hand over hers and together they poured it.

Penny downed her glass before saying, "I'm leaving the day after tomorrow." Marie nodded, but Jeanne started crying. "My orders came in before this happened."

"I don't want you to go, not now."

Marie put her hand on her daughter's arm. "She has to. Isabelle has her work to do, just as we have ours. I'm sure she will come back when she can. Certainly, when this war is over. Then we will relax, drink decent wine and get on with our lives. Until then, duty calls." Marie turned back to look at Penny. "Is Victor able to help with transport for our guests?"

Penny nodded. "He said he will send someone tomorrow evening." She tried to keep her voice steady. She'd known she was close to these women but now she felt like they were family. Saying goodbye would be very difficult.

Jeanne stared at her through her tears, "Can you tell us where you're going?"

Before Penny answered, Marie shook her head. "Jeanne, you know better than to ask. We can't betray Isabelle if we don't know where she is." Marie turned to Penny. "Thank you for everything you have done for us and for France. Do you need anything for your journey?"

Penny was tempted to ask Marie if she could find out through her network where Paul was, but decided not to. It might be best to forget about him. Instead, she shook her head. "No, thank you. I have everything I need." Penny stood. "I should go and check on Jason and Geoff. They may have heard some of the argument."

Judging by the looks on the other women's faces, they too had forgotten about their guests for the moment.

Jeanne stood and took a step to put her arms around Penny. "Isabelle, will you promise to come back some-day? When this is all over."

Penny hugged Jeanne. "I promise. Maybe then you will have made an honest man of Marc and I'll get to meet him." Penny gave her a hug, exchanging a glance over Jeanne's shoulder at Marie. She didn't have to say anything – both knew that the chances of her being alive at the end of the war were slim. But Jeanne was entitled to her dreams. They couldn't lose hope that this madness would be over soon.

∽

PENNY EXPLAINED to the airmen the events of the evening.

Jason paced back and forth, his hands shaking. "It's all my fault. If I had done what you said, he wouldn't have seen me. Now I have put you all at risk. I'm sorry."

"Jason, you did what you felt you had to do. Nobody can change what happened. We have to focus on the next steps."

"I can't believe you killed him. With a knife. What sort of woman are you?"

His words hurt, but she tried to keep her face expressionless. He was in shock and didn't realise what he was saying.

"I mean, he was a traitor. I can imagine someone shooting him but a knife, that's more personal, isn't it?"

Irritation made her snap at him. "Just make sure you do what you're told from now on. You have no idea of the risks these people are taking to get you home."

He blanched at her tone, giving her a look that reminded her of a dog being kicked by their owner. He moved to Geoff's side and sat down, not looking at her.

She didn't know what to say. How could she explain how she felt about killing someone when she didn't really know herself? It was easier to walk away.

~

THE NEXT DAY, Jeanne's friend Michel arrived to help dispose of the body and to move the airmen to another safe house.

"Victor sent me. He trusts me to do what needs to be done."

Penny didn't argue. If Victor trusted Michel, who was she to ask questions. Taking care to ensure they weren't being watched, they dug up the body and loaded it onto the back of Gaston's horse and cart.

The body seemed heavier than it had last night. They were all breathing faster when Michel moved to take the reins of the horse.

"Michel, you must make sure that there's no chance of the remains being found. We don't need the Germans around here asking awkward questions."

Michel grinned at them, a sly expression in his eyes.

"Don't worry, Marie. By this time tomorrow, there will be no remains to speak of."

Curiosity got the better of Penny, but it was Jeanne who asked, "Where are you taking him?"

"To the Laurent farm."

Marie blanched. Penny was worried enough to put her hand around the other woman, thinking she was in delayed shock. Jeanne moved closer to Michel, hissing, "Those collaborators? But why?"

Michel seemed to be enjoying himself, a smug expression on his face, "Never accept things for what they seem. They aren't collaborators. They just pretend to be."

"I'm sure you know what you're doing. I have to go inside, I need a drink." Marie hurried off in the farmhouse's direction.

"Pah! All farmers have to provide some produce to the *Boche* but the Laurents..." Jeanne looked at Penny. "They provide the fattest pigs you ever saw. Me, I would serve them the skinniest runt of the litter and making sure it was full of worms!"

Penny couldn't help but smile at Jeanne's outburst. Michel reddened, but with amusement or irritation, Penny wasn't sure.

"Jeanne, look closer. Yes, their pigs are fat because they are fed well. Their diet is supplemented by the odd traitor or two."

Penny and Jeanne stared at Michel and Penny gasped, "You're joking."

"They leave nothing behind, not even the bones! Everyone's happy. We get rid of our enemies, the pigs get well fed and the Germans think it's the best bacon they have ever tasted."

Penny felt the wave of the nausea hit her as Jeanne mumbled an excuse and ran, clutching her stomach.

Michel couldn't stop laughing, which made Penny angry. "Did you have to? There are some things we are best off not knowing. That man was still her stepfather."

Michel's face hardened. "He was a traitor. Do you

think he ever gave a second's thought to what happened to his victims? I spit on him. Tell Marie I will see her later."

Penny stood, staring after him, wondering whether they would ever regain their humanity. She didn't notice Marie come up behind her.

"Don't judge young Michel too harshly. His father was one of the first my husband ratted out to the Germans. He has since lost his brother and an uncle." Marie looked in the direction Michel had gone. "I have tried persuading him to leave. But he won't. He insists his mother needs him. He is brave but young, reckless and bent on revenge. A fatal combination, especially in these times."

Arm in arm, the two women made their way back to the farmhouse in silence.

CHAPTER 50

The train took hours to get to Paris because of problems on the track, being sidelined to let troops through and what seemed like continuous searches. Penny was nervous at first, but soon exhaustion overtook her and she fell asleep. Soldiers checked her papers twice but found them to be in order. She didn't see David – it was safer for them not to travel together. They would meet at an address in Paris.

She was curious to see how much Paris had changed since the last time her father had taken her. None of the landmarks had been damaged, but it was difficult to see the Nazi flags flying from government buildings like large black-and-red spiders. Soldiers were everywhere, from the streets to the trams. Mostly, they were ordinary military, but she also saw the black uniforms of the dreaded SS. The Parisians were different too. Despite the women making valiant efforts to remain glamorous, she'd lost count of the number of different styles of hats being worn. The impact of the occupation was clear in their drawn faces, forced smiles and grey skin.

She walked along, trying her best to be inconspicuous, something made more difficult by her leather shoes, her healthy appearance and glowing skin. Perhaps she should have used some cosmetics to make her skin greyer. As she walked, she saw some soldiers pasting posters to walls or posts.

One soldier whistled, only stopping when his blushing colleague nudged him, before nodding in her direction. "*Bonjour madam.*"

She'd planned to ignore any greetings, but even if she wanted to, she couldn't speak. She fought to keep a poker face as David's image looked down at her. How did *Fritz* know what he looked like?

"*Une terrorist, madame.*"

His accent as he murdered her language enraged her. She was tempted to correct him, but she gave him a look her cousin, Harriet, would have been proud of.

She walked slowly on, wondering if she should go to the safe house. Was David in hiding right this minute? He couldn't know the Germans had put his image up all over Paris. If he had, he wouldn't be here. Would he?

She strolled around as if she were a tourist taking in the sites, stopping occasionally to look in a window. It was a good way to check if anyone was following her. A few times, she entered the store and looked back out into the street. Were any of the people on the street watching her?

Once convinced she wasn't leading the Gestapo to David, she went to the safe house address and was relieved to find him inside. She was glad to see the apartment was on the ground floor in a building without a concierge. The fewer people who knew about him being here, the better.

He barely glanced up from the papers he was working on, "What took you so long? I was worried."

"Never mind worried, I was frantic. What are you doing in Paris? Don't you know they have your picture plastered everywhere offering a reward for information leading to your capture..." She stopped. He knew. He hadn't stopped working.

She slipped into the chair on the opposite side of the table.

"You knew. Yet you're still here."

"I told you, we have a job to do. You can help me with a new disguise. In the meantime, we have had to increase security."

"You need to tell the other groups that!"

David looked up from his papers to stare at her, his eyes widening. So what if he didn't appreciate her tone? Seeing his picture filled her with terror.

"I went to a café on the north side of the city. While I was there, I noticed a group of people chatting rather loudly. Their being loud wasn't what caught my attention, as French people often get quite animated while talking. But these people just didn't look right. It may have been their haircuts or perhaps their clothes or maybe even the fact that it was a group of them that all looked like they were playing a part. One lady in the group asked for a cup of tea. Her companions suddenly stopped talking to glare at her before realising that they were attracting even more attention. Then they all talked at once. I didn't hang around much longer as I figured I was in more danger being in the same place."

"That sounds like Renaud's group. I keep telling him to stop with the big meet-ups, but he's not listening. He tells me we English don't know anything as we're not an occupied country. They seem to think they're invincible. His argument is that they haven't really done anything yet, so the Germans aren't interested in them. But I believe it's only a matter of time before they're all pulled in. You did well to leave. The less contact you have with that group, the better."

Penny nodded, then realised that David hadn't finished.

"I don't believe in socialising with other members of our group. Yes, meet them in a café but don't stay for the afternoon. It makes for lonely times, but what would you prefer? Being free and lonely or spending time with the Gestapo?"

She rolled her eyes. "Time with the Gestapo."

He looked startled at the sarcasm. "Sorry, Penny, I keep treating you as a novice. It isn't fair, and you're right to correct me. Now we, or rather you, have a job to do."

She waited for her orders.

"Do you remember Michel, Jeanne's friend?"

"Yes, David, he wasn't someone you could easily forget. He's the reason I can't look at pig meat. Why?"

David looked at her with a quizzical expression on his face. "Pig meat? Never mind. You need to meet with Michel. He has some news from London. I can't risk being seen with him."

"Where and when?" she asked.

"At the Café de la Nouvelle Mairie. It's near the Sorbonne. Sit at a table near the window and wait for him. He should arrive at four."

On her way to meet Michel, Penny thought about Gracie. She wondered how her friend was finding life with William and Ruby. They wouldn't be babies for much longer. How much she had missed already. Thoughts of Gracie brought Meme to mind. Her grandmother would be worried, as she was bound to spot the letters Penny had written, to be sent via Vera, weren't answering any queries Meme no doubt raised in hers. Penny gave herself a mental shake. I have a job to do. It's not like I can send her a postcard.

She arrived early, despite taking time to ensure she hadn't been followed. She took a seat by the window and ordered a coffee. The waiter brought it over to the table but seemed distracted by a van driving down the road outside. The van driver seemed more interested in what was behind him. He kept looking over his shoulder.

"He's going to drive through the checkpoint. *Mon deux*, what is he doing?" the waiter commented as he stood staring, glued to the scene in front of him.

Penny clenched her fists by her side, her heart beating so fast she was tempted to run away. She had to stay seated and watch as the occupant of the van finally saw the checkpoint. Rather than stop, he attempted to drive through it. The driver was driving erratically and at speed, and it took a few seconds to register in her brain that she knew him. It was Michel, David's contact. Jeanne's young friend. A black car drew up fast, some occupants shooting at the van. People scattered at the sound of shots, but she watched in horrified fascination as the van crashed into a wall, blocking the driver's door. Michel, travelling alone, was kicking and pushing at the other door, trying to get it open. It was obvious he was trapped as the soldiers moved closer, but he didn't give up. He kept kicking. Penny froze, wanting to help but realising there was nothing she could do.

Finally, the door opened. Michel jumped out, waving a gun. A shot rang out and Michel fell to the ground, a red puddle forming under his head. Had he shot himself or been shot? She wasn't sure.

She gathered up her things, paid for her drink and left the coffee shop as casually as she could. The last thing she needed was the Germans asking her questions. Thankfully, they were busy following orders to search the van. It was too much of a coincidence – Michel being shot on the day she had seen David's image on the posters.

She made her way back to the safe house, doubling back a couple of times. She wanted to make sure nobody was following her. David was waiting for her.

She couldn't speak for a couple of seconds, her hands shaking.

"What is it?"

"Michel's dead." She stood against the wall, her legs feeling weak.

"Damn it. What happened?"

"There was a German checkpoint. Rather than drive through it as he should, he panicked and tried to speed up, then he lost control and drove into a wall. The door jammed, and it took a while for him to get out of the truck."

David glanced behind her as if expecting the Gestapo to jump out.

"Are you sure he's dead? We have to get out of here. He knows about us and the safe house. We have to warn the others."

"David, he's dead. He had a gun, I saw him wave it around and then he or a soldier shot him in the head."

She shuddered, blinking to get rid of the image of his body lying on the pavement, the pool of blood widening under his head. "He was only a kid."

David stared at her. "And you are how old? Michel knew the risks better than anyone. He was reckless. Why did he drive into town and through a checkpoint? What was he thinking?"

Penny didn't have any insight to offer. She couldn't help thinking of how Marie had predicted this, but she didn't feel the knowledge would comfort David.

"Victor, what do we do now?"

"The Germans did us a favour. A dead man can't tell them anything." She gasped at his coldness but realised he'd turned to look out the window. Was he hiding his actual feelings? His voice was less confident when he next spoke. "This mission is far too important. We can't let London down. I have to go out now. I'll be back later this evening. Try to get some sleep," David said before slipping out the door.

Sleep! Was he serious? She had just seen one of their own shot dead. Michel's mother had already lost so much. Someone would break it to her that her teenage son wouldn't be coming home.

She lay on the bed thinking of Paul.

Mama, please keep him safe, she whispered.

David came back before long. "Grab your things. We're leaving."

"Now?"

"Yes, now. London wants us to build a network of partisans to help with the invasion when and if it comes. They have reliable information which suggests our cover here in Paris has been blown. We must hurry."

"Is that why Michel was driving like a demon possessed?"

"I hope so. It's the only reason for his actions. I don't like the fact he was driving towards the rendezvous with you. You came too close today."

She didn't need telling. "Where do we go now?" She didn't want to dwell on Michel's death.

"We have a job to do, and I need the skills you learnt in training. And I have to introduce you to some people. They are loyal. Friends – just in case I'm not around."

Now she understood, and her blood turned cold. Who had told the Gestapo about Michel? Did they know enough about David or Victor, as he was known, to catch him?

She hurried to get her things. She wasn't the reason he would die. He had a life to return to in England. A wife, maybe.

CHAPTER 51

They travelled separately by train to meet Lucien, David's second in command.

David gestured towards a man standing by the station, wearing a policeman's uniform. "There he is."

"He's police?"

"Yes, some of them are with us. Quite handy to have friends in the services, don't you think?"

How could David be so light-hearted when there was a price on his head? Ten thousand francs was a lot of money.

Lucien greeted her with a kiss on both cheeks. He shook David's hand, but the look he gave him said something was up.

"This is Simone," David said. "You can trust her completely. We've known each other a long time. I've seen her in action."

Penny must have looked confused as David whispered, "Café de Paris."

Of course, but that seemed so long ago. How innocent she'd been back then. Her greatest worry had been trying to get Harriet's fiancé to keep his hands to himself. If she met him now, she could break his groping fingers in a couple of seconds. For some silly reason, the thought amused her.

"She is certainly calm under pressure. The place is teaming with Gestapo spies and she looks like, how you say it, the cat got the cream?"

Penny wiped the smirk off her face, but Lucien winked at her to show he was joking.

❦

AT THE SAFE HOUSE, this time a printing shop, Lucien's friend gave them glasses of wine. Penny would have preferred a tisane, but she didn't want to appear difficult.

"Do you have details of the weapons drop? Ferdinand is getting impatient, and he has influence with the men."

David pointed to Penny. "That's why Simone is here. She'll scout out some landing grounds and contact the radio operator. We have to wait for a full moon, few of them around this time of the year."

Penny jumped to her feet, putting her hand on her

gun, as a man came through the door, shouting, "You promised to teach the men how to plant *plastiques* and blow up trains and then you disappear?"

"Simone, meet Frederick. He's half Spanish, hence his bad temper."

The man glared at Penny. Seeing her gun, he sneered at her. "Know how to use that, do you? Women like you should be home in bed."

Penny bristled but, at a shake of David's head, she didn't respond.

"Well, what have you got to say? How long do our men wait with their hands tied while you keep promising us arms, ammunition and money?"

"Frederick, calm down and stop shouting. The printing presses don't mask every sound and you'll bring the Gestapo down on top of us. Simone is our explosives expert – she'll show you how to lay the *plastique* to blow the trains."

Frederick couldn't have looked more amazed. "You're joking? She's barely more than a child."

Penny stepped forward. "Don't underestimate me. It's a mistake."

He raised his hand to swat her away, but she grabbed it, used his bodyweight against him and had him on the floor before he could say a word.

The men sniggered, but Penny was far too angry to deal with them.

"I warned you. I can take care of myself."

David pulled her back as Frederick found his feet. If looks could kill, she'd be dead. But he didn't make the mistake of reaching out towards her again.

"Simone, explain what you need the men to know."

David produced a bag that must have come from the safe house. She smelled the almond scent of the *plastique* and guessed David had charges too.

"This is the *plastique*," Penny said. "As you can smell, it has a distinctive scent. Take care when touching it – don't unless you have to and, if moving it, use gloves if you can. The Germans know the smell. Don't give them reason to suspect you."

She explained how the charges worked and what the different coloured fuses meant.

"Ideally the men could practise but we don't have enough plastique for that to happen. Nominate certain men from your groups and I'll train them by showing them how to do an actual sabotage mission."

"I'm not sending my men off under the command of some girl." Frederick said, moving so the distance between them was wider.

"You'll do as I tell you. If I'm not around, Lucien is in charge. Now what targets have you found for us, Frederick?"

The man, now the centre of attention again, came to life. He certainly appeared to be as committed to the cause as he was to keeping women chained to the kitchen sink.

She didn't like him and was loath to trust him, but David obviously valued his opinion and if she wanted to be close to the action, she had to obey David. It rankled she was a highly trained agent, but the best way to shut up Frederick and others like him was to prove her worth. In the meantime, putting up with his chauvinist views was a small price to pay. Their aim was the same. To free France.

CHAPTER 52

CHRISTMAS 1943

Gracie strapped Ruby into her pram, ignoring the child's protests. She would never get a tree put up if her daughter insisted on moving across the floor at the speed of light. Charlie was back in hospital for his latest skin graft. William was content to lie down, playing with his train.

As she put the knitted and handmade ornaments on the tree, Gracie wiped away one tear after another. She couldn't bear another Christmas away from her family and friends. The children would be grown-ups by the time her mother and father met them. How she missed her mam. What was she going to do for Christmas dinner? The fifth year of the war meant there wasn't a goose or turkey to be found, even a rabbit was scarce these days.

The post arrived, giving Gracie an excuse to sit down with a watery cup of tea. She'd used the leaves

twice already, but she couldn't waste fresh ones. Then
Charlie would have to do without when he came home
at the weekend. How she missed the days when you put
a spoon of leaves in for everyone, and one for the pot.
Now the pot never got a look in.

She picked up the letters, glancing through them.
Two for Charlie, one from her mam and the last one,
Penny. She tore the envelope open. Was her best friend
home? Would she come to East Grinstead for Christmas? That would make Christmas. Shed eat turnips and
still be happy if it meant catching up.

She sat on the couch, one hand pushing the pram
with Ruby now falling asleep.

DEAR GRACIE,

*I hope you, Charlie and the twins are fine. I'm so
busy with work these days. Scotland is boring, nothing
much to do but work, work and more work. I'm sorry I
can't get away to see you all.*

Love

Penny

THE PAGE of the letter fell to the floor. Gracie didn't
bother to pick it up. It was the same as the last three
letters she'd got from Penny, almost word for word. She
never responded to any of the things Gracie told her in

her own letters. She didn't even mention the news about Mr Churchill being ill with pneumonia or President Roosevelt expected to visit London. Not to mention what was happening with the war. It was almost as if she wasn't aware these things were happening.

She was being sentimental. Of course Penny would know. Anyone with access to the radio knew what was going on. She picked up her mam's two-page letter. Smiling, she settled back to read.

DARLING GRACIE,

How I miss you and the babies, but thank God the news on the war front seems to improve. Maybe this will be the last Christmas of the war.

Wait til I tell you what old Mrs Jones did. Some American soldiers came to visit the town hall. They gave some chocolate to the children and seeing Mrs Jones all alone, I suppose they felt sorry for her, and gave her some chocolate-covered toffee sweets. I can't remember the name. The old dear sucked the chocolate off and gave the toffee to the children.

GRACIE HELD a hand over her mouth as she laughed. She could just imagine toothless Mrs Jones doing such a thing. She read on, smiling at the interesting titbits her mam shared. Stan was doing well and had received her mam's parcels. He'd asked for some more socks and woollen hats. Gracie had some old jumpers she could unravel and knit up. That would be a better use of her time than feeling sorry for herself.

She continued reading.

GRACIE, *have you had any news from Penny? I got a letter, more of a note really, but it said nothing apart from Scotland being cold. I found it odd.*

GRACIE RETRIEVED Penny's letter and read it again, her mam's comments in her head. Yes, it was distinctly odd. Just where was Penny – and what was she doing?

CHAPTER 53
FRANCE FEBRUARY 1944

Penny cursed the train delays making her late getting back to the safe house. She only had an hour to get to the landing zone. She'd be fit for the next Olympics if they ever admitted cycling as a sport. She grabbed a piece of day-old bread, cutting the mould off the cheese as she gobbled up her first meal in twenty-four hours.

PENNY ARRIVED at the landing zone just in time to hear the first burst of gunshots. Instinct drove her to go forward, but her training took over. She withdrew her Sten and attached the silencer. Carefully, she inched forward, crawling silently through the grass. She needed to find out if she could help.

She surveyed the scene in front of her. The Germans were out in force and had laid in wait for the team.

Someone had talked. Just then, she spotted one of the *Maquis* gesturing to the German officer. Aaron. He was part of Frederick's group and shared his beliefs. She had never taken to him, but he had been a member of the *Maquis* long before she arrived.

She watched from her hiding place as the brave members of the landing team were picked off, one by one. The Germans weren't shooting to kill. Their shots were too low. They must want to take them alive for questioning. Penny's stomach heaved. She had to get back to the others to warn them. There was nothing she could do here. She watched for a couple more seconds, hoping to spot David, but she couldn't see him.

She retreated, still crawling, praying the German wouldn't see her. As soon as she thought it was safe to do so, she broke cover and ran to where she had left her bike. *That should have been me.* It was the closest she'd come to being caught. She cycled furiously back to their camp. She had to warn them before one man broke under torture. The losses they'd taken were bad enough without losing the entire camp.

Frederick looked up as she jumped off her bike, letting it fall to a heap on the ground.

"What's the matter? Where are the others?" he said, the habitual cigarette hanging from his lip.

Trying to catch her breath, Penny leaned forward, panting. "Frederick, everyone has to get out of here now. I have just seen the Germans with Aaron. He led them to the landing party. There were too many of them. I couldn't do anything. We have to go now before they come here."

"Aaron with the Germans? Don't be ridiculous. He went down south to visit with his mother. He'll be back tomorrow." Frederick spat out the cigarette, grinding it into the dirt with his foot. "You were supposed to be with the landing party. If the Germans have them, why weren't you caught? How did you escape?" He glared at her suspiciously.

"How dare you?" She struck his face. "I was late, as I had a meeting that I couldn't miss. Victor knew it was unlikely I would make it on time. That's why he took Adam with him. I raced to the spot as quickly as I could. I only spotted the Germans as the gunfire started. I got lucky." She stared defiantly back at him.

Another man came running in. "The Germans have our guys. We have to get out of here."

Frederick turned his attention back to Penny.

"Lucky? Is that what you call it? I have another name for that type of luck." He turned to some men behind him. "Disarm her, tie her up, and shove her in the cart. We have a traitor in our midst. She could have led the Germans to us. Give the order to disperse for now. Send the men who come from local villages home. The rest are to disappear into the woods. Tell them to be careful. The Germans are on the rampage."

"Frederick, you're wrong. I wouldn't betray France. Victor is my friend and now he could be dead."

Frederick spat on the ground. "Adam is my nephew. My sister's only child. Perhaps you want to come with me to tell her that her little angel is now dead, or worse, in the hands of the Gestapo. I never agreed with girls doing a man's job. Men, take her."

Penny was tempted to put up a fight, but seeing the looks on the men's faces, she decided not to. They disarmed her, or so they thought – she still had a knife hidden, tying her hands behind her back. They gagged her, too, but only after the two of them had both taken several minutes to pat her down. She bristled as they touched her intimately.

She had never felt anger like this before. After everything she had done over the last six months, she couldn't believe this could be happening. She had lived, slept, ate and fought with them. It was not only the personal risks she had taken, but putting her old friend's lives in danger, too, and she thought that had won her their trust. How could they believe she could betray them?

She tried to think logically. It looked bad that she was due to be at the landing site but arrived later than the Germans. She wondered whether they would put her on trial or just shoot her when they set up a new camp.

The cart moved slowly as the horse picked its way

through the trees. The wood was dense. Only the locals could locate the camp now. David had advised locating the camp here before, but the others hadn't seen the need for such precautions. David. She didn't want to think about him now. He'd become like a brother to her. She was very fond of him and totally in awe of his bravery. He never stopped to think of himself or to rest. London had ordered him back, but he refused to leave his men. Despite the continuous arguments, he had to fight with the *Maquis* over the lack of arms and ammunition. Hopefully, he was dead. The Germans would make him wish he was.

He had arranged for a meeting with some other *Maquis* leaders in a couple of days. He had asked her to get the code to London, confirming the date. The time and location still had to be agreed. She didn't know the names of who was supposed to come. She didn't think David knew the full details, either. Given the current circumstances, that was probably just as well. Where was Lucien? He would vouch for her.

The cart slowed to a stop. Penny was dragged off and thrown to the ground. Frederick came over to where she lay, holding a gun in his hand.

"If I had my way, we would shoot you now," he growled. "I have to wait to see what Victor wants to do."

"Victor?" Penny said. "He was at the landing site."

"Did you see him there? Was he the prize you

promised to the *Boche*?" He spat at her. "You sicken me."

"Frederick, I didn't bring the *Boche*. I saw Aaron speaking to them. He didn't look too concerned for his safety."

"*Ta gueule*! You can say your piece in the morning. Then we will shoot you. Guard her."

Penny grew silent. There was little point in antagonising the situation further. With her arms tied behind her back, it was impossible to sleep. She lay on her side, wishing the morning would arrive. She had to reach her knife in her sock, open the ties, otherwise she'd remain helpless.

The next morning, the camp was a hive of activity. Nobody approached Penny directly, but listening to bits and pieces of conversation, she learnt that six of their people had survived the shoot-out. One was seriously injured, four had been shot in the lower legs, but the rest were unharmed. For now. They had been taken to the local police station where the *Milice* were having fun tormenting them. They would be handed over to the Gestapo the following day.

Penny learnt the plan was to mount a rescue operation. That was madness. It was clearly a trap. Aaron must have told them how many of them there were. They were trying to use the captives as bait.

She continued to work on the ties on her hands. She had released her knife during the night and was almost free of her restraints. The self-appointed leaders, including Frederick, gathered around the fire having a heated discussion. She watched them with one eye as she drew herself to a crouching position, ignoring her muscles screaming in protest, having been immobile all night. Glancing around, she saw everyone was looking at Frederick so she took her time, moving silently, all the time getting closer. Now she had the stag and her trainer to thank for teaching her how to move quietly. Nobody saw what Penny was doing until it was too late. She had her blade to Frederick's throat before they knew she was free.

"You're making a big mistake, my friend," she said. "This is exactly the response the Germans will hope you'll make."

"Well, you would know, given your love for the *Boche*," he spat.

Penny ignored his outburst. "It's too risky. Victor would forbid it."

"He's not here to do anything, thanks to you." Frederick looked around him. "What further proof do you need of her guilt? She holds a knife to my throat."

"If I was guilty, I would have run into the forest, you cretin. I want to rescue Victor and the others, too. But not at the risk of our men." Penny looked at the other men, seeing Lucien, whom she knew David trusted implicitly, coming into camp. Her hopes soared; he'd believe she was innocent. He knew her. His eyes widened as he took in the scene, gaping at Penny with her knife to Frederick's throat.

"What's going on? The Germans are torturing our men and you're fighting among yourselves."

She ignored his fury and pleaded with him. "Lucien, you know I would never betray Victor."

"It's true. I don't know why she was late, but Simone knows Victor loves her. They share a past. She would never betray him." He looked at Penny. "Do you have an alternative plan?"

"Maybe." Penny continued to hold the knife to Frederick, but not as closely. "First, we need to get a message to London to postpone the meeting with the other *Maquis* leaders. That was due to take place tomorrow night."

Lucien nodded before looking at the other men. "Only Victor and I knew that meeting was going to take place. It's a sign of Victor's trust that he shared this knowledge with Simone. I believe in her innocence." He scribbled out a message, calling for Luc to take it to the wireless operator. When the boy had gone, Penny talked, but he told her to be quiet.

"Before we listen to Simone's alternative plan, I want to clarify that I have one hundred percent faith in Simone. Does anyone doubt my judgement?" Lucien stared at the men, his gaze lingering on each man's face for a couple of seconds. Nobody spoke until his gaze moved to Frederick, the last man in the group.

"How do you feel now, Frederick? Do you question my loyalty?" Lucien asked.

"Of course not." Frederick glared at Penny. She ignored him, as did Lucien.

"Good. Then Simone, proceed please."

"Victor and the others are to be passed to the Gestapo tomorrow. We don't know if that means they'll transport them to 11 Rue des Saussaies. I assume they will, but I would rather not wait to find out. There aren't as many Germans around now that they have sent them to the ports in case of an invasion."

Penny took a breath. This had to work. "I suggest tonight we blow the train lines in two or three different locations on the other side of town. We need to give the Germans the impression that we're more than they have been told. Also, by having several sites, the *Milice* should be tied up, and the Germans. London wants us to delay the movement of troops to the coast. So we'll kill two birds with one stone."

Penny took a breath, letting what she had suggested sink in.

"But what about Victor and the rest of our men they have arrested?" asked one man.

Penny answered, "A small group of us…"

"Us? I take it you expect us to trust you?" Frederick spat. "Lucien, I said I trusted you. That doesn't mean I have to follow her."

"It does if I put her in charge and send you under her command."

Frederick turned white.

Penny continued as if she hadn't heard the exchange between the two men. "As I was saying, I'll take nine men with me and go to the prison and free our men. I'm not making any promises. It's a dangerous mission. Only those who accept the risk involved should volunteer."

Lucien scratched his beard.

Frederick shook his head. "You can't seriously be considering this. It's another trap designed to kill more of us."

"Victor trusts Simone, and so do I. We have had this discussion, Frederick. I'm in charge and what's good enough for me…" Lucien looked at Penny. "That doesn't mean I agree with your plan. The prisoners will be well guarded."

"Exactly. That's why we need the diversions, aside from the fact that London expects us to do a job. Victor wanted those lines blown." Penny looked at the men staring back at her. She was trying hard not to show any weakness. "Aaron will have told them all he can about us. The Germans know how many we are, the number and type of weapons we have, and that Victor is important to us. They'll expect a rescue attempt. If we all go to the town, we walk into a trap."

Frederick grunted his disbelief. "I say we shoot

Simone as the traitor she is and then attack the town *en masse*. It's our only chance of success."

Lucien looked at Penny and Frederick. Then he looked at the other men sitting around the camp. "I trust Simone. However, this is a suicide mission and for that reason I ask for volunteers. Are there any here who would volunteer to go with Simone?"

Some men stepped forward. Lucien turned to Penny. "I'll go with you as well."

Penny shook her head. "No, Lucien. We need you here. If Victor doesn't come back, you must take over. Frederick can come with me."

Frederick glared at Penny. "I don't take orders from a woman, never mind a traitor."

"If I'm a traitor, you can shoot me at the prison. You're one of the best shots. We need your marksmanship. Of course, if I scare you, I'm sure some others will volunteer."

Frederick reacted to her goading by volunteering, just as she expected. She didn't relish working with him, but she needed his skills. "There's one condition. I'm in charge of this mission. You obey me or don't go."

Frederick glared at Lucien, who shrugged. "She's given you a choice."

Frederick turned back to Penny. "I'll keep a gun on you at all times. If I suspect a trick, I will shoot. Understood?"

Penny nodded. "We are wasting time. Patric can lead us into the prison. He seems to know it intimately."

The men laughed as the ex-convict, Patric, took a bow.

Penny continued, "We need to be quick and quiet. Bring a knife and your other weapons." She looked at Lucien. "What time can you set the detonators?"

"Give me two hours."

Penny shook his hand and, turning to her men, she said, "Get ready. Wear your darkest clothes and cover your face and hands with black mud or soot. I don't care. Be back here in ten minutes."

"*Bonne chance*, Simone."

"You, too, Lucien." Penny turned to go, but walked straight into Frederick. "Why haven't you changed? Put that cigarette out."

Frederick took a long puff and blew the smoke in her face. "You may have convinced the others. Not me. I will be watching you." He strode off, leaving Penny shaking behind him. What had she got herself into?

CHAPTER 54

The moon was on their side, hiding behind the clouds. The band of ten made their way quickly to the edge of town. There, they gathered to discuss the plan. Patric drew a crude map of the prison on the earth.

They waited for the first explosion, with Penny ordering them, "That's it. Let's go."

Keeping to the shadows, they moved quickly towards the prison. As they moved, there was another explosion in a different direction from the first. Lorries full of soldiers hurried out of town. Soon, a third explosion lit up the sky. "Now," Penny shouted.

The ten of them ran towards the prison, taking the two sentries that remained by surprise. They didn't make a sound as their necks broke. The group moved cautiously towards the entrance. As Penny had suspected, most guards were members of the *Milice* not

Germans. In order to get into the prison, they would have to get past two of them in the front guardhouse.

"Friends of yours?" Frederick whispered to Penny.

"Hardly! Stay here."

Penny took off her beret and tossed her hair around her shoulders. She pulled at her blouse, revealing more skin. She walked to the door, calling for help. The door opened, causing her band of men to shrink back into the corners as the light from the room blinded them.

"Mademoiselle, what's the matter? Why are you crying?"

"Oh, monsieur. I have just been attacked. I was walking home, and a man jumped me. He kept pawing at me and, and … oh, monsieur, help me, please. My papa will kill me if he sees me in this state." Penny pulled her blouse down further, giving the *Milice* more of a view.

The man put his arm around her shoulders. "My dear girl, you have come to the right place. Come in and have a drink. My friend and I will look after you." A bawdy laugh rang out from the room, but Penny ignored it.

"Oh, thank you, monsieur." She turned on her brightest smile and threw herself into his arms. She looked directly at Frederick and motioned him into the prison before closing the door to the room holding the two *Milice* guards.

It didn't take her long to catch up with Frederick. Patric was leading them to the cellars. As they moved, they heard another explosion. As Penny had suspected, there were few guards. They had the element of surprise in their hands; taking care of them was easy.

They had just come to the cells when they were discovered. Aaron was chatting to a member of the *Milice*. Frederick swore loudly, causing Aaron to spin around.

"You?" Aaron paled.

"You traitor." Frederick shot him before Penny could stop him. She fired at the other *Milice* man, shouting at the others to open the cells. The four injured *Maquis* would need one-to-one help to leave. Two others would go in front to shoot their way out. Penny ordered all the cells be opened and gave guns to the newly released prisoners. "Follow our men. Fire at will. It's every man for himself, now."

Penny, Frederick, Patric and another man hung back.

"Where's Victor?" asked Penny, looking in each of the cells. There was nobody left. She looked at Patric. "Where else do they keep prisoners?"

Patric looked grim. "There's another set of cells at the back. They are rarely used."

"Take us there. Quickly." Penny refused to abandon the mission now, despite the noise from above. "I hope there's a back way out of this place."

Patric lead them through a labyrinth of damp passages. Finally, they emerged into a larger opening where Penny could see a row of cell doors bolted shut, but there was nobody guarding the cells.

Opening them, they were shocked at the state of their inhabitants. David had already been tortured. Adam was in a worse state.

Penny thought she saw Frederick's eyes glisten. He moved forward to lift his unconscious nephew in his arms. "*Mon Dieu*. What have those bastards done to you?" Adam couldn't answer.

Penny moved towards David, who was trying to stand up. "We need to get out of here. Lean on me."

Patric beckoned them on. It seemed as if they were going further into the bowels of the prison. "Through here. It's not ideal, as it will take us up to the local police station. But it's our only chance."

Penny nodded. She continued supporting David while another *Maquis* tried to help hold him up from behind. Finally, they reached their destination.

"I'll go." Patric moved forward. "They know me already. I think they'll be sympathetic, but if not, shoot it out."

Penny held her breath, waiting. Frederick cradled Adam, who had still not regained consciousness. David moaned but couldn't speak. It seemed hours before Patric reappeared, grinning broadly. "It seems we've been arrested. We're to be transported immediately to Arras."

The sympathetic gendarme couldn't have come up with a better solution. They piled into the back of the police car with the two wounded men covered with blankets. Penny and Frederick travelled in the boot. Patric squeezed into the back seat.

Luckily, the police sailed through the checkpoints set up by the Germans. They told the soldiers they had been sent to investigate reports of a band of *Maquis* who may be responsible for the explosions. The gendarmes drove to the edge of the forest. "We'll have to leave you here and go towards the site of the explosions. Otherwise our cover could be blown."

"*Merci beaucoup*," said Penny, smiling at the two gendarmes.

"*Vive la France*," muttered one, kissing her on both cheeks.

"He's a real Frenchman. Wasn't going to give up a chance of kissing a pretty girl," Patric commented, causing the others to laugh.

"Come on. We aren't safe yet."

Patric and another *Maquis* carried David between them. Frederick refused help with Adam. It took a while for them to reach a point they deemed safe enough to rest. Penny's first aid training kicked in. She didn't think Adam was going to recover. His injuries from both the shooting and subsequent torture were too severe.

David was unconscious now. He had also been tortured, but wasn't as badly injured as Adam. Penny guessed the *Milice* had tortured Adam in front of David. They knew brave men wouldn't talk if they were in pain, but couldn't bear to watch it inflicted on one of their own.

"How is Victor?" Patric asked.

Penny didn't look up from tending David. "He should live if we can get him back to England."

"I think Adam will die before morning."

Penny nodded, not trusting her voice. Patric put a hand on her shoulder. "We must get going."

The party made their way slowly back to the new camp, taking care to make sure nobody followed. With relief, Penny saw that Lucien and his men were waiting for them. Lucien rushed forward on seeing the casualties.

"Victor?"

"He needs proper medical attention. We have to get a message through to London. Arrange for a bird to come in and collect him."

"Adam?"

Penny shook her head. "I don't think a doctor could help him. His injuries are just too severe. Frederick wants to stay with him. He should rest, but…"

"He can rest tomorrow. What about the rest of our men?" Lucien asked.

Penny had momentarily forgotten about them. "Four were injured. They left with the others before us. I thought they might have made it back here."

"They may have taken shelter elsewhere. We'll find out in the morning. It's too dangerous to go out. The Germans will be furious. We don't need to give them an excuse to come after us."

Penny saw he was right. She was exhausted, physically and mentally.

"Simone, you need to get some rest. I'll monitor Victor." He looked sternly at her. "You're no use to anyone in this state. Go to bed."

Penny gave him a mock salute before turning in.

∼

THE NEXT MORNING, she was surprised to find she had slept. Adam had died before she woke. She found Lucien sitting beside David.

"I've sent a message to London to get him out. We can't stay here. The Germans are searching everywhere. It's only a matter of time before they come deeper into these woods."

"Any word on the other men?" she asked.

"Two were shot dead trying to escape, but the others all made it back safely. They stayed in town last night as they didn't want to be caught after curfew. They've moved further south to a bigger *Maquis* camp with better medical facilities."

"Simone."

Frederick stood behind Penny.

"I apologise for calling you a traitor. Thank you for what you did last night." Frederick looked uncomfortable.

Penny held his gaze. "You disobeyed a direct order, putting the lives of our men at risk. If you ever do that again, I'll kill you myself. Are we clear?"

Frederick looked at Lucien. "Are you just going to stand there and listen to this?"

Lucien shook his head. He moved forward and put his hand on Penny's shoulder. "Pull a stunt like that again, and if Simone doesn't shoot you, I will. Victor is going home. Simone is taking over as leader."

Frederick growled. Penny stared at Lucien.

"Lucien, it should be you. You know all the men, the area and …"

"Simone, Victor had told me a few days ago that he was sending me to train another *Maquis* unit. I won't be here. There's nobody else."

Frederick puffed up his chest. "Then I'm the most logical choice. I'm a man, after all."

"Not the most essential prerequisite for a leader, Frederick. You're too hot-headed. You react on impulse, sometimes to our cost. From what I hear, you were lucky to get out last night. You could have landed Simone, Patric and yourself in a Gestapo cell."

"Aaron needed to be dealt with."

"Yes, Frederick, he did. I have no issue with you killing him. Your method was clumsy and careless. You should have killed him with your bare hands or your knife. You could have acted innocent and persuaded him to come back with you. You should have done anything but shoot him."

Lucien looked at Simone. "You are young and female. That's going to cause issues with some men, like this old goat here. The majority will accept you as you have shown your worth again and again." Lucien clapped her on the back. "You scare me, Simone. I'm glad you are on our side and not theirs."

~

A COUPLE of days passed before London confirmed they were sending in a Lysander to collect David. He had regained consciousness and was trying to persuade Penny to go back with him.

"You can't stay here alone," he said.

"I'm not alone." She smiled at him. "David, this is my home. Imagine how you would feel if the *Boche* were marching through London. You would do anything to stop them."

"Yes, but I'm not a…"

"Twenty-one-year-old girl? You're not French, either, but that didn't stop you fighting."

"I don't have the energy to fight you. I've spoken to Frederick and some others who could prove difficult. I've told them that if you insist on staying, you're my choice as temporary leader."

"Temporary?"

"Yes, Penny. As soon as I get back to London, I'm going to request they order you back. You need a rest. I will ask them to send a suitable replacement."

"I can rest when the war is over. You can order all you want. I'm not going back to England. Not now. Maybe never."

"Never? But I thought that when things were over, you and I might … What I mean is that we…" David stopped in the face of Penny's stare.

"There is nothing between us, David. Maybe at some point there was. But not now. I'm not that inno-cent little girl looking for a hero. You have Marianne. She will make a more suitable wife for you."

"But I don't love her, I…"

Penny leaned forward, pressing a quick kiss to his lips, effectively stopping him from continuing.

"You love the idea of me. The reality is quite differ-ent. I have a job to do here in France. When the war is over and my role complete, I want to stay here. I won't live in London."

"I'll make you change your mind."

"Nothing is going to do that. Goodbye, David, and take care. Be happy."

Penny walked off. She had to meet with a new contact in the next town. Men. Why did they think they had a right to rule her life? She knew David was worried about her. But she wasn't a little girl. She knew exactly what she was doing.

Penny was away from the *Maquis* camp for a week. She went to see Madame Bayard. She thought her connections may prove useful. She had been right, and returned to camp with new contacts for food and better papers.

If only they could live in actual houses rather than in the woods like this. The wet ground did nothing for the mood of the men, nor did living on a diet of what they could scrounge from the forests. At least the weather was improving, it wasn't as cold at night. Out here in the woods, there was little shelter from the freezing winds.

Often, the men were left standing around doing nothing but smoke. She'd insisted they train every day, but without rifles and ammunition to give them, they were running out of patience. It had been a good idea to have some women join them. They did the cooking and washing. A few acted as couriers, it now becoming almost impossible for healthy men to travel around France without being picked up by the Germans. Every day newcomers came to enlist in their group. They were committed to freeing France from the enemy and for that she was glad. Her good mood didn't last long as Lucien had bad news for her.

"I'm glad to see you. We have trouble. I sent one man into Boulogne. He came back. It's not good."

Penny motioned for the man to speak.

"We have to disperse. The Germans are widening their searches. Nobody is safe. If they find a family sheltering a *Maquisard*, they shoot the man in front of his wife and children. They are then imprisoned, and they burn their home to the ground."

The men looked at Penny, wanting to see her reaction to this grim news. She knew they wouldn't like what she had to say.

"Those that were staying with farmers must come and hide in the woods where possible. Unless they have papers allowing them to work on the farms, they leave immediately. We can't expose the brave farmers to any unnecessary risks," she said.

The man spoke again, this time not looking at her. "It's not just the farmers. The Mother Superior at the local convent was severely beaten before being imprisoned. She had allowed an injured *Maquisard* to be treated at the convent."

"Did they send our man to prison, too?" she asked.

"No, they dragged him out of his bed and shot him."

The group of men sitting in front of Penny started talking at once. Penny had to stop them before their fears grew out of control.

"Silence. We knew what the *Boche* were like. Their barbarity will encourage more brave Frenchmen to join us. We will prevail."

A large man, the son of the baker who joined them having run away when the Germans ordered him to Germany, ignored her.

"It wasn't just Germans. In Boulange, it was mainly *Miliciens* who made up the two hundred or so men disguised as *Maquisards*. Their latest trick is to run through the town begging for help from the Gestapo. If anyone is brave enough to open their door and offer help, they suffer the same fate as those found hiding our men."

"Those *Milice* cowards are worse than the Germans. They make me ashamed to be French. The stories of their treatment of female captives make the Gestapo look preferable." Patric swore.

The men muttered, shaking their heads.

"That's enough." Penny moved her gaze from man to man. She had to convince them to concentrate on the task at hand. "These traitors will be dealt with later. We have work to do now. London has asked that we step up activity to keep the Germans busy. Lucien, is your team of saboteurs ready? We must disable the train network.

We have to put out the rail lines for a week or more. The *Boche* need to transfer their panzers by rail. Our job is to stop them."

"Yes, Simone. Jean-Luc suggested we take out the railways without using the explosives London sent us. We're running low on supplies. He can disable the rail network quietly, but effectively."

"Good. We can do without bringing more unwanted visitors to this area." She turned to the heavyset farmer with the cigarette permanently attached to his lip. "Frederick, have you warned the villagers about the planned searches?"

Frederick nodded.

"We need more landing areas. London wants to drop both arms and supplies. I'll leave it to you to find suitable spots. They'll be here the night after next. You'll also need to put together two teams to greet the planes. One will carry supplies, the second will carry some members of our team."

Frederick agreed with another nod of his head. He still didn't enjoy taking orders from Penny.

Lucien cleared his throat, causing Penny to look at him expectantly. He had recently returned from the south. They were having the same problems; more young men were joining the *Maquis* rather than going to Germany as forced labour, but they didn't have the money to feed them – never mind arms to provide them with a means to fight. She could murder London. Didn't they realise how difficult it was keeping a secret army under wraps but ready to go when the invasion came. If it ever came. She ignored the voice in her head.

"Will London be sending more money? We need it to pay bribes and buy supplies. The local farmers have been wonderful, but they have to feed their families, too."

"Yes, Lucien, the drop will include some francs." She moved her neck around, trying to reduce the tension. "Questions?"

Her tone told them not to ask anything else. They listened for once. "Good. Right, let's get moving."

Penny walked away, Lucien following quickly behind her. He caught up with her and said, "Don't take too much notice of the men. It's difficult for them. They're not used to taking orders from a woman."

"Frederick still doesn't like me, does he? He blames me," said Penny.

"He has to blame someone. He always thought that he would take over if anything happened to the boss. Then you came along. He doesn't like taking orders from anyone, least of all a girl young enough to be his daughter."

"And you, Lucien. You're happy with my command?" Silence greeted her question. "I'm asking you to speak freely."

"Simone, you're brave and have proved your love of France more than once." He stopped.

"But?"

"Sometimes you're too impulsive. You take risks."

"We all take risks. I don't ask anyone to take more than I do."

"I didn't mean you put us at risk. When was the last time you had a break?"

"I just had a week away."

"We both know that was work. Since before Victor left, you have been doing the work of ten. We all want to drive out the *Boche*, but with you, it's something more." He stopped talking. She glanced at him before looking away. Exhaustion flooded her body, but she couldn't stop. If she did, she'd have to think about all the things she did. Shooting men at point blank range, arranging for traitors to be executed, standing by without being able to rescue her men from torture and execution. An image of Lily and her doll came to her mind. How things had changed from the day she'd stood watching the truck take the little girl and her family away. Then she'd dissolved into tears. Now she couldn't remember the last time she cried.

Plus, keeping busy kept her mind off Paul. He seemed to have disappeared into thin air. Nobody knew where he was. Not that she asked, but she kept an ear out for news and there was nothing. Only silence.

"You're thinking too much, my friend. Go get a drink of Calvados and I'll see you again in a few days. I have to go to meet with the wireless operator. I know I said we would get more francs in the next drop. I have to convince London to send them. Meet me at the church."

"Simone…"

"Enough, Lucien. I appreciate your concern. There will be plenty of time to have a rest when the Allies have landed. Now, I need to be off. I have to meet with the mayor. My *Carte D'Identite* needs updating. I want to make sure he's on our side and also see whether he has any news."

"Take Luc with you. He knows the countryside. You can't go alone. With the latest arrests, we can't afford to take any chances."

She reached out to caress the side of his face. "Thank you, Lucien, for caring."

"Sshh, don't say things like that. The men who find the *Boche* scary have never met my wife. She would skin me alive if she thought you and I were … well, you know."

Penny laughed. "Mrs Lucien has nothing to fear from me. You're a brave and fearless fighter. I trust you with my life. But as a lover, I prefer my men groomed," she teased.

Lucien scratched his bearded face, beaming.

"Now, I must go. It will be curfew soon. Where's Luc?"

Lucien whistled softly and Luc appeared. Penny

kissed Lucien once on each cheek before heading out into the darkness with the younger boy at her side.

They reached the town without incident. Penny sent Luc to a safe house, with instructions to return to Lucien the next morning. She wanted to work alone.

They updated her identity card without issue. The mayor was more than sympathetic to their cause. He gave Penny some vital paperwork that would enable the resistance to travel more freely. He also provided some intelligence regarding troop movements. The Germans, it would seem, were finding it difficult to contain their men and had requested reinforcements.

Penny smiled. They were succeeding. The more Germans, the better. Their role was to support the Allies' invasion. If the *Boche* had to send more soldiers to fight them, they would have fewer to direct towards the invasion.

"*Ici Londres. Les Français parlent aux Français...*"

The men surrounding Penny leaned forward towards the radio as if they were one person. She knew how they felt. Her own heart was beating fast. Was this it? The moment they had waited for. "*Le combat viendra.*"

Penny clapped her hands together as the men stared at her.

Lucien spoke first. "Was that it? The moment of battle is approaching? When, where and what do we do?"

"We wait. London will tell us more in due course. In the meantime, tell your teams to be ready and on their guard. The Germans will have heard the same message and may turn even nastier."

The men grumbled, but Lucien nodded in agreement. "Now is not the time for us to lose faith or do something stupid. We stay anonymous until the right time comes. Then we will show everyone how Frenchmen fight."

The men cheered but soon shut up at a look from Lucien. They dispersed into smaller groups, checking their ammunition and getting ready.

～

4 JUNE 1944

THE MESSAGES *personal* on the BBC took almost eight hours to be read out on June 3rd. Penny took turns with Luc, listening to them, waiting to hear the specific message for her team. Her host, Madame Kneper, a widow now living on a deserted farm, kept her company for a while.

"The *Anglais*? They are coming?" Madame stared at the radio as if it would announce Churchill himself was coming to France.

"We don't know yet, Madame. We must be patient."

Madame stood up with a growl. "I've no patience left. First, they took my husband in the last war and now my sons are somewhere in Germany. I want them gone. Why does it take so long?"

Penny couldn't give her any reason. She wasn't sure

what was going on either. There had been so many
rumours of landings, a few of her men didn't believe it
would ever happen. But it had to. They were running
low on food, ammunition and explosives. She needed a
drop from London, but perhaps more important, she
needed a sign to let the husbands, brothers and sons who
were fighting in her team know they weren't alone.

"The bird has flown the nest once her eggs have
hatched."

That was it. They'd agreed to the drop. It would
happen late tomorrow night. She jumped up, kissed
Madame on the cheek and grabbed her jacket and beret.

"Where are you going now? It's raining."

"I know, but I have to see someone. You should
sleep. Have faith, my friend."

The woman muttered about faith and being young
and other things Penny couldn't quite work out. She left
the farmhouse on her bicycle and headed to the camp
where Lucien and the other men waited.

∼

IN THE WARM sunshine the next morning, the local
Catholic priest set up an outdoor altar. Most of her men
came from Catholic families and wanted the chance to
attend Mass. Going to the church in the nearest town
wasn't possible.

Penny had set up guards on the perimeter of the camp. Now was not the time to get careless. She watched the priest as he kissed and raised the chalice, the warm sun's rays reflecting off the gold. The familiar Latin words flowed over her. She hadn't attended church in England, but Madame Bayard had taken her to Mass often as a child.

She watched as her *Maquisards* bent their heads in prayer. She could imagine what they prayed for. Freedom for France, obviously, but also prayers to live to see the end of the occupation and for a win. These men weren't just fighting for their freedom, but for that of their families. The Germans had increased the reprisals against families of known *Maquis* members. The women, mothers, daughters, wives and girlfriends risked being arrested and deported to Ravensbrück concentration camp.

Luc approached her.

"I thought you'd be at Mass."

Luc glanced toward the men before whispering, "The landing zone is ready. The men you asked for will be there."

"Good."

"Simone?"

Penny waited.

"You think this is really it this time? The Allies are coming?" Hope and doubt mixed in his eyes.

She laid a hand on his shoulder. "*Oui mon ami*, they will come soon."

"The years of *attentisme* – sitting on the fence – are finally over. Our French brothers must finally rise and fight back. It's time to decide to be men, not sheep."

Penny grimaced at the hint of anger in his tone. Being young, Luc didn't always understand the sacrifices men with families had to make. Some were cowards and were waiting to see which side would win. But many were just trying to get through the war alive. They had a duty to protect their families, and no father wanted his daughters to be at the mercy of the German soldiers.

"Don't judge them so harshly, Luc. People react in different ways. Keep your focus on the job at hand. I want to see you waving the French Flag as *Fritz* crawls back to Germany."

∾

PENNY SAT with Lucien and a couple of his men, watching the radio as if it was about to explode. The silence was deafening until it crackled into life.

"*Ici Londres, Ici Londres*. London Calling."

Penny and her men moved closer. The announcer spoke clearly and slowly. She listened as their instructions came, then turned and spoke to the group.

"We have to intensify our actions, but not as an army. They want us to continue in guerrilla mode. It's safer for all of us. The sabotage of telephone cables and railway lines is to go ahead at maximum level. We also need to obstruct the roads, make it more difficult for the Panzar divisions to get to the site of the invasion." Penny stood up, kissed their host on each cheek. "Thank you, Madame Kneper, for your hospitality and for the meat for my men."

"*Bonne chance. Vive La France.*"

Penny and the other men stole away in the darkness to the forests where the groups of partisans waited. Penny shivered as the chill of the foggy night bit into her bones. She saw the smoke from the fires before they arrived at the camp and heard the soft singing of their marching song.

"The Allies are coming. Tonight."

At her announcement, some men cheered while others shrugged. They'd heard similar rumours before.

"We listened to the BBC, this time it's the real deal. As we speak, ships are making their way from England to our shores, filled with Allied soldiers from all countries. America, Canada, England and, of course, De Gaulle and the free French."

The mention of De Gaulle got their attention. She beckoned to Lucien to take over and stood back as he organised the men into their different roles. Some would cut down trees to form barricades across the major roads, others would attack the gendarmerie and liberate their friends and any arms they could find. Penny would lead a group to set detonators on the railway lines in order to derail any German trains coming from the south. Lucien would cut the power cables.

～

THE WORD SPREAD QUICKLY, causing both men and women who had not been in the resistance before to join them. The new arrivals were enthusiastic but untrained and sometimes hard to discipline. Penny left it to Lucien to appoint other men to keep the troops in order. She had enough to do with looking after her wireless operator, George, whose careless behaviour was causing enough headaches. She also had to keep the focus on preventing the Germans from getting more troops to Normandy rather than wasting resources on petty revenge.

As if Lucien read her thoughts, she heard him say, "The time for us to revenge our colleagues will come, but for now, we must concentrate our efforts on the Germans. The best chance for the invasion to succeed."

She allowed her thoughts to wander, thinking again about where Paul was. She was still set on revenge, but if she'd known that the last time she'd see Paul for almost a year was that day, would she have argued so fiercely? No, but she would have tried harder to explain how she had to make Alain pay. Not just for murdering her mother, but for all his sins against the people of France. There was no doubt in her mind, his dealings with the Germans had resulted in many deaths and deportations.

CHAPTER 57
JUNE, LONDON

Nell listened to the wireless, tears running down her face. Tom walked in the back door and blanched when he saw her crying.

"What is it, love? Stan? Frank?" He put his paper on the table and moved to take her in his arms.

"No, it's good news. The invasion has happened and Rome has fallen. We're going to win this war. Stan, Frank and all the others out there are coming home."

Her husband turned away, heading for the door once more.

"What?" she called.

"Love, this is only the beginning. There's going to be many more killed before that devil Hitler is finished. I'm off to the allotment. I will try to see what veg I can get for you."

She sank into the chair. He was right, Hitler wouldn't take this lying down. Still, she tuned in to listen to the king as he told the nation how proud he was. He even brought the queen in and told them all to pray. Nell would pray harder than she'd ever done before. Not just for her family, but for Penny and the thousands of other youngsters fighting to get rid of the evil that was the Nazis.

Everyone involved in the Home Guard was on high alert, and those in the Red Cross were on call too. They had known nothing of the robot bombs until the siren went the other night. These were different to the bombs during the Blitz, at least then you had a chance to hide. This time, nobody knew where the robot bombs would land. Some said if you could hear them you were safe. One had destroyed the roof of St Mary Abbots hospital, causing many casualties. Another one had fallen at Marble Arch – and they were only the ones Nell had heard of.

Nell tried not to think about the raids that might still come before it was all over, and instead kept busy, one ear on the wireless, listening to the reports as she scrubbed her house. She spent hours queueing for food, not that they could afford the prices being charged for potatoes and other vegetables these days. Thank God for her husband's allotment. She gave some potatoes, peas and carrots to her neighbours. She couldn't have them pay 4/6 for a bundle of carrots.

As she went about her chores, she prayed for her family to stay safe. Occasionally her thoughts flew to

Penny. Gracie was convinced she was back in France. Was that true? It didn't seem likely, but then who knew what was going to happen in this war? Before it started, she'd have laughed if someone said she would send her children to the country to live for over four years. How much longer would it be before Kenny and girls came home – and then would they want to?

Stop it, you silly old woman. Stop borrowing trouble.

CHAPTER 58

Penny looked at Annette's house with sadness. It appeared so neglected now. She guessed nobody had wanted to move in. The Germans may have thought they were involved, too.

She had taken a risk coming back here, but she hoped to see Paul. Since realising it was Paul she loved and not David, and with the end of the war at last in sight, she had an increasing need to know Paul was still alive. She didn't know any members of his circuit. It wasn't like she could walk around openly asking if anyone had seen him.

She risked a visit to the bakery. It had been nine months since she had been there. Nobody was going to remember her.

The bell rang as she walked in. She was hoping to meet Yvonne, but a man was serving.

"*Un pain, s'il vous plaît*," she said as she reached

the counter. "Is Yvonne here?"

"No, my wife has gone to stay with her sister. Are you a friend of hers? I don't think we have met." The baker seemed friendly, but Penny couldn't take the risk.

"Not a friend, really. She was very nice to me a few months ago. I just wanted to pop in and say hello."

The baker stared at her with suspicion.

"*Merci, au revoir.*" Penny picked up the bread and walked out of the bakery. She had only gone a few steps when the man called her back.

She turned, about to say no, but walked back to meet him.

"This kindness you mentioned. Did it involve a man?"

"Are you asking me if your wife was having an affair?" Penny pretended to be affronted.

The baker laughed. "No, of course not. Goodbye, madame. Paul says *bon voyage.*"

Penny stopped, convinced the man could hear her heart beating.

"I was right, wasn't I?" whispered the baker. "It's okay. There's no danger to you here. Paul said you may call back. I think he was hoping you would."

"Paul, is he here?"

"Sadly, no."

"He's not…" Penny couldn't bring herself to put her fears into words.

"Nothing like that. He had to go on a trip. He's due

back tomorrow. Would you like to stay here? You can have my son's bedroom?"

"Thank you for your kind offer." Penny still wasn't totally convinced that the man was genuine. Something was off, but she couldn't put her finger on it. "Please tell Paul I said hello. If this war ever ends, remind him he promised to take me to Berlin."

"Berlin?" The man looked perplexed.

"*Au revoir, aussi.*" Penny quelled her instinct to run. Instead, she walked as sedately as possible. Her churning stomach was making her feel ill.

Once out of sight of the baker, she hurried through the streets. Paul was safe and due back. She couldn't wait to see him. She wanted to apologise for the things she had said. The way she had treated him. She hadn't changed her mind about killing Alain, but if Paul wanted to come with her to seek revenge, she wouldn't argue. She had spent too long on her own. Lucien had been right.

She was so tired it was difficult to think clearly. The baker was one of Paul's oldest friends. He wouldn't betray him. She shook her head. She'd been doing this too long; she would suspect de Gaulle of collaborating at this rate. Penny gave herself a mental shake. Maybe if luck stayed on her side, she would be curled up in bed with Paul in a couple of days.

She was due to meet with Gerard, the new wireless operator London had sent to their district, at a café in the town centre. She sat at the table, resisting the urge to pick at her nails. Where was he?

"Can I get you something else, Madame?"

"No, but thank you."

"Are you waiting for someone?" asked the waiter.

"He said to meet him here today, but…" She shrugged, trying to imply a lover had stood her up.

The French waiter winked and walked away. *Great, so now he thinks I'm a tramp*. The lack of sleep was affecting her mood.

"*Bonjour*, Simone. I'm sorry I was late."

Penny looked up into the smiling face of Gerard. He reminded her so much of Leon, the would-be agent who'd washed out of the training course. Like Leon, the Frenchman Gerard was too full of himself. She could hit him for being late and putting her at risk, yet he looked as if he didn't have a care in the world.

"Where have you been?" she hissed, not wanting the other customers to hear her.

"Sorry, had a date. I overslept."

Penny was speechless. The invasion had started, and her team member had just confessed to putting his love life ahead of their operation.

"Can I get a drink before we leave?" he asked.

"No, we must go now. I've been here too long already. I will walk out in a huff and you follow me."

She stood up, throwing some francs onto the table. Walking out, she heard him say something like,

"Women!" before following her down the road. The waiter whistled.

When they were out of sight of the café, Penny rounded on Gerard. "What the hell do you think you are doing? This isn't some country jaunt. We have important work to do."

"Blimey, what got into you today? So I was a few minutes late. No big deal. I'm here, ain't I?" Gerard glared back at her.

"Gerard, whether you like it, I'm in charge around here. You don't keep me waiting in a café unless there is a bloody good reason. Do it again and you will be back in Blighty before you can pull on your trousers. Do you hear me?"

"Yes, ma'am. Loud and clear." He saluted her.

"You idiot. You are going to get us all shot." She looked around quickly, but thankfully his gesture appeared to have gone unnoticed.

"Do you have a message?" she asked.

"Yes." He handed her a small piece of paper, which she read quickly.

"I don't have time to write a response. Can you remember it?"

He nodded.

"More arms, cash and first aid supplies." Penny allowed a mother and child to walk past them. "Tell them to use the drop zone for Victor."

"Victor?"

"They will understand. Now, what about you? There are more detection vans on the streets. How are you transmitting?"

He smiled, but it didn't reassure her. "Trust me, you don't want to know."

Her rebuke stopped at her lips. Over his shoulder, she saw some soldiers checking papers further down the street ahead of them. She threw her arms around his neck.

"*J'taime*," she said loudly, then whispered, "Go quickly. Don't look behind you. For God's sake, be careful."

He walked off whistling down the street. Penny stared after him, wondering if she had ever been so fearless. She turned to face the soldiers as they asked for her papers.

"Good morning, madame." The soldier looked pointedly at her ring finger. "Why you cry?" asked one.

The other soldier laughed, replying in German, "I think she has just been dumped. French trollop. What does she expect? I bet he's not her husband."

Penny said nothing. The first soldier gave her back her papers and smiled. "Put a smile on your face, madame. You are far too pretty to go around in tears. I'm sure your friend will come to his senses."

Penny stared in shock. The German soldier had seemed almost human, and he was way too young to be in uniform.

CHAPTER 59

A few days passed, and it was time to meet Gerard again. She prayed London had agreed to the drop. The men were getting impatient. She couldn't blame them. The Germans, knowing something was up, were imposing stricter restrictions. They hassled everyone for papers. She could almost hear the bomb ticking. They couldn't last much longer.

Gerard didn't show up at the appointed time. She waited as long as possible before leaving. She tried again the next day following their agreed process, a second appointment, just in case something went wrong, but he didn't show up. Penny's anxiety grew. She had to know whether the drop was on. She couldn't send a landing team to the drop zone without knowing whether the planes were coming. She cursed Gerard, and London for sending him.

Finally, she decided she had to go to Gerard's safe

house. It was against all the security rules, but there was no one else to send. She had no choice. She would go early the next morning.

The walk to Gerard's was uneventful. She didn't meet any patrols. She took several precautions to prevent being followed. She didn't see anyone, but that wasn't reassuring. She couldn't put her finger on it, but her instinct was telling her she had missed some detail. Something over the last few days was niggling at her. I'm losing my nerve.

She moved quietly into Gerard's apartment, opening it with the key he had put under a stone. Once inside, she stared around her. The place was a hovel. It looked like the scene of an attempted burglary. Had the Germans been there already? No.

Gerard wasn't there, but his codebook was strewn on the bed. She picked up some of his notes. It looked as if London had responded.

He transmitted from here. Even as the thought crossed her mind, she heard trucks outside. She ran to the windows. The Germans.

She had to get rid of the codebook. She cursed Gerard. It had been a stupid risk to take. He had been careless, too, leaving everything lying around. She hoped Madame Reynaud, his landlady, stayed in Lyons with her sister. She didn't want the old lady implicated in anything.

She ran to the stove. Thankfully the fire, although

small, was still lit. She tore up the paper into small pieces and crammed the lot into the flames. She used a poker to make sure that the evidence was destroyed.

Outside she could hear the Germans knocking on doors and shouting at sleepy residents.

She ran back to the room, intending to hide the wireless set. Maybe they would be lucky and the Germans might not search so thoroughly. She dismantled the set as much as possible and hid bits and pieces around the room. She put the bulky part into the wardrobe, covering it with some old clothes.

Then as she heard a noise on the stairs, she threw off her dress, climbed into bed and tried to look as if she had been asleep.

The door burst open. She grabbed the bedcover and held it to her breast.

"What the hell are you doing bursting into this room?" she said.

Her outburst took the German soldiers by surprise. They evidently weren't used to young girls screaming at them from their beds. But they recovered quickly.

"*Schnell, schnell* … downstairs."

"Why? I have done nothing. I'm just waiting for my boyfriend to come back. He went to get some food. We were hungry." She tried to smile, hoping to charm them into believing her story.

"*Schnell!*" they roared.

When she didn't move quickly enough, they aimed their guns at her.

She decided it was best to comply, so she grabbed her dress, threw it over her head and went downstairs, still shouting at them for waking her up. She shut up as soon as she saw the officer.

"So, Madame Michiels, we meet again? Or should I say Mademoiselle? That is your correct marital status, isn't it?"

She answered in French, despite him asking the last question in English.

"I don't know what you are talking about," she said.

"I think you do. You are an English spy, and there is no point in denying it. I know everything. Now, please take a seat while my men search this house from top to bottom."

The shouts from upstairs came quickly, telling her they had found the wireless. Unfortunately, they had found more than that as Gerard had left his gun behind as well. She thanked God that the fire had destroyed the codes and all written documents.

"It's such a pity that a beautiful young woman like you had to get involved in a nasty business."

She kept maintaining her innocence, telling him she didn't understand what he was talking about.

"We shall see about that. Take her away."

"Can I ask where you're taking me?"

"How about 11 Rue des Saussaies?"

She hoped they were trying to scare her. That was the building all agents feared; the place the Gestapo had taken as its headquarters. She couldn't hide the involuntary shudder that hit her body. It was a prison that everyone in the resistance had heard about and for good reason; rarely did anyone come out of that place alive.

When Penny got outside, it was obvious someone had talked. The sheer number of cars that had arrived searching for her told her the Germans knew she was someone in the network.

They didn't believe she was just a French girl who was in the wrong house. She panicked – would she reveal any details about her fellow agents? She thought back to what the man had said at her interview – "Everyone talks, my dear, but some last longer than others."

Mama, help me please, she prayed. *Don't let me betray my friends. Give me the courage to withstand whatever they throw at me. If I do talk, let it be later. Let me give the others a chance to escape.*

She put her shoulders back and sat up straighter, although the handcuffs made it difficult. She was determined that her tormentors wouldn't see her fear or think that they could intimidate her. Despite the evidence to the contrary, she was going to keep on insisting that she was innocent.

CHAPTER 60

"Out now."

One soldier gave her a push to get her moving towards the building. She noticed some townspeople staring at her. She put her shoulders back and held her head high as they walked into the building and up a series of stairs. The soldiers stopped outside a room. They knocked at the door before opening it. They gestured for Penny to walk inside.

Two men, only one of whom was in uniform, were waiting. They asked her to take a seat and offered her some coffee and a cigarette. She was a little taken aback. Why were they being so nice to her? She hadn't expected them to act like genuine people, but then that was what made them so dangerous. On the surface, they looked like ordinary human beings, but they were capable of acts no decent person could even dream about.

The men introduced themselves, apologised for taking up her time, and kept up the pretence that the interview was a formality to clear her name.

"So, Madame Michiels? Tell us a little about yourself: where were you born, what you do, that sort of thing."

"Yes, monsieur. My name is Isabelle Michiels, and I was born in Normandy. I'm an only child. My father was killed in the last war, my mother died some years later. I married in 1938 but my husband was reported missing, believed killed in the first week of the war. We have no children and, having no money, I had no option but to get a job. I work as a secretary…"

"A secretary? I would have thought the countryside was a funny place to find work as a secretary." The man looked closely at Penny.

"Well, yes, of course it would be easier in a town, but my health hasn't been too good, so I go to stay in the countryside for a few weeks." She smiled at the officers, hoping to convince them she was innocent. She thought she might win until the man who wasn't in uniform suddenly turned and hit her hard across the face.

"Stop lying to us. Do you think we are stupid?" he said.

She knew this was the time she was supposed to break down and confess, but she didn't. Instead, she stood up.

"Just who do you think you are, hitting me like that? What type of parents did you have that taught you it was okay to hit a defenceless woman? How dare you? I demand to see your senior officer right now."

The men stared at her as if she had lost her mind. A suspected spy asking to see a German officer? She watched their faces as they tried to hide their disbelief and confusion. They weren't used to being spoken back to. They were used to delivering orders and having them carried out.

She knew that they couldn't or wouldn't believe her for long. The physical evidence of her guilt was there for all to see, although it was ironic that they thought she could use the wireless. Good job they wouldn't be testing her ability, she thought rather hysterically.

She was determined to waste as much of their time as possible. She wanted word to leak to her circuit, to give them time to make the necessary changes to protect their future. She couldn't do anything to save herself now. She would not be responsible for the deaths of the brave people working for the network. She worried about Madame Reynaud returning to her home to the waiting Germans. She hoped the soldiers would believe that she was a slightly senile old lady who didn't know who had rented the rooms in her home.

She answered their questions, changing her tone from exasperation to sullen. Occasionally, she was friendly. There was no clock in the room, so it was difficult to tell how long the interrogation lasted. At least they didn't hit her again.

Finally, they had enough. They pulled her from her chair and sent her to the cells. They pushed her into a dark and smelly chamber with one occupant. The other lady swore at the soldier as Penny fell into the room.

"Here, let me help you. Swine – I'm sure they get a real kick out of pushing young women around. Probably the closest he ever gets to a date – did you see his face? One only a mother could love. Now why don't you sit down over here? I would offer you some coffee, but provisions are rather low around here."

Penny tried to smile at the other woman's attempts at humour, but her face was too sore.

"I'm Suzanne."

"Isabelle."

"What did they arrest you for? I dabbled in the black market. You wouldn't believe the fuss they are making over a couple of boxes of cigarettes and some under-the-counter meat. I won't be here much longer. They are shipping me off to Germany. Seems I have volunteered to work for them in one of their factories," Suzanne said.

Penny told her she didn't know the reason for her arrest. She didn't mention the wireless. It was best to protect her cellmate in case the Germans thought she knew anything.

"I don't mind the idea of going to Germany, but I'm

worried about my kids. Two I have, one is thirteen and the other, a girl, is nine. Thank God Mama is with them, but she is getting on a bit. Their dad is somewhere in Germany. He became a prisoner early in the war. He isn't much of a letter writer, but neither am I. *Ecoutez moi*, you don't need to hear about my life. What about you? Do your children know where you are?"

"I don't have any," said Penny.

"Sorry. I saw the ring and just supposed you did."

Penny twisted the ring on her finger. "No, my husband went missing, believed killed at the start of the war. We weren't married that long. So there is no one."

"Nobody at all? Well, that's good."

Penny looked questioningly at the other woman.

"Well, if you don't have any family they can't threaten them, now, can they? You hear many awful things in here. I heard they shot the entire family of one man who wouldn't confess to being a member of the resistance. They made him watch, too."

Penny shivered. "Please stop."

Suzanne apologised. "I'm sorry. It's being stuck in here all day with no one to talk to. I go on a bit – always have."

"Don't apologise. I appreciate you telling me. I'm tired. I have been here all day, answering question after question. I want to sleep."

"*Bien sur!* You should rest. While you can."

CHAPTER 61

Penny slept. When she woke some hours later, Suzanne was sitting on her bed looking at her.

"You were having nightmares," she said.

"Was I? I don't remember."

"Well, take that worried look off your face. You said nothing ... well, nothing that I could understand, anyway. I thought you might be cold, so I put my blanket on top of you."

"Suzanne, you are very kind, but you must take it. It's freezing in here and I don't want to be responsible for you getting sick."

"Don't mind me. I'm tougher than I look."

"Thank you, Suzanne, for looking out for me."

"We have to stick together, don't we? Otherwise they have won and I refuse to give those bastards victory."

Penny felt guilty. Her cellmate had shown her

nothing but kindness, and all she had done was lie to her. You couldn't and shouldn't trust anyone, but this was a person in trouble with the Germans. She was just like her.

So caught up in her thoughts, she failed to notice that Suzanne had been talking to her.

"Sorry, Suzanne, I was miles away. What did you say?"

"I meant to say it to you last night, but if you want me to get a message to anyone, just let me know."

"A message?"

"Yeah, if there is anyone in here you know and want to contact, I know how. One girl who was in here with me a few months back made friends with one of the French workers. They get them in to clean the place, although obviously they do nothing with our cells. Anyway, she will contact another prisoner for you and can even get messages outside."

For a second, the offer tempted Penny; it was a way of letting the network know where she was. But almost as soon as the thought crossed her mind, she dismissed it. The risk was too high. She looked at Suzanne. Something wasn't quite right about her, but she couldn't put her finger on it. Although she seemed to be a nice Frenchwoman, Penny had only just met her. She couldn't trust her, not yet. Maybe never.

"Thank you, Suzanne, but there is no one to worry about me, not any more."

Sometime later, the guards came back. Relief flooded through Penny when they took Suzanne, even if she hated herself for feeling that way. She wanted to get some strength back before facing more questions. She suspected that they had gone easy on her the first day. This place didn't get its reputation because the guards slapped you a couple of times around the face.

Judging by the movement of the sun, a couple of hours passed by. She spent the time thinking about her friends. Gracie, Nell, Uncle John and Meme back in England. How were the Taylor girls coping? Was Kenny still keen on farming? Jeanne and Marie here in France. Was Madame Bayard safe?

Then her thoughts turned to Paul and David. David, she was very fond of; he was like a brother to her. She hoped he was back in London out of the field. He'd done enough. Her thoughts moved to Paul. She loved him. She knew that now. Where was he? He wasn't dead, at least she didn't think he was. She'd know, she was sure of it. She'd give almost anything to see him again. To tell him she loved him.

The cell door opened, and the guard pushed Suzanne inside. Her cellmate's face was no longer recognisable, both eyes were already swollen, her mouth dripped blood, and she was missing a couple of teeth.

"What have they done to you?" asked Penny.

Suzanne tried to joke, "Aw, this is nothing. Wait till you see what I did to them." Then she cried.

"Don't cry, please."

Penny draped both covers over Suzanne and tried to soothe her by stroking her hair.

Suzanne sobbed. "I kept telling them I knew nothing, but they wouldn't believe me."

"What are you supposed to know about? I thought you were in here for black-market trading."

Suzanne held Penny's gaze for a second. "I am, but they thought I might tell them something about you. They didn't believe me when I said that you were a widow with no children. I told them over and over that is all I knew, but they seemed to think that there should be more. What did you not tell me?"

She moved away from Penny and lay down on the bed.

Penny knew she couldn't confess now. It wouldn't help Suzanne, and it could hurt the other members of the network.

"Nothing, Suzanne, I don't know what they want from me. I told you what I said to them. I think my husband died in the early months of the war and we have no children."

Suzanne pushed herself up on the bed.

"I know there's something you're not telling me, but it's okay. I don't want to know. I just hope that whatever you are into, you are making some headway in dealing with those bastards. If I had my way, I would kill every one of them. Murdering scumbags – how dare they march around my country as if they owned it. Well, they won't be here forever. France will rise again and be free once more. I only hope it's a day I will see. I'm glad you didn't trust me enough to tell me because what I don't know, I can't tell them."

"No, Suzanne, it's not like that."

Suzanne looked straight into Penny's eyes. "Please stop lying to me."

Then she turned her head to the wall and didn't say another word until the morning. The guards came again once more, taking Suzanne with them. They shouted at her to take her belongings with her.

Penny tried to give her cellmate a hug, but she remained stone-faced.

"*Bon voyage, ma pauvre amie,*" she whispered into the empty room.

CHAPTER 62

Time passed slowly. Penny couldn't take the suspense and began to wish the guards would come for her. Sitting in the cell, imagining what was going to happen, was driving her mad. She tried to remember all the stories her mama had told her when she was little. She repeated them over and over, talking to herself out loud, doing anything to pass the time. She started a primitive calendar by using a small stone to mark off each night that she spent alone.

Four marks later, the guards arrived to take her back for questioning.

"So, Madame Michiels, we meet again."

"I wish I could say it was a pleasure, Monsieur."

"Herr Hauptmann." He looked her up and down but displayed no emotion. "A couple of nights of our hospitality hasn't done anything to make you more amenable. Perhaps it has helped you come to your senses. Now I'm going to ask you the same questions as before, but this time, try giving me the correct answers."

"I don't know what you mean. My name is Isabelle Michiels. I believe I'm a widow. My husband is missing, believed killed in the early days of the war. I have heard nothing of him since."

"Yes, yes. I know the fiction, Madame Michiels, but it's the truth I'm interested in, Simone ... or should I say Penny?"

Her proper name caught her by surprise, but she managed not to react.

"My name is Isabelle Michiels, and it's rather a waste of my time to be sitting here playing these games. They are rather boring."

"I assure you, young lady, that nobody is playing games. At least, not any more. Now let me tell you what I know about you and please correct me if I make a mistake."

He looked down at the papers in front of him before saying, "Your name is Penny Hamilton. You are in fact French, having been born here in France to a French mother and an English father. Your father died from the wounds sustained in the last war, and your mother brought you up alone. After some years, your mother died, and you went to live with your father's family in England. So tell me, how am I doing so far?"

"You tell wonderful but tragic stories, Herr Hauptmann. My name, as you know, is Isabelle..."

"Please spare us the story. It's all getting rather, as you say, boring. Now, where did I leave off? You are an only child but lived with your aunt, uncle and two cousins in London's Belgravia. You wanted to become a nurse, but your aunt didn't think it was a reasonable occupation for a young lady."

He sneered.

"Tell me, what did she think of you becoming a spy? Somehow, I can't see that being high on the list of accomplishments a young English lady should achieve."

"I don't know, being French, not English."

"Well, at least we agree on one point. You are French, that much is true. Alas, it's the only true part of the web of lies you have spun. But let's get back to Penny as I find her rather fascinating. You spent the early years of the war helping in a children's home."

As he continued talking, Penny tried to keep her face impassive. She couldn't believe how much information he had on her.

"Bored, are we, Penny?" the officer asked, pretending to care.

"Yes, but you seem to enjoy your brief story, so I thought it rude to interrupt."

"Well, I have to give you one thing. Of all the English spies we have seen, you are one of the coolest, sitting here making smart remarks as if you didn't have a care in the world."

"Well, that's because I don't."

Her head swung back from the impact with his hand.

"I never liked cheeky children, and smart-mouthed adults annoy me intensely. You may think you are being brave and heroic, but you are, in fact, stupid. You can see how much we already know about you. It's only a matter of time before you fill in the missing gaps for us."

"I don't know what you are talking about. I have given you my name and told you everything. I have nothing more to say," hissed Penny.

"You will. We have, as they say, ways and means of making you talk. Our men are used to dealing with proper soldiers, not a slip of a girl caught up in a world she doesn't understand. It would be a genuine pity if you didn't come to your senses." He reached out to stroke a finger down her face. "Their methods are rather primitive and the damage they inflict lasts a long time, if not forever. It would be a shame to ruin something as beautiful as you." He moved to touch her face again, but Penny recoiled. "Take the prisoner back to the cells." The soldiers dragged Penny to her feet and went to push her out the door.

"One moment." Herr Hauptmann walked over to stand by her before whispering, "I trust, my dear, that you will take some time tonight to consider your position. Tomorrow the gloves come off, and believe me, I will find out what I need to know by any means necessary. This is not a game, no matter what those idiots in Beaulieu told you."

～

ONCE BACK INSIDE the comparative safety of her cell she couldn't stop shivering. Whether it was from cold or fear, she wasn't sure. Who had betrayed her? It couldn't be David. They hadn't caught him, and, anyway, he would never inform on her. Or would he? How far would he go to save his network and support his cause? Would he see her as just a minor blip in the scheme of things? After all, he had led her a merry dance before telling her of his fiancée. Or what about Paul? He knew her proper name and where she was from. But he hated the Germans. He loved her. Didn't he?

There was nobody else. All night she tossed and turned, trying to figure out who had given the *Boche* so much accurate information. David or Paul – she didn't want to believe either would do it, but in her dreams, they both seemed to merge into one. The only benefit of driving herself mad was her not lingering on thoughts of what tomorrow would bring.

She knew that Herr Hauptmann was serious about making her talk. He didn't seem like a man who would accept failure. Well, now he would find out what is it like to want something you just can't have. Someone had betrayed her. She was damned if she was going to do that to anyone else.

She tried to concentrate on what her training had taught her. To never give in or give up as that was the path to failure. But sitting in her dingy, cold cell, she was struggling not to do both.

CHAPTER 63

The guards came early. Penny shook their hands off her and walked with her shoulders back and head straight.

Walking into the room, she came to a halt when she saw who was sitting there. She knew she was gaping at him, but she couldn't help it.

"Good morning, Penelope."

He looked younger than she had imagined he would, his belt straining against his belly. But he wasn't as tall as she remembered. He seemed slighter too, not the gigantic monster of her nightmares. The war had been good for him. He still wore a moustache but now had a beard as well. His eyes were the only thing that hadn't changed. They were still as black and soulless as they'd been when she was a child.

"You…" She lunged at him, but the guards pulled her back.

"Fiery, aren't you? Wonder what other qualities you inherited from your mother?"

Penny spat at him. The guards looked at him expectantly, but her actions only seemed to excite rather than annoy him.

"I shall enjoy taming you. It will take some time, but that's okay. We have all the time in the world. Guards, leave us."

The guards left the room, leaving Penny alone with Herr Hauptmann and Alain.

"The Allies will be here soon."

"Penelope, darling, I *am* the Allies." Alain laughed at his own joke. "General de Gaulle is an old family friend. He won't save you."

"Traitor. You're working for the Germans. He will have you shot. That's if you live long enough to see him."

Alain laughed again. "Beautiful, but not too bright. The Germans are working for me. As you said, the Allies have already landed in France. Some of our German friends will fight on. Others are more, shall we say, sensible? Herr Hauptmann has kindly agreed to give you to me in return for a rather sizeable sum of money and some valuable paintings. After you disclose all your secrets, of course." He looked her up and down with distaste. "I think my investment will pay off rather nicely, although it's hard to see under all that dirt."

"You will never have me," Penny hissed.

"I think we both know that is not the truth." Alain walked around her. "Bit on the skinny side, too. And the hair will have to go. It has taken on a life of its own. Pity, but it will grow back."

Herr Hauptmann spoke. "Alain, are you sure? Now I'm not about to return your generous gifts, but there are many women in France. Why this one?" Hauptmann looked dubiously at Penny. "Yes, she is – or was – pretty, but…"

"My dear Herr Hauptmann, we both know that our tastes are very different. I love women of all ages. We have history, don't we, Penelope? What were you? Twelve? Fourteen? I have been waiting for this opportunity for a long time. Too long."

Alain came closer, reaching towards Penny. Instinctively, she drew back. He smiled before whispering, "Take time to think about all those things I will make you do. Believe me, by the time I'm finished, you will beg me for more."

Penny straightened her back, looked directly at him. "I will die first."

"Yes, the cyanide pill. I almost forgot. Where is it?" He patted her down, touching her intimately while Herr Hauptmann watched. Patiently, he searched every bit of her clothing until, with a triumphant grin, he retrieved the pill from the hollowed-out heel of her shoe. He ground it under his boot. He put a gloved finger under her chin, forcing her to look at him. "Accept your fate, Penelope."

He laughed, walking to the door.

"Wait," she said.

"Pardon?" Alain turned.

"Please. I have to know. Who betrayed me?" She hated herself for asking.

"Nobody betrayed you, Penelope. You betrayed yourself." Alain turned back and walked over to a different door to the one Penelope had entered. He opened it and spoke to someone outside. "Come in, you might enjoy the spectacle."

Penny stared at the man who walked in.

"You? Why? After everything you lost? Adam?"

Frederick glared at her. "Adam is the reason you are here, you stupid witch. If you had been on time, you would have been at the landing site. Victor would never have taken Adam."

"But you hate the Germans." Penny was struggling. "That's why you shot Aaron in the prison. He would have told us about you."

Frederick didn't deny it. "I don't hate the Germans now they're leaving. France belongs to French men. I'm a patriot, just like Alain and the others. I just believe that money, lots of it, makes life a little more enjoyable."

Penny lunged at him. "You betrayed your country for money."

Frederick moved as if to strike her. Alain grabbed his hand. "Don't touch her. She is not Juliette."

Penny's attention was caught.

"What are you to Juliette?" Penny asked, thinking of the pretty girl with the air of sadness who had helped her pass her initial training.

"Juliette, as you knew her, was my wife. She was a bit like you, although not as fiery. Stupid cow believed we were fighting for freedom. She had lost her family to the Germans back in 1940. They had hid some Jews or other undesirables. The *Boche* didn't bother with a court, just shot them and burned the farm. Juliette was at the market. She didn't know until she came back. I was on hand to rescue her. She was indebted to me." The grin he shared with Alain sickened Penny. "I suggested to Victor that she train as an agent. He agreed and so you met her. Meeting you was a bonus. It wasn't part of the plan. Some girl broke your cover story. It wasn't hard for Juliette to find out the rest of the details. It took me a while to work out the connection with Alain, but when you took to visiting Marly-le-Roi to see your little old lady…"

"You swine. You…" Penny fought against her restraints.

Frederick turned back to Alain. "I have to get back now or they will be suspicious. Enjoy your catch."

Alain clapped him on the back. "Thank you, my

good friend. I had forgotten Juliette was dead. We shall have to find a replacement wife for you."

The sound of Frederick's laughter echoed behind him as he left the room.

The fight had gone out of Penny. Frederick would betray the entire group, and there was nothing she could do about it.

Alain looked at Penny. "Nothing to say? From what I hear, that is unusual."

He walked over to the main door. Opening it, he called, "Guards take her away and get her washed. See that she has some decent food. Watch her 24/7. If anything happens to her, I will shoot you."

The guards came in, grabbed Penny roughly, and pushed her out the door.

"Wait." Alain gestured to the guards. "This woman is mine. Mine. Have the servants wash her." He looked at Penny before turning back to the guards. "I won't take away all your fun. You can stay and watch. But, if any of you lay a hand or anything else on her, I will cut it off. Personally."

The door closed as the guards dragged Penny back to the cells.

CHAPTER 64

Penny shivered. She didn't want to think about Alain's plans. She had been taught not to accept defeat, but that was when dealing with a common enemy. She had thought the Americans would save her. Not now. They would view Alain and his friends as allies.

Despair threatened to overwhelm Penny. There was no way out. She looked around her. No glass left in the window. She searched the floor for a stone. Maybe she could make it sharp enough.

She heard someone approach. The cell door opened and in walked two soldiers, dragging a tin bath behind them. Some women followed them carrying boiling water.

Penny was stripped and pushed into the scalding water. The women washed her hair, none too gently, before moving on to her body. Every inch of her was scrubbed.

Penny did her best to pretend the soldiers weren't present. Now her body had got used to the heat, the bath was refreshing. All too soon, she had to get out and stand naked before them. The cell door opened again, admitting yet another woman who had some clothes in her hands.

"Get that filthy bath and clothes out of here," the woman ordered. The soldiers glared at her.

"Don't just stand there. Move. Now. Nobody keeps Herr Hauptmann waiting."

The soldiers muttered something in German. Judging by the looks in their eyes, it wasn't flattering, but the woman ignored them.

The woman turned to Penny. "My name is Fantine. Herr Hauptmann asked me to help you. The three of us and Alain shall dine together tonight. I have to work hard to get you looking good. Put these on." She watched as Penny scrambled into the clothes, glad to be covered again. "Now come with me. Your hair needs attention. Herr Hauptmann won't be happy with me if you go to Alain looking like that. He knows French women like to look their best."

"No," said Penny.

The women who had bathed her in the cell stared at her.

"Leave us," the woman ordered. She turned to Penny. "You will come with me."

"I said no. I'm not going anywhere. If Alain wants

me, he will have to come here." Penny sat down on the floor.

"Get up. I won't be in trouble with Hauptmann because of you, you ungrateful cow." The woman reached down to pull Penny roughly to her feet. "Paul sent me," she whispered in Penny's ear. "Act reluctant but we need to get out of here."

Penny refused to listen despite her heart leaping at the mention of Paul's name. It was another trick. It had to be.

"Paul said Annette would expect you to follow his wishes," Fantine hissed, keeping her eyes on the door.

Annette. It was true, Paul had sent this woman to help her. But where was he? How did he know she'd been captured?

Penny got to her feet. "You can drag me with you. But I will die rather than belong to him."

The woman slapped Penny. "You will do as you're told." She turned towards the cell door. "Guards. Please take this prisoner to Gate A."

The woman led the way, with the guards pushing Penny along behind her. They passed several cells, causing Penny to wonder what poor souls were behind them.

They neared the exit. The daylight hurt her eyes. A car was waiting. Inside were two German soldiers and a driver. She hesitated, torn between thinking this was a trap and trusting Fantine knew what she was doing. The gun in her back decided for her.

"Leave us now." The women dismissed the soldiers. She drew a gun, aiming it at Penny. "Get in the car. Make one false move and I will shoot. I won't kill you, but it will be painful."

Penny scowled at the woman.

"We have orders to stay with the prisoner," said one soldier.

"Orders? Do you want to land on the Eastern Front, as that can be arranged? Hauptmann has told me what he wants. He has given me two soldiers and a driver. How many more men does it take to guard one woman? Do *not* stand in my way."

The soldiers looked at one another before withdrawing. The woman pushed Penny into the back of the car, getting in beside her. The uniformed driver drove off.

"Drive quicker, Henri. The draught I gave Alain and Hauptmann will wear off shortly." She put the gun on the seat beside her. "Relax, Simone. We are on the same side. These men are all patriots dressed up for the day."

One man pulled at his uniform, a look of disgust on his face. The other stared out the window as if expecting trouble.

"Paul ordered me to take you to Chambray or as close as we can get to it. I have family nearby, so we have a place to stay. The Americans are already there. We will both be safe there, you from the Germans and me from the French. They don't look kindly on those of us who became intimate with the Germans."

Penny's stomach churned; this woman had been Hauptman's mistress.

"Don't look at me like that. You don't know the reasons for my actions. Before you judge me, think about what you have done. Your brief visits to your friend weren't authorised by London or Victor, were they? Alain has been waiting to catch you for a while now."

Penny pulled herself up in the seat. Alain. She needed to go back and finish what she had come to France to do.

"I want Alain dead. By my hand. Take me back there."

"Not on your life. I want to survive this war. Someone else will take care of Alain. You and me are going to Chambray." Fantine's voice softened slightly. "Simone or whatever your name is, you have done your bit. Let us look after you now. You couldn't fight Coco the Clown right now. You need to rebuild your strength."

She couldn't argue with that logic. She leaned back in the seat, briefly closing her eyes. Paul had sent his woman to rescue her. So he had to be close by.

"Where is Paul? Is he at Chambray?"

The woman didn't answer.

"I asked you a question. Where is Paul?"

"Look, you need to rest. You also need a haircut and some decent clothes. Let the men do what they have to do. They don't need a half-starved, beaten woman getting in their way."

"My men need all the help they can get. Especially with so many gone now. Victor and the others. Do they know about Frederick? He's a traitor."

"He's dead. Forget about him. Give your team some credit. You can see Paul later. First, we need to get you out of here."

Penny knew the woman was right, but she wanted to be with Paul. She needed to see him. She spoke, but the woman stopped her.

"Drink this, it will ease the cold."

Penny drank slowly. Having been deprived of decent food for days, her stomach heaved at the richness of the liquid.

"You will see him soon. Stop thinking with your heart and start using your head. You will be of more help once you get your strength back. Now, please try to sleep."

Penny felt tiredness overtake her. She suspected they had laced the drink with something.

"You will stay with me?"

"Well, I can't exactly go back now, can I? I wouldn't want to be there when Alain finds you gone." The woman looked at Penny. "Simone, you are with friends. Real friends. Go to sleep."

The motion of the car combined with the hot drink, bath and tiredness meant Penny couldn't help succumbing, and she slept most of the way.

~

SHE WOKE when the car stopped. It was pitch-black outside.

"Come now." The woman held her hand out to help Penny from the car.

Penny walked through the door into the house. Marie came running towards her. "Isabelle, I mean Simone, you're alive. Look at the state of you, you poor girl. You are skin and bone."

"Marie, what are you doing here? Jeanne?"

"We had to leave the farm. Things got a little hot, but we came through it. Thanks to Victor and his friends."

Marie hugged Penny to her. Over her shoulder, Penny smiled with relief at Jeanne.

"Why are you here? Are we on the farm?" Penny was totally confused.

"No, Simone, we are in Jeanne's grandparents' home. The farm is no more. Between the bombs and the landings, it was too dangerous to stay there. There is little left standing now." She smiled sadly. "But it can be rebuilt. Buildings are not what make a home. Family and friends are. Come sit down by the fire. Jeanne, get her something light to eat. An egg, perhaps. With some bread." Marie turned to Fantine. "Any problems?"

"None. Men, they are so predictable. Can't go back there now, though."

Marie hugged Fantine to her. "You never have to leave home again."

Penny struggled to accept what was happening.

"You two know each other?"

Marie smiled. "Fantine is family. She was engaged to my son. The Germans killed him before they could get married." Marie looked at the woman who had saved Penny. "She found her own way to take revenge. I didn't agree with her actions, but I have always been proud of her bravery. She is like another daughter to me."

Marie hugged Fantine close again. "It's over now, for all of us. The Americans are here and soon all the Germans will have left."

"It's not over for me," said Penny.

"England is still fighting, but they won't expect you to work. Not yet. Recover."

"This has nothing to do with England."

"Simone, leave Alain to the Americans." Fantine frowned. "You have done enough."

Marie looked from one woman to another. "Who is Alain?"

"Alain is a traitor." Penny paused, trying to speak clearly without emotion. "He is working with the

Germans, although de Gaulle thinks he is a trusted adviser. His men are with the *Maquis*. They work alongside the actual heroes. The blood of people like Michel and others who have died lies at his feet."

Fantine turned to Marie. "I don't know the history, but there is much more to it than that. The Germans arrested Simone but Alain bought her from them."

"He secured her freedom. Why would you call him a traitor?" Marie turned to Penny.

"He didn't buy my freedom. He bought me."

What they were saying took a while to register with Marie. Penny sighed – it was time to come clean with her friends. She owed them an explanation.

"As you guessed before, I'm French. I was born in Marly-le-Roi, where I lived until I was a teenager. Alain was the local gendarme. He killed my mother after mistreating her for years. He wanted me, but a friend sent me to England." Marie went to say something, but Penny continued. "He has been working with the Germans, having infiltrated many of the *Maquis* networks. His hands are covered in the blood of our men. He's very wealthy. People paid him money to save their families. He took their properties, cash and jewellery but sent their families to the camps anyway. He is evil. Now he has switched sides. He says he supports de Gaulle and uses his money and influence to give that impression. He has bought off several high-ranking German officers, including Fantine's friend,

Hauptmann. He paid him a lot of money not to send me to the Gestapo headquarters."

"Why? If you know him and can expose him, surely he would want you dead," Marie asked.

"I'm sure he does, but first he wants to own me. To prove that nobody escapes. Not from him."

Marie shuddered. "We must warn the men. Jeanne go…"

"No. Don't. Frederick was informing on them; he's dead and we have sent men to warn the others," Fantine said before turning to Penny. "I understand the need for revenge. I felt the same when Jean-Luc was taken from me. But it's best you leave it to Paul and the others."

"Who is this Paul?" said Marie, looking from Penny to Fantine.

"Paul is the leader of my group. He and Simone worked together when she first came to France. Simone saved his life. He loves her and I believe she loves him. He's been in London with De Gaulle and then over in Algiers. He only came back recently." Fantine looked directly at Penny. "A man like Paul doesn't come around very often. You should hold on to him with both hands. At least your love is still alive. Live for that, or else what have we been fighting for?"

Despite her love for Paul, Penny couldn't let the need for revenge go. Not after all these years. Her mother had died at Alain's hands. This was personal. Penny jumped to her feet. "NO. Alain is mine. He is, and always was, the reason I came back to France." She swayed, causing Marie to grab her and pull her down onto the chair beside her.

"Enough talk for tonight. Simone needs to rest. She isn't thinking straight. We will decide what to do tomorrow."

PENNY SCRIBBLED a note before the others woke that morning. If things went well, she'd be too far away for them to stop her by the time they got up. *Thank you for everything. This is something I have to do. Alone.*

CHAPTER 65

Penny walked as quickly as she could. Every step caused her pain. She knew she was getting some odd looks. Thank goodness Fantine had got her some decent clothes. Some took pity on her and gave her a lift on a cart. Others ignored her. With the bombs raining down from the sky all over northern France, combined with the chaos caused by the expected arrival of the Americans and retreat of the Germans, she travelled unmolested. Finally, she arrived at Madame Bayard's.

When Madame opened the door, Penny could have wept with relief. "Madame, thank God you are okay. I was certain he would hurt you."

"Penny, leave now. You shouldn't have come back here. It's not safe." The old woman looked stricken.

The hairs on the back of Penny's neck stood up as she sensed his presence. She looked around her. "He's here, isn't he?"

"So beautiful, yet predictable, my dear Penelope," he said, moving out of the shadows pointing his gun at them.

Penny gazed in shock at the man standing in front of her. She had imagined he would flee, but he had set a trap and waited for her to walk right into it. Not only had she put herself in danger, but Madame Bayard, too. The guilt overwhelmed her.

"Alain, it's over. I will go with you. Just leave Madame alone."

"It's too late for that now. She knows everything." Alain put the silencer on his gun. He aimed, and despite Penny lunging for the gun, Madame crumpled.

Penny rushed to the old lady. Taking her in her arms, she could feel the blood soaking through her clothes. "You bastard. Why?"

"She knew too much. Now, move. We have little time," he said.

"I'm staying with her. She was my family, and I betrayed her. If I hadn't come looking for you, she would still be alive." Penny held her dearest friend, willing her not to die. The old lady was trying to say something. Penny bent towards her face.

"Paul loves you. Let him…"

Penny knew then what it meant when someone said your heart was broken. Hers shattered as the old lady struggled to breathe. She had let her bitterness and determination to seek revenge destroy the one woman who had loved her always.

Shaking with fury and rage, she lay Madame back on the floor and kissed her gently before standing slowly and making a lunge for Alain. Taken by surprise, he fell backwards onto the floor. Penny pounded on his chest over and over. "You've taken everything, everyone I loved. You will die. Today."

Alain fought back, twisting Penny over onto her back so he was astride her. "Wildcat. Continue fighting me, please."

The mist cleared. Penny realised he was enjoying the struggle. She immediately made herself go limp and didn't respond when he started touching her body. "Where's the knife? You don't have a gun, but you wouldn't have been stupid enough to come here unarmed. Is it here? Or here?"

Penny couldn't reach her knife. She noticed something or someone moving behind Alain. She continued to lay limp, as Alain's hand moved lower, lifting her skirt before moving higher up her leg.

"Got it. I knew you had one." Triumphantly, he threw her knife to one side. As he moved, Penny took her chance to knee him. He reared back in pain, giving her a second to wriggle free. Half crawling and half running, she made her way into the kitchen.

Alain followed as she ran into the room towards

Paul, sheltering behind his broad-shouldered figure as he stood between her and Alain.

"Alain, it's a great pleasure to meet you. I have heard so much about you," Paul said cordially.

"Who are you?" snarled Alain.

"I'm de Gaulle's right-hand man. But then you know that, don't you, seeing as you and Charles are such good friends," said Paul.

Alain puffed up his chest. "Don't be insubordinate. I'm not only a friend of the general but an important member of his staff. Now, please instruct the lady you are hiding to come with me immediately. She's a wanted criminal."

"Who? This lady? I thought she was with the resistance," asked Paul, clearly enjoying himself.

"No, that's what she claimed. In fact, she was working and sleeping with the Germans. Wasn't too particular, either. Seems anyone in a uniform would do."

Paul's grip tightened on his gun, but Alain didn't appear to notice.

"I'm ordering you to hand her over, now," he shouted at Paul.

"Simone, or should I say Penny, I think you should do as the man says. After all, we wouldn't want any traitors going free now, would we?" Paul turned to Alain. "What do you plan on doing with her? I assume she will hang?"

"That's for the courts to decide. We're not murderers," Alain said, visibly pleased Paul appeared to have fallen for his trick. "Now we have agreed we are on the same side, can you please give me a weapon? I seem to have lost mine."

Paul walked closer to where Alain was standing. "Ah, yes, your weapon. The one you used to shoot the old lady who lived here."

Alain paled before stammering, "She was a traitor, too. She harboured a fugitive."

Paul struck Alain so quickly the other man didn't see it coming. Alain fell to the floor at Paul's feet. "You traitorous bastard. I should shoot you right now. But that's not my decision to make. Unlike you, I'm no murderer." Paul turned to Penny, handing her his gun. He got some rope and secured Alain's hands tightly in front of his chest before also tying his legs together. "He can't get away now."

"Wait." Keeping the gun trained on Alain, Penny rushed to Paul's side. "Wait for me outside, please."

Paul looked at her "That is up to you. If you kill him now, we are finished. Our future dies with him. I told you a long time ago to let this go. You couldn't or wouldn't, and now Madame Bayard is dead. I can't order you not to kill him. But if you do, you are no better than he is."

Penny reached to touch his face, her eyes pleading for understanding, but he pulled back. He closed the door behind him.

She turned towards Alain. For the last ten years, she had waited and dreamed of this moment. She had imagined how it would feel to have his life in her hands. Would he beg for forgiveness? Would he say he was sorry for leaving her alone in this world? For taking everything she held dear, her mama, her home and … now she had allowed him to take her oldest and truest friend.

She looked at him lying on the ground in front of her. He didn't get up or beg for his life. He just watched and waited. She levelled the gun, aiming at his heart. Her finger hovered over the trigger. Her hand was shaking so much she had to use her other one to steady her aim. Fire now. Kill him now. For Mama's sake, for Madame Bayard, for Michel, Adam and all of his other victims.

She looked into his mocking eyes. He thought she couldn't do it. Her hesitation gave her away. A small smile played around his lips. He was almost baiting her to kill him.

The sound of the gun going off jolted her out of her trance. She took a second shot before walking towards the door back to where Madame lay.

Penny gathered the woman's body to her. Rocking back and forth, she held her friend. "I'm so sorry, I should have been more careful."

"Penelope…"

The whisper pierced through Penny's grief. She

looked around her, but there was nobody else in the room. Only her and…

"Madame? You're alive!" The tears came at last, rolling freely down her face. "You're not dead. But how? There's so much blood. You need a doctor." Without waiting for a response, Penny lay the old woman gently back on the ground. She ran to the back door, almost tripping over Alain, but Paul was nowhere to be seen. She raced inside again, this time heading for the front door. A young boy was playing on the street outside.

"Get a doctor to come. Now. Madame is injured. She needs help. Quickly." She barely waited for the boy to run off before heading back inside to Madame. She wrapped the old lady's coat around her.

"Penelope, stop fussing." Madame Bayard still whispered, but she sounded a little stronger. She winced as she tried to move. "Where's Alain?"

"He's in the kitchen. Don't worry, he can't hurt you now. He won't cause anyone pain, ever again."

Madame Bayard stayed silent for a couple of seconds before asking to see Paul.

"He's gone."

"Find him, Penelope. Don't lose him, too."

"The doctor is coming. I'm not leaving you. Not now."

Madame didn't have time to argue as the doctor arrived just as Penny finished talking. Thankfully, he had some experience with bullet wounds and with dealing with Madame Bayard, whom he had known for years. As he treated her wound, he told her off for trying to act like a woman a third her age.

Madame's wound had bled a lot but wasn't serious. Alain's shot had hit her arm, not her chest as Penny had suspected. It was the shock that caused her to pass out.

"Penelope, I'm fine. Dr Robin will take good care of me. Please find Paul. He's your future."

Penny looked at Madame and then at the doctor, who nodded. Leaning forward, she kissed Madame on the cheek. "I will go, but I won't be long. Okay?"

"Go child. Now."

CHAPTER 66

Once more, she headed to the kitchen. Opening the back door, she found a *Maquis* standing guard.

"Where is Paul?" she asked.

The *Maquis* pointed towards a lone figure at the bottom of the garden.

Penny ran towards the man she loved, calling his name. He turned towards her but didn't take her in his arms.

"Are you happy now?" he asked coldly.

"Not yet. I love you, Paul," she said, stopping just short of touching him.

"Clearly." His sarcasm spoke volumes. He turned away from her.

She put her hand on his shoulder, but he shrugged her off.

"Paul, I love you. More than anyone. I want to spend the rest of my life with you and our children. Here in

France. In Marly-le-Roi." Penny reached towards him again, willing him to believe her. She ached for him to hold her.

"You want to stay here after today? What will you do? Lay flowers on the grave every weekend?" His bitterness hurt her.

"No, Paul. She's alive."

A look of total incredulity came over Paul's face. Penny kept talking.

"I thought I had killed her with my stupid need for revenge. The doctor said she was lucky. The wound isn't too bad, she will recover." Penny took a breath, trying to slow her speech. "Paul, she sent me to find you. She told me you were the man for me. She was right. I would do anything for you," Penny pleaded with him.

"Anything? You just committed murder. That puts you in the same category as the people we spent the last five years fighting." Paul turned and grabbed her, shaking her. "I loved you with every fibre of my being. You were the reason I survived. I wanted to spend the rest of my life with you. And you just threw that away with those two shots. Was it worth it? Was it?" He let her go, his disgust evident on his face as he stalked off.

"Paul, wait."

"Leave now, or I will order the men to arrest you and turn you over to the Americans. They will probably put you back where Fantine found you."

"Stop being so pig-headed. You aren't listening to a word I'm saying…" Penny shouted back at him.

Paul whirled around. "Me? You're calling me stubborn. You, the woman who came all this way for a vendetta. You have some nerve…"

A young man cleared this throat.

"Em, excuse me, boss, but what do you want me to do with him?" The *Maquis* stood there, patting his rifle nervously.

Paul looked from Penny to the young man. "What?"

"The old man inside. We should get him a doctor. His legs are in a right mess."

"Doctor? Legs? What the hell is going on?" He turned to Penny. Her anger vanished, and she started laughing. "What on earth is so funny?"

"Alain needs a doctor. Well, he can bleed to death for all I care, but you said you didn't want him dead. So I didn't kill him. As you said, the Americans can deal with him. But I couldn't let him run away. So I shot out his knees." She stared straight at Paul. "Both of them. He's lying on the kitchen floor. Unconscious, or at least he was a few minutes ago."

Paul glared at her and then at the young man whose discomfort was patently obvious to both of them. "Go find some American soldiers and bring them here."

"Americans." The youngster looked disappointed. "Aren't we going to hang him?"

"Not today. Tell the Americans to hurry. Now go. I have some urgent business to attend to."

Paul pulled Penny towards him, kissing her savagely on the mouth. "Don't play games with me." He kissed her deeply. "I thought I had lost you."

"Never," she swore before kissing him back just as fiercely.

The teenager shrugged his shoulders, taking in the scene before him. Shaking his head, he went back inside to send someone else for the Americans.

～

MADAME BAYARD LOOKED UP, smiling weakly as Paul and Penny walked into her bedroom hand in hand. Penny moved to one side of the bed, leaving Paul to stand on the other.

Paul shook the doctor's hand. "How is she, Doctor?"

"I think her days in the resistance are over. She will recover, but she must take things slowly."

Madame tried to sit up but before she could speak, Paul intervened. "Madame Bayard, we can't thank you enough for everything you have done. Not just for us but for France. I will personally tell the general all about you. I wouldn't be surprised if he came and visited you himself."

Penny looked at Paul. "General de Gaulle here? Do you think he will come?"

Paul nodded, but put a finger to his lips. Penny looked back at Madame and saw she was asleep.

"I'll sit with her a while. I'm sure you both have some things to discuss." The doctor smiled. "You can come back later. Let her rest now."

Penny kissed Madame's forehead gently before leaving the room. She followed Paul downstairs. Neither wanted to sit in the kitchen with the blood stains marking the floor. Instead, they walked into the garden, past the *Maquis* guarding their prisoner. The Americans had yet to arrive.

They stood arm in arm for a few moments.

"I saw the general once in London," Penny said, remembering. "It was on Bastille Day. Churchill gave a speech the same day. He promised France would, one day, be free. He was right."

"That day hasn't come yet, Penny. The Germans may have withdrawn from the north, but there are still plenty of divisions fighting in the south. Many of the *Maquis* are moving south to help with the fighting. They won't rest until all the Germans have gone."

Penny looked up at the man she loved more than anyone else. "Are you saying goodbye? I'll go with you. I won't stay behind."

Paul smiled before kissing her gently. "Aren't you forgetting you work for the English government? Their war isn't yet over. They may post you somewhere else."

"I won't go. I'm not leaving you again. Ever." Hands on her hips, Penny glared at Paul.

He moved towards her, cupping her face in his hands. "I love you so much. I don't want to be apart either. But this isn't the end of the struggle, Penny. It's only the start. We have so much work to do. The war isn't over yet and then we will deal with collaborators. Traitors like Alain."

Penny scowled. "Don't say that man's name."

"There are loads of turncoats like him. Who knows how many French men and women worked for the Germans? There will be several bloody battles as quarrels and petty grievances are aired. You might be safer going back to England."

"I told you. I'm not going anywhere. Not without you." She put her arms up around his head, drawing his face closer to hers. Looking into his eyes, she murmured, "With you, I'm home. At last."

NOTE ON SOE

The bravery of the members of both the Special Operations Executive (SOE) and the Resistance has inspired me for years. When I was a teenager, first reading about their exploits, I hoped I'd have been as brave as the men and women I read about.

But that being said, we must remember that the people who joined SOE were, in the main, ordinary individuals doing extraordinary things. They were civilians, not trained army personnel. They had some training, but not at the level the Green Berets or the SAS of today would receive. Some joined for the challenge, some wanted excitement. Some were deliberately sent into situations they weren't ready for - there is an argument to say this happened to Noor Inayat Khan (her story is one of the most inspirational stories I've read).

The clock was ticking, and the allies were desperate for victory. D Day had to happen, and the Allies made many decisions which may have led to the deaths of agents, civilians and troops. War is never neat and tidy and choices were made which would be unacceptable in times of peace. Examples include the D Day training exercises, which resulted in the death of 949 American servicemen during Operation Tiger in Devon, UK in April 1944.

The incidents described in Penny's Secret Mission draw on true events, as outlined in various diaries kept by those who went to France. The group in Paris speaking English, the specialist team sent in by London to work with the fictional Paul and Penny's capture because of her radio wireless operator's carelessness are all based on actual happenings.

One early reviewer suggested I was anti-English as I seemed to think the English agents were stupid. Nothing could be further from the truth. I admire those who were brave enough to go into the field knowing the price they could pay. They volunteered despite knowing the type of torture the Nazis would use, and the chance of their survival wasn't very high. Yet still they went. But some of them made mistakes such as crossing the street looking in the wrong direction - Britain drives on the left whereas French drivers, like most of the world, drive on the right. Or they spoke in English or ordered meat on a non meat day etc. Mistakes which may have cost them their lives and that of their colleagues.

Yet as I continue to study this area, I can't help

feeling that a lot of these volunteers were let down. The release of previously secret papers relating to the activities of SOE during the war, suggest that the people in charge in London may have cupablity in the deaths of some of their agents. For example, when the Prosper resistance team (Paris and surrounding areas) was infiltrated and betrayed, the captured agents did their utmost to warn London. London ignored those warnings, sometimes sending back messages to their people telling them off for not including safety signals. That would have been enough to sign the death warrant for a captured agent forced to send a radio signal but desperate to convey he/she was in enemy hands.

This also happened with other resistance groups. In particular, the Dutch resistance and SOE members sent to Holland. This led to many deaths.

If you would like to read more about SOE or the French Resistance, I would suggest the following books.

Life in Secrets by Sarah Helm
    The Heroines of Soe F Section - Beryl Escott
    A Train in Winter - Caroline Moorehead
    Little Cyclone - Airey Neave (himself a WW2 hero)
    A Woman of No Importance - Sonia Purcell
    Prosper - Major Suttill's French resistance network.
(written by his son.)
    And so many others.

ACKNOWLEDGMENTS

This book wouldn't have been possible without the help of so many people. Thanks to Shaela for my fantastic covers. Shaela is a gifted artist who makes my characters come to life.

I have an amazing editor, Victoria Blunden and also use a wonderful copyeditor and a proofreader. But sometimes errors slip through. I am very grateful to the ladies from my readers group who volunteered to proofread my book.

Please join my Facebook group for readers of Historical fiction. Come join us for games, prizes, exclusive content, and first looks at my latest releases. Rachel's readers group

Last, but by no means least, huge thanks and love to my husband and my three children.

ALSO BY RACHEL WESSON

Orphans of Hope House

Home for unloved Orphans (Orphans of Hope House 1)

Baby on the Doorstep (Orphans of Hope House 2)

Hearts at War

When's Mummy Coming

Revenge for my Father

Women and War

Hearts on the Rails

Orphan Train Escape

Orphan Train Trials

Orphan Train Christmas

Orphan Train Tragedy

Orphan Train Strike

Orphan Train Disaster

Trail of Hearts - Oregon Trail Series

Oregon Bound (book 1)

Oregon Dreams (book 2)

Oregon Destiny (book 3)

Oregon Discovery (book 4)

Oregon Disaster (book 5)

12 Days of Christmas - co -authored series.

The Maid - book 8

Clover Springs Mail Order Brides

Katie (Book 1)

Mary (Book 2)

Sorcha (Book 3)

Emer (Book 4)

Laura (Book 5)

Ellen (Book 6)

Thanksgiving in Clover Springs (book 7)

Christmas in Clover Springs (book8)

Erin (Book 9)

Eleanor (book 10)

Cathy (book 11)

Mrs. Grey

Clover Springs East

New York Bound (book 1)

New York Storm (book 2)

New York Hope (book 3)